# SAVAGE KISS

# ROBERTO SAVIANO

PICADOR

First published 2020 by Farrar, Straus and Giroux
120 Broadway, New York 10271

First published in the United Kingdom 2020 by Picador

This edition published 2021 by Picador
an imprint of Pan Macmillan
The Smithson, 6 Briset Street, London EC1M 5NR
*EU representative*: Macmillan Publishers Ireland Limited, 1st Floor,
The Liffey Trust Centre, 117–126 Sheriff Street Upper, Dublin 1, D01 YC43
Associated companies throughout the world
www.panmacmillan.com

ISBN 978-1-5098-7919-9

Originally published in Italian 2017 as *Bacio feroce* by Feltrinelli Editore, Milan

1 3 5 7 9 8 6 4 2

A CIP catalogue record for this book is available from the British Library.

Printed and bound by CPI Group (UK) Ltd, Croydon, CR0 4YY

WAR
10/2,

# SAVAGE KISS

Roberto Saviano was born in 1979 and studied philosophy at the University of Naples. His novel *The Piranhas* earned widespread acclaim and was adapted as a major motion picture, which won the Silver Bear for Best Screenplay at the Berlinale. *Gomorrah*, his first book, has won many awards, including the prestigious 2006 Viareggio Literary Award. It was adapted into a play; a film, which won the Grand Prix du Jury at Cannes; and a television series.

To G., *killed innocent at age 17.*

To N., *guilty killer at age 15.*

*To my land of the killers and the killed.*

Don't turn around, run
Children with guns
Yelling, "This is fun!"

—NTÒ, "IL BALLO DEI MACELLAI" (THE DANCE OF THE BUTCHERS)

# CONTENTS

# CHARACTERS

| | |
|---|---|
| MARAJA | Nicolas Fiorillo |
| BRIATO' | Fabio Capasso |
| TUCANO | Massimo Rea |
| DENTINO | Giuseppe Izzo |
| DRAGO' | Luigi Striano |
| LOLLIPOP | Vincenzo Esposito |
| PESCE MOSCIO | Ciro Somma |
| STAVODICENDO | Vincenzo Esposito |
| DRONE ANTONIO | Starita |
| BISCOTTINO | Eduardo Cirillo |
| SUSAMIELLO | Emanuele Russo |
| RISVOLTINO | Gennaro Scognamiglio |
| PACHI | Diego D'Angelo |

# PART ONE

# KISSES

**W**hen we blow kisses, when we send them in a letter, they always travel in a generic plural, kisses. Lots of kisses. But every kiss is unique unto itself, like a snowflake. It's not just a matter of how that kiss is given, it's also how it comes into existence: the underlying intent, the tension accompanying it. And then there's the way it's either accepted or rejected, the vibration—cheerful, excited, embarrassed—that buzzes around that reception. A kiss that smacks in silence or amid noisy distractions, bathed in tears or the companion to laughter, tickled by sunshine or in the invisibility of darkness.

Kisses have a precise taxonomy. There are kisses given like a stamp, lips stamping other lips. A passionate kiss, a kiss not yet ripe. An immature game. A shy gift. Then there's the far end of that spectrum: French kisses. Lips meet only to part: an exchange of papillae and nodes, of humors and caresses with the flesh of the tongue, within the perimeter of the mouth, within the ivory presidio of the teeth. Their opposites are a mother's kisses. Lips pressing against cheeks. Kisses heralding what will follow soon after: the enveloping hug, the gentle caress, the hand on the forehead feeling for feverish heat. Fatherly kisses graze the cheekbones, they're whiskery kisses, prickly, fleeting signs of proximity. Then there are kisses of greeting that brush the flesh, and the dirty old man kisses that sneak up on you, little slobbery ambushes that batten off a furtive intimacy.

Savage kisses can't be classified. They can put a seal upon silence, proclaim promises, pronounce verdicts or declare acquittals. There are the savage kisses that barely reach the gums, and others that practically shove down your throat. But savage kisses always occupy all the space available, they use the mouth as a way in. The mouth is merely the pool into which you wade, to find out if there's a soul, whether there really is anything else sheathing the body, or not—the ferocious kiss is there to probe, to fathom that unsoundable abyss or to meet a void. The dull, dark void that conceals.

There's an old story told among neophytes of barbarity, a story that regularly makes the rounds among breeders of fighting dogs: desperate creatures, devotees in spite of themselves of a cause of muscles and death. That legend, devoid of any scientific basis, tells how fighting dogs are selected at birth. The dogfighters scrutinize the litter of puppies with icy intolerance. They're not interested in choosing dogs that seem powerful, they don't wish to overlook dogs that look too skinny, they don't care to favor dogs that push their sisters away from the mother's teat, they're not trying to identify dogs that punish brothers for their greed. The test is different: the breeder yanks the puppy away from the nipple, seizing it by the scruff of the neck and pushing the little snout close to his own cheek. Most of the puppies will lick that cheek. But one—practically blind, still toothless, gums accustomed only to the mother's softness—will try to bite. One wants to know the world, have it between its jaws. And that is the savage kiss. That dog, male or female as it may be, will then be taught to fight.

There are kisses and there are savage kisses. The former remain within the precinct of the flesh; the latter know no limits. They want to be what they kiss.

Savage kisses come not from good nor from evil. They exist, like alliances. And they always leave an aftertaste of blood.

# HE'S BORN

**H**e's born!"

"What do you mean, he's born?!"

"That's right, he's born."

On the other end of the line, silence, nothing but breathing crackling over the microphone. Then: "Wait, are you sure?"

He'd been expecting this call for weeks, but now that Tucano was telling him, Nicolas felt the need to hear it again, repeated so he could be convinced that the day had finally come, to savor it well and truly in his head. So he could be ready.

"Right, like I'm kidding around! No, trust me. He was just born, I swear it, *adda murì mammà*, 'a Koala is practically still in the delivery room . . . No sign of Dentino, I came straight to the hospital."

"Sure, no surprise, he doesn't have the balls to show his face. But who told you the baby was born?"

"A male nurse."

"And who the fuck is he? Where did this nurse come from?" Nicolas wasn't about to settle for generic information, this time he wanted the details. He couldn't afford to improvise, nothing could get screwed up.

"He's a guy who used to work with Biscottino's father, Enzuccio

Niespolo. I told him that Koala is a friend of ours, and we just wanted to make sure we were the first to know, when the baby came into the world."

"And how much did you say we'd pay him? You don't think he's spouting bullshit just because we haven't given him a hundred euros yet?"

"No, no, I promised him an iPhone. That guy couldn't wait for this baby to be born so he could get his hands on a new phone. He was practically bent over with his ear against Koala's belly."

"Then let's do this thing. Tomorrow morning, the minute the sun rises."

Dawn found him ready and fully dressed, eager for action. The bed he was sitting upon was barely rumpled, he hadn't slept in it for even a minute. He shut his eyes and took a deep breath, then exhaled, a flat sharp sound. Day had risen. He needed to keep his mind clear, not let himself be sucked down by memories. He had a mission to perform; after that there'd be plenty of time for everything else.

Tucano's voice acted like the switch that opens the electric current. He stuck the Desert Eagle in his jeans and was down in the street quick as a flash.

Tucano had already put on his full-face helmet.

"Do you have the telephone?" Nicolas asked him as he put on his own helmet. "It's in the original packaging, right?"

"Maraja, everything's set."

"Then let's go buy the flowers." Nicolas swung his leg over the seat and started off at reduced speed. He felt a sense of calm warm his whole body. An hour from now, the whole matter would be settled. Case closed.

"These fucking assholes . . ." Tucano said. "They say they're not making money, but they sleep all day."

The metal roller blinds on the florist's shop were pulled down, they had no idea where to find another one, and in any case, they had to move quickly, thought Nicolas. Then he jammed on the brakes and the front of Tucano's helmet slammed against the back of his.

"Maraja, *maronna* . . ."

"That's right, the Madonna," said Nicolas, and, pushing the bike backwards with his feet, he rolled back to the mouth of the narrow alley, the *vicolo*. There, enclosed within a metal cage that glittered like gold set against its shabby, decaying surroundings, a votive shrine was lit by a small spotlight. Photographs of ex votos and holy cards of Padre Pio practically covered the Madonna, but still, she smiled reassuringly, and Nicolas returned the smile. He got off the TMAX, blew a kiss, the way his grandma had taught him to do when he was little, and, standing on tiptoe, slipped a bouquet of white calla lilies out of a vase.

"Isn't that going to piss off the Madonna?" Tucano asked.

"The Madonna never gets pissed off. That's why She's the Madonna," said Nicolas, pulling down the zipper on his sweat jacket to make room for the lilies. They took off again, engine roaring. At that exact time, as agreed in advance, Pesce Moscio was about to go into action.

Just inside the gates, the nurse was waiting for them; he was stamping his feet on the asphalt, bundled up in a down jacket. Tucano raised one hand in greeting, and he went on hopping up and down in place, even if what was driving him now was no longer any thought of warding off the bone-chilling cold, as much as the lurking fear that these two new arrivals on a scooter wearing full-face helmets might not be there to repay him for the favor.

"All right, then, take me to pay a surprise call on this baby," Nicolas began.

The male nurse tried to stall for time, trying to understand the spirit of the visit. He replied that they weren't relatives, he couldn't let them in.

"What do you mean, we're not relatives," said Nicolas. "It's not like the only relatives are first cousins. We're the closest kind of relatives, because we're friends, we're real family."

"Right now he's in the nursery. Soon they'll take him to his mother."

"It's a boy?"

"Yes."

"So much the better."

"Why?" asked the nurse, trying to gain time.

"It's easier that way . . ."

"What's easier?" he insisted. Nicolas ignored the question.

"Easier to bring 'em up, it's easier if you're a boy, am I right?" Tucano put in. "Or maybe it's easier if you're a girl. At least if you know how to fuck, you can get where you want, right?"

In Nicolas's silence, the nurse made the assumption that they would wait. He started to throw both arms wide, as if to say, what can you do, these are the rules.

"I want to see this baby before he gets to latch on to his mother's tits." The impatient voice, throbbing with rage, slapped him like a whipcrack, and before he could come up with a response, the nurse found himself with his face smeared against the visor of Nicolas's helmet. "I told you that I want to see him, this baby boy. I even brought flowers for the mother. Now you tell me how to get there." And with a shove he pushed the nurse back into an upright position.

The information poured forth with precision, the route was simple. At that point, Tucano grabbed the box containing the iPhone and tossed it into the air, while the nurse, eyes turned skyward to track the box's trajectory, waved his arms in terror, desperately trying to make sure the cell phone didn't hit the ground. He was so focused on his technological gem that he entirely overlooked the dense cloud of black smoke that was billowing into the air only yards away, and perhaps he even failed to catch a whiff of the acrid stench of burning tires. Pesce Moscio had been punctual to the split second. Nicolas had asked him to be punctual, indeed he'd ordered him to be. I want plenty of smoke. You have to cover everything up with a smoke screen. He'd told him that he wanted to make sure that the booth where the security guards spent their day was empty, the last thing he needed was a platoon of security guards chasing their scooter. "A diversion, Pescemo'," and Pesce Moscio had picked a restroom in the Polyclinic near the guards' booth. He'd stolen the tires from a shop that morning, and with a bottle of kerosene and a lighter, he was going to throw a hell of a party, a celebration of stench and toxic smoke, he'd focus everybody's attention on that restroom.

In the meantime, the Yamaha TMAX was rolling through the gate at walking speed. Up till that point, the plan had followed a certain logic.

Nicolas had worked out a timeline and a series of possible snags, and Tucano himself, diligently playing his part, had felt like a cog in this well-oiled machine. Then Nicolas had twisted the throttle and thrown all logic to the winds. The heavy scooter reared up in a wheelie and roared up the first flight of steps, almost like a horse leaping over a hurdle; bouncing step after step, it climbed the stairs and reached the entrance. The hospital's automatic front door whisked open and the TMAX plummeted into the lobby.

Indoors, the engine roared like a Boeing turbojet. They still hadn't encountered anyone, and at that hour of the day the steady stream of appointments and visiting families and friends hadn't yet started to come in, but their noisy incursion brought hospital staff running, bursting out of the ward and clinic doors in disbelief. Nicolas ignored them. He was looking for the elevator.

They stormed into the maternity ward, where they were met by silence. No one in the hallways, not a voice or a whimper to point them in the direction of the nursery. The bedlam they'd unleashed downstairs didn't seem to have ruffled the peace and quiet on this floor.

"What the fuck is this baby's name?"

"They must have them listed by last names, right?" Tucano replied. He knew Maraja far too well to run the risk of asking him how he thought they were going to exit from the blind alley they'd rushed into. In fact, that was what made Nicolas what he was, his willingness to push you to your limit before you even realized what was happening.

They left the TMAX blocking the corridor. Gleaming and black, the scooter looked like an enormous cockroach between those walls, which were a pale lime green and covered with posters proclaiming the benefits of breastfeeding. They galloped down the corridor in search of the nursery. Tucano went first, helmet still firmly gripping his head, Nicolas right behind him. An enfilade of doors to the right and the left, and the clucking of their soles on the linoleum flooring.

They emerged into a lobby with two empty desks, and beyond that glowed the plate-glass window of the nursery. There they all were, babies freshly delivered into life, lined up, red-faced in their pastel onesies; some slept, others were waving their tiny fists over their heads.

Maraja and Tucano leaned over, like two relatives curious to know whether the baby resembled mother or father more closely.

"Antonello Izzo," said Tucano. The light blue blanket with the name stitched to the corner was rising and falling almost imperceptibly. "Here he is." He turned to look at Nicolas, who was standing there, motionless, palms pressed against the plate glass, his head turned toward that newborn, who was smiling, or at least so it seemed to Tucano.

"Maraja . . ."

Silence.

"Maraja, now what are we going to do?"

"*Come s'accide 'nu criaturo, Tuca'*?" How do you kill a baby, Tucano?

"How the fuck do I know, you just thought of that now?"

Nicolas drew the Desert Eagle from the elastic of his boxer shorts and, with his thumb, snapped off the safety.

"If you ask me, it's just like popping a balloon, isn't it?" Tucano went on.

Nicolas pushed gently on the door, as if he wanted to be courteous enough to keep from making noise, to avoid waking up the other babies. He went over to Antonello, Dentino's son, the child of the guy who'd killed his brother, Christian, who'd shot him in the back like the lowest of traitors.

"Christian . . ." he said, in a whisper. It was the first time he had uttered that name since the day of his brother's funeral. He looked as if he'd fallen victim to a spell, his dark eyes focused straight ahead of him, but actually fathoming deep into who knows what other reality. Tucano felt like pounding his fists against the glass, shouting at Nicolas to hurry up, shouting that he needed to shoot that son of a traitor right away, immediately: instead Nicolas had placed the barrel of the Desert Eagle on the tiny belly, but the finger on the trigger wasn't moving. The pistol kept moving up and down, slowly, as if the lungs of that tiny creature really were capable of lifting the four and a half pounds of pistol. Tucano turned to look down at the end of the corridor and realized that in the time Nicolas had hesitated, a nurse had appeared behind them. She was moving rapidly down the corridor toward them, grabbing the pole of an IV stand as if it were a spear: "What are you doing here?" Then she focused on Nicolas and started screaming in dialect: "*Stanno arrubbando i criaturi! Stanno arrubbando i criaturi!*" They're stealing the babies! Tucano quickly leveled his Glock at her and the nurse instantly stopped short, with the IV stand held in midair, but that didn't stop her from continuing to shout.

"*Stanno arrubbando i bambini!* They're stealing the little ones! Help! Help!" Her voice was growing sharper and louder, like a siren.

"Maraja, pull the trigger, hurry up, they've figured it out, put him down once and for all . . ." But now Nicolas had tilted his head to one side, as if to get a better look at Dentino and 'a Koala's son. The baby was sleeping serenely, in spite of the pistol: Christian, too—when his mother had brought him home from the hospital, after delivering him—had slept exactly the same way. She would sit Nicolas down in an armchair and then put Christian in his arms, and Christian would just go on sleeping. But all around Antonello, in contrast, the other babies were starting to wake up. In no time at all, the nursery had turned into a hellish cacophony, the wailing of one newborn quickly infecting the one in the next crib, a deafening wave that was enough to stir Nicolas out of his trance.

"They're stealing the children! They're stealing the children!" the nurse went on shouting, whirling the IV post all the while, trying to work up the momentum to hurl that stainless-steel javelin with all her strength.

"Maraja, shoot, kill him now!" Tucano shouted. The nurse kept coming closer, and he didn't know whether to deck her with a punch to the face or shoot her, and if so, whether to wound or to kill. He just didn't know.

"Maraja, things are going sideways, we need to get out of here. Now. I mean fast, let's move!"

Nicolas lifted his left hand and touched the tattoo that he'd had done on the back of his neck, so that it could give him strength, confirm that there, too, in the presence of another innocent, what he was about to do was the right thing. For himself, for his mother, for the Piranhas. Because this was the time of the tempest, and he was the tempest that was crashing down furiously upon the city. He pressed the handgun down hard on the newborn baby's body, and now Antonello started crying, too.

Tucano had retreated, taking one step back after another until his helmet banged against the plate-glass window. "Listen, fatso," he was saying to the nurse, "I'll kill you, stay back." But she kept coming, and two other nurses, summoned by her shouting, had appeared in the corridor. As soon as they saw their colleague, they too started shouting: "*Uddio si stanno arrubbando i criaturi! Stanno arrubbando i criaturi!*"

"Get back! I'll kill you! I'll kill you all!" Tucano was shouting, and now his whole body was plastered against the glass. There was only one way out. He gripped the Glock with both hands now, taking careful aim at the forehead of the nurse with the IV pole.

*Boom.*

An explosion. Then silence. Tucano looked at his hand, which hadn't been fast enough to fire.

The bullet in fact had come from behind, shattering the plate-glass nursery window into a hail of sharp-edged fragments, shards that rattled off Tucano's helmet, glittering on the lab coats of the nurses, who were covering their faces with their hands, bounced off the ceiling, stabbed into walls and floor. When Tucano turned around to see who had fired, he saw Nicolas holding the Desert Eagle still pointed right at what had once been the nursery window. High up on the facing wall was the hole where the bullet had finally lodged. The cries of the babies, which had ceased for a brief fraction of a second, resumed desperately and Nicolas angrily started into awareness: "Come on, come on, get out of here."

Just like on the way in, they crossed paths with no one. They descended the broad steps of the Polyclinic, and then the steps that led down to the lobby. There Nicolas twisted the throttle all the way to barrel through the security guards who were struggling to draw their guns and the firemen with gas masks on their faces. The last person they roared past was the male nurse who had let them in in the first place, but his eyes were glued to his iPhone and he didn't even notice them going past.

Nicolas returned home just as his building was emerging from sleep. He heard the showers running, parents calling to children to get moving or hurry up, that the school gates weren't about to wait for them to wake up. Only his own apartment was mute and deserted. His mother was already at the laundry and pressing shop, every morning she got there a little before opening time; and his father had moved out right after Christian's death, he'd left the house with them to go to the funeral and then he'd never come home. They could live without him, though; his father didn't make the difference—he never had. Nicolas's mouth twisted in a grimace, he tossed the keys onto the table and turned on the television set. The volume was turned down all the way, not even the morning news dared to break a silence that smacked of reproof. Trailing after the segments about local politics, on-screen there were images from the hospital, the shattered plate glass, the nurses taking newborn babies with convulsive bawling faces out of their cribs and carrying them off, tire marks on the floor. "Hooligan Pranks at the Polyclinic," read the banner graphic on the TV screen. A minute later the report was over, the time you'd devote to a stupid stunt.

He reached his bedroom, lay down on his brother's bed, and knitted the fingers of both hands together behind his neck, allowing his fingertips to trace the name he'd had tattooed there: Christian. A meticulous braille-reading of the name, back and forth, and then again, a circumnavigation of the oval outline of the hand grenade, and then, slowly, he repeated the process. He'd insisted on having the hand grenade exactly the same as the one on his chest that enclosed his name, Maraja, an identical twin tattoo.

What have I done? he asked himself. He stuck both fists into his eye sockets and started digging.

Cat and mouse. A furious cat on the hunt for a phantom mouse.

The piazzas were thriving. Coke was moving briskly. They had no trouble selling Scignacane's heroin. The monthly take from the protection racket was coming in on time. The sun shone on the Piranhas' territories, in the center of Naples. But Dentino was still alive, and Nicolas simply couldn't make peace with that idea. It was like a backache that just wouldn't quit, a cavity in a tooth that torments your sleep: the traitor was still somewhere in the city, hiding who knows where.

For the past five months, he'd been wearing himself ragged, on endless stakeouts. He'd begun by setting up an ambush outside the courtyard of the parish church. That rectangular patch of dirt still bore the marks of their soccer matches. Then he'd spent night after sleepless night outside the dentist's office where Dentino had spent his first month's wages on whitening the teeth that smoke and drugs had blackened. Then his parents' apartment, the apartment of his maternal grandparents, then that of his paternal grandparents, and Capodimonte Park because someone said that they'd seen him sitting on a bench there, and finally the train station, because it had just struck Nicolas as a logical option to give that a try. Homeless bum by homeless bum, toilet by toilet. Tightly pinching his nose shut, he'd turned over those worn and weary men sleeping in their rags. At the apartment where Dumbo's mother lived, he'd devoted a full week of continuous stakeouts, ready to ambush him at any time of the day or night, confident that sooner or later that traitor would give in to temptation. But he'd come away empty-handed.

The mouse hadn't shown itself anywhere, so he logically had to crush the baby mouse. But he hadn't been able to do it . . . *Come si accide 'nu criaturo?* How can you kill a baby?

"That's enough," shouted Nicolas, "that's enough." A single movement, his arm sweeping away everything. Saint cards, holy cards, cards of the Madonna, San Gennaro, Padre Pio, photographs of Christian at his first communion, in a swimsuit beside him on a beach of which he had no memory. He looked down at the clutter of objects at his feet, then he took off shoes, trousers, and sweat jacket. After that, he pulled the blanket aside and slid under the sheets, holding his knees up with both arms. And then he finally made up his mind to do what he ought to have been doing for some time now.

He started crying.

# QUICKSAND

A wasp's nest. Nicolas could hear them swooping around his head, and without opening his eyes, did his best to wave them away with wide sweeps of his hands. Then consciousness took over. Nicolas opened an eye. Wasps? The old Motorola StarTAC cell phones that he and the *paranza* used as burner phones. Impossible to bug or hack. Who could say how long they'd all been sizzling away on the desk.

He leaped out of bed. He'd slept the whole morning away, and part of the afternoon, but his sleep had done nothing to refresh him. He splashed icy water on his face, then pulled the hood of his sweatshirt over his head, as if that could protect him from the pain that was rising in the back of it. One of those splitting headaches that focus on a specific point, an infinitesimal dot, and then dig in deeper, scraping and shoveling like a sadist with a fine-point drill bit. When he was little, if he had a fever or a tummy ache, his mother, Mena, would mix up a glass of water, lemon, and sugar. That was her universal remedy: that, she said, would cure whatever ailed you.

But Mena wasn't there now, and first he'd thought of chasing the pain away with a joint, then with a line of coke, but in the end he'd opted for a strong espresso and a text to the whole *paranza*: he wanted them all at the private room, at five on the dot, they had a lot of things to talk about. Even if he actually didn't much feel like talking, and after all, he had nothing to say. He just wanted to bathe in the hail of words from his team, in the hope that those words would push back that *thing* he could sense under the buzz of that fine-point drill bit. A clot of helplessness and dissatisfaction with himself, and the more time he spent alone, the more it continued to grow.

The New Maharaja was still under renovation. Or at least that's what the proprietor, Oscar, told the people who showed up outside the club every evening. A total embargo. He'd walk over to the people who stood gazing up at the scaffolding that concealed the white of the façade, and, resting his hands on his flaccid belly, Oscar would swear to each and every one of them that when the club reopened, they'd find an even more magnificent New Maharaja. The "renovation work" actually consisted of nothing more elaborate than a coat of white paint and a wax-and-buff of the dance floor—but Oscar was counting on expectations to do the work for him. He was counting on mirages.

For the Piranhas, though, the New Maharaja was always open, even when it was closed.

Oscar saw Nicolas's TMAX arrive, cruising along at an unusual velocity, placid as one of those big cruise ships that you could admire from the balcony of the New Maharaja. He watched him abandon the scooter like any old piece of junk and continue straight ahead on foot without so much as a glance at him or either of the two young women he was talking to: both blond, tall, very young.

"Maraja"—he tried to detain him for a moment—"come here, let me introduce you to the new dance corps." But Nicolas didn't even hear him, he just wanted to get to the private room, lie down on one of the little settees, and maybe get a few minutes alone in the dark before the others arrived. He tried to put his priorities in some kind of order, after his failed raid on the hospital. Talk to Tucano? Make it clear to him, with kind words or threats, that he mustn't breathe a word to the others of what had happened? Or else confront Mena, tell her about his failure? Because there really was no other word to describe it. Maybe she already knew all about it, maybe she hadn't missed the report on the local news.

The first one to arrive was Lollipop, followed by Briato'. His old friend from mini-soccer still had a very visible limp. After being broken in four places, his leg had never quite healed right, and the doctor had told Briato' that he would limp for the rest of his life. Still, he didn't make too much of a big deal about it, and, in fact, if anything he overdid his walk, "De Niro style." In the gloomy cavern of the private room, they couldn't spot Nicolas right away, over where he sat bent at the waist, with both hands pressed against his temples. Nicolas was seated on his throne, so that the others would see him exactly where he belonged, but he simply hadn't been able to bring himself to turn on the lights.

"Maraja, where are you?" shouted Briato'.

"I'm right here," said Nicolas. "Why are you shouting?"

Lollipop flopped down on the little sofa, while Briato' switched on the lights, filling the room with a blast of artificial daylight. A glaring white sun exploded behind Nicolas's eyes.

All it took was a vicious glare from Nicolas, and Briato' switched the light right back off, returning the room to darkness. One by one, the others drifted in. The last to arrive was Drago', who sat down next to Drone, reassembling the old hemicycle that right there, on that spot, had first officially sanctioned the distribution of the piazzas. They were so many colorless silhouettes now, more or less dense according to the quantity of light that they were able to capture as they moved. Only Nicolas, sunken in his throne, seemed to have lost all features of his lithe physique.

Biscottino couldn't seem to keep his hands still. They rustled in the darkness, in time with his words: "Maraja, how come all this darkness? Doesn't Oscar pay his electric bills anymore?"

"That guy never paid a bill in his life," Pesce Moscio piped up. "They just tied his power line into the apartment house next door."

The ensuing laughter was a wave of needles that drove into Nicolas's skull, but he said nothing. Needle by needle, his brothers would cure him.

"But did you see the two big blond ladies out there? Oscar must need a ladder to fuck them . . ." said Lollipop.

More laughter, more needles, and already he was feeling a little better. It was the usual ritual for which he had always been the master of ceremonies: first the bullshitting, then the tide of wisecracks would subside and at last they'd come to the important matters. The piazzas. The money. Their kingdom.

At first, it had been a genuine boom. Prices that low had never been seen before—in Forcella it seemed like Christmas every day. Everyone came to the neighborhood, even from as far away as the provinces, and the Piranhas regularly ran out of narcotics in a single morning and had to arrange for a speedy resupply. Everything had gone as smooth as silk, and the line of customers had turned into a mob. Drone had appointed himself the chief logistics officer of the operation—he was in charge of crowd management. He'd managed to get his hands on his own tally counter, like the ones that airline personnel use during boarding procedures, and he'd rush from one piazza to another. *Clackety-clack, clack, clack.* He'd set up in a corner and with every person that walked past to buy drugs, he'd lower his thumb. *Clack.* When there were too many customers, he'd arrange to interrupt the stream somehow, or else quickly order a resupply. The tally counter had become an extension of his hand, and even when he was at the New Maharaja, you could occasionally hear that *clackety-clack, clack.*

"On my patch, there's nothing left," said Tucano. "I can't hold on to them. They want to go back to selling Micione's shit. I can't hold on to my dealers."

The euphoria had waned over the course of the last three months. At first the merchandise that the Piranhas were pushing had sold like hotcakes, but now they were running out of product. So the managers of the piazzas had made the sober decision to turn back to their old supplier, who'd taken advantage of the opportunity to flood the market with tons of his shit.

"Same thing in San Giorgio," said Lollipop. "You know what they used to call me, until just last week? Don Vince'! You get that? But now that we're running out of product, they're going back to what they've always done. They talk to Micione and we go back to being the fucking last of the brothers."

"Lollipop," said Drago', "your problem is you don't try to figure things out." He went over to Lollipop to give him a pinch on the cheek, but Lollipop dodged aside and the two of them tangled up in a gentle wrestling match, without real effort, to such an extent that to Nicolas those bodies momentarily reminded him of a video of kittens—or were they bear cubs?—that Letizia had posted. Just as quickly as they'd come together, the two young men broke apart and Drago' sat back down.

In a throbbing voice, bursting with satisfaction, he described how he often had to turn customers away, he had so many of them at Vicaria Vecchia.

"I just doubled the price," he explained, "and the product moves more slowly but that means the dealers keep their mouths shut."

"Fuck, listen to him, the businessman!"

"Holy shit! You blew them away!"

"Yeah, but that way they make less money," said Tucano.

"They make less money, maybe a little slower," Drago' conceded, "but then they're not stuck between a rock and a hard place."

"Ua', nice, Drago'," said Biscottino, "the rock won't budge, and the hard place either. Ua', that's what's great about the Vesuvio district."

If Nicolas had opened his mouth, he would have said that it really wasn't a joking matter. They were caught in quicksand and they were going down. One piazza after the other, they'd all go down, some sooner, others later. Maybe a few would keep control over a street here and a street there, but they'd eventually be suffocated between Micione's firepower and the fate that awaits those who have never even looked their supplier in the face. L'Arcangelo's supplies were down to their last scrapings. Nicolas knew that and so did the others, but no one had the courage to say it out loud. Certainly, Scignacane's heroin continued to arrive, as regular as clockwork, but it alone wasn't enough to assure the loyalty of the *paranza*'s piazzas.

That's what he ought to have said, but his headache wouldn't let go. So he said nothing and limited himself to keeping an eye on Tucano, who in turn kept his eyes downcast. Was Tucano waiting his turn so he could reveal what Nicolas had been unable to do in that hospital, waiting his turn to denounce Nicolas's weakness? All it would have taken was a single word and then, So long, Maraja. I would have done it, he thought, so why doesn't Tucano say anything? Didn't he want a *paranza* all his own, too?

"Maraja," said Drago', "Tucano and Lollipop are right. We're running out of product. Before long, we're going to lose these guys."

"Let's just kill them all," Briato' weighed in. "That's how they do it, right? When someone sells someone else's product without authorization, they need to be shot."

"That's just the way it is on the piazzas," said Drone. "Either you sell drugs for a boss or else you have to pay taxes to that boss. They aren't paying us any taxes, and we're running out of drugs."

"Nico', let's call them all in to the club and then let's gas them," suggested Briato', unleashing the *paranza*'s laughter. Nicolas could only manage a grimace, and they were off again, joking and bullshitting.

"Maraja and me," Pesce Moscio started telling a story, "were there, on Piazza Bellini, you know. There were these *chiattilli*, preppies in polo shirts. They were staring at us, I already had my hand on my gat. And then these assholes come over to us, I look at Maraja and he shrugs his shoulders."

"Pesce Moscio," said Drone, "what kind of a story are you telling? You sound like Piero Angela!"

"One of them says that he's from the news," Pesce Moscio went on as if nothing had happened, "and he wants to know if he can interview us, right, Maraja?"

The seven silhouettes turned toward Nicolas, but not a word came from the throne. Drago' stood up, slithered around Lollipop, who had guessed his intentions, and switched on the lights.

Nicolas Maraja had left the building.

## STOP CRYING

He headed back to Forcella, riding the TMAX the same unhurried way he had on the trip out. The throttle at half speed, never a line over or under, the occasional tap on the brake when necessary. The meeting at the New Maharaja hadn't done a lot of good, other than to reassure him that there weren't any signs of an impending coup. It was as if his brothers hadn't noticed that something had stopped working inside him, that he felt somehow blurred. Even worse: he felt as if he was in that old movie that his teacher Signor De Marino had shown the class: *Invasion of the Body Snatchers.* Soon enough they were sure to notice that there was nothing actually left of him but an empty shell. Guided by force of habit, the TMAX turned onto Via Vicaria Vecchia, then angled into a gentle rightward curve. Via dei Carbonari. He was home.

What the fuck kind of thoughts do I have in my mind, wondered Nicolas. It was all the fault of that clot that had formed in the back of his neck since he'd awakened that morning, a clot that was tormenting him with a feeling he'd never experienced before in his life. The sensation that he was no longer good for nothing.

Eyes downcast, he parked the scooter and left the *vicolo* on foot. How long had it been since he'd walked through his city?

Before he even realized it, he arrived on Via Mezzocannone. A couple of university students called him by his name. Who knows, maybe they were old customers from the times when he used to deal for Copacabana. He ignored them, kept going, by now Forcella was behind him, and with it, the murals of San Gennaro. He lengthened his stride, eyeing every intersection, every street corner, every shop out of that need of his to size up the territory—a need that had by now been transformed into an instinct. The jagged gap in the bronze gate of the Maschio Angioino was there to remind him that, just a few years earlier, while strolling past with Letizia, he had taken an oath that one day he too would leave his mark on the city, on its stones, on its people.

By the time he reached Castel dell'Ovo he was out of breath. He was panting, as if he were drowning. He climbed the steps and walked out onto the balcony. He leaned against the wall, shoulders pressed into the tufa, knees gathered up to his chest. In front of him was the sea. A shiver of pleasure made the hairs on his arms stand up. The sea. That's what he needed, that was the antidote to those thoughts. That inexhaustible blue asked nothing of him and never could. Alone in front of the sea, he could manage to stop thinking, stop planning, perhaps because all that horizon left him free to wander aimlessly, freed of all calculations.

He felt better, but there was still something missing. He pulled out his iPhone, and, indifferent to the missed calls and the stacks of texts, he wrote to Letizia:

**Nicolas**

I'm at the usual place, looking out over the sea.

When Letizia arrived, Nicolas was still in the same position. He barely turned to look at her, and all she did was sit down beside him, laying her head on his shoulder. They looked like what they were: an eighteen-year-old boy and a sixteen-year-old girl. The wind was teasing Letizia's hair out over Nicolas's face, but he didn't recoil, he let the hair whip his face, fill his mouth, and then he sat waiting for the next gust. He let his eyes abandon the deep blue of the sea, which by now had taken on the same coloration as the sky at sunset, and he kissed her. At first on the eyelids, and then on the chin, then he lingered for a while on the lips, and then moved on to her earlobes. He had exposed his neck and Letizia dived in, kissing him, nipping at his neck with her teeth.

"Every time I kiss you on the neck," she said to him, "I see Christian, because I read his name."

Nicolas's mouth, soft with kisses, twisted into a grimace.

"You need to forget about his name" was all he said.

Letizia tied her hair back with a scrunchie, and the magic of a moment earlier had evaporated. "But I feel there's a thief in my body—*mi sento 'o mariuolo in cuorpo*—as if we were the ones who did it . . ."

Nicolas had been trying to come to terms with that thief in the body for months now, and he wanted to say so to Letizia.

"*Ma accirelo a stu mariuolo*," he said instead. "Just kill that thief. I was the one who didn't know how to defend him. When Scignacane told me he wanted to kill Dumbo, I should have had the balls to kill Dumbo myself, and Dentino, too. I left the job half done, and they took half of myself away from me. My brother. *Fratemo*."

Letizia shook her head, flinging her ponytail back and forth.

"Nico', I don't want to know these things."

"Then why the fuck are you telling me about a thief in your body? Just don't say a word. If you don't want to know, then these things shouldn't exist for you, that's the way it has to be."

Letizia stood up, she didn't want to feel Nicolas's body anymore, his legs seeking hers. She took a few steps back and leaned against the wall. He let her be.

If she didn't want to know, then she could get the hell out of there.

"Why this pineapple at the end of the *n* in Christian, right here, on the back of your neck?" asked Letizia, restoring a tone of affection in her voice.

"That's a hand grenade," said Nicolas without looking around.

"I know, silly. I know these things," she said, but as she said it, she lightly caressed his neck. Gently. "But why this ugly thing near your brother's beautiful name?"

"That ugly thing is to remind me that the people who killed him need to die. All of them."

"You can't tell me these things, I already told you that, they scare me. *Tienatelle pe' tte.* Keep them to yourself."

"Then don't ask me things, mind your own fucking business."

"*Maro'*, Nico': Madonna, when you talk like that, you're like an animal . . ."

"No, an animal would know how to defend his brother. Shut that toilet mouth of yours. Just shut the fuck up."

"You know that you're a sewer rat, Nico'? Go fuck yourself!" The words came out in a tremulous voice. She'd never spoken like that to Nicolas, never with that violence, but he hadn't turned a hair. This indifference between them was a new thing, too.

She felt like crying, but she didn't want to let him see that she was hurt, and frightened.

Before heading down the stairs and leaving, she raised her middle finger to Nicolas's back, as he continued to stare out at the sea.


He rolled the street back up like a ribbon. Castel dell'Ovo, Maschio Angioino, Via Medina, San Biagio, Mezzocannone. Forcella. Home. From downstairs he could see the wide-open kitchen window, a clear indicator that Mena was home, that she hadn't lost her deeply ingrained habit of letting fresh air into the apartment morning and evening, not even after Christian's death. She'd shut down everything else, Mena had, but she hadn't given up light and air.

He found her folding freshly laundered T-shirts. She lifted those bundles of fabric, then a quick snap of the wrists and the T-shirts regained their shape. Those wrists twisted under the armpits of the T-shirts, then a last fold leading to the final transformation: a perfect rectangle.

Nicolas waited for his mother to finish with that basket of laundry before saying: "Ciao, Ma."

She needed only a quick glance at his face to glimpse the burden he was carrying inside him.

"Have you been to the beach?" she asked him.

He nodded. He didn't particularly want to talk, but he felt the need to hear *her* talk, as if since he'd awakened that morning all he'd been doing was wandering the city in order to wind up there. To come back home to his mother, to appear in the presence of the tribunal that would finally shout out his failure, his inadequacy. He approached the table and set one hand down on the T-shirt on the top of the pile. On it was a picture of the London Eye. Christian had given it to him, in exchange for the promise that one day, Nicolas really would take him to London with their pockets full of cash, and that they'd take a ride together on that panoramic Ferris wheel. "And from up there, we'll piss on the heads of all the Arab oil tycoons in London," he had told Christian. He looked at the T-shirt and he felt as if it, too, were trying to accuse him of the absence of the once-living body that had occupied that T-shirt just a few months ago. He took his hand off the pile and clenched it until he could feel the fingernails biting into the palm of his hand.

"You see all the things Christian had?" his mother asked with a gentle smile. "It's unbelievable, you never even notice all the things that revolve around a person, and some of those things are useless, eh? Things that aren't needed at all. All these T-shirts, all these shoes, all these toys . . . and you wouldn't even have time to wear all these things." She ran her fingers through her hair, locks that had whitened at her temples in lifeless strands. He looked at the floor, unable to bring himself even to nod, his fingers still clutching as if his hand were holding the pistol he'd been unable to use, dangling useless at his side.

"Nicolas," his mother summoned him back to her. When she uttered his entire name, neither Nicolino nor Nico', it meant that a speech was in the offing. "I'm not sure I'm happy with how I see you, Nicolas," she said, using his full name again as she set down the steam iron, standing perpendicular to the surface of the ironing board, and ran her fingers through his hair now, the way she used to when he was small, smaller than Christian had been.

"I'm just fine, Ma," he replied in a tone of voice that he tried to make sound confident.

"You don't seem fine to me. You seem gloomy, sad . . . Listen to me. They're things people say, but they're true, too: A mother knows. A mother knows her handsome son has been to the beach. A mother knows that her son is carrying a burden that's eating him alive. A mother always knows everything, Nico'."

"Mammà," Nicolas tried to say, but there wasn't enough air in his lungs.

"And for a mother," Mena continued, looking closely at him with the eyes of a woman who had nothing left to lose, "for a mother, all her children are the same. But that's not true for me. Christian was my heart and soul, you know that, but you've always been different. Christian was my puppy. You're my limited edition. I coddled him too much, and I coddled you too little. I made that mistake, it's my fault."

Pause. A voice from downstairs, the voice of someone looking for someone, and then more silence.

"I'm the one who just didn't pay attention, who didn't know how to protect him. I thought I could see everything, that your father didn't understand a thing but that I could . . . after all, though, what good did it do to understand what you both were doing? Where was I looking? I was just fooling myself."

"Mammà . . ."

"You didn't do anything wrong, Nicolas, I'm telling you. Someone else killed our boy. He hadn't done anything wrong, you were always careful to keep him out of it. He was as innocent as an angel. Their little boy is an angel, just the same. *Comm' 'o puo' ammazzà 'n'angiulillo?* How can you kill a little angel? You can't, Nico', I'm here to tell you. You can't kill an angel."

Nicolas felt his body turn soft and the clot at the back of his neck turn hot, as if the blood had finally started to circulate again, free to flow.

"Mammà, so you knew about Dentino's son, I . . ."

"A mother knows everything, Nico', I told you that. When you were small, you remember? When the nuns were taking care of you and you walked around the palm tree in the courtyard. And then, just like that, you started smacking your little friend. Do you remember?"

He just lifted his head and sucked out a flat "no," in dialect, "'nzù." He couldn't stop thinking of that angel. No, he could never kill the angel. His mother was right. It was simple enough, that's why—and the more often he said it, the more he started to feel like himself again.

"Mother Lucilla, *a capa 'e pezze*, the raghead, the nun, you remember? She called me and you were all angry. And when I asked you why you would have done such a terrible thing, you told me: 'Mammà, one time that kid beat me up and so I beat him up, because anyone who's hurt me once should never hurt me again.' Nico', you were just small and already you were the strongest one. You're still the strongest one. You've always walked on your own two legs, you've never hesitated, and even when you made mistakes, you did it for the right reason. You've always been a man, even when you were small. More of a man than your father." She got up from the chair and went over to the window. A light breeze had closed the shutter and she leaned out to hook it open. Then she turned to look at him with the faint light of the *vicolo* behind her. She looked like a saint in a painting. "You did what you needed to do, Nico'. Anything that sons do, the mothers are guilty of. Even when they lose a son, the mothers are to blame."

Mena stepped close to him again, and that same gentle smile appeared on her face. "I never paid enough attention to you, but a mother should always be close to her children. Maybe I didn't give you many things, but what you needed you took for yourself. The things I didn't give you, you just took for yourself. Well, if you want to take everything for yourself, then go ahead, but take them for real. There's no point shedding tears, here. And I say the same thing to myself, Nico'. No more tears, Mena. If the path of goodness brought us nothing, maybe the path of evil will be more fruitful. You're a special son. You're eighteen, you're a man now. So do what you have to do, and do it right. Whoever took Christian away from us? *S'adda fà male.* They need to be hurt badly."

Nicolas felt like laying his head on her breast, the way he used to do when he was five and he'd hide in the armoire and then call her to come find him. But that only lasted a second. He was a man now; in fact, he'd always been a man. He felt uneasy. On the one hand, it seemed to him that his mother's words somehow protected him, but on the other he could tell that the mandate she was imparting to him, her approval, was a bad thing, as if he needed a mother's orders to do what he needed to, as if he couldn't do it of his own accord. He tried to overcome that confusion in the only way he knew how: "Mammà, I love you."

"And I love you, too, Nicolas." She took his face in her hands and brushed her lips over his forehead. "I'm always with you. Now more than ever." Then she unplugged the iron and moved off toward the bedroom with the stack of T-shirts. "The one who hurt us must never again be able to hurt us," he heard her whisper.

# JACK OF HEARTS

**B**efore he reached the border of the Ponticelli neighborhood, it had really been a lovely day. It was warm out, even though they were in the heart of the fall, and the sun was beating down hard on Nicolas's freshly shaven head, but a breath of breeze was blowing behind him; it almost seemed to be pushing the TMAX along.

That morning, he had told his brothers, reappearing out of the empty air just as he'd vanished: "To get out of the quicksand, I need to talk to Don Vittorio today." Nicolas had summoned them to their lair, and the *paranza*, present down to every last member, had nodded their approval, that's right, *accussì s'adda fà*. No one had breathed a word about the failure of the incursion at the hospital, and anyway, by now he understood that the vendetta would follow different paths. He'd gone back to being Maraja, and he gazed into their eyes, his men—one by one, from Biscottino to Drago'. The sky was the limit.

He wanted to arrive at the Conocal from behind, instead of getting there directly from Ponticelli, just to savor that air. It was an air that cleared everything else away, and it did it kindly, as if warding off the bad thoughts, leading them away by the hand.

It had been a while since he'd gone to see L'Arcangelo, he'd covered a lot of miles since then, and the money in his pockets was there as proof, pressing against his thighs.

He saw Micione's men from a distance, because they and they alone could be just sitting there nonchalantly rolling a joint, perched on the hood of a Mercedes-Benz. They were exuding the confidence of guards taking an important prisoner to solitary confinement. Nicolas tried other ways in: he explored the entire perimeter of the neighborhood, he circumnavigated the Lotto Zero neighborhood (two other men, this time on motorcycles), he brushed the boundary with San Giorgio a Cremano, confident that on that side the security would be a little more lax. Instead, he found himself face-to-face with an SUV with tinted glass windows.

They want to bury Don Vittorio alive, he thought to himself. He'd stopped at a safe distance, outside a café with an array of empty tables. The day had lost its beauty, even the breeze that had sprung up earlier had waned to little or nothing. He called Aucelluzzo: if he knew how to get out of Ponticelli, then he certainly must know how to get back in there. Five minutes later he heard the unmistakable sound of Aucelluzzo's scooter. He saw the man come buzzing out of the curve, zipping along at top speed, ears practically grazing the ground. The scooter screeched to a halt right in front of him, and Aucelluzzo still hadn't set both feet on the pavement when he was already pulling up his T-shirt to proudly display his new tattoo. He'd had four bullet holes inked on his skinny pale chest.

"*Ua'*, that's too great, exactly like Wolverine!" Nicolas exclaimed, a little bit to flatter him, but almost as much because he really thought so.

As soon as Aucelluzzo pulled his T-shirt back down, he set off on his usual litany of woes. Nicolas couldn't just call Aucelluzzo whenever he pleased, his life was already a shitstorm, he had to peddle drugs for pennies, and now he had to deal with Micione's guards, too.

"Maraja," he said at last, "I'm the only one who can come and go, I move like the wind."

Nicolas gently laid his fist on the other man's shoulder.

"Why, you think I don't know that? That's why I called you, Aucellu'. I need your superpowers."

Aucelluzzo puffed out his chest, and without a word he took off at speed, followed by Nicolas. They turned into a large parking lot just off the A3, and arrived at a cemetery of rusty trailers, and then at a sheet-metal barrier that bordered Via Mastellone: the entrance to Ponticelli. Aucelluzzo went over to a panel that was dangling loose and removed it without effort. He threw it to the ground, kicking up a cloud of dust: "Now you can get through, Maraja." Nicolas gave him a half bow and sped off.

The zone of Ponticelli was, if possible, more desolate still. All the life that remained in it was drying up. The few shops had their roller blinds down and defiled with graffiti, and there was practically no one in sight on the streets.

A nuclear war, Nicolas said to himself. A war of asphyxiation, an extended siege, the sole objective of which was to drain L'Arcangelo's resources, driving him into famine, paralysis, utter starvation. Sooner or later, Micione would win his victory, everyone else believed.

Everyone but Maraja.

He parked under the portico of the apartment building where Don Vittorio L'Arcangelo had his cell-like apartment. He glanced up to see if he could spot a pair of eyes peering out from under the lowered wooden roller blinds: the eyes of 'o Cicognone, Don Vittorio's factotum, and then he knocked on the door of the schoolteacher, Professoressa Cicatello. She answered wearing the usual stained apron. Nicolas greeted her with the most courteous "*buongiorno*" he could muster, but then he ruined everything by blurting out an oath—"*mannagi'a morte*"—because he had just remembered the porcelain ballerina he'd left downstairs in the underseat compartment of his scooter. He turned and ran downstairs to get it. When he got back upstairs, Professoressa Cicatello was still standing there, and Nicolas placed it in her hand with: "Payment in advance, signo', otherwise I'm sure to forget it." He'd already run into too many unforeseen obstacles that day to waste time on conventional chitchat, and after all, he knew the way by heart. He walked past the young kids Professoressa Cicatello was tutoring and reached the kitchen: up the ladder, reach the trapdoor, three well-aimed blows with the broom handle on the ceiling. 'O Cicognone opened the trapdoor, giving him a fleeting glance, because in the meantime L'Arcangelo was shouting: "*Ua', che chiavata! Che chiavata!*" I'm getting fucked here!

Nicolas found them sitting in front of an *ISS Pro Evolution* video game. L'Arcangelo was holding the joypad as if it were a TV remote control, with just one hand, and he was waving it in front of the television screen as if that would allow him to steer the players. "What the fuck!" he kept saying. He'd jumped to his feet, on edge, and Nicolas noticed that the jeans he was wearing were at least a couple of sizes too big. A T-shirt that must once have been bright red hung torn on one side, while the pullover draped over his shoulders, hanging slightly askew, was pilling and covered with lint balls. Don Vitto' has lint balls, Nicolas thought to himself, and that image cut the tension that had seized him the minute he'd climbed up into the apartment. Today he was risking a chunk of his future, and he was going to have to face off with that man who reeked of filth and old age. Who reeked of death.

"How the hell do you do it, though," Don Vittorio was saying, "how the hell do you have any fun with this piece of shit?" And then he slapped his hand down on the joypad and silenced the PlayStation. "Cicogno'," he said, "go make an espresso, *ja'*, we have an important guest."

"Sure, Cinderfella will make you an espresso," 'o Cicognone muttered, and vanished into the kitchen. As soon as they were alone, Nicolas made his business report to L'Arcangelo, telling him that everything was going pretty well, leaning hard on that "*pretty* well," and then pulled a couple of wads of cash out of his pockets. "This is the cut from the Grimaldi clan."

L'Arcangelo hefted the wads of bills for a short while, uncertainly, his eyes half closed.

"Don Vitto', wait, what are you saying, don't you count the money?"

"There are two kinds of men in this world. The kind that counts money, and the kind that weighs it, Nicolas. The ones who count money don't have any. The ones who weigh it have plenty. You know how much a billion lire weighs?"

"A billion what?"

"A billion *lire*, asshole! The money people used before the euro. Thirteen kilos, four hundred grams."

"Fuck. And how much do you figure I just gave you?"

"More or less fifty thousand euros," he replied promptly. "Nico', if *I* was selling it, I would have made twice as much. You and your fucking Google method . . ."

Nicolas took the slight without complaining, there was no point in digging up that old argument, he was there for a specific reason. He knew what he wanted to ask, but he didn't know when, and if the old man was in a bad mood, that would ruin everything. So he tried to sound him out: "Don Vitto', don't you ever have a woman come to see you?"

"No, because I lost your mother's phone number. Why would you ask me a question like that? What, have we eaten from the same plate?" the old man replied with a hint of surprise, but they were words uttered with a smile.

"No, Don Vitto', but I'm seriously worried that you, with Cinderfella over there"—and he jutted his chin in the direction of the kitchen—"what with one espresso and another, you and him, him and you, maybe the two of you . . . you know what I'm saying, I mean maybe you still get it up."

Don Vittorio's smile didn't waver: "In fact, I have to try and remember if I ever fucked your mother, a *guagliona* from around Forcella, eighteen years ago . . . maybe you're actually my son."

"Eh, I only wish, Don Vittorio."

L'Arcangelo took pleasure in that aside and, with a smile still on his face, finally invited Nicolas to take a seat. "So tell me, Nico', you don't keep the weapons I gave you in the lair on Vicolo dei Carbonari, do you?"

"And how do you know about the lair?"

"I know all about you. I created you. The apple never falls far from the tree. You're my apple."

"This thing with the apple sounds a little gay, if you don't mind my saying so, Don Vitto'. I'm Adam, not Eve, you know."

"Madonna, what a rude thing you are . . . So where did you put these weapons, anyway?"

"Where they'll be safe."

"No, but *exactly* where, tell me that." L'Arcangelo had made an investment. It was his entrepreneurial right to make sure things were being done right. "You might trust the children you work with, but I don't, or not as much as you, anyway. They never caught me with anything, not in the past twenty years."

"They're in the safekeeping of a caregiver, in Gianturco. Safer than that there's only the carabinieri barracks."

"Good job. And good job your *paranza* is doing, you've got your system chugging along nicely. You're becoming the prince of Naples, bravo."

Nicolas cocked an eyebrow. "*Ua'*, Don Vitto', if you talk like that you're making a mistake, don't you know what Maraja means in Sanskrit?" He spoke carefully, pausing briefly before uttering that last word, almost as if getting a running start before uttering that difficult foreign term. "It means great king. And you could bet your bottom dollar that I wasn't born to be a prince; I'm the king."

"Great king . . ." L'Arcangelo said again, with a face that gave no sign of whether he was losing his temper or thinking back to the years when *he'd* been the king of Naples. "A great king has a sword, you know that? It's like his license to command. Are you eighteen? Do you have a driver's license?"

Nicolas nodded, embarrassed.

"Good for you," L'Arcangelo went on. "But the most important driver's license you need is the license to stab."

And on the oilcloth that covered the table, a switchblade knife appeared. Nicolas took it as if it were already his own property. The handle was a section of black horn to the end of which a metal plate had been attached. The guard. He knew what it was for. He'd seen a never-ending succession of knife cuts to the palm, caused by the sudden yanking of knives out of the bellies of animals, or men. He pressed the button on the side of the knife and the blade darted out like a lightning bolt. That sound, too—that *stack*—was all too familiar to Nicolas. Only then, seeing his image reflected in the steel, did he remember to say thank you. But curiosity immediately devoured any boilerplate politeness:

"L'Arcangelo, have you ever killed anyone? I mean, with your own hands?" he asked.

"What shocking rudeness, Nico'! I'm sure that your mother taught you decent manners, it's just that you've forgotten how to use them." L'Arcangelo threw both arms wide and then let them fall flat on his knees.

"Then tell me now, *ja'*, L'Arcangelo," said Nicolas. Palm to fold the blade shut and thumb on the button.

"Anybody can shoot," Don Vittorio replied, "it doesn't take anything special. Technology destroys real worth, didn't they teach you that at your school? The old bosses wouldn't deign to pick up a pistol, that's why everyone respected them, because the old bosses knew how to defend themselves with their own hands."

Nicolas kept snapping the switchblade open and shut, faster and faster. And the metallic sound relieved him of at least a bit of his tension. A couple of old books about the Mafia came to his mind, and the stories of bosses who considered it unseemly to carry a firearm, and honorable only to settle accounts with knives.

"Confronting a person and subduing him face-to-face gives you respect, shooting him in the street makes you no better than anyone else!"

He picked up the pace. Practice makes perfect, he thought.

"Now that's enough fooling around, Nico'!" The old man walked over to a shelf that was head-high, pushed aside a bottle of fine wine and a couple of worn-out old decks of cards, and picked up a half-smoked Toscano cigar. He lit it and drew hard three, four times, then 'o Cicognone arrived. The espresso was served.

Nicolas put the knife in his back pocket and tried another question: "But are you always locked up like this?" 'O Cicognone took the two demitasse cups and set them on a glass table, fogged over by now. "Don Vitto'," Nicolas went on, "don't you feel a lack of oxygen?"

"It's the will of the Lord," L'Arcangelo replied. The Toscano cigar had finally caught and he went over to sit down in his usual recliner.

"Do you really think the Lord wants you shut up in a cage?" Nicolas felt that they'd checked off the boxes on all the preliminaries, and that sensation of circling around the real reason for the visit infected his whole body. "Don Vitto', can I ask you something?"

"What have you been doing so far? Go on, keep on busting my balls, but hurry up about it." Don Vittorio L'Arcangelo was giving him permission to get to the point.

Nicolas stood up, as if using the impetus of his body to help the words get out, but he found himself standing there silent, and started stepping on the carpet fringe with the toes of his Nikes.

For a while, L'Arcangelo just let him dawdle, amused. Then he got tired of waiting: "Nico', what's the matter, has your tongue gotten stuck to the roof of your mouth?"

"You need to give me your contact," said Nicolas. Just like that, the way you'd confess to your girlfriend that you'd been cheating on her.

"What are you saying?" There was no anger in that question, just disbelief.

"Your contact," he repeated, "the guy who supplies you with shit, with weed, hash, coke . . ."

"Mmm." A low sound, like a brass instrument, emerged from his throat. Then L'Arcangelo stood up and undid his belt.

Nicolas stiffened, but he was ready. He'd be ready to take the whipping, sure, no problem, that old man had every right to take a belt to him.

But L'Arcangelo threw the belt away, across the room, against the wooden blinds, then dug his hands down between his skin and the elastic of his underwear, and with a single movement yanked down his trousers and everything else, revealing a body that was wrinkled but not entirely abandoned to the ravages of age. He turned around slowly and got down on all fours.

"Put it in, Nico'! Go on, *ja'*, stick it in my ass! Hurry up! Ass-rape me."

When confronted by the sight of that flaccid derriere, Nicolas couldn't help but burst into a rollicking wave of laughter. The other man leaped to his feet with considerable agility, pulled his pants back up in rough and ready fashion, and then suddenly stepped up close to Nicolas. He jammed his belly against him, forcing him to step back. Caught off guard, while still laughing, Nicolas felt his breath being sucked out of his body, then the unexpectedly powerful hands of L'Arcangelo slamming him against an empty bookshelf, which rocked back and forth, threatening to come crashing down onto him.

"There's not a fucking thing to laugh about, *piccirè*." L'Arcangelo, calling him "youngster," kept shoving him back against the bookshelves. "How dare you?" he said once. "How dare you?" he said a second time, his voice growing louder. "How dare you?" he said for a third time, his voice so loud now that it hurt Nicolas's eardrums. "Now even the fleas sit up and talk. You think you can be the king in my house? *Muschillo!* Little gnat!"

"What *muschillo—*" Nicolas tried to retort. "Let me speak, Don Vitto' . . . let me speak!"

"Wait, are you still talking, *muccusiello*? Little snotnose!" Another shove, this one more powerful still, almost at neck height. Nicolas banged his head, and for an instant he was tempted to head-butt Don Vittorio right on the bridge of his nose, cloud his vision with blood and turn and leave this place, but he brought himself under control. The stakes at play kept his head clear. He planted his eyes like a pair of glittering needles in Don Vittorio's eyes: "Will you let me speak? I know perfectly well that your contact is your personal property. But we're running out of shit. Your timeline is too slow. The rest of the world's using a PlayStation, Don Vitto', but you're still at a card table with a bunch of old geezers. They're cutting off your oxygen."

"The more shit there is to sell, the more shit I'll let you have," said L'Arcangelo. His rage was subsiding. Did the boy want more drugs? Then he'd give him more drugs. But not the *contact*, his contact was sacred, the contact is like your wife, like your children. Even more important than them, really, because it's how you feed your wife, how you feed your children.

"Don Vitto', no disrespect intended, you don't have the money to buy the shit. The piazzas that my *paranza* took control of are empty. Micione is taking them all back." Nicolas had managed to wriggle free. He was panting, bent over on his knees, his T-shirt twisted to reveal a fresh scratch, close to his carotid artery. "We can take the whole sea for ourselves," he continued, "and you're still settling for taking a bath in a fishbowl."

"And you're just a goldfish," L'Arcangelo replied, "so shut up and swim in your fishbowl in Forcella."

Nicolas stood up now, stuck out his chin, and finally lost the patience that had guided him thus far. "Don Vitto', *nuje 'e Furcella simmo r'o centro 'e Napule, stiamo 'ngopp'o mare, siete vuje che state rint'a gabbia*." We, in Forcella, are at the heart of Naples, we're looking out over the sea, you're the one in a cage. Then he went on: "You've become the jailer of your own neighborhood."

"*Omm'emmerda!*" L'Arcangelo shouted in a shrill voice. Piece of shit! Then he lunged at Nicolas, but 'o Cicognone, who until that moment had stood there, waiting to receive a clear signal, beat him to it. He came up behind Nicolas, tripped him, and when he fell to the floor, gave him a quick kick and rolled him toward the trapdoor, which was standing open.

Nicolas plunged straight down into Professoressa Cicatello's kitchen, making the walls of the apartment shake. Professoressa Cicatello's husband came running, followed immediately by his wife, and the kids were all rubbernecking in the doorway. Nicolas got to his feet as if nothing had happened and, looking pretty beaten up, with a cut on his cheek smearing his face with blood, shouldered his way through that little crowd.

"I slipped and fell, so what? What is this, can't I slip and fall?!" he muttered, more to himself than to those startled faces.

# IN THE ANIMAL'S DEN

entino had been living in his mother's garage for more than five months now. A frayed lamp cord that hung from the ceiling, and two hundred square feet of completely empty space, because a year ago they'd sold everything they owned. A few thicknesses of cardboard served as a pallet, two more as a blanket, and a fruit crate was the side table where Dentino placed the bottle he filled with water he drew from the common tap in the courtyard. Dentino spent his days reviewing the past few months. The things he could have done or left undone, or maybe done differently, a steady stream of them flowed through his mind, but he knew that there's no changing the past. Every so often a metallic knocking sound brought him back to the present. A pan of lasagna or a bowl of pasta. After that, Dentino went back to his shadows, like a beast whose basic needs had been tended to.

One day, after the usual banging against the metal roller gate, another knocking announced his food, but instead of a meal he found two ten-euro notes. His mother hadn't been well, she hadn't been able to get out and do her grocery shopping, so this was how she was making up for it. He held them crumpled in his hand for an hour, then his stomach made up his mind for him.

With his spare pennies he wandered the city like a vagabond. His eyes bloodshot from being indoors too long, the acrid stench of his filth, his weary trudge. People avoided him, taking him for yet another junkie in withdrawal, but he didn't even see them. He felt muffled. He imagined himself trapped in a giant block of gelatin, outside of which orbited Dumbo, Scignacane, and Nicolas. He tried to grab them, but his movements were slow and awkward.

A fast-food outlet, that's what he needed. With twenty euros, he'd take care of lunch, dinner, and even lunch the next day. He walked along, shooting rapid glances right and left, and caught glimpses of Nicolas everywhere. When he did, he'd take shelter in a doorway or behind a car, then continue walking. All of a sudden, there it was, as if out of a mirage: Piazza Principe Umberto. His own piazza, the one that had been assigned to him by his *paranza*. An anthill where every tiny being had a specific role all its own. The lookouts standing at the street corners in their relaxed poses, with one hand ready to send a WhatsApp message in case the police showed up, the customers striding with a confident gait into the doorways, and the piazza bosses strolling along, taking in every movement at a glance. It was a perfect and highly coordinated dance. From a certain point of view, it was a pleasant sight because it comforted him: his cloistered existence hadn't yet deadened his senses. He could hear the customers murmuring *"ch'hé avé?"* as a sort of password for ordering baggies of cocaine rather than pellets of hashish. After which a different kind of dance ensued. One hand met another hand, in the scissor space between middle finger and ring finger the narcotics were handed to the customer, who in turn transferred the cash between middle and index finger. Hands that take and hands that give.

Dentino had been there for fifteen minutes, and he'd calculated at least a thousand euros of completed cash transactions. A thousand euros that should have gone straight into his pocket.

*The show must go on.* He heard the words in Italian-accented English in his head; everything was going on without him. His stomach cramped and his throat was swamped with a mouthful of acid. He spat a yellowish clot onto the pavement and hurried off toward the fast-food outlet. The line stretched out the front door, a restless oversized snake that was mainly tourists. You could see lots of them in the city, lately: sunshine, sea, a subway system that's a work of art, no terrorism.

Dentino once again spat on the ground and took his place behind a woman with a broad-brimmed straw hat. As she turned to talk to her friend, she managed somehow to slap Dentino in the face with the brim of her hat, and he snapped back into full consciousness. He wasn't about to wait in line in his own city.

He strode the length of the line, walked into the restaurant, and stopped behind a young man who was just collecting his change. As soon as he saw him, the manager addressed him with a: "*Guaglio', t'aggio visto, sai?*" Hey, kid, I saw you, you know? "Go straight back out that door and stand in line like everybody else." Dentino didn't even bother to reply but instead turned and identified a marble-topped table for two, and, with the fury that was filling his body, he didn't feel even an ounce of effort in lifting it. He hurled the table at the manager in a gust of rage, and the manager barely dodged it by flinging himself to the floor. Dentino grabbed the paper-wrapped parcel of food out of the kid's hands and headed back out onto the street, scattering the line of terrified tourists. At last, he finally felt alive again.

He wound up eating in the garage, standing up. "So now what?" he wondered aloud. "So now what?" He couldn't stand still, as if that mouthful of fresh air made it intolerable for him now to be confined in that funky animal's den, that mousehole. He threw the paper into a corner and started wandering in a circle, endlessly, punching himself in the forehead and the chest. Then he dropped to the floor, exhausted. When he reawakened, he didn't know whether it was day or night, but none of that mattered, the time had come to go see 'a Koala and Antonello. He opened the metal roller gate and saw it was still light out; with a brisk step he hurried to 'a Koala's apartment house and went upstairs.

'A Koala was wearing an XXL T-shirt and a pair of Dentino's Chicago Bulls basketball shorts that hung down to her calves. She looked like a little girl playing at being a grown-up. She ran straight to Dentino, hugged him, and kissed him on the mouth even though he recoiled as if she were the one who stank. But she persisted and touched him all over, checking to make sure he was all still there while she told him how worried she had been, even though there had been no sign of the police at all. Dentino let her vent, his arms hanging down at his sides, as if doing penance. "Why didn't you ever come?" she asked, but he had no answer, not even for himself. "It doesn't matter," she went on, as if fearing to see him vanish again, "all that matters is that you're here with me now, that you're here with us." She took him by the arm, gently, as if warning him to be cautious as he approached her baby, and led him into the living room, where Antonello lay sleeping on a sofa, surrounded by cushions. This was the first time Dentino had seen his own son, and that tiny little creature, so peaceful and delicate, awakened a tenderness in him that moistened his eyes; Antonello emitted a scent of talc that instilled a moment of peace inside him.

Dentino was tempted to pull aside the blanket and take Antonello into his arms, and even give him a kiss, perhaps, but then he was afraid he would awaken him, and so he decided to simply stroke his hair, already thick and black, exactly like his own. 'A Koala let him do as he wished, she'd been so afraid of losing her man, so afraid of having to raise the baby on her own. As soon as Dentino took a step back for another look at that tiny creature of his, 'a Koala threw her arms around him again and dragged him into the bedroom. When they'd first started dating, they spent hours on end in bed together, with her wrapped around his skinny body, while Dentino with one hand stroked her back from the nape of her neck to her ass. 'A Koala lay him down and clung to him in a way that was hers alone, a way that had once belonged to them both. She could sense that Dentino hadn't come here for that—it was like hugging a log—but she hoped that it would be enough to win him back, to start over again. The three of them.

Her images of the future were interrupted by Antonello's sudden wailing. 'A Koala leaped to her feet; Dentino joined her as she took the baby's diaper off. Reddish rays of sunlight poured in through the blinds, hitting the little one's skin and turning it into the purest light. He looked like the Christ Child. But when 'a Koala lifted the baby's onesie, Dentino noticed something that clashed with all the rest of the little vignette.

"What did that, what is that thing?" he asked, stepping closer to Antonello. On his snowy-white flesh there was an unmistakable purplish bruise directly under his right nipple. A circle with a smaller circle right inside it, the edges ragged and uneven, as if the pressure exerted hadn't been even, as if whoever had pressed the pistol against the baby hadn't had the nerve to take matters to their logical conclusion.

'A Koala's eyes glistened when she thought back to her son's first day of life, which could so easily have also been his last. But she choked down the knot in her throat, and, putting diaper and onesie back on the little one with confident, quick movements of her hands, she said gently: "He's fine now. The Madonna will protect him, you know, there's no need to worry."

Dentino didn't need to ask any other questions, he'd already glimpsed the whole scene in his mind's eye. Just as he continued to see that bruise on his son's body, floating before his eyes. Would it remain there forever, like a tattoo? A kiss of death. How long would Nicolas be afraid to pull the trigger? He couldn't allow that; Nicolas wasn't going to be allowed to count out the days of his son's life with an hourglass.

At the sight of Dentino's face, disfigured by rage, 'a Koala had picked up Antonello and hugged him to her breast. The little boy had stopped wailing by now, but she went on rocking him just the same.

"Giuseppe, calm down, you're scaring me," and she took two steps back.

At that point, Dentino burst out in an incongruous laugh, as if she'd come up with a hilarious wisecrack. Certainly, she needed to be scared. He walked over to a cabinet, pushed aside a couple of lace doilies, and plunged his hand into a bowl full of coins, candies, and keys of every kind. He rummaged around in there for a little while until he found what he was looking for: the key to 'a Koala's scooter. She'd buried it in there herself when she found out she was pregnant, and had locked up the scooter. Dentino laughed again, surprised he'd remembered this detail. "I have to go out," he said. He ran out of the room, and, as he was passing by his son, 'a Koala took a step back, pressing Antonello even tighter against her breast. He wasn't her Dentino anymore. Between sobs, she called 'o White, maybe he could talk some sense into him. His cell phone number rang and rang, once, twice, three times, but there was no answer; she felt like cursing, but of course there was no way she could turn to that piece-of-shit brother of hers.

She sat down in the armchair, her baby in her arms, the sun setting, as if the two of them were alone in the entire city, just the two of them on the whole empty planet.

# HIGH SPEED

**W**e need to be done with this idea that we're the last link in the European chain!" "Naples is a great tourist city," "Naples, jewel of the Mediterranean" . . . The voices echoing inside reached all the way out onto the little balcony of the New Maharaja to which he and he alone had access. A *privé* within the *privé*, a private room within the private room. You got to it through an emergency exit that Oscar had had installed to win him the favor of the project inspector. In reality, it wasn't a way to anywhere, just a semicircular balcony that overlooked a sheer plunge down to the waters of the bay. Nicolas hadn't brought anyone out there but Letizia; once they'd even had sex on that balcony, tangled against the wrought iron railing. All that fit in that cramped space was a lounge chair and a minibar powered by a cable that ran under the door.

It was his haven on the few occasions when the New Maharaja was in use for some party, such as this evening. The lawyer Caiazzo—who had helped Nicolas and his crew get suspended sentences when they were convicted of dealing narcotics—had organized a reception for a few government bigwigs. His whole law firm was there, along with an assorted handful of local politicians and bureaucrats. It was the lawyer himself who'd written to him, a message that Nicolas had only half read, bored with the flattery that oozed out of every word. "I'd love to exchange a few words with the new prince of the city . . ." and so on and so forth. He hadn't bothered to reply, but the lawyer just went on calling him. Nicolas turned off his phone. "Tonight I'm on vacation."

He'd failed with L'Arcangelo, but there had to be some way of getting his hands on the contact. "And if there is, I'll find it, for sure." He needed to recover, he needed to get back on top.

He walked over to the parapet and stood with his back to the sea. He looked up and his legs began to shake. The looming wall of the sky was giving him that sense of vertigo. A weakness that had more to do with attraction than fear, a weakness he enjoyed inducing from time to time, as if to remind himself that he was still the master of his emotions.

In the private room it was a continuous coming and going. Pesce Moscio had requisitioned all the bottles of Moët & Chandon because he had got it into his head to replicate a champagne pyramid he'd once seen in a commercial. He pushed his way through the guests at that party, announcing that on the other side of the club they were going without champagne for their toasts; after all, he said, the penguin should be along soon with more *moetta*. And sure enough, the waiter arrived, only to notice soon enough that that bottle, too, had vanished.

Drago' and Lollipop were standing in the doorway of the private room. They'd laid out three lines of cocaine on a little hand mirror they kept passing back and forth, ignoring the people going by right in front of them.

"Mariposa cocaine makes you fly," said Lollipop, and he snorted a whole line in a single snort, the way you fill your lungs with oxygen after being underwater for too long. Drago', on the other hand, preferred a different technique, short, sharp snorts of coke in succession, fast, instantaneous. They were both fascinated to watch Briato'. He was wearing a pair of torn and tattered jeans, which he'd accompanied with a pair of loafers, worn without socks, and a purple dress shirt unbuttoned to the sternum. His look was completed by a walking stick with the pommel shaped like a silver skull. He brought it out only on special occasions, to give himself the tone of a British lord who could afford such an eccentricity.

"*Ua'*, look who's here, Count Dickhead!" exclaimed Lollipop, but

Briato' ignored him, running his hand over the head of hair he was letting grow out that he kept in order with gallons of hair product. He was buzzing around a young woman. Tightly bundled into a gray skirt suit, she seemed to have just stepped out of a business meeting.

"*Ua*', did someone lick your head?" asked Drago'.

"What are you talking about," said Drone's girlfriend, who had watched the whole scene out of the corner of her eyes, "he's the spitting image of Johnny Depp!"

His confidence restored, Briato' puffed up his chest and headed toward Drago' and Lollipop, walking as if he owned the ground he walked on. He stopped between the two of them, his eyes laser-pointed on the mysterious young woman.

"Thirty years old?" he asked.

"Who knows," said Drago'.

"For sure she's graduated from university," Briato' said.

"How can you tell?"

"The glass. She holds it from the top. Another girl would hold it from the bottom."

"Sure," Lollipop broke in. "Now you need a college degree to wear a pair of slut stiletto heels."

"Too gorgeous! Too gorgeous! I'm going in!" said Briato', and he headed forward at the top speed his leg allowed him.

"Oh, did you hurt yourself?" he asked the young blonde, overacting his concern.

"Excuse me, what do you mean?" she replied, furrowing her brow in puzzlement.

"No, I just want to know if I should call an ambulance."

"What on earth are you talking about?" she asked, increasingly on the defensive.

"Did you hurt yourself, shining star, when you fell to earth from heaven?"

She smiled, a white flash of teeth, then took half a step backward. Still, that simpleminded, overbearing charm amused her and flattered her at the same time.

"My name is Valentina," she said, and curtseyed by bending one leg, resting it on the calf of the other leg. She perched, balanced on that single narrow heel, as elegant as a flamingo. An irresistible pink flamingo. She looked like his twin soul, both of them perched on a single leg, so much so that for a fleeting instant, he himself felt light and elegant.

"No one knows my real name," Briato' replied, "but I can tell you: Fabio."

She laughed again, this time more openly, so hard that she came close to spilling her mojito. Briato' grabbed her wrist and placed his other hand on her hip. She didn't pull away, but put both her heels flat on the floor, breaking the momentary enchantment. She asked him how old he was; she seemed curious.

"Twenty-eight," Briato' ventured—he'd been about to say eighteen, but he just kept the eight and went for broke.

"Oh, really? You look much younger. You're lucky, you know?"

"It's just that you make me feel so much younger, Valentina."

Briato' had let himself go, and now Valentina was shortening the distance between them. Solid marble, these tits, he thought to himself when he saw them up close.

"And just what is it that you do for a living?" she asked, harpooning him with those intelligent eyes, from which ran a few lovely wrinkles.

She had to be thirty years old, maybe a little younger. "I'm in business," he replied.

"In what area?

"Flour, chocolate, taxes . . ."

"What?"

Briato' took her by the hand. He led her to the bar and slammed a fist on the counter to draw the barman's attention. "Friend, pack up the whole bar for the signorina here." Then he turned to Valentina, who had in the meantime taken up a perch on a tall bar stool.

"Do you want to go on vacation with me, Valentina?"

"I don't even know you!" she replied after a moment's hesitation.

Briato' smiled. "What do you mean we don't know each other, Valentina? I've seen you every time I lifted my eyes to heaven."

"Are you pulling my leg?"

Briato' pouted for a few seconds too long.

"Is everything all right, Valentina?" asked a man in a suit and tie, a colleague who had immediately laid his hand on her shoulder.

"The signorina is doing just fine. Do you have a problem?" Briato' retorted. He'd replaced his playboy expression with one straight off the street; all it required was for him to squint slightly and harden the features of his face. And Valentina didn't miss that transformation. Her colleague ignored Briato' and addressed her once again. "Is everything okay?"

Briato' pinched the man's chin with two fingers. Delicately, just to turn the other man's eyes to look into his. "You're putting your hand on a high-tension wire," he said. "Don't you know you should always read labels carefully?" he continued. A new tattoo, still gleaming, covered the upper portion of his abdominals. A skull over the classic double crossbones and the words "Danger of Death."

Her colleague raised both hands in a gesture of surrender and apologized, everything was fine, he just wanted to steal Valentina away for a second because he needed to tell her something about work. "Of course," said Briato', running his arm around Valentina's waist, "work is work." He drew her close and whispered in her ear: "Thirty seconds, little one, then I'll come get you."

No, Valentina decided, he wasn't pulling her leg. The guy was just the way he seemed, he wanted her, and that was that.

She and the man walked a few yards away, close to the bathroom door where the stream of passersby would cover what they said.

"Valentina, have you lost your mind? That guy's in the Piranhas!" her colleague urgently told her.

"Oh, really?" Valentina replied. Then she recovered from her surprise: "Well, so what? He's just a kid and we're just having a drink. What's wrong with that?"

"What's wrong with that!" he echoed her. "Every once in a while, why don't you take a little spin on the Web and find out what's happening in Naples!" But Valentina had already stopped listening to him. Their boss had been trying to get in touch with Maraja for days now, and that was exactly why he'd held the party here of all places, to flush him out into the open.

"Listen," she started saying, but she was interrupted by Briato', who appeared beside her: "No, but for real, do you like this queer?"

Valentina burst out laughing and locked arms with Briato', striding away from her colleague, who watched them go, open-mouthed.

"You see?" Briato' said to her. "I'm made of iron and you're my magnet."

"Where did you say you wanted to take me on vacation?" she shot back.

"I'll buy you the island of Capri, we'll clear out all the people, and we'll just be there alone, you and me," and as he talked he was leading her toward the little sofas of the private room.

"So you're a member of the Piranhas?" Valentina asked as she ran her eyes over his tattooed abdomen.

Upon hearing that question, Briato' stopped smiling, even though he felt a burst of pride deep down. "Well, I could tell you, but then I'd have to kill you, beautiful," he replied, and then he reached out a hand to straighten a lock of her hair, tucking it behind her ear.

Valentina turned serious and grabbed his arm, stopping him. "Wait," she said, "first I need to speak with Maraja."

"Who, Nicolas? My brother? I'm much better-looking than he is."

She nodded her head, and Briato' decided to attribute her assent to the second part of what he'd said. He could feel the excitement swelling within him.

"But then if I tell you . . ."

"Then?"

"Then I'll have to kill you," and they both broke into laughter.

Nicolas's cell phone was still turned off, so Briato' ran to the little balcony and pushed open the emergency door—after all, he knew that Nicolas would ignore any knocking, no matter how loud. Nicolas was standing at the parapet, looking down at the rocks and the waves breaking against them, and he greeted Briato' with a terse "Leave me alone."

"There's a super-hot babe here who wants to get to know Maraja" was all Briato' said. He put all his chips on personal vanity: by now, they were VIPs in that city. And then he added: "But she's totally ready to fuck me!"

In the meantime, Valentina was sending the lawyer a text. She immediately recognized Nicolas, even if she'd never seen his face before. As he walked through the crowd, everyone made way for him, keeping their eyes glued to him the way you do with a famous actor.

"Ciao, Nicolas," she said as she approached him. "I've been wanting to meet you. Valentina Improta," she went on, squeezing his hand. "I'm one of Counselor Caiazzo's assistants. You know, the lawyer. He's on his way here, and he wants to say hello to you."

Nicolas understood now, glaring daggers at Briato'. "Fuck, you led me right into the trap," he whispered to him under his breath, the minute Valentina turned her back on them to wave to the lawyer.

"All right, so let's meet him," said Nicolas. "That way we can have him stand in as best man for the wedding."

"Ah, you're getting married?" asked Valentina.

"*Your* wedding: yours and Briato's."

Valentina turned around and looked at the young man who until then she had called Fabio and saw him blush.

"Here's Maraja! Here's the king himself!"

The lawyer Caiazzo's deep voice drowned out "Toca Toca," which the DJ had sworn to the crowd would get everybody dancing.

"Today, here and now, Naples becomes the capital of Europe again! Do you know that the first railroad line in the world was built here? The Naples–Portici line!"

While Caiazzo talked, Nicolas studied Valentina's thighs. He was sure she went to the gym, and in fact, maybe she was also a runner, but she wasn't skinny, she was solid, and he'd happily let himself be squeezed by those legs. He wondered if that old sardine of a lawyer was screwing *her*, that beautiful horn of plenty.

"The railroads here are going to be the hub for the whole Mediterranean basin . . ."

"*Uànema*," Nicolas said to Briato', and whirled his hand in the air like a rotor, as if to say that when all was said and done, it had been worth it.

"Maraja," said Caiazzo, "is there a quiet corner somewhere that we can talk?"

This was overtime for Nicolas, but he could hardly say no . . .

Now the private room was empty; the members of the *paranza* were on the dance floor, too.

"Maraja, only you can solve this problem for me," Caiazzo began, sitting in the damask egg-shaped armchair. "Have you seen that the CEO is here? Engineer D'Elia, you know the one I mean? He's on TV all the time."

"Wait, what, the one who runs the trains, who one day he's running the airplanes, the next he's at the soccer championship? What the fuck, is he the stationmaster now?"

"Ah, Nicolas, so you do watch the evening news, after all. That's right, he's the one, he's in charge of everything. Have you seen the work he's done on high-speed trains? When I was your age, to go to Rome took four hours. Now you don't even have time to take a piss, and you're there already. These are sectors that bring good things to our homeland. Have you noticed how many tourists get off those trains every day? It's an invasion. But have you ever noticed just how beautiful those trains are?"

"Counselor, what the fuck does that matter to me, are you asking me to become a conductor?"

"What are you talking about, *conductor*? I came here to ask you a favor, and after all, as you know, I always find a way to repay my debts."

At last, the conversation was starting to make sense. Nicolas got a little more comfortable on the sofa across from the lawyer; he extended his legs and prepared to listen.

"Maraja," Caiazzo went on, "these fucking Gypsies are going to derail the whole line! They're stealing copper on the Milan–Rome line, on the Milan–Bologna, and the Milan–Florence line. In Naples, Salerno. Everywhere, round-trip. They steal everything, morning, afternoon, evening, and night. And without copper, how is Engineer D'Elia going to power his trains? The guy's career is being ruined by this problem!"

Nicolas barely nodded, waiting for the ask.

"Maraja, you need to get this fucking gang off my back and get back whatever amount of copper is still in the storeroom before they ship it off to China." The lawyer looked around for a moment, then moved out to the edge of the armchair to lean closer to Nicolas and, in spite of the music playing in the club, lowered his voice: "It's the Gianturco gang, Maraja. They're Mojo's Gypsies."

So Mojo was back again. Nicolas had some unsettled matters with him, and he hadn't forgotten that.

Nicolas got up from the sofa, looked out the door of the private room, and shouted to a passing waiter to bring him more Moët & Chandon: *"Altra moetta, presto!"*

"You need to eliminate them for me," the lawyer went on in the same tone of voice, after finishing his second glass of champagne. "And everything they've taken from me, you need to get back for me."

"But why are you asking us?" Nicolas asked the question even as, deep inside, he was connecting the dots: at last his brain had started working the way it used to, and he was beginning to conceive a plan that smacked of comeback, that smacked of the future.

"If I go to the police it'll take me ten years before it's taken care of. The *paranza* can turn it around in ten minutes."

Selfies, notoriety, handshakes. For the members of the *paranza*, it meant they'd attained their goal, that they really had become VIPs. These were good things. But what the lawyer was talking about was something completely different. This meant official sanction of the fact that for those who mattered in the city, the *paranza* was an efficient organization. Suitable to entrust with special missions. And an efficient organization can claim the chairman's seat at the negotiation table.

"I get it, but why should the *paranza* do you this favor?"

Nicolas had intentionally chosen to use that word, *favor*, because the lawyer himself had uttered it.

"Tell me how much you want, and we'll gladly pay."

Without answering, Nicolas grabbed a stack of paper napkins off the table and started balling them up. He made clumps of paper and stuffed them into his mouth, pushing them to the back with his thumb. The lawyer stared at him like he was a lunatic. What was Nicolas trying to do? Make a jury-rigged mouthguard and then start a boxing match?

Instead, Nicolas, unruffled, crossed his legs and started talking in a hoarse voice and a Sicilian accent: "But now you come to me and say, Don Corleone, you must give me justice. And you don't ask in respect or friendship." He'd always wanted to act out this scene, such a pity that no one was filming it, there would have been a lot of shares and likes with a video like that! "And you don't think to call me Godfather; instead you come to my house on the day my daughter is to be married and you ask me to do murder . . . for money?"

"Maraja, I don't understand, if I've said anything to offend you . . ."

Nicolas had always had a weak spot for Don Vito Corleone. He felt just like him: courage above everything else. But that ignoramus of a lawyer was having trouble even registering his Brando impression . . .

Caiazzo, even more confused now, attempted his usual exit strategy: abandon the negotiation by taking it for granted that they'd come to an understanding.

"All right, then, so it's settled? Are we all good? Let me go talk to the engineer and give him the good news. I'm indebted to you, Maraja." He was already on his feet when Nicolas spat the balls of paper onto the floor, where they lay, wads sodden with saliva.

"Hold on there, Counselor. Have you taken me for a houseboy at the service of Engineer D'Elia?"

"What houseboy, I'm asking you for a favor and I'm ready and willing to pay . . ." said the lawyer. He'd sat back down on the armchair, slightly pale and more confused than before.

"No disrespect meant, Counselor, but the money you're thinking of paying us? We can make that in two hours."

At last, the veil that had been dimming Caiazzo's vision was torn away: these were no longer the children he'd defended in court, these were no longer the same kids he'd kept from having to serve time in reform school.

"And?" he shot back.

"I'd make a fair-trade exchange, sustainable and transparent." He smiled and mentally drew a line between two dots that were very far apart. "You need to tell me where 'o Tigrotto lives."

"Who?" He really wasn't expecting this, and it took him a moment to grasp the point.

"'O Tigrotto, Counselor, the Faellas' man. The one who killed Gabriele Grimaldi, Don Vittorio's son."

"'O Tigrotto, yes, I understand, but he's not one of my clients," Caiazzo said, already composing himself. He was a lawyer, he thought to himself, assuming a rather more formal tone of voice, he knew how to face up to certain situations. "It's not one of my trials, I wouldn't know where to begin. That's in Masturzo's portfolio . . . and it's confidential information, Maraja, you'd have to speak with him."

"I think it's confidential to go shoot a bunch of Gypsies. Here *everything* we're talking about is confidential, Counselor."

"But I wouldn't even know. I'm not on such close terms with Masturzo, how would I ask him such a thing in the first place?" He was grasping for words, while the firmness he'd so painstakingly constructed vanished into thin air.

Nicolas smiled: now it was his turn to walk away from the conversation.

"Counselor, all of you down at the courthouse swap wives, you certainly won't have any real problem asking him where I could find 'o Tigrotto, no? For the rest of it, you and your friend the engineer can rest easy, you're in the hands of professionals!"

# SUNDAY

The florist had come to Letizia's house on Saturday. He'd rung the doorbell, and her mother had leaned out the window.

"Are you delivering a bouquet of flowers?"

"No, signo'."

"Then why did you ring?"

"Because I've brought you the whole vanload."

Nicolas was certain that this would mend the quarrel of a few days earlier, and in fact, when he woke up on Sunday, what he found on WhatsApp was a photograph of Letizia wearing the fuchsia panties that drove him crazy, her hair unbound over her breasts to conceal them, but only a little, and the Hello Kitty oven mitt. Along with the photo, an invitation surrounded by hearts: "Sunday lunch with your kitty cat?"

The fall through the trapdoor still smarted, and going to lick his wounds in Letizia's arms was a comforting prospect. But since what hurt worst, more than the fall in and of itself, was the insult that Don Vittorio had leveled against his neighborhood, his *rione*, he brought a can of black spray paint and, along the way, revving the engine of his TMAX, grabbed the spray can and left a fast, flowing message on the asphalt, his signature, a love note: "F12." Where the *F* in Fiorillo was also the *F* in Forcella, and it fused together, in the same destiny, his own name and the streets he commanded. The 12 represented the position of N in the Italian alphabet, and what's more, it stood both for *'o surdate*, the soldier in the Neapolitan card game of smorfia, and for the twelve apostles. A proper self-respecting signature, he thought, and nodded with satisfaction. Then, as long as he was at it, he shook the can again and added, beside it: *I love you, Lety.*

Tucano, rolled up in his sheets, opened a single eye, the other one still glued shut by sleep dust. Someone was twisting his big toe. It was Sunday, what the hell was happening?

"Piece of shit," his father shouted, smacking his foot, "you got a D-minus in math, and a D-plus in Italian. Are you seriously going to make me work as hard as I do for no good reason! And what the hell is this new tattoo on your forearm?"

"It's Michael Jordan," Tucano mumbled.

"Who? It looks to me like a triangle with a dot." Fucked-up Sunday, Tucano thought to himself.

Tucano had decided that he wouldn't quit school, for one simple reason: it was a good way to rest up from the effort of running a piazza and a good cover ever since he'd been a member of the *paranza*. But it also meant he had to put up with the furious outbursts of his father, a violent man who was fixated on academic achievement. He was a mailman, but he wanted more out of life, so he tried to redeem himself through his son's education. And Tucano let him.

Fucked-up Sunday, thought Lollipop. He'd woken up with a hunger in him that he would have had to go to a wedding banquet to satiate, but on the kitchen table all he'd found was a pitcher full of some greenish liquid and a few flat buckwheat cakes. His mother was on a diet again and the beverage was her celery-ginger-orange centrifuged drink. His whole family was there, father, mother, and two sisters, and the conversation was revolving around the same topic: the gym they all ran together. Nothing much, a room with treadmills and exercise bikes, another room for running, and the third room crowded with barbells and weights and a couple of full-body training machines. Then there were the showers, a mini-sauna that could hold two people at the most, and the locker rooms. It had been an old investment of his father's with the unexpected money from an inheritance, and now that gym was struggling to stay afloat, just to make ends meet.

"What time did you get home, Vince'?" his mother asked. She was wearing an Adidas tracksuit that highlighted her butt, rock-solid from hours of pilates. Everyone else in the family was in Adidas, too: his father called it their family uniform.

"Ma, please," said Lollipop.

"Vince', you know that Ciro Somma got Fabrizio Corona to come to his gym?"

"I know that, Pa," Lollipop replied, grateful to his male parent for sparing him the umpteenth sermon from his mother. "Corona goes there because Somma paid him!"

His father was fixated on the idea that to make the great leap forward, what he needed was to attract a VIP clientele, ideally soccer players.

"The reason those guys don't come is that they have gyms of their own. And after all, you have to pay them three times as much. The price to get them to come and also the price for the competition you represent for their own gyms. They're filthy pigs."

"But we need . . . we need some event! If you can get an event, then you exist! And if you exist, then people want to come see you! It's because of the event that they know you exist."

Lollipop rolled his eyes, and when he lowered them again they met his mother's. She picked up where she'd left off: "So that's why you want to live, eh? I wish I knew how you can stick those things on you that you wear! You and that gang of friends of yours . . . but if I find out that you're working for someone on the street, with the Strianos or, even worse, with the guys from San Giovanni, your life is over, I'll shoot you before they can."

Lollipop turned serious: "No gang, Ma. We don't work for anyone else. If we need something, we just take it, full stop."

"What do you mean, you just take it?"

Lollipop pretended a sudden stomachache had come over him, and he took shelter in the bathroom. The text from Tucano had come in just two minutes earlier.

**Tucano**
Before-dinner drinks, no girlfriends.
Piazza Quattro Colonne at 6.
See you there.

Lollipop emerged from the bathroom shouting an "all's good" to his mother, who was worried that his constant stomach troubles were a result of the garbage he ate when he wasn't home, and then headed down to the garage to get his scooter. Under the seat, he'd already prepared all his necessities. In the meantime, Tucano was doing the same thing.

Tucano's and Lollipop's piazzas were in a state of crisis. Micione was evicting them, inundating the peddlers with a waterfall of narcotics. According to Nicolas, it was a sign that Micione was shitting his pants and felt obliged to show off his muscles. No doubt true, thought Tucano and Lollipop, but in the meantime they felt helpless, and to make up for the shortfall in their piazzas' revenues, they had turned to shakedowns and extortion.

Lollipop arrived first and rode the traffic circle of Piazza Quattro Colonne while he waited for Tucano. Everytime he passed through there, he gave a glance at the statues that seemed to be holding up those stout *palazzi*. He was going to be famous one day, but he wasn't going to sweat and toil like those losers.

He steered the scooter with just one hand, legs crossed to one side, as if he were perched on a stool. Tucano's idea was a good one, he had to admit, even if he didn't understand why he'd asked him to show up unarmed—or, as he'd put it in their rudimentary code, "no girlfriends"—for that before-dinner drink, and therefore, for the shakedown they had in mind.

He saw him arrive, aerodynamically reclined, from the avenue leading to the station. Without bothering to glance at the traffic, Tucano cut straight across the traffic circle and pulled up next to his friend, extending his fist.

"Wait, so, have you ever fucked a *femminiello* in the ass?" Lollipop asked after returning the greeting

"No, but one time I let one suck me off."

"But if you have sex with a *femminiello*, a tranny, does that make you gay?"

"It's not like we're having sex with them, we just need to take their money. If they don't pay us, we break their legs. We kick them good and hard in the face."

They were riding along side by side, chatting as they putted slowly, 5 m.p.h., circling under the stern gazes of the Telamons, the mighty atlases holding up the balconies, and the indifferent glances of the motorists.

"Did you make the maces?" Tucano asked.

Lollipop nodded. The day before, he'd stolen two barbell shafts from his folks' gym and he'd wrapped the banners of the S.S.C. Napoli team around them. That way, if the Falchi—the cops—spotted them, they'd just be heading to the stadium. Diego Armando Maradona was in the city. His tour had begun a week earlier, in the TV studio of a talent show where he'd danced with a professional ballerina, and that tour was going to conclude that evening, at the San Paolo stadium, in a farewell to his fans and his old teammates.

"This is the queer that's in charge in the neighborhood," said Tucano, "so if he starts to pay us . . ."

"But if you ask me, queers, even if they're paying us," said Lollipop, "even if they're paying us, they need to be beaten. I mean, why the fuck are you going to be gay?! You were born a man, so be a man! If you're sick—"

"What's that have to do with it! Look, they use their ass to make money! My father always says that the *femminielli* give the best blow jobs."

"For real?"

"Sure, because they have a dick too! So they know, you get it, what to do with a dick . . . how to treat it, but women don't have dicks, so they have to learn."

"I don't know, it's gross. Would you let guys stick it up your ass for money?"

"That depends on how much money they'd give me." Tucano laughed.

"And after all, people are free to do what they want, I mean, if you're a *femminiello*, you're a *femminiello*! That's how God Almighty made you!"

"Are you serious?" asked Lollipop, giving the finger to a Toyata Yaris that had honked at them. "God Almighty made Adam and Eve, not Adam and Steve. *Ja'*, what bullshit!"

"Ha ha, at the very worst he made Eve and Eve."

"*Ua'*, Eve and Eve! Now, I don't mind that! Once in the gym my mamma caught two women in the shower licking each other off!"

"Really? *Ua'*, I'm getting a hard-on!"

They drove out of the traffic circle. Via Duomo, in the direction of Nuova Marina. A couple of cross streets and then a right turn. They'd already arrived. The building was elegant, with a doorman greeting the respectable tenants as they walked out to go to Mass. He asked no questions of those two young men carrying the Naples soccer team banners on their shoulders: even envied them a little bit.

Esterina was receiving customers on the sixth floor, and the boys took the stairs to avoid the residents as much as they were able. On the second flight, Tucano was already huffing and puffing, pulling the T-shirt with the Mexican skull on it away from his sweaty chest. Lollipop, on the other hand, clambered up the stairs, light-footed, defiant of his mother and her refusal to feed him pasta.

Esterina's door stood ajar, an old habit of hers to put her clients at ease, especially the green ones who were there for the first time: it meant they didn't have to ring the bell twice and give themselves time for second thoughts. That door was the first step to perdition.

Tucano and Lollipop entered in silence, walking down a dimly lit hallway. There was just one door, at the end of the hall, with a panel of pebbled glass. Behind it was a shadow and then there she was, Esterina. She wore a purple peignoir trimmed with lace, loosely fastened to keep from revealing entirely what nonetheless remained just visible. A pair of enormous, perfect tits. Esterina sashayed forward, her face turned slightly downward, doing her best to imitate the walk of Belén Rodríguez. Perhaps that's why she failed to notice the barbell shafts sticking up from behind the backs of Tucano and Lollipop.

"Hey, queer," Tucano burst out, all in a single breath. "From now on you're giving us five hundred euros a week. Five hundred for this week and five hundred euros for last week, which you haven't paid us yet. The *paranza* will come around to collect the money. If we hear that you're telling other queers like yourself not to pay, you're dead. You see this club? We'll split your skull with it!"

Esterina finally looked up, and, before her face twisted in rage, Tucano and Lollipop were both able to admire it, the way her many clients had previously done. It was a gorgeous face. Smooth, diaphanous skin, with just a hint of makeup, and those deep, dark eyes, enhanced further by the kohl. She's a fairy princess, thought Lollipop, enchanted, but then he noticed the Adam's apple dancing up and down and he was liberated from the enchantment of those eyes.

"I've never paid anyone," said Esterina. Her voice came out especially shrill, heightened by fear. "I've never had a pimp," she went on, "I work for myself, and only for myself. I don't come around asking for money from you, and you shouldn't come around asking for money from me." What Esterina was displaying wasn't courage, it was just a quirk of her profession: aggression pays off.

"You see, she isn't Eve!" Lollipop said to Tucano. "Take a look at the piece of apple that stuck in her throat!"

"Listen, slut," said Tucano, "we're saying it for you. If you pay us, then you're authorized to work here; if anyone gives you any trouble, then you're authorized to call us."

"Authorized to work here? I was born here, what the fuck are you talking about? Who do you think you are, the mayor of Naples?"

"That would be nothing, we're the *paranza*, and the *paranza* gives the orders!"

"Even when the Strianos were in charge, they didn't make us pay."

"The Strianos are dead now, they don't exist anymore. We're in charge now. And you queers have to pay just like everybody else, because you don't exist unless we say so."

"Well, well, well, now the runts of the litter have decided they're lions!" said Esterina. Her shrill voice had given way to a baritone timbre. She whipped around, in a fluttering cloud of perfumed fabrics, and strode briskly toward her bedroom door. Cinnamon, Lollipop decided, she smells of cinnamon. Then, having stripped the barbell shafts of the banners, he hurried after her, and Tucano was right behind him.

Esterina threw herself onto the bed, using the pillows to fend off the blows, while the two members of the *paranza* wrecked everything in the room, smashing lampshades, perfume bottles, breaking pieces of furniture, and ripping down curtains and shades. Only the mirror was left intact, because nobody is ever intentionally looking to tempt bad luck.

"That's enough, please, stop now!" Esterina shrieked, but those weren't words that Tucano and Lollipop were interested in hearing.

The timer on a tropical aquarium hidden behind a torn-down curtain caught Lollipop's attention.

"No, not the fish!" Esterina squawked. "Forget about those fish and let me see *your* fish."

Lollipop froze with the barbell shaft in midair and turned to look at Tucano. In the meantime, Esterina had gotten out of bed, turned her back to them, and with a shimmy of her ass, let her robe slide to the floor. Then she slipped off her panties, which were silky black and translucent, and tossed them behind her without looking.

She had grabbed her sex in her hand and was hauling it upward, displaying the dark patch between her testicles and her anus.

"*Ja'*, come fuck me here."

Tucano furrowed his brow, squinted, and darted his neck forward like a turkey.

"Lollipo', this girl doesn't have a dick!"

"You're right," said Lollipop, drawing nearer. "It looks like a pussy!"

"You see? Come on, come fuck me, *ja'*!"

"But then will I turn gay?" asked Lollipop.

"Only if you take it up the ass are you gay," said Tucano.

"That's right, yes, I'm the only one who's gay, because I take it," Esterina confirmed.

Tucano dropped his pants, frantically, and almost tripped over them, but immediately recovered his balance and grabbed his penis, heading straight for Esterina.

"What do you think you're doing?" she asked, and handed him condoms.

Lollipop waited his turn, watching the intercourse, secretly relieved that it had been up to Tucano to dance the first dance. Once his friend was done, Lollipop stripped from the waist down.

"Ah, now I understand why they call you Lollipop," said Tucano, wiping himself off with a hand towel that Esterina had given him. "Your cock looks like a stop sign."

Lollipop grabbed his long, skinny penis and waved the oversized head of it in the direction of Tucano, who burst out laughing while Esterina rolled her eyes.

They screwed her twice apiece, and then, after pocketing the thousand euros, on their way out of the apartment, Tucano told Esterina: "You can tell all the other *femminielli* that you're the mayor of the *femminielli*! Then maybe we'll give you a discount."

"So you see, you're already falling in love," Esterina replied, blowing him a farewell kiss.

It was a Sunday like any other. Dull and overstuffed with lunches, soporific and seemingly endless. A time for homework done with uncommon diligence. Biscottino was writing furiously, without much interest in whether he was answering the questions correctly, because all his mother required was a sufficient display of effort.

He'd concealed his smartphone under his butt. His mother had already confiscated one phone, but he'd immediately arranged to procure another one, to keep an open channel of communication with the *paranza*. When Tucano's text made his testicles vibrate, his face split into a beaming smile that she, sitting across from him, had no idea how to interpret.

It was a Sunday of bitter quarrels, like the one between Drone and his sister, Annalisa, who refused to abandon her standpoint: that boy was too intelligent for the friends he spent his time with, as well as a computer genius. She didn't know anything about the tech field, but still she realized that her brother was genuinely talented. And then those guys had come into his life, and what happened had happened, and now he'd even stopped attending school. She looked at him, bent over his iPad, though she took care not to ask him where it had come from.

Drone could feel his sister's eyes on him, but he had no time to return her look. Just yesterday a restaurateur who was under the *paranza*'s control had complained to him because, in spite of all the money he gave them, he was still getting terrible reviews on TripAdvisor. "Then that just means that the food you cook is disgusting," Drone had replied. The TripAdvisor scam was a technique he'd come up with to maximize his revenue. It was based on the principle that these days, no one bothered to go to a restaurant anymore without first checking the reviews and the average rankings given by users in terms of number of bubbles. Four and a half bubbles? Why not five? The difference between a profitable bar and one on the verge of bankruptcy was a matter of a few decimal points. And so Drone had decided to exploit them, those bubbles, and it was a win-win for everyone: the customers in the piazza where Drone dealt narcotics, who got their drugs at a 5 percent discount in exchange for at least twenty favorable reviews for the restaurant indicated by the *paranza*; the proprietor of the restaurant who saw an increase in customers; and the *paranza*, who pocketed a percentage from the restaurateur without lifting a finger.

"Will you stop reading that damned thing?" asked Annalisa. Now she was on the offensive, her face beet-red: at least they could be a family on Sundays, couldn't they?

"Shh," he silenced her, "this is important," and he proceeded to read the message from Tucano that had just appeared on the screen of his iPad.

Sunday is a day of preparation for the coming week. You go to the barbershop, to the beautician's, to the curator of your image, as Briato' liked to call Santino, the *paranza*'s hairdresser. Every Sunday evening, he'd force Santino to open his parlor just for him. A nice haircut, a hot towel, his sideburns. Now and then, five minutes under the tanning lamp, just to tone his skin. When Briato' read the text, he turned to Santino: "I've just found you another customer."

———

While the *paranza* was still fast asleep, Pesce Moscio had already tried on three different looks for the birthday party being thrown for the octogenarian grandmother of his latest girlfriend, Sveva. Sveva met Pesce Moscio's standard buxom requirements, but he'd never had a girlfriend quite like her. Born and raised in Vomero, she was the daughter of a psychologist—her father—and a gallery owner, her mother. She loved sailing and she loved Russian novels. They'd met at an Enzo Dong concert.

"Princess," he had said to her, and then he had lifted her into the air, setting her on the other side of the threshold that marked off the VIP area.

"What are you doing?" she'd asked, but then she'd noticed where she was and the boy with an oversized hockey jersey and a bandanna tied around his head Tupac-style, and she hadn't thought twice: she'd darted her tongue into his mouth.

"*Ua'*," Pesce Moscio had said, recovering his breath, but Sveva had latched on to him like a lamprey again, and neither of them had seen much of the concert. Sveva's free-spirited approach was the surprising result of years of school with the Ursuline sisters and a family upbringing free of taboos.

Pesce Moscio had discarded his jeans and checkered vest, as well as the dark blue suit from his uncle's wedding, and had opted for a dress shirt and pin-striped trousers instead. A regular fashion plate. Still, he wasn't fully convinced, and so he searched for tutorials on YouTube: "respectable young man first time dinner in-laws." He'd already met Sveva's group of friends: coddled youth of well-to-do parents dressed up as gangsters, who had welcomed Pesce Moscio the way you pluck a 24-karat-gold brooch out of a bin of costume jewelry. Thug life, just a short walk from their glittering neighborhood. And the fact that he could procure narcotics at discount prices made him even more popular. "Business and love go hand in hand, you see that, Maraja?" Pesce Moscio had explained to Nicolas. "*Hai scassat'i ciessi,*" Nicolas had replied with an affectionate smack. "You broke the toilets."

The apartment where Sveva's parents lived was furnished in an industrial minimalist style. An open space surrounded on all sides, and subdivided internally, by sheets of glass. And so it might well happen that if you walked in the front door, you'd see, in the distance, the lady of the house getting dressed after her shower, because even the walls of the individual rooms were transparent. When Pesce Moscio crossed the threshold, his first question was how Sveva's parents ever managed to have sex in that place. Then he spotted the birthday girl, the grandmother who, even in the midst of that overabundance of reflective surfaces and statues made with metal wire, commanded pride of place in all her floral decrepitude. Skinny, wan, and angular, she wore a sky-blue dress spangled with daisies. She was smiling and shaking hands, like a woman pope. She shook hands with Pesce Moscio, too, and he introduced himself as Sveva's boyfriend, but she didn't even deign to glance at him, just a limp hand that the young man hardly touched. Sveva's parents, in contrast, were happy to meet him. The tattoos that could be glimpsed peeking out from under the cuffs or the collar of his shirt matched up correctly with their scale of values: you could see them but really you couldn't, they were transgressively housebroken, a little bit like them, one foot on this side and one foot on the other. All things considered, the evening was enjoyable. Pesce Moscio and Sveva went from one buffet table to the next, hand in hand, as if the party were being thrown for them. Yes, Pesce Moscio thought to himself, there, among those people, perhaps he really could live comfortably. He raised his glass in a toast, joining in the chorus of grandchildren—"Many happy returns of the day, Grandmother!"—almost happy to be there, so much so that he felt free to pull out his cell phone and take a picture.

The last message in the chat was from Tucano.

**Tucano**

What a damn fuck, with a kiss! But next time, we should get there in the morning, because in the evening *femminielli* have whiskers.

And the champagne went down the wrong way. He ran into the bathroom, hoping that there, at least, there were four walls.

"Who has whiskers, Luigi'?" It was a Sunday of pure boredom, the kind of day when you leave your phone lying around because you don't want to talk to anyone. Drago' told his little sister to give him his smartphone and started to reply, but it died in his throat. On the *paranza*'s chat, Nicolas, still wrapped around Letizia's body, had written:

**Maraja**
Tonight. Lair. Meeting.

## THIS IS BUSINESS

The year before, during Christmas dinner with the whole family gathered, Lollipop had wound up sitting next to an uncle who worked in the PolFer, Italy's national railway police. For hours his uncle had told him about his job, complaining especially about the thefts of copper, telling him in considerable detail about the hows and whys of the problem. A story that had at first piqued his curiosity, then entertained him, and in the end had simply bored him to death, but which now proved useful. During the meeting at the lair, in a short half hour, he instructed the members of the *paranza* on the fundamentals, because, if they hoped to fix the little red wagons of the people stealing the copper, they had to know exactly how it was being stolen. That, too, was part of membership in Maraja's *paranza*: always being well informed.

Counselor Caiazzo had given Nicolas the details. The Gypsies used the Bausan Wharf to deliver the copper, showing up in big cars packed with the metal and then jamming it into containers. "But who buys it?" Nicolas had asked. "The Chinese," the lawyer had replied, but they were too powerful, better forget about that angle. Certainly, they'd be pissed off, but they'd find other suppliers. It was the Gypsies of Gianturco who had to be wiped out.

After the meeting at the lair, the members of the *paranza* had set out from Forcella in formation, all six of them, in single file, roaring along at moderate speed. The only one missing was Biscottino—his mother marked him closely and the excuse that he was sleeping over at someone else's house didn't work with her. Nicolas hadn't insisted, there were enough of them, and, after all, Biscottino was too young, there was a risk he might prove a liability in this kind of operation.

They'd opted for automatic pistols because Uzis against those metal walls ran the risk of ricocheting; better to have a lighter weapon, easier to handle and not as noisy, even though there was bound to be plenty of ruckus. Nicolas would take care of Mojo.

They were stopped at a traffic light, with cars honking behind them. No bullshit before reaching the wharf, the mission was too important.

"And how are we going to take them?" asked Drone.

"We surround them and we take the containers," Nicolas replied. He'd decided that Engineer D'Elia was going to be too busy celebrating his high-speed trains to worry about demanding the return of the swag. The *paranza* would sell it off, maybe to the very same Chinese they were about to leave empty-handed.

"We surround them and we take the containers? Like that?" asked Lollipop.

"*Adda murì mammà*, just like that," said Nicolas.

Green light. They took off again, still in single file. There was no fear in those questions, just the need to understand the coming moves, clearly, to get the sense that Maraja knew what to do.

Another red light. This time it was Drago' who pulled up next to Nicolas.

"Nico'," he said, "we're running the risk of being knocked over here." Nicolas unleashed a kick at the bodywork of Drago's TMAX, and Drago' immediately set his other foot down on the asphalt, recovering his balance.

"You see?" asked Nicolas. "You didn't get knocked over." Green light.

Until they reached the Bausan Wharf, no one said another word. Nicolas led them to the farthest slip, where it looked like one single multicolored shipping container, so close were they stacked together to save even two feet of space.

A path just wide enough to let an average-size car through without scratching its sides cut the mass of shipping containers in half. They got to the open patch of asphalt and waited.

The lawyer Caiazzo had explained to Nicolas that it could only have been the Gypsies, they were the only ones capable of pulling off that job, wedging their way into that one-way street where the only way out was to jump into the water of the bay. That's why they had the monopoly on copper: they weren't afraid of becoming fish food.

Floodlights illuminated the blacktop where a number of automatic stacking cranes stood motionless, as bright as broad daylight, while leaving the shipping containers surrounding it on three sides in utter darkness. The only sound was the sloshing of water against the wharf. Nicolas walked over to a Fantuzzi forklift, a sort of oversized jeep with enormous wheels fitted with an extendable arm, broke the driver's-side window to get inside, and swung up behind the steering wheel. From there, he could see the entrance to the blacktop area. The other members of the *paranza* took up scattered positions on top of the containers that had not yet been stacked, so that at a signal from Nicolas—a text in their chat room—they could leap down, weapons at the ready.

Silence. The water had stopped sloshing, the cables dangled from the cranes without emitting so much as a creak. The whole world seemed sunk in a dead calm, as if an invisible hand had placed the Bausan Wharf under a giant glass bell jar. Nicolas caressed the button of the switchblade knife L'Arcangelo had given him. He applied pressure, not enough to make the blade snap out, until he could feel it make contact with the spring that was just on the verge of triggering, and then his finger released its pressure.

A metallic noise, followed immediately by another, softer one. And then, again, silence. Maybe one of his men had gotten a cramp, from waiting like that, beached flat on top of the shipping containers. A sudden flash of light made him raise his head. A repeated flash, as of headlights rapidly being turned on and off. A signal. His eyes focused straight ahead of him, he held his breath. Nothing, it was just a car flashing its brights at another.

Was he leading his *paranza* to slaughter? If the Gypsies were armed with submachine guns, would they even have time to draw their pistols? The lawyer had told him loud and clear: those guys are penniless bums, they don't even carry knives. Nicolas went back to pushing the button on his own switchblade, and this time he snapped it open. *Clack.* In that dead calm, the sound seemed to echo among the containers. They all heard it, and Nicolas knew it, because in turn he heard the sound of creaking sheet metal. They all raised their heads to see if someone was coming, he decided, and they all stayed there waiting, for fear that lowering their heads too suddenly might make noise. And in fact, a few seconds later, Nicolas heard a succession of other booming metallic noises. The boys had gone back to their initial resting positions.

It was twenty minutes past eleven. Caiazzo hadn't given them a precise schedule, he'd just muttered something about "around midnight." Another forty minutes like this is more than we can take, thought Nicolas. Five minutes went by, and then a distant buzz broke the stalemate. Cars. Big engines. Coming closer. The Gypsies were arriving. And they were there ahead of time.

Four big Mercedes cars with only their parking lights burning stopped at the center of the blacktop, with their engines still running. A dozen or so men got out of three of the four cars, and went around to open the trunks, while the doors of the fourth remained shut tight. He'd already prepared the text that he'd send the others—"Rock 'n' Roll"—but before sending it, he made sure that Mojo was one of that group of men. An enormous silhouette was moving between one automobile and another; the floodlights of the wharf backlit him so that only his silhouette could be seen. Nicolas recognized him from the way he moved: you never forget your own jailer, you never forget the man you've promised to murder.

### Maraja
Rock 'n' Roll.

"Freeze!" "Sons of bitches!" "Hands up!" "Piece-of-shit Gypsies!" From atop the shipping containers, Pesce Moscio, Lollipop, Drago', Tucano, and Drone fired a few shots into the crowd.

Four or five of the Roma took to their heels immediately, eluding pursuit as they dodged away around and behind the shipping containers. There was no need to go after them, Nicolas's plan was to slaughter their captain, and then the rest of them would slink back to their filthy trailers. Briato', who had taken up a hiding place behind a forklift because, with his leg in that condition, he wasn't eager to make the jump, went over to one of the Roma who had obeyed the *paranza*'s shouted commands and stood there, both hands held high. He swung the butt of his pistol and cracked it against the man's temple, knocking him to the ground. "No did nothing," the man said over and over, but Briato' ignored him and delivered another solid blow, this time to his nose. Two Roma next to Mojo gestured to the car with its doors still closed to drive away. The driver put the car in reverse, but Lollipop and Drone each unloaded a clip of six bullets, riddling the tires and hood, which now started to exude a plume of smoke. Pesce Moscio drew his pistol and took careful aim. He shot one of the Roma who had tried to wave the lead car off. "*Ua*', I've become quite the sharpshooter."

The lawyer had had a point, thought Nicolas, these guys didn't even think of bringing weapons. He pulled back the hammer on his gun, and the other members of his *paranza* followed suit. They opened fire on the Roma as they tried to get away.

Then there was no sound left but the rumble of Mercedes engines turning over. The members of the *paranza* exchanged glances as they stood, panting, pistols hanging at their sides, like so many cowboys who had fought off the attack on the stagecoach and were now surveying the field of battle. Mojo was missing. Nicolas left his men to exchange high fives and chest bumps and walked over to the lead Mercedes. He threw open the rear passenger door. There were three children and a dog that immediately started snarling at him. On the floor between the seats, Mojo had joined his hands in a mute plea, and was darting his eyes at the children.

"Make that dog shut up!" Nicolas shouted, pointing his gun right at the dog's jaws. It was a powerful-looking dog, a snarling mass of muscle. The children led it behind their backs and Nicolas lowered his handgun, using it to wave Mojo out of the car, and fast. Mojo continued to hold out both hands, clasped in a mute plea, without moving.

"Maraja," Mojo said. "We friends, right? Me saved you. You can't shoot me. Me saved you."

"Mojo, my man, this is nothing personal. This is strictly business. And business is what you're out of." He shut the door and went around to the other side of the car, ordering Drago' and Tucano to come over. "Get that sack of shit out of the car!" Drago' and Tucano threw open the door and dragged Mojo out onto the asphalt. He sat down, legs crossed, the members of the *paranza* in a circle around him. "Me beg you. Me always loyal to you. Me make you rich," he said, swiveling to face each of them, hands clasped, as if in benediction. Nicolas slowly walked around the outside of the circle, snapping his switchblade open and then folding it shut immediately. The wind had once again started to blow gently; his nostrils were met with the smells of exhaust fumes from the boats and ships moored not far away.

"Me make you rich!" Mojo repeated.

"We're already rich," said Nicolas, without stepping into the circle. Mojo looked around wildly to understand where that voice was coming from, but all he could see was the other members of the *paranza*, sniggering.

"Maraja, if you kill me—"

Nicolas stepped into the circle, and, before Mojo could even finish his sentence, he completed his performance of *The Godfather* with which, at the New Maharaja, the whole episode had first begun. He snapped open the switchblade that L'Arcangelo had given him as a gift and planted it deep in Mojo's belly, then hauled up on it, slashing diagonally, up and up, until he sliced into his chest, leaving behind a streamer of blood—just the same as De Niro had done when he'd killed Don Ciccio, the man who, back when Don Vito Andolini, before his last name became Corleone, was just a snot-nosed kid, *un muccusiello*, had murdered his family. Mojo stared up at him, round-eyed and uncomprehending, and unlike the members of the *paranza* all around him, he didn't even know the script of his own death.

"And now," said Nicolas, once he was sure that the man had stopped breathing, "let's take this nice present back to the sewer where Mojo lived."

"*E i guagliuncelli?*" asked Drago'. What about the kids? Nicolas nodded his head; this time Drago' was right. He went back to the car. The children hadn't moved from the back seat and they seemed to be clutching at the dog like a lifeboat.

Nicolas observed the three boys huddled on those filthy seats, covered with open food packages, rags, crumpled paper, and empty bottles. They sat there staring at him, paralyzed; only the dog had continued to snarl, the slobber streaming down her neck to her collar. She was a young dog, though no longer a puppy, but clearly not one of those animals that issue meaningless threats. The whiteness of her coat wasn't kindness, it was purity. A pure concentrate of power and destruction. Nicolas aimed his Desert Eagle at the center of her massive forehead, but the oldest boy implored him: "Don't kill us, we're begging you!" Then a sly glint appeared in his gaze: "You can make a bunch of money with this dog! And then when she's all grown up, she can have puppies, and you can sell them," he said again.

"What money?" Nicolas asked as he lowered his gun, for no real reason other than that he liked that bitch, and she deserved respect.

"She's a Dogo! A Dogo Argentino! You know about Dogos?"

He knew about them, everyone knew that they were the best when it came to dogfights, but he'd never seen one before. Still, now he realized that their reputation was well deserved.

It was the eldest of the three boys who was talking to Nicolas, and he must have been sure that, if he kept distracting the man who had killed his father's boss, he'd save both the life of the Dogo and his own life and those of his brothers, who were clinging to each other, stunned, their senses dulled by the slaughter.

"I like this championess, here." The boy realized he'd done it, put the collar on the Dogo, and handed the leash to Nicolas. Then he gave her one last kiss on the head goodbye, whispered a few words that were neither Italian nor Neapolitan, and then pushed her out of the car. "Go on," he said, "get going."

The dog had a pair of eyes that understood everything, and maybe that's why she walked away from the Mercedes without looking back.

"*Guagliu'*," Nicolas said to his crew, leaning over the Dogo, who was no longer snarling, "let me introduce you to Skunk."

They drove all the way to Gianturco, their mission not yet fully accomplished. After pulling the copper out of the trunks and hiding it in certain empty shipping containers to which Counselor Caiazzo had directed Nicolas, they had set out for the Roma shantytown. With a little effort and a few scratches, Nicolas had managed to hold Skunk still, clamping her between his legs. The dog had started barking ferociously, but then she'd realized that there was nothing to be done and had subsided into yelping. With that siren going in the background, they arrived in Gianturco, where they found the Gypsy camp swarming with people. Maybe they were all expecting their men to return home after the job on the wharf, thought Nicolas, who waved his hand in a signal to his men to start shooting: this was the beginning of the *stesa*.

They fired at human height, right into the sides of the trailers, at the cars, and against the scrap metal that the Roma used as laundry baskets, clotheslines, tables, and chairs.

"Fucking piece-of-shit Gypsies!" "If you touch the trains again, you'll wind up deader than Mojo Vileda!" "That copper belongs to us!"

It was like being in a pinball machine where, every time you hit the bumpers, they bounced into the air. They rode through the camp twice, wallowing in the mud and stirring waves of filth. The Roma ran this way and that, like ants when you rip open their earthen anthill.

Nicolas stopped at the entrance to the camp and the others gathered around him. They had performed well and there was going to be a nice reward for each and every one of them. But it was time to head home now, he needed to feed Skunk.

# A DERANGED PLAN

He'd taken 'a Koala's Kymco to the garage. That night, locked up in there, Dentino slept dreamlessly, untroubled. He'd put his vendetta off for a day; he had something to do first.

When lunchtime rolled around and his mother knocked, this time he opened the metal roller gate. They found themselves face-to-face after all these many months. His mother's eyes immediately filled with tears, in part due to a surge of emotion, but especially because of the state to which that son of hers had been reduced. If it hadn't been for those distinctive chipped incisors of his, she would have taken him for a stranger. In particular, his eyes frightened her. He gave her a hug.

"Mammà," he said, "I went to see Antonello yesterday, he's the spitting image of you, have you ever noticed? You know that when he grows up, he's going to be crazy about your Neapolitan tart? I'll bet you spoil him rotten already."

She said nothing; those words smacked of a farewell, and that was the last thing she wanted. Before she could say a word, he had already turned to go, and in a moment he was already back inside his den.

———

He could remember the place perfectly, a building dating back to the sixties, and an apartment on the sixth floor, in Gianturco. Nicolas had chosen it especially because it was anonymous and nondescript, not a place anyone would notice. He'd never been back, but Dentino hadn't forgotten a single detail of that first day they'd had an arsenal all their own. Back then, though, there'd been no need to post a lookout to keep an eye on that tactical asset. Back then, they'd all been friends, they were all still the *paranza*.

Dentino identified him in no time: that *guaglione* could have been him just four or five years earlier. He walked up and down on the sidewalk outside Aza's apartment building, in fact, he bounced along in his white Converse All Stars to the rhythm of the music he was listening to in his earbuds. Dentino knew how to take him in, just a few years ago he would have fallen for it himself. He went back to Piazza Principe Umberto. *"Ch'hé avé,"* he said, as if he were just any old customer. Ten euros of cocaine, that would be plenty, and then back to Gianturco again. Back and forth, half an hour each way, but Dentino didn't mind the sweat or the hours spent crossing the city.

The lookout was still there, idle and bored. Dentino walked over to him and said hello as if they'd been friends forever. A slap on the shoulder, good and hard, so that the lookout was forced to take out his earbuds. Dentino didn't give him time to react.

*"Ua',"* he said, "what kind of shitty job does Maraja have you doing? Still, this is just the beginning, right?"

The other young man took a step back and did nothing more than gaze at him, hands hanging at his sides, not on his handgun, a handgun he didn't even have, just as Dentino had supposed. Maraja didn't trust little snotnoses, he told himself.

"Who are you?" the boy asked him.

"You don't get it, I'm the one who asks you who *you* are. I'm Nicolas Maraja's right-hand man."

"But you don't look like a member of the *paranza* . . ." he said, taking in Dentino's appearance at a quick glance.

"Huh, sure, but I'm in disguise, I have to go on a mission. But first, why don't you try a snort of this." He pulled out the cocaine and offered him some. They started snorting coke right there in the street, while Dentino talked to him about the *paranza*, about the enemies they'd whacked, about the missions that he'd carried out with Maraja, that's right, with that very boy's boss, the same guy who had put the boy there to keep an eye on the sidewalk.

"Go ahead, be my guest," said Dentino, offering him another snort. "What's your name?"

"Luciano," the boy said, and took another snort.

"Good boy, Lucia', bravo. But now I've got to say goodbye to you. I have to go do a job. I need to go up and get a weapon."

"Hold on, first I need to report this to Maraja."

Dentino smiled condescendingly and put the rest of the coke away, as if to punish him for those words.

"Let me teach you something. You should never leave traces on your phone before you go do a job," said Dentino.

Luciano nodded, and, to conceal the red blush of shame, he started tormenting a cigarette butt on the ground with the toe of his shoe.

"Don't worry about it," said Dentino, laying a hand on his chest, "I won't say a thing to Nicolas." Then he changed his tone of voice and turned suddenly serious: "Do you carry a piece? Or doesn't Nicolas let you youngsters carry one?"

Luciano blushed an even brighter red. Dentino started up the stairs, but first he turned around: "Be good," he told him, "and when I get downstairs, I'll give you another present."

Up in the apartment, Aza had managed to get the old lady to sleep and had just sat down for a rest in front of the television when she heard a knock at the door. When she heard the words "Power company, we're here to read your meter," Aza opened the door but immediately realized this was no employee of the gas company. "Gypsy," she squealed, and tried to slam the door. But Dentino had already jammed his foot in the door.

"Go away, or I'll call Maraja's *paranza*, understood?"

He smiled: "Step aside, Aza, I'm Dentino, one of Nicolas's brothers, don't you remember?" He had to swallow to get the word *brother* out, but he never stopped smiling.

At the sound of Nicolas's name, Aza lessened the pressure on the door and examined him carefully.

It was true, he really did look like Nicolas's friend, the one with the chipped front teeth. But what had happened to him? Aza wondered, as she gestured for him to come in and then put her finger to her lips to caution him to silence. And that look in his eyes! Could he be on drugs? The question had just appeared in her face when Dentino wrapped both hands around her throat, pulling her head close. "Still in there?" he asked.

"Yes, she's in there, but she's asleep, please don't wake her up," she replied.

Dentino burst out laughing again, and his breath washing over her face made her squint in disgust. She held her breath.

"Not *her.* The arsenal," Dentino muttered, "is it still in there?"

Aza nodded forcefully.

There they were, the big duffel bags. All he'd had to do was move a few bags of Christmas decorations and other junk and he could already see the green of the canvas. Dentino seized one, tossed it onto the bed where Aza slept, pulled down the zipper, and started rummaging inside. He chose a Kalashnikov, then thought it over and opted for an Uzi, hefted it, and then changed his mind once again. He leveled the Kalashnikov and pretended to fire at the Justin Bieber poster—'a Koala had one just like it in her bedroom. Just as quickly as that thought had come into his mind, it slipped away again: it was no longer a time for thoughts like that, that past struck him as someone else's life. That was another Dentino, another Giuseppe Izzo, the one who had discovered that, behind the death of his friend Dumbo, there was an understanding between Nicolas and Scignacane—heir to the Acanforas, exclusive supplier to Micione for the finest Afghan heroin, who'd twisted the rules to supply the Piranhas with the same shit. Scignacane wanted to eliminate Dumbo over some matter of principle and Nicolas had agreed. He'd sacrificed him in exchange for narcotics.

Dentino also grabbed two hand grenades and a Beretta Storm, which he stuffed into his waistband, the gift for Luciano. In the meantime, Aza had left the room, shutting the door in the hope that it might muffle a bit the metallic rattling of the guns, and then she'd gone into the kitchen. She selected Nicolas's number, but on the sixth ring she gave up and left a message on his voice mail. In a whisper: "Your friend has the weapons."

She looked down at the display, hoping he'd call her right back, then allowed herself another thirty seconds and went back to Dentino, but he was already gone.

Luciano had started walking back and forth again, and the pistol that Dentino tossed him with a whistle to catch his attention almost hit him right in the head.

There had been a time when the soldiers of ISIS had aroused a feeling of repugnance in Dentino. Nicolas thought they had real balls, but Dentino thought they were cowards who planted bombs and couldn't look their enemies in the eyes. Adrenaline and rage had filled his body with a determination that he mistook for lucidity. He was convinced that now he finally saw everything clearly, and, riding 'a Koala's scooter, with two hand grenades hanging from the belt loops of his jeans, a Kalashnikov, and two full clips of ammunition, Dentino felt like a vigilante, out to do justice on his own. He roared toward San Giovanni a Teduccio, pulling wheelies all the way, indifferent to how his hand grenades jerked and lurched every time the front wheel slammed back down on the asphalt.

He was racing to the castle of the Acanforas, a place that Dumbo had described to him a thousand times—even though the only aspects of a castle that it possessed were the bristling defenses and the sentinels standing guard. That narrow lane wedged between buildings was a path that Dumbo had taken back and forth before with La Zarina, Scignacane's mother, clinging behind him. It was a passageway about a hundred feet long, overlooked by windows that were always left open, summer and winter, because no one lived behind them. The sharpshooters of the Acanfora family spelled one another in eight-hour shifts, so venturing into that cramped alley would have amounted to a suicide mission.

Completing the fortifications was a sheet-metal gate that ran back and forth on a track cut in the asphalt. It wouldn't entirely stop a car roaring at full speed, but it would slow it down enough to make sure that, trapped in a latter-day barbican, it would be turned into a sitting duck, an ideal target.

Dentino had fantasized about charging into the castle in a scene straight out of *The Fast and the Furious*. But he gave that dream up promptly, they'd riddle him with lead even before he could make it through the gate, and he couldn't afford that, not yet anyway. Scignacane wasn't the last name on his list. Once he'd taken care of him, Dentino told himself, it was going to be Nicolas's turn, and then at last their accounts would be evened up.

He needed to catch Scignacane out and about, in the no-man's-land that separated the sheet-metal gate, the city street that ran to the state highway, and the larger feudal holding of the Acanforas, right in those last few yards, where the attention of the bodyguards had slackened. A few more seconds, the clanking of metal, and there was the warm belly of the fortress, safe from the attacks of the Faella clan. He walked down the sidewalk and felt the hand grenades that were slapping heavily against his crotch, like an extra pair of testicles. "*Mo' verimmo chi tene 'e ppalle,*" he said to himself. Now we'll see who's got balls.

In his accounts, Dumbo had also described the ghost buildings you encountered before entering Scignacane's neighborhood. The Acanfora clan had bought them and emptied them out, as if trying to create a buffer zone between them and the rest of the city: in order to survive, they lived in a perpetual state of siege.

Dentino checked once again to see that the Kalashnikov across his chest had the safety switched off, and then he lay on his belly on the sidewalk, right where the street curved ever so slightly to the left before the gate, creating a sort of blind angle, or at least that's what he hoped—proof against video cameras and snipers.

With his nose jammed against the gravel of the walkway, Dentino felt happy. I'm a walking target, he told himself, but at least I'm out of that garage. He laughed at the nonsensical thoughts that filled his mind. "I'm out! I'm out!" he went on, speaking aloud; after all, he was in a no-man's-land, you could just up and die on that asphalt and your body would bake in the hot sun for days before anyone even bothered to think about cleaning up.

He would wait there, flat on the pavement, until Scignacane's Smart Car arrived. Dentino knew that the Smart Car might very well just keep driving straight and run him over, that's certainly what he would have done. But he felt confident that Scignacane, with the flaccidity attributable to his blue blood, would order his driver to come to a halt.

It was a plan full of holes, potential twists and turns, and agonizing waits, but it was one of those unattainable plans that only a capricious god could make feasible in the hands of a madman. And by this point, Dentino was stark raving mad.

He heard the Smart Car arrive. He'd always had a good ear for engine noises, ever since he was a kid. He lay there, motionless, calculating the distance between himself and the approaching automobile. Another thirty yards. One hand grenade would rip open the Smart Car like an M-80 in a can of sardines. But then he wouldn't have a chance to look Scignacane in the eyes, and Scignacane wouldn't look him in the eyes. Twenty yards. The Kalashnikov, I'll use the Kalashnikov, he said to himself with a laugh. Five yards. Dentino bent his elbow, stiffening it, ready to leap to his feet.

A sudden screeching halt. The sound of a car door. Then a sudden acceleration and another screeching halt, as if the Smart Car couldn't make up its mind whether or not to run him over. Dentino remained motionless. The tar beneath him was giving him strength, it was as if he were breathing in the rhythm of the earth.

"Get out, go and take a look," he heard Scignacane tell his driver. "Scignaca', why shouldn't we run over him? This guy's dead already." And, after a pause, Scignacane replied: "Go on, get out." The engine of the Smart Car cut off, then started up again. A foot on the accelerator, though the car was in neutral by now, and finally another order, again disregarded: "Come on, get out of the car," but no footsteps in his direction. At last, he heard the driver get out of the car. *Ja'*, he said to himself, let's go. And he rolled over.

Dentino let loose the first burst of bullets before even getting fully to his feet, one knee still braced against the ground, and the other leg fully extended. From that stance, he shot Scignacane's driver in the hips, which exploded like balloons full of blood. The man screamed, or at least Dentino thought he did, but when the hail of bullets whipped back in the other direction he devastated the man's mouth, and sent him reeling to slam against the Smart Car's hood. In the meantime, Scignacane was already clambering over the handbrake and gearshift to get into the driver's seat. A third burst of lead riddled the side of the car, and Scignacane tried to shield his head by crouching so low it was crammed under the steering wheel.

"Fucking Smart Car!" he shouted. A bellow of anger that turned into a screech of pain, rising two octaves, when a bullet hit him. In the instant of the blaze of gunpowder, Scignacane managed to tell himself that the piece-of-shit shooter had managed to tear half his face clean off, and he reached up and patted the side of his head desperately, in search of the missing piece. "My ear!" he yelled. "You piece of shit, you took off my ear!"

"Lost your earring, did you, you queer?" Dentino laughed, and at the same time he jammed a new magazine into the AK-47. Scignacane took advantage of that short pause and managed to get the Smart Car's engine turning over, shifted it into first gear, and screeched straight at the gate, hitting his driver's body while he was at it. Dentino stood there watching the automobile vanish behind the gate, then he turned his AK-47 against the Acanforas' fortress. A spray of lead that he kept coming as long as the magazine held out. It was scorching hot. He yanked it out all the same, ready to shove in a new one, but Scignacane's men returned fire. With the Kalashnikov slung over his shoulder, Dentino took off, running in zigzags, and leaped over the orange plastic barrier that separated the neighborhood from a field overgrown with yard-tall weeds, and disappeared.

He emerged on the other side of the field covered with scratches and with another, deeper cut on one of his cheeks. Reaching Forcella by foot would be a demented undertaking even for Dentino. He walked over to an intersection and fired a shot in the air. There was always someone who'd panic and abandon their means of transport, and even if it was a two-bit Kymco scooter, it would do in a pinch. Dentino leaped aboard and took off.

He raced through red lights without even bothering to look in either direction to see who was converging on the intersection, bent over the handlebars of his scooter, head even with the top of the low windshield. The street struck him as unusually wide, in fact he even thought that cars and pedestrians seemed to be scattering at his approach, as if they'd sensed the urgency of his mission. He drove with the Kalashnikov clamped between his legs and just one thought in mind: Antonello. That tiny creature was the only innocent character in this whole story, and now he understood that he was far more innocent than Christian had ever been, because Nicolas's brother had lived long enough to make certain decisions, and for those decisions to be choices made of his own free will. After all, hadn't he freely gone to the station? To a certain extent, he was responsible for his own death. But little Antonello hadn't even chosen to come into this world.

A carabiniere standing by the curb held up his paddle, intimating a halt. The Kymco showed no sign of slowing down, and roared past just a handbreadth away from the policeman. The blast of air spun him around and knocked him to the ground. His partner helped him back to his feet and they hopped in their squad car and took off in pursuit, siren wailing.

Nicolas was eating dinner. Skunk had gobbled down the half-thawed meat for the spaghetti sauce and now the Dogo was fast asleep on the old blanket laid out at the foot of the TV table in the kitchen. Mena was resting in her room; these were hard days at the pressing shop, and in her exhaustion she hadn't even had the strength to get up and make her son something to eat, so he had heated up a 4 Salti in Padella, a frozen dinner. Linguine with a seafood sauce. Between one forkful and the next, he ran through his directory of contacts on WhatsApp. He had 128 messages scattered through a dozen different chats, and then there was an unknown number, a landline, that had tried to call him and had finally left him a voice mail: "Your friend has the weapons." He knew that voice, but he couldn't quite place it, then and there. He poured himself a glass of Coke Light and pressed the button to listen to the message on speaker, but the sound coming out of his cell phone was drowned out by a voice coming from outside. A voice that this time he recognized instantly.

It was shouting in the street, that voice; in fact, it was approaching aboard a scooter revving wildly, a scooter that reminded Nicolas of his old Beverly. He was talking fast, every word driven by cocaine, words that Dentino had been repeating obsessively to himself for months, words that had been steeping in the vinegar of rage and that now emerged in a violent rush. When he finally was able to make out the words, even his last doubt died: "I followed the law. I had my vendetta. 'O *criaturo!* The little baby! Don't take it out on the baby, all you know how to do is kill little ones, you're no one. You had Dumbo killed, even though he had nothing to do with it, you did it for Scignacane, to suck that piece of shit's dick, Dumbo was my brother, he did his time behind bars in silence, he was a man, not like you. I want to lay you out dead, along with all your blood, all your kin . . ."

Dentino shouted as if those words could turn into bullets and lodge in Nicolas's body. And at last he fell suddenly silent. And pulled the trigger.

Nicolas didn't wait to hear the bullets from the Kalashnikov, he tore out of the kitchen overlooking the street, ran with Skunk hurrying after him into his mother's bedroom, lifted her bodily and threw her, diving after her, onto the floor at the center of the apartment. He counted seventeen bullets striking the building, he heard a window shatter, and almost immediately a siren, then another shout—the voice, now unrecognizable, deformed, of the young man who had once been his friend—and then it was all over. He lay on the floor a little longer, just to be safe, then got up and went to look out the kitchen window, just in time to see Dentino shaking the Kalashnikov in the direction of the police, as if to squeeze the last shots out of it. He tried to slam in a new magazine, but he was tackled and knocked to the pavement by two policemen, who yanked his arms behind his back.

Nicolas leaned out into the void, craning his neck, to pick out every detail, and so did dozens of other people, out of every window, like so many turtles.

The cop car tore away with a screech of rubber, and Nicolas let himself slide back against the wall. "Asshole," he muttered to himself, smacking himself in the forehead with a fist. "Asshole."

Mena put a hand on his head. "Get out of here," she said.

Nicolas nodded, a gesture that was a mark of gratitude and a plea to be careful with the cops when they questioned her, and then he started up the stairs that led to the attic areas and the roof. He could hear the voices of policemen, down in the atrium, telling people to stay inside, in the safety of the apartments, they'd go door to door themselves.

The whole neighborhood had been shut down. From up there, the streets seemed battened down as if in wartime. Police squad cars were blocking the points of access, and there was even a helicopter whirling and clattering overhead: Dentino's hail of gunfire had been taken seriously, and not as the isolated case of a madman in search of vendetta.

Putting an inexperienced and unarmed kid in charge of guarding the arsenal had been an unforgivably careless act. And now he was paying the price. Dentino could easily have killed his mother!

He checked his smartphone. Scignacane had called him a dozen times, but he hadn't answered. The heroin supply was the last thing on his mind.

He went downstairs. Police checkpoints everywhere, even the army with submachine guns. He looked up at the façade of his building. Dentino might have scraped the inside of his skull clean, but he could still aim a gun, Nicolas thought to himself. At least five bullets had hit within the radius of a yard from the window of his kitchen. Not bad for a guy riding a beat-up old scooter going fifty with the police after him. The shattered glass belonged to the upstairs neighbors; later he'd stop by and give them some money to get the window repaired.

The news of the shooting had reached everyone, and among the dozens of messages he'd received (especially from Letizia), he'd managed to read one, from Scignacane.

**Scignacane**
I'm waiting for you at the university.

And one more:

It's urgent.

And then another one:

Get moving.

What does that asshole want? Nicolas wondered, before diving into the *paranza*'s chat. They all knew, and they knew confusedly, that before swinging by Nicolas's house, Dentino had tried to rub out Scignacane.

Scignacane was waiting for him in an alley right behind the university, as he'd written. He was leaning against the side of an ambulance and was still wearing the jeans he'd had on when he was shot. His T-shirt was slung to one side, torn, and his jeans had a patch of curdled blood on one thigh. The gauze on his left ear had fallen away and was dangling from a few Band-Aids. When he tried to slap it back into place with swats of his hand, the sound was like a boot sinking into a deep mud puddle.

"We need to take him out," said Nicolas, or at least he tried to, because Scignacane was paying him no attention.

"This is all your fault," he shrilled unexpectedly. "I want your fucking *paranza* out of my hair. You kids. You *muschilli*. You *guagliuncelli*. Enough's enough. I've had it. All you know how to do is stand around with your dicks in your hands and sell hash. You don't know how to manage your own people. We're done. What are you trying to do, be Pablo Escobar? You don't know how to do a fucking thing."

"Scignaca'," said Nicolas, "that kid doesn't belong to the *paranza*. That little bastard killed my brother. And now he's tried to rub out you and me. Our business dealings have nothing the fuck to do with this whole thing."

Anesthetized by the shit he'd shot into his veins before meeting Nicolas, Scignacane went on with his rant: "You *muschilli*," he spat out, "you *guagliuncelli*. You think you're the new Camorra. Enough's enough! You're nothing!"

Nicolas laid a hand on his arm, firm and reassuring, like a doctor speaking to a hysterical patient, and said only: "Now calm down—" and Scignacane subsided. They stood there looking at each other in silence for a while, then Nicolas said again: "We've got to kill him."

"They're going to put him behind bars," said Scignacane. What remained of his ear was pulsating at the accelerated rhythm of his heart. "By now he's under guard. He took off one of my ears, and if I do it inside after the bedlam he unleashed, they'll give me life imprisonment without parole."

"If you kill him, I'm indebted to you." But then he emphasized: "Remember, though, it's going to have to hurt him."

Scignacane went behind the ambulance and put his hand on the door handle.

"Maraja," he said, "you don't want to understand."

"Oh, I understand. But he has to pay, Scignaca'."

"He'll pay," said Scignacane, and half opened the door. The interior of the counterfeit ambulance he moved around in was furnished with a bed and computer. It looked like a mobile office. He cleared his throat and spat out a clump of red. "I'll turn him into a living ghost, worse than death."

"Worse?" asked Nicolas, his voice midway between doubtful and curious.

"You're just a kid, you don't know that there are much worse things than death."

# PIRANHAS

*Capelloni*, the Longhairs, were in the clubhouse, the lair used by 'o White's men—one-third tobacconist, one-third bar, one-third Punto Sisal, or lottery window. There was the usual back-and-forth, comings and goings, the shouts of the bettors and the cries of those ordering an *amaro* at the bar's greasy, wood-faced counter, and there was also 'o White himself, wireless earbuds in his ears, jerking his head to some unknown beat. Rap or heroin? his men asked themselves, but they didn't dare step close to him: under that apparent normality they could sense a tension pushing to the surface that had never subsided since Roipnol's death. Nothing had happened since then—no warning shots, not even a muttered word—and that was what they found unsettling, more than anything else. The samurai knot that 'o White wore at the back of his side-shaven skull stopped without warning, in full silence. Mauriziuccio 'o Pagliaccio had entered the room, and the sheer weight of his importance had sucked all the bedlam out of the room. 'O Pagliaccio rapped his knuckles twice on the pool table, but 'o White had resumed his stationary dance, eyes still shut.

"'O White!" said 'o Pagliaccio.

"Oh, Mauriziu'. What are you doing here?" he asked, slowly removing his earbuds.

"I came by to see how the face on top of your dickhead neck was wearing over time. And it's pretty worn out!" He burst into a thunderous laugh. 'O Pagliaccio had two dense shrubs of reddish curls, one on either side of his skull, and on the top of his head glittered the reflection of the room's overhead fluorescent lights. A third shoal of tangled curls clung stubbornly to his forehead. He was the spitting image of Krusty the Clown, and since the day someone had pointed out the resemblance, Maurizio Viscardi had become Mauriziuccio 'o Pagliaccio.

"You need to come to San Giovanni."

"Wait, you want me to come to—"

"No. You all need to come. Your whole *paranza*. To Micione's house. Tomorrow morning."

"I got it," said 'o White. "But has something happened?"

'O Pagliaccio ignored the question. "All right, then, around ten in the morning. Because after that Micione has things to do. Take care of yourself, *guagliu'*."

As soon as 'o Pagliaccio was out of the room, the place emerged from its hibernation and began jumping again. Orso Ted and 'o Selvaggio were churning around 'o White.

"Oh, the fact that he came all the way out here . . . that's definitely not a good sign. But, 'o White, tomorrow it's not like 'o Pagliaccio is going to sentence us all to death, is it?" asked Orso Ted.

"Or else do you think they finally made you king of Forcella and tomorrow they're going to hold your coronation?" said 'o Selvaggio.

"Oh. Enough with these stupid questions," 'o White snapped. "You've busted my balls. No doubt, whatever it is, it's serious, otherwise they wouldn't have sent 'o Pagliaccio, they'd have sent a kid. *'Nu guaglione. 'Nu muschillo . . .*"

"Then why did they send him especially?" asked Orso Ted.

"Because you can't say no to 'o Pagliaccio," replied 'o White.

"I'd never met this guy 'o Pagliaccio," Orso Ted went on, "but the minute he set foot in here, I got scared!"

"*Uaaa*'. You really are a lightweight," said 'o White, brash and bold, "if 'o Pagliaccio scares you!"

"He scares me, too," said Chicchirichì.

"He doesn't scare me in the fucking slightest!" said 'o Selvaggio. "But he does look like a professional killer, I'll say that."

"That's some bullshit. Now you can glance at a guy and say he looks like a professional killer! If someone looked like a professional killer, then everyone would be able to tell you were a professional killer first thing, and you wouldn't be good for a single job," 'o White snapped. Could he be outdone in ferocity by someone who looked like Krusty the Clown?

"No, no," said Chicchirichì, "he definitely has the face of a professional killer. And after all, what does that have to do with it, 'o White. If a guy has the face of a professional killer, then everyone's just going to respect him."

"So you know what that professional killer does for a living now? He's cornered the market on Japanese motorcycles in Italy. He's the biggest dealership. And I'm not saying the biggest in Naples. In all of *Italy*!"

"But I thought he was the guy who carried out Micione's executions?" Chicchirichì asked.

"Sure, he killed people, alongside 'o Tigrotto," said 'o Selvaggio. He'd walked into the center of the cluster of Longhairs, he had something important to say: "And nobody suspected him. That means he had a pair of balls on him. If all you do is sell motorcycles, then you're a businessman. If all you do is kill people, then you're a professional killer. If you do both, then you know how to be a boss."

"So what are we doing now, reciting 'o Pagliaccio's biography? Come on, let's start a Wikipedia page for him . . ." 'o White interrupted him. The discussion had gone on too long now. The king of Forcella had summoned them, that alone was enough to set his imagination aflame. "It's about time they gave me Furcella, I mean what the fuck! After Don Feliciano turned state's witness, and Copacabana's behind bars, and now they've rubbed out Roipnol . . ."

"'O White, the tournament of Furcella is something you have to win, no one's going to give it to you—" said 'o Selvaggio. 'O White's hands seized 'o Selvaggio's throat and squeezed tight.

"No one ever gave me a thing in my life!" hissed 'o White. "When you speak my name, you need to gargle first with Tantum Verde mouthwash, you filthy *lòuta*!" He loosened his grip just enough to allow 'o Selvaggio to get a word out.

"'O White, no one in our *paranza* has a piazza. We're all on salaries. All we do is protect the piazzas, and do whatever Micione tells us. In the meantime, the Piranhas are supplying the whole city with shit."

"Bullshit. They give them a handful of fleas."

"Eh, like hell, a handful of fleas!" snarled 'o Selvaggio.

'O White met the gaze of all his other men.

Orso Ted said: "'O White, don't get mad. But the piazzas are all selling the Piranhas' shit."

"Okay, it's true," said 'o White, "so we'll settle the matter, at Micione's place."

"You see? We always have to go talk to someone to settle a matter."

"Shut your mouth." And he lifted his finger to the tip of his nose, to impose silence.


Via Sorrento in San Giovanni a Teduccio is a strip of asphalt lined with big apartment buildings, warehouses, and a mini-soccer field where the grass no longer grows. Micione lived there, on the top floor of an apartment house, and from there, from one of the countless outlying districts of Naples, he controlled the city's historical center. The road that runs from Forcella up to San Giovanni a Teduccio runs straight almost the whole way. You keep the sea on your right and in fifteen minutes, if there's no traffic, you're there. From the *palazzi* of the seventeenth century to big blocky apartment buildings in just minutes.

The Longhairs had crowded into 'o White's VW Golf, and the minute it crossed the boundary into San Giovanni he switched the engine off. He had no other instructions and he was in foreign territory. He hadn't ventured out of the historic center of Naples in more than a year: walking away from business for even just a handful of days is a dangerous thing, it means becoming a target.

Three scooters pulled up next to the car, surrounding it. A glance inside, another at the license plate, and finally a pair of knuckles knocking on the hood. "Stop when you get to the elementary school," said one of the guys on a scooter, and then roared off with the others.

Outside the elementary school a guy wearing jeans and denim a jacket waved him over. "Turn in here," he said to 'o White, opening the car door. "From here on I'll be driving."

The VW Golf pulled a U-turn and accelerated in the direction the Longhairs had come from.

"Oh, wait, now we're going back?"

"That's how it works . . . There are only four people who can approach the Faellas' house with a car. I'm one of the four."

"Well, what about if Amazon wants to deliver a package . . . ?"

"Ah, go blow yourself, you and *Amazòn*."

In the murky seabed of San Giovanni, the only security system was to allow access only to certain motorists, who, like maritime pilots, knew the low tides, the shoals, the reefs.

They arrived in a small open space surrounded by a horseshoe of public housing structures. The top floor of the three apartment buildings sutured together belonged to the Faellas, thousands of square feet of floor space that, viewed from the sidewalk, seemed like nothing more than depressingly normal apartments.

The Longhairs were ushered out of the car and lined up against the building's wall.

"*Guagliu'*, undress," said the man who had conducted them there. 'O White set a good example for his men and dropped a Beretta M9, his personal favorite, onto the reddish tile pavement. The others followed suit, all except for Orso Ted, who declared he wasn't carrying. The driver ordered them to take their shoes off, too; if they went up to see Micione with even a razor blade hidden in a sock, then he'd be a dead man. But they were all fine, they could go in. They caught a freight elevator that opened out onto a hallway that seemed to stretch out endlessly. The white walls were decked with antique view paintings of Naples in a faint sepia tone and, at regular intervals, a series of modern ottomans, these too sepia-hued. It looked like a waiting room, or the aisle of a church, so great was the solemnity it emanated. A narrow-plank parquet floor extended down the hallway, only to come to a sudden stop: beyond that point, you continued walking on a sort of plexiglass catwalk, but the LED can lighting overhead reflected a glare off the surface, producing a sort of fata morgana to the eyes of the Longhairs.

"Hold it right there," said Micione's man, and with long strides he walked away, vanishing into the distance.

"'O White," said Chicchirichì, "is it true that Micione looks like the Cheshire Cat?"

"Like who?" 'O White had raised his hands to his forehead to ward off the glare of the spotlights, and in the meantime he ventured a few steps to get past the parquet.

"The Cheshire Cat!"

"What the fuck is that?"

"The Cheshire Cat in *Alice in Wonderland* . . ." And then, seeing 'o White's baffled expression, he specified: "The cartoon."

"Ah, go fuck yourself . . ." But he never finished the phrase, because the sight of what lay beneath his feet had silenced him. A stream of rushing water flowed past under the transparent floor. It felt as if he was in one of those paintings of the miracles of Jesus; his grandmother had a holy image identical to this on her nightstand. Only here the sea was real, tropical, with seaweed, rocks, garishly colored fish, even a stingray that was swimming along with its belly glued to the thin transparent barrier separating it from 'o White's appalled face. "Oh, there's real water under here, and no kidding!" he said, and was immediately joined by the others, who got down on all fours, their heads swiveling to follow the clownfish and surgeonfish. Jaws hanging open, like four children visiting the Genoa aquarium.

"Look out, if you fall in it'll eat your face off . . ." The Longhairs hadn't noticed that Micione had come out a door and was enjoying the amusing sight of all of them, heads down, faces on the ground, and asses in the air.

"Why, are there piranhas in there, too?" 'o White promptly asked.

"Exactly. Do you know much about fish?" asked Micione. Then he shook hands with 'o White, ostentatiously ignoring the others. The Faella boss had shown up barefoot, jeans ending just below the knee and a white

Ralph Lauren shirt, untucked. "This way, boys," he said, and the Longhairs followed the master of the house, suspended above that stretch of Caribbean seascape in the heart of San Giovanni a Teduccio.

"I'm still trying to make up my mind whether I should fill a bathtub with acid and dissolve you in it one by one, or if there's anything about the bunch of you worth saving." Micione told them to sit down on a swaybacked sofa without a backrest. It was the only piece of ramshackle furniture in a living room that was crammed with mirrors and statues, candelabra and credenzas, all of it in a profusion of gold leaf and silver intarsia.

'O White tried to keep his back straight, but he felt as if they'd extracted his spinal cord all at once when 'o Pagliaccio's voice broke in: "What is it, have they made you whiter than white?"

"Crescenzio Roipnol has been shot," Micione went on, "'a Culona, his wife, has been shot. And you and your *paranza* were supposed to protect them. In Forcella, you and your *paranza* are me. I pay your salaries. I pay your bonuses. I pay for your tickets to the stadium. So? Who have you sold out to?"

"To no one, Micio'," murmured 'o White. Micione's eyes turned to the others, and like a chorus of soldiers, they all cried: "To no one!"

"Why are you talking about selling out?" 'o White continued, working up a little bit of nerve.

"Well, wasn't Carlito's Way in your *paranza*? Wasn't he supposed to stand guard outside the door? He was the one who sold out," said 'o Pagliaccio.

"No, what do you mean? They're writing all over Facebook that he had nothing to do with it . . ."

"That's true!" said 'o Selvaggio. He tried to stand up and pull his iPhone out of his back pocket, but 'o Pagliaccio shoved him back down with a hand to his chest. "All the lawyers that we have here, eh . . ." he said, and easily slid his phone out and took it, handing it over to Micione.

Carlito's Way had created lots of different profiles on social media, and for each and every one of them, he'd selected the same picture of Al Pacino in *Scarface*. "For informers all I have are the jaws of the wolf," Micione declaimed, scrolling with his thumb. "If someone talks dirty about the others with you, then he talks dirty about you with the others . . ."

"Quite the poet," said 'o Pagliaccio.

"'Death to informers. Anyone who accuses me of being a traitor and a fake is a traitor himself. My bros have to defend my innocence.' Well, well, well, he's turned into a writer to save his ass. That doesn't mean he didn't sell out. So? Where is he? What the fuck has become of him? 'O Pagliaccio has been looking for him for months and hasn't found him . . ."

"We'll find him for you," said 'o White. He'd braced himself, pushing his fists into the fabric.

"So who shot Roipnol? Was it you?" Micione stepped rapidly close to 'o White and hit him with an elbow, knocking him off-balance again. "Did you shoot him? Who gave you the money? Was it Mangiafuoco from Sanità, who was trying to defend himself? Was it L'Arcangelo? Was it those Grimaldi bastards? The people from Secondigliano? Who have you sold out to?"

"To no one!" 'o White reiterated.

"Bring me this fucking Carlito's Way."

"He's shitting his pants, he's terrified we're going to shoot him."

"And right he is!"

"People say he shipped out with his father. He's a sailor now," put in Orso Ted.

"Then get a boat and sail out and get him. Or maybe you could just dive in and swim out and get him. I really don't give a fuck either way. Do you know why I haven't dissolved you in acid, one by one, so that there's nothing left of you but your teeth, bobbing on the surface? Because I have to bring proof that my men, my arms, are clean, that I'm not letting myself be fucked in the ass by these gnats—*sti muschilli*."

"Oh, but by which *muschilli*?" asked 'o White.

"Ah, because you're not a *muschillo*, eh?" said 'o Pagliaccio. "So what are you? You a boss? You a zone chief? I throw a bone for you, and you're supposed to bring it back to me. And you don't even know how to do that."

'O White bit his lip, and struggled not to respond.

"I need you to bring me Carlito's Way," Micione went on. "I can't fight a war against everyone. You're too damned ignorant, all you know how to do is shoot. The more you shoot, the less you command. I have the police after me, the newspaper after me, I'm constantly leading the news roundup on regional TV. They say I'm hurting this city. But in fact, if there's anyone who's helping this city, it's me. I bring jobs to this place where no one else can give you a job. We need to organize business here, not just spend our days being bandits like you guys . . . bunch of ignorant louts . . ."

"I'm not afraid to shoot," said 'o White. He'd surrendered. Surrendered to the sweat, to the uncomfortable position, to the disappointment of not having been summoned there to be appointed to a new post. And now he could talk about it freely.

"But is he talking or is he shitting?" 'o Micione asked, with a glance at 'o Pagliaccio.

"No, if you ask me, he just belched."

"If you ask me, it was a fart."

"Me, afraid? I just fuck fear!" said 'o White. 'O Selvaggio tried to hold him back by tugging on his T-shirt from behind, but by now there was no stopping him. "Fear can blow me! What the fuck do I care about fear? I care about making money. 'O Micio', if you don't mind my saying, you should have given the scepter of Forcella to someone like me, not to people from outside . . ."

"Ah, so you wanted to be the prince of Forcella? 'O White the First, king of Forcella . . ."

"The first asshole!" said 'o Pagliaccio. "You didn't even know how to protect your own boss!"

"But he wasn't my boss," shouted 'o White.

"Then it was you who killed him. In that case, you need to die!" 'O Micione seized him by the throat, and 'o White started spewing incomprehensible phrases. Everyone else on the sofa bowed their heads, silent and motionless. Micione clutched even tighter, his fingers twisting the muscles of 'o White's throat. "So who's your boss?"

"You are," 'o White finally managed to gasp out, and Micione released his grip.

"What do you want to become? If you want to be a boss, you have to have a pair of balls on you that when you walk down the street, the street itself bows down before you. Bring me Carlito's Way, *ja*'! Save his life for him."

# PLIERS

O White needed to think and not think at the same time. Develop a plan and avoid putting his foot back into all the bullshit he'd spewed out then and there into Micione's face. But he'd never been much when it came to strategizing. Maraja was better at that than 'o White, and that's why he was running circles around him. But strategies are important only up to a certain point. He'd learned that if you were willing and ready to pull the trigger, then might and right were on your side. The driver who had brought them there had ordered him to wait, he'd go and get the VW Golf.

"How many shots do you count in here?" 'o Selvaggio was saying. He'd pulled out the clip of his Beretta 7.65 and was holding it high, like a saint card. "One, two, three . . . there's nine. 'O White, this clip alone will do it, it's one shot apiece, with a few left over. We blast lead into that piece of shit Maraja and all of his *paranza.*"

"I don't know if it was him. But whoever it was that killed Roipnol and that fat wife of his did a good job, he wasn't from Forcella, he just bought his way in," said Orso Ted.

'O White decided that maybe 'o Selvaggio and Orso Ted were right.

But what did that matter right now? Micione had set his sights on Carlito's and they had to bring him Carlito's.

"The Piranhas are just a bunch of limp dicks," he said. "I'll eat 'o Maraja fried and crunchy whenever I please."

"But when are we going to do it?" asked 'o Selvaggio. "He's controlling all the piazzas. Micione hardly even noticed . . ."

"He noticed, and how, but he's shitting in his own hand. He's afraid of blood. If he hangs them one by one, you know what happens? They'll shut down the piazzas. If you're afraid to shoot, you wind up shot."

"Sure, but Maraja's *paranza* has the piazzas now."

"Who knows where they get this surplus shit . . . someone must be selling it to them under the table," 'o White replied. He heard the engine of his car even before he saw it come around the curve, and he headed off down the street, followed by the others.

"It isn't garbage, what they sell, they're good rocks . . . and at ridiculously low prices, they're taking over Naples," said Orso Ted.

'O White went on walking, leaving them to argue among themselves.

"Let's just ride down to Forcella and take them out. Boom boom boom and we're done."

"And if we kill all the *paranzas* of Forcella, asshole, then the outsiders will just take over."

"So what are we going to do?"

"Then let's go hear what Copacabana has to say . . . he was the one who was supposed to decide . . . so he's the one we're supposed to bring back."

The VW Golf pulled up next to 'o White, who grabbed the keys that the driver tossed him and then slid behind the wheel, violently slamming the door behind him. Then he hit the door locks and started the engine. Chicchirichì and 'o Selvaggio grabbed the handles and started yanking on them: "Hey, open up!"

"Like fuck I will, you can hoof it all the way back, you pieces of shit. You aren't real brothers. When Micione took me you didn't lift a finger, so now you can walk all the way back."

"What's that have to do with anything, 'o White?"

"You're out to lunch!"

"What were we supposed to do?"

With the screech of tires, 'o White had already disappeared behind the buildings of the Faella clan.


The plan that 'o White had come up with wasn't outstandingly original or anything, but everyone agreed that it was the most effective one.

They all knew that the Costagliola family had taken off sometime ago, escaped, down to the very last member. Where they had gone, however, no one seemed able to say; the neighbors were keeping their mouths stitched tight, information was at a premium. The plan was to help the neighbors to see matters more clearly.

'O White appeared with his men outside the apartment house, cradling in his arms the only AK-47 the Longhairs possessed.

"What happened to the Costagliola family?" he demanded, shouting up at the empty windows, giving them one last chance.

Then, seeing that no one had even stuck their head out, he pulled the trigger. The balconies might as well have been made of styrofoam, so readily did they absorb the bullets, while the window fixtures shot splinters and shards in all directions. A burst of lead hit a line of geraniums, and the red petals scattered, fluttering gently through the air, while the windowpanes shattered, inundating the terrified passersby below with sharp bits of glass. 'O Selvaggio took the pistol he carried with him and started firing. Chicchirichì and Orso Ted, who carried no weapons, shouted amid the roar of gunfire: "You're all garbage, you're shitholes . . ."

Once he'd fired all the bullets in his first magazine, 'o White waved to his men to fall silent: "All right, then, where are they? What's become of these ghosts?" he shouted. He gave the people in the building five seconds to make themselves heard, and when that time was up he shoved a new clip into the assault rifle. After the first hail of bullets, once a piece of stone cornice more than three feet long had crashed to the pavement not far from his feet, they heard a voice coming from one of the shattered windows. "In Villaricca! At their grandmother's! They're in Villaricca!"

"Where the fuck does this grandmother live?" shouted Orso Ted.

"Near the Conad supermarket!" rang out another voice.

Carlito's Way's beehive had started to buzz again. The veil of *omertà* had been rent asunder because the silence that ensures protection always has a sell-by date, and it corresponds to the moment when you actually risk your own life, in the first person.

The Longhairs rode their scooters back to the clubhouse, where 'o White had parked the VW Golf, and then off they all headed toward Villaricca, equipped as follows: the AK-47, the five magazines of bullets that they kept hidden behind the Stoya poster in the clubhouse, an old Colt M1911, and 'o White's Beretta. A GPS set for Villaricca, and a crack pipe. 'O White had made sure to buy a car with an automatic transmission, so that he could keep the car on the road with one hand but had the other hand ready when his turn to take a hit came around. With that traffic, it took them two hours to get there.

Passing the pipe around the whole time, they started driving up and down the stretch of street that ran past the Conad supermarket.

"If we keep driving back and forth like this," said 'o Selvaggio, "they're going to start thinking we're planning an ambush. And then we'll have the police on our ass, busting our chops."

"Get out and walk it, then," said 'o White, and he parked the car on a crosswalk.

Orso Ted and Chicchirichì walked along the sidewalk, hands stuffed in their pockets because the evening had turned chilly.

"What do you think, does Carlito's Way really have nothing to do with this?" Chicchirichì asked, and he'd been wanting to ask that question for a while now.

"If you ask me, he doesn't have a fucking thing to do with this," Orso Ted said immediately, and it was clear that he, too, had had that answer in his head for some time.

"According to 'o White, there's someone behind it, either Sanità with Mangiafuoco, or the people from Secondigliano, or the Quartierani. Which means there's going to be a war."

"You ask me, it's the Piranhas."

"You ask me, Carlito's Way sold out. He took money to say when the sentinel wasn't standing guard."

"But if he did that, it would have been too easy to find out. He can't be that much of an asshole. And then, if they'd given him the cash, he wouldn't be in Villaricca by now. He's not with the Piranhas. He's just an asshole. I've known him all my life, Carlito's Way. He's just shitting his pants because Micione thinks it was him."

They went back to the Golf. 'O White and 'o Selvaggio had fallen asleep with their heads pressed against the windows, and, seeing that it looked like the neighborhood was deserted, Orso Ted and Chicchirichì slumped into the back seat.

They were awakened by the rapid beeping of a garbage truck backing up. Without uttering a word, 'o White started the car and resumed their patrolling. Compared with the night before, the street had come to life, for the most part populated with retirees pulling shopping carts and heading for the supermarket. There wasn't the slightest trace of the Costagliola family, though.

"Where the fuck are they!" 'o White snapped. He was starting to run out of patience, and the fact that they'd smoked all the crack wasn't doing a thing to sweeten his mood. He pulled the car up alongside the pedestrians and followed them closely until, terrified by the dilated pupils over that rotten complexion, they scampered to safety down their front drives. 'O Selvaggio kept saying they needed to get back to Forcella, by now they'd made their presence all too clearly known, they'd attracted too much attention, but 'o White wasn't interested in listening. Now he was tracking the progress of a couple of matrons on their way back from the Conad. The two women, in their turn, were watching 'o White, and once they reached their apartment house door, the younger of the two yanked on the other's sleeve to get her to hurry up a little. To 'o White, that uncertainty was more than sufficient. He slammed on the brakes and threw open his car door: "Signora Costagliola? Signora Costagliola?" The two women hurried their pace, without looking around, with the younger one practically dragging the older one.

"Signora Costagliola, don't run away! I just want to tell you something for your son."

With those words, as if 'o White had shouted, *Ready, set, go*, the women dropped their shopping bags and started to run. They hurried through the gate and slammed it shut behind them with a metallic clang, vanishing through the atrium while the Longhairs were already clambering over the gate and charging off after them. The elevator door shut right in 'o Selvaggio's face and so, one after the other, they charged up the stairs, taking the steps three at a time. In the meantime, one of the two women was shouting into her phone for someone to open the door, that it was the people from Forcella, not to waste any time. 'O White waited downstairs, ready to ward off anyone displaying excessive curiosity with the most definitive of phrases: "Nothing's happening. Family business."

The first of the Longhairs to reach the walkway on the top floor, Chicchirichì, saw one of the women dive into the apartment, leaving the old woman at the door. Chicchirichì grabbed her by her headscarf and yanked, uncovering a compact, well-tended hairdo. The Longhair grabbed that head of hair, hauling on it with all his might. And he kept tugging, until he finally ripped the wig free and liberated a cascade of really long gray hair.

"Madonna. What is this? Rapunzel as an old woman?" said Chicchirichì.

Carlito's Way's grandmother had always been an attractive woman and she attributed her success with men to the head of hair that as a young woman she'd worn waist-length. As she aged, she'd always refused to cut it, even if everyone constantly told her that for older women to wear their hair long was a sign of lasciviousness. And so she kept her hair tucked up, hidden—it had been her secret, at least until the arrival of Chicchirichì.

Now Carlito's Way's grandmother, being held hostage by the members of the *paranza*, was shouting for them to let her go; 'o Selvaggio held both her arms tight behind her back and warned her to pipe down, but she kept up her squawking all the same, calling upon all the saints and the Madonna Herself to blast those interlopers from Forcella straight to hell.

In the midst of that rosary, the door that the other woman was hiding behind swung wide open: in the space framed by the doorjamb, Carlito's Way appeared with a Glock in his hand. He leveled it immediately at 'o Selvaggio, but he in turn used the grandmother as a human shield and Chicchirichì aimed his AK-47 at her.

Carlito's Way's grandmother kept yelling at him to shoot, to send them both to meet their maker, after all, she'd lived long enough, and her grandson kept trying to drown out that bedlam by shouting the words he'd been repeating for months now: "I didn't do anything! I don't have a thing to do with Roipnol and 'a Culona, *adda murì mammà*! They killed them without any help from me. I didn't sell out! I never sold out."

"Sure, we can believe you, but it makes no difference, you need to tell your story to Micione!" Chicchirichì explained. "Micione wants to hear you say it to his face. You need to come, otherwise he'll take it out on us. Fucker! Why the fuck are you running away? Keep it up and you'll get us all killed, little piece of shit."

In the meantime, Carlito's Way's mother had appeared behind him, and like the grandmother she was calling on the neighbors to come to her rescue. The only one keeping his mouth shut was Pisciazziello. He'd taken shelter at the far end of the living room, and every once in a while he'd stick his head out to get a better view.

Orso Ted kept them both covered with his Colt, while the grandmother shrieked and kept trying to wriggle free by stamping on 'o Selvaggio's feet, while he dodged and shuffled like a tap dancer.

"I didn't do a thing! Let go of my grandmother, you bastard!" Carlito's Way shouted.

"Drop the pistol on the floor, and I'll give you back the old woman," said Chicchirichì, jamming his AK-47 into the lady's belly.

"But what if you shoot her anyway?"

"Oh, so you really are an asshole. If I wanted to, I'd have already shot you, your grandmother, your mother, and Pisciazziello, too."

Carlito's Way compressed his lips, turned for a second to look at his mother, then carefully set the Glock down on the floor and kicked it away. The pistol slid to the center of the landing. 'O Selvaggio let go of the grandmother, and the minute she felt his grip relax, like a horse that no longer feels the bit, she took off running into the apartment, with her daughter and her grandson, taking advantage of the fact that the Longhairs had all lunged together for the Glock. The armor-plated door slammed shut so violently that the doorjamb shivered.

From downstairs, 'o White asked what they were doing up there, why it was taking them so much damned time, and 'o Selvaggio reassured him with an "It's all good," then he let loose with a burst of gunfire that peppered the door panel. "Now you're all dead," he shouted, "every last one of you," and he held the trigger down until the clip was empty. The move must have been persuasive because after the noise of shots had stopped echoing on the landing and down the stairs, the door opened a crack. Through that narrow opening, Carlito's Way begged them to stop firing, he'd come with them to talk to Micione. "Cut out the mayhem! *Basta co' stu burdello!*"

In the background, you could hear his mother saying over and over again: "Don't hurt him! He didn't do anything!" But it was finally Carlito's Way who told her just to shut up for once: "Don't worry, Mammà. It'll all turn out fine, they're brothers. Pisciazzie', you take care of it if anything comes up!"

During the drive to San Giovanni a Teduccio, the only sound was Carlito's Way's labored breathing. He'd used up all his courage in his attempt to assure his family that it was just a trifle, nothing serious, and that things were well under control, in spite of the firefight on the walkway.

"Smoke this," 'o White told him, extending a joint. "You need to keep calm when you're talking to Micione."

Carlito's Way shook his head, he wanted to keep his head straight, he wanted to give the best possible answers to Micione's questions.

"But why the fuck did you run away?" asked Chicchirichì. "Eh, why the fuck did you run, what good did you think it would do, why'd you make the whole neighborhood think you'd sold out?"

"You were sure to kill me," Carlito's Way replied with a faint threat in his voice.

"Asshole, you belong to my *paranza*," said 'o White, "you should have come to me. We'd have taken care of it. What was going to happen? You might have gotten slapped around a little. That was all. You were a piece of shit. You took off. But if I'd killed you, I'd have been killing myself, you asshole! It would have meant that I'd let a traitor inside my own *paranza*!"

Carlito's Way raised his hands to his chest to make sure that his breath hadn't left him. And he wondered whether Al Pacino would have gambled away his own life just because he didn't have the courage to tell the truth.

The procedure was exactly the same as the first time, but along with Micione, slumped deep in a rosé-hued damask armchair, and 'o Pagliaccio, there were two other people that the Longhairs had never seen before: Micione's brother, 'o Gialluto, and Roipnol's sister, 'a Ranfona. They were standing in a semicircle behind Micione; in a corner, almost hidden behind a grandfather clock that loomed all the way to the ceiling, Agostino 'o Cerino, or Matchstick, watched the scene with both hands locked behind his waist. He looked like a bodyguard, or a sellout, as 'o White would have called him, still baffled at the fact that the guy had managed to get himself kicked out of the Piranhas and then recycled himself as Micione's bagman.

Carlito's Way did his best to hold his head high and thrust his chest forward, but the result was a ridiculous pose, like a fighting rooster. Micione smiled and intercepted the shove with which 'o White tried to rid himself of Carlito's Way as if of some useless prey. "No," Micione said, "there's room here for everyone, but you all need to stand, because you've busted my balls with what you've done. You, Carlito's, you can sit down, though," and 'o Pagliaccio stepped forward to lead him out of the group of Longhairs and nail him to the sofa. It was no longer a time for poses and attitudes, and soon Carlito's Way was sucking in oxygen with a labored breath.

"Now then," Micione began, "it was your job to protect Crescenzio Roipnol and you failed. You can just thank the Madonna that you're still breathing; that your mother is still breathing; that your brother is still breathing; that your grandmother is still breathing; and that we didn't board the ship to grab that gay father of yours."

"He's not gay," Carlito's Way said, reacting instinctively.

"No? Then how do you think he passes the months without women on that ship? Don't you think he swaps fish with the other sailors?" Behind Micione everyone burst out laughing, and even a few of the Longhairs laughed along with them.

"And only the son of a queer can leave his job uncovered like you did. You were supposed to stand sentinel but you sold out. So now you die." Micione hoisted himself up on the armrests and lunged at Carlito's Way. He started off with a light punch, and then he increased the intensity, focusing with brutal fury on his ears. Carlito's didn't react, he limited himself to grunting and at least to holding his back straight.

"Where the fuck were you? Queer!"

"I went to pick up the gambling money at the bar, I was supposed to bring it to Roipnol. I always did it at the same time of day. They must have followed me, so that's when they went and rubbed him out."

Two more straight punches. A right and then a left. And then Micione retraced his steps, sitting comfortably back in the armchair. Then 'a Ranfona stepped forward, and once you looked carefully you could see that she was the spitting image of her brother. Tall, dark, curly-haired, arms so long they almost reached her knees, so they looked like *ranfe*, or octopus tentacles. A big octopus tentacle—'a Ranfona.

"They got in," she said. Her voice, too, seemed to come from the depths of the sea. "The door was open, they didn't bust it open, so it must have been someone they knew. Someone you must have introduced them to, you piece of shit!" And she swung back and hit him. That was the signal. 'O Pagliaccio and 'o Gialluto unleashed a storm of punches to his back and his rib cage, which seemed to echo as if there was nothing inside but a void.

"I didn't introduce anyone to them," Carlito's Way spat out. "I just went down to get the money . . ."

"How long did you take?" asked 'a Ranfona. "Walking with your balls scraping the dirt, the distance between Crescenzio's house and the bar is five minutes. How fucking long were you out if by the time you got back, the police were already there? They'd already called the ambulance. It had been half an hour. So what the fuck were you doing all that time?!?" And she punched him again. That was the second signal. 'O Gialluto lifted him to his feet, grabbing him by the ears.

"Well? What the fuck did you do?"

Carlito's Way's eyes were brimming over with tears, but his cheeks were dry. He didn't want to cry in front of what he still considered his *paranza*. Then he told himself the time had come to confess.

"I stopped to eat," he said.

"You stopped to eat?!" Micione shouted, immediately taking back the floor. "You were supposed to stand guard at the front door. You're seventeen years old and you don't even know how to guard a door? If I'd let your brother do it, if I'd let 'o White do it, things would have worked out better, right?" He turned toward 'o White and slapped him hard in the face; he didn't want him to feel safe just because he wasn't the one getting the third degree. The chief of the Longhairs took the blow, but his ponytail whipped through the air, and his hand went straight for his lower back, where he usually kept his Beretta.

"What, did you want to shoot me, 'o White? Did your hand try to go for your boxer shorts?" asked Micione. "Good job, you ought to shoot me, because I trusted the fucking *paranza* of the Longhairs and now we'll never even know who the fuck it was. 'O Maraja? The bastard Grimaldis? Mangiafuoco from Sanità, who wanted to take revenge?"

"There are video cameras . . ." Carlito's Way whispered. His right ear had already started to swell and his vision was beginning to blur.

"Asshole!" Micione shoved 'o White to get him out of the way and crammed his face nose to nose flat up against Carlito's Way, who ventured: "But there was a video camera . . ." Bang. Micione's fist slammed against the base of his right ear. Carlito's Way felt no pain, just a piercing whistle, as if a siren had been installed in his brain.

"Of course there was a video camera, asshole, but it wasn't recording, otherwise we might as well just hand over the film to the cops!" It was an age-old rule of the many thousands of video cameras that kept watch over the front doors of mob bosses. You could see what was happening in real time, but you never, ever hit record, you never, ever leave evidence. No one had noticed that 'a Ranfona had left the room and now come back with a pair of carpenter's pliers. She was opening and closing them to see how they worked.

"You were eating . . ." she said. "That was your failing. So now we're going to teach you how to stop eating."

Carlito's Way lunged for the door, but 'o Pagliaccio stuck out his leg and tripped him, then grabbed him by the hair and dragged him back to the sofa and forced him down onto his back, jamming his knee against his sternum. 'A Ranfona handed the pliers over to Micione, stepped behind Carlito's Way's head, and seized both his wrists. She pushed down, using all her weight as if on the handle of a car jack, until she could hear his joints cracking. In the meantime, 'o Gialluto pressed his nostrils shut and used his other hand to yank his jaw open wide. An act of medieval torture.

Micione started with a molar. He made sure that the pliers had a firm grip on the tooth and then he started twisting, as if he were trying to extract a screw from a wooden plank. Carlito's Way emitted a succession of animal sounds, punctuated by the muffled slurps of his blood-engulfed epiglottis.

The molar came away with the whole root, accompanied by a blood-curdling scream. "You went to eat, did you?" he said, puffing with the effort. "This'll teach you to stay in and do your job next time." And then Micione went on to a canine. "Fuck, the teeth on this piece of shit must have been cemented in place." He handed the pliers over to 'o Pagliaccio, who pulled sharply in a way that shattered the incisors while he was at it. Then it was the turn of the two others. In the meantime, Carlito's Way had passed out, and they were able to finish the job without encountering any more resistance.

The Longhairs were staring at the floor. After Carlito's Way, it could have been anyone else's turn next. 'O Cerino, on the other hand, was supposed to report back on every detail to Copacabana, in his prison cell.

"Your life belongs to me," said Micione, after 'o Pagliaccio had brought Carlito's Way back to consciousness by pouring a pitcher of water over his face. "Now I'm going to lend it back to you."

"No, I want him dead! I want him dead!" 'a Ranfona objected, but Micione brought her around with a solid argument: "The *guaglione* needs to stay alive, but don't you worry, I'll give you the dealership in Forcella."

After hearing those words, 'a Ranfona crossed her long arms and said not another thing.

"First thing." Micione turned back to Carlito's Way. "You need to thank the Madonna that you're still alive, to prove that my *paranza* betrayed nobody. Otherwise, it would be better to get rid of pieces of shit like you, with a bucket of water on the sidewalk. Your life has only one purpose to me: as a poster on the wall. You just need to tell everyone that you're still here, you need to say, 'They let me live because I wasn't the one who betrayed.' And if you leave Forcella, anytime in the next ten years, you're a dead man. Now get the fuck out of my face. I'm sick of looking at you."

They found a plastic tarp, stealing it from a nearby construction site, covered up the leather rear seats of the VW Golf, and laid Carlito's Way on them. He couldn't seem to stop coughing. When his solar plexus sank he barked out a cough, spraying blood and chunks of broken teeth.

They arrived in Villaricca after a long and roundabout excursion to avoid any possible checkpoints, but apparently the shootout had been dismissed as an attempted robbery, and the street was clear.

They dragged him down the driveway, and then up the elevator, and finally deposited him against the armor-plated door, which had been repaired, or jury rigged, with a section of plywood.

The mother came out even before 'o White could ring the doorbell: "What have you done to him? What have you done to him, you bastards?!"

"What have they done to him . . ." said Chicchirichì.

Pisciazziello had emerged, along with his grandmother, his eyes filled with hope. "Did they believe him?"

"Yeah, they believed him," replied 'o White, in the bitter tone of someone who knows they're still not bringing good news.

At the sight of his brother—face ravaged, unrecognizable—Pisciazziello's vision blurred. It was only the pity of a passing moment, then everything emerged again before his eyes, up close, all too clear. Around him moved the frightful, deformed face, the splotches of blood, the fists that his mother was pounding against her chest, the long locks of white hair fluttering in the air, the walls, the floor, a merry-go-round of horror that melted his muscles.

He slumped to the ground, and, something that hadn't happened to him in years, his bladder released, drenching his underwear and trousers.

# DELIVERY

There were eleven missed calls on his iPhone, all from an unknown caller. Nicolas was about to delete them when the same unknown number lit up the screen again.

"Hello?!" he answered, his voice still slightly slurred.

"Oh, Nicolas, how are you?"

"Who's this?"

"It's Emanuele, your cousin. I'm calling because—"

"I don't have any idea who you are," Nicolas interrupted him. "I don't have any cousins named Emanuele."

"What are you saying, Nico', don't you remember me? I'm the son of Lelluccio . . . your mother's first cousin."

"Who's ever heard of you? Stop wasting my time, *ja'*—"

Nicolas had just ended the call when the phone started ringing again.

"What the fuck do you want? Asshole!"

"No, Nico', hold on! I wanted to work for you, that's why I'm calling!"

"Who the fuck do you take me for? The IKEA in Afragola? What do you think, who told you I'm hiring? I mean, who are you, who's ever heard of you?"

"Nico', wait—"

Nicolas ended the phone call again. So now a cousin he'd never even had was going to start tormenting him? "Fuck!" he said in a loud voice. "*Che spaccimma!*" Filthy pig! He let fly a kick at the first thing to come within reach; a small crack opened in the refrigerator door. A new call from the imaginary cousin distracted him from that dent. He answered the call because now he wanted a man, he wanted to know who this was, and he wanted to go and find him and beat him badly enough to make himself feel a little better.

"Oh, now you have to tell me where the fuck you are, and I'll come and get you!" he shouted.

"Nico', it's me, Susamiello, your cousin!"

There was a moment of silence. Susamiello! Of course: the son of his mother's cousin.

"Ahhh, Susamiello! Why the fuck would you say that you're Emanuele, why the fuck would you call me with that name? What are you up to, Susamie'?"

"Eh, next week I'm turning fourteen. Which means I can drive a scooter."

"Ah . . . and do you have a scooter?"

"Yes, yes, Papa gave me one."

"Good old uncle. So what do you want from me?"

"I want to work."

"What do you think, I have a factory?"

"Why, no . . ."

"Okay, *ja*'." Nicolas cut off the conversation. "Let's get together . . ."

"Can I come by now, to your house?"

Nicolas smiled. He could see him downstairs in the street outside his building, his ass on the saddle of his scooter, his smartphone glued to his ear, and his head tilted back to detect any movement at the upstairs window.

"Well, what makes you think I'm at home?" Nicolas asked. He found this persistent cousin amusing. A little bit, he reminded him of himself; only he, Maraja, would never have asked anyone permission to work.

"My aunt told me so," said Susamiello. From his decisive tone of voice, it was clear that he had prepared that answer and the whole preceding pitch.

He was tempted to laugh. "Come up, *ja'*."

"Can I bring a couple of my friends?"

"Who do you mean?"

"Classmates of mine."

"What school do you go to?"

"The Convitto Nazionale."

"How old are they?"

"One is twelve, the other one is thirteen, just like me."

"All right. Come on, but hurry up, because I have things to do and I don't want you to bust my balls too much."

Nicolas let himself sink into the cushions of his armchair. He told himself that those guys downstairs would let at least five minutes go by before ringing the doorbell, just to make the whole masquerade look plausible.

The beep of the intercom made him start and he instinctively moved his hand, reaching for where he usually kept the Desert Eagle. The kids had been punctual, but that didn't mean he couldn't leave them dangling a little while longer.

"I'm taking a shower," said Nicolas. "Come back later . . . what the fuck."

Fifteen minutes later, when he went to the door wrapped in his S.S.C. Napoli bathrobe, he thought to himself he ought really to have had security cameras installed. The fake video camera with the clearly visible sirens that his father had had put in—because, he said, after all, Gypsies see it from outside, and knowing that it's there, they go looking for another house to burgle—no longer intimidated anyone at all.

He studied them through the peephole. Zit-ridden, earrings with fake diamonds, one of them even wearing a pair of counterfeit Rolex watches on the same wrist. *Muccusielli*, thought Nicolas, snotnoses, and he smiled again, without however being able to entirely rid himself of a hint of paranoia that was telling him: bait, cops. After Dentino almost killed him and his mother, and even got arrested in the street down below, he felt he needed to be a little more cautious. He opened the door just wide enough to see all three of their faces and, at the same time, realize if there was about to be a raid.

Nicolas's cousin spoke up, with a faint "May we come in?" 'O Maraja ran his eyes over Susamiello from head to toe, following the S shape of his gangly body, just like the Neapolitan Christmas cookies from which he took his nickname.

"*Trasite*," he said at last. Come in.

"*Cia', Nico'!*" said Susamiello, and gave him a hug, catching him off guard.

"*Ua'*, you're crooked as a snake, just like you were when you were little," said Nico', and he fastened the sash a little tighter around his dressing gown.

"This is Risvoltino," said Susamiello, and invited his comrade to step forward. He barely reached Nicolas's shoulders, and the cuffs he insisted on wearing on his jeans—*risvolti* were cuffs—certainly did nothing to make him look any taller. He wore a plaid shirt at least a size too small that created rolls on his belly and hips. The sleeves, of course, were rolled up, too. *Risvoltate*.

"My pleasure, Maraja." He shook the clammy hand, and then it was the third boy's turn, and he introduced himself as Pachi. Nicolas extended his hand again, and the boy took it and lifted it to his lips, planting a resounding kiss.

"I like the manners of your buddy here," Nicolas said to Susamiello. "So what is it you want to do?"

"Eh, we want to work. We want to work with you. With your *paranza*."

"And what do you know how to do?"

Susamiello's face lit up, he hadn't been waiting for anything but that question. He started loudly declaiming the qualities and talents of his friends. He seemed like a farmer working to sell his cattle at a fair. This one knew how to ride a scooter with special skills, that one boasted of how good he was at eluding the cops' pursuit, and the other was talented at concealing hashish. And he wound up with: "One time we snatched a purse, and we even stabbed this one guy."

Nicolas let him talk. He rocked on his heels and every once in a while tilted his head to one side, studying them the way a cattle breeder might do with a few select calves. Then he turned and went toward his bedroom, allowing the three kids to follow him. "We even stabbed this one guy . . ." he muttered with a laugh. He untied his sash and slid the robe off his shoulders, nice and slow, so they'd have time to take a good look at his back. And even though he wasn't looking at them, he could see them in his mind's eye, elbowing one another, pointing at Christian's name next to the hand grenade, which for them must have been like partying with Dan Bilzerian, fame and reality coinciding for once. When they saw the wings, their jaws had certainly dropped. So was that the logo of the Piranhas? And then a woman's face, on his waist, to the left. Maraja's girlfriend?

"I'm not going to have you work in a piazza. I'm going to put you to work doing *delivery*," Nicolas said without turning around.

Susamiello stumbled over the unfamiliar English word: "Doing deli . . . ?"

"Doing *delivery*. People call, and you head out and deliver to their home."

He finished getting dressed, unhurriedly, still keeping his back turned to the three youngsters. Then, without any need for words, he invited them to follow him. It was a pain in the neck, having to handle those little snotnoses, or maybe they could turn out to be a useful asset, who could say.


Zi' Pe' had worked in that delicatessen in Forcella since, like, forever. If you asked an old man who worked there *before* Zi' Pe', behind that gleaming counter, you'd always get the same answer: "Zi' Pe'." On the one side, *rosticceria* with trays full of prepared foods, already laid out first thing in the morning, and on the other side, an old-school delicatessen, with provolone cheeses and prosciuttos dangling on strings. Behind him, a glass wall to give a sense of depth to the five hundred square feet, at best, of shop and shelf space lined with neat rows of spumante bottles stacked up in miniature castles of glass.

"*Buongiorno*, Zi' Pe'," Nicolas began, speaking loudly to drown out the ding-dong of the door.

"*Buongiorno*, Maraja," Zi' Pe' replied. Skinny and bald, he seemed to vanish within the folds of his white deli clerk outfit, but when he turned his piercing diamond-hard blue eyes on you, most people tended to drop their gaze, abashed.

"I brought you three young men, they're going to come work with you," said Nicolas, and he shoved the youngsters forward. They looked around wildly, trying to figure out if this was some kind of joke. "See if you have some white smocks and hats in their sizes."

Susamiello and the two others kept turning their heads from a hanging pig's leg to the meat slicer, from the containers of Olivier salad to the medallions of paté.

"Come right this way," said Zi' Pe', and he handed them three smocks, which the three boys put on without objections, and with the same dreamy expression as when they'd come in there. In the end, it was Pachi who gathered his courage. All in a breath he blurted out: "Maraja, but what do you think we're here for? This isn't happening, we don't want to work like a crew of assholes. Why would we want to be delivery boys for a delicatessen? Is this the *delive—*, *deliver—*, whatever the fuck word you said, that you were talking about?"

"I thought you were a smart boy," said Maraja, who had come around behind the counter, "wide awake, someone who knew how the world works. I guess I had that all wrong. Get out of here, *ja*, you're just a bunch of limp dicks that wouldn't stiffen up even with a bottle of Viagra."

"No, Maraja, forgive him," Susamiello weighed in, glaring daggers at Pachi. "He's just an asshole."

Nicolas went on, indulgently: "Well then, who is it that people constantly see coming and going, in and out of the apartment houses? The delicatessen delivery boy. Okay? When the call comes in, out you go. We get the call, we forward it to the deli man, and he writes the address of the place you need to go on a piece of paper. One time you'll work here, another you'll work at the slaughterhouse, sometimes you'll work at the supermarket . . ."

Supermarket, slaughterhouse, haberdashery. Big warehouses to store the shit: hashish, marijuana, cocaine. They came in in perfect condition, in foil-wrapped lengths, tufts of weed, foil dots for the heroin. Products packaged with care and skill, to be kept in readiness for the couriers: in the spaces between bottles of mineral water, snug in their six-packs, under the labels of the small bottles of preserved red peppers, in among the meat in the freezer cases. Everywhere that the shopkeepers thought it was safe to keep them, in exchange for a monthly fee and the promise that there would be no extortion, no shakedowns.

The three of them brightened, a glow in their eyes, and suddenly even those delivery boy smocks seemed like so many uniforms of soldiers of the *paranza*. Risvoltino rolled up his sleeves and said: "So this is *delivery*!"

"Good for you, you're a genius," said Nicolas.

"No, though, this is disgusting," Pachi insisted. "I wanted to work dressed in the latest, not wearing a white smock like a delivery boy, what the fuck."

"Do you want Air Jordans, or do you want to go on wearing those parallel shoes you have on your feet?"

"They aren't parallel . . ." The term meant counterfeit.

"Sure, they're parallel . . . you could see it clearly if we stayed here and you flew to the moon. The toe is misshapen and the color is all wrong . . ."

Pachi looked down at the toes of his Air Jordans. He'd tormented his mother for six months. Those were the kind he'd wanted, the latest model, the 13 Retro, red heel and sole, the rest white. And those were the shoes he'd been given. No doubt, the red had faded to a pale pink in no more than a week and the sole was already coming loose, but he'd never have dreamed that his mother had bought them counterfeit. Suddenly false. Suddenly he, too, felt he was parallel to the truth, and he buttoned his smock to keep Maraja from making further comments on his Lacoste polo shirt, because he wasn't certain that the crocodile was facing the right way.

"You'll be paid fifty euros a day," Nicolas went on, "if you work for six hours. They'll give you the shit to deliver at the location. Then you'll take turns. Sometimes you'll be delivering shit, other times you'll actually be making deli deliveries to housewives . . . pecorino, provolone, prosciutto, Pan di Stelle cookies. And then baggies of cocaine, assorted fruit, hot chocolate. If you have any problem, call the number I'm going to give you. If you skim off the top . . ." He came around from behind the counter and stood legs akimbo, facing his cousin. He stared at him hard for a few seconds and then did the same to the two others. "You can do it ten times."

"For real, Maraja?" Susamiello asked, his eyes wide with gratitude. "We can skim off the top ten times?"

"Yes."

"But why exactly ten times?" Risvoltino asked; more than listening to the words, he was looking at Maraja's face and the wording didn't add up as far as he was concerned. With that smock that hung down almost to his shoes, he seemed even shorter. A garden gnome.

"Because . . ." Nicolas began as he moved along the walkway, behind the counter, twirling his fingers in the air, as if he were searching for something. And he found it: a butcher's cleaver with a worn wooden handle. He swung it through the air like a katana. "Because every time you skim a little off the top," he explained, "we'll cut off one of your fingers. How many fingers do you have on both hands? That's how many times you can skim a little off the top. If you decide to be a traitor, this blade will cut off a finger ten times, and then on the eleventh time, it goes straight for the tip of your dick." The three kids' mouths were completely dry. "When the cops catch you, and if they do, keep your mouths shut; worst case, they'll slap you around a little. They're not sending you to Sing Sing. And even if you do wind up doing time, man up and show you have a pair of balls, already. Anyway, then the lawyer will come around, and you'll get some money, even if you're in the can. Got it?"

They all nodded. The fright had already worn off, they seemed to have been galvanized, their eyes following the circumvolutions of the cleaver, and on their faces were the smiles of youngsters who finally knew they had been allowed into the ranks of real players.

"Then we'll give you a call to organize your work schedules," Maraja went on. "The vehicles you use to work can't be stolen, or they'll catch you first thing. If you fall and hurt yourselves, that's your fucking problem. If you have a crash, that's your fucking problem. For the gas, there are a couple of gas station attendants who are brothers of mine, and I'll send you to them. I'll let you know. Now I'm fucking sick of looking at you."

He hung the cleaver back on the hook he'd taken it down from. He put his arm around Zi' Pe's shoulder. "Will you make me an *'mposta 'e pane?*" A sandwich, in dialect.

"Sure, how you want it?" asked the deli man.

"*Ricotta e cicoli.*" Ricotta and pork curls.

Nicolas had always loved the preparation of that sandwich. The curly slices of the pressed cakes of fatty pork, which if you looked closely resembled nothing so much as marble, with the same grain and striations. And then there was the ricotta, light and fluffy, like a cloud, flakes that lay down on that solid mass of pork. And in the end, the touch of magic: a sprinkling of pepper staining the mountain of ricotta with black, and then it's all pressed together, crushed in the cavern of a rosetta bun after its crumb has been removed.

Maraja practically failed to notice that his three new men had taken off their smocks and were leaving the store. It was the ding-dong of the door that made him look up.

"Susamie', come here," he said, and immediately added: "The rest of you, get out of here." He placed his hands on his cousin's shoulders, and Susamiello looked up at him the way that, perhaps, he had once gazed at Don Feliciano at his trial. That seemed like a lifetime ago, a different life. "Susamie', even if you have a gob of my blood in your veins, if these two fuck up, or if you fuck up, if you go around telling even just your dad what you're doing, you're dead, Susamie'. And it won't be a pretty death. I'm not going to let you die easy."

"No, Nico', you're clear with me, I swear it. I can really tell that this is the right path for me. I mean it, I'm really happy. I've found my calling. I'll make you proud of me, it's an honor for me to work with you."

'O Maraja said nothing. He turned around. His sandwich was ready.

"Now get the fuck out of my sight."

# THE SOLDIER'S MOTHER

**B**iscottino's mother was listening to the words the man in front of her was uttering, and she felt as if she'd fallen into a dream. He was talking about Africa, Syria, wars, and terror attacks. And then about antipersonnel mines, shrapnel, armor-piercing bullets. Bellies burst open and shattered. Nightmares: but for her, Greta, those nightmares might actually be an escape route from Naples.

Half an hour had already gone by since that meeting with Doctors Without Borders had started in the conference room in the basement of the Loreto Mare hospital. Everyone was listening, attracted by the thought of those faraway worlds, and with an eye to the refreshments: two tables pushed together on which stood a couple of bottles still cool from the freezer and a Ballarò market tray of pastries, a dozen or so crunchy *sfogliatelle ricce*, and another dozen smooth *sfogliatelle frolle*.

"Here we have the finest physicians specializing in abdominal surgery," the representative from the NGO named Lorenzo went on, "we're accustomed to working in frontier conditions, and you all live on the frontier already, anyway. So your assistance will be fundamental."

Greta had never before set foot in there, because it was a place off limits to everyone but medical staff, whereas she worked in the cafeteria as a cook, and the fact that she was even there and could listen to all these fantasies of escape was thanks to the kindness of a nurse who was a friend of hers. Every once in a while she'd spend the night at her friend the nurse's house to look after her father.

Naples, Greta was thinking, really did resemble one of those countries at war that Lorenzo was talking about. Naples had taught her to cook. It had given her a name that had nothing Neapolitan about it, a job (two, actually, if you counted her work as a caregiver), but it had also given her a husband shot and killed during an armed robbery, three children and the endless challenge of keeping them safe, making sure they survived. The ground-floor hovel, or *basso*, where she lived, though, she owed only to herself, and the courage to move out of an apartment she deeply loved but was now renting out to university students. She'd found a *basso* for three hundred euros a month that she'd managed to snatch from the grip of the countless families from Bangladesh and Sri Lanka, the only ones who were willing to live there anymore. But she felt no shame, in fact, quite the opposite. Her *basso* was more dignified in its way than the second-, third-, and fourth-floor apartments where her sisters lived. She had furnished it, slowly, carefully selecting the furniture and accessories. She could feel that apartment on her skin, she felt it like a form of prestige that at first had helped her to make it through the day, but that had eventually worn out, until it was transformed into frustration to start and then into a lust for redemption, in the fullness of time. But what could a cook do?

"You can all do a great deal," the man from Doctors Without Borders was saying, and Greta blushed because for a second she thought she might have been thinking aloud.

War didn't frighten her, because that was another thing she'd basically received as her birthright, and going to seek out a war on the far side of the planet would at least allow her to help a lot of people.

"*I' nun so' nisciuno, i' saccio sulo cucinà*," she said to herself in dialect. I'm no one, and all I know how to do is cook, and this time the words really did come out.

"We're looking for people, and each of them offers what he or she can do," the man said, speaking to Greta. They all turned to peer at her, and she bowed her head in embarrassment. "You'd be useful. How could you

122 | ROBERTO SAVIANO

not! You know, a calling is something that's inside a person, not outside. If a person wants to, they can become whatever they desire. And everything emerges when there are no exams, no credentials. When you have to do something because your survival depends on it. When you have to do something for someone else because *their* survival depends on it."

"But I have three children."

"All of us have children . . . But we don't feel as if we're taking anything away from them. Quite the opposite. When you live, giving life, then you simply add to the equation, you don't take away from it. I spent three and a half months in Aleppo, and I've told you a few of my stories: not the most terrible ones, otherwise you wouldn't have gotten any sleep tonight."

Lots of smiles spread through the room, but Greta had another question: "So what would I do? Make pasta with *ragù*?"

"Does that strike you as unimportant?"

The smiles were transformed into laughter, and then into a round of applause that marked the end of the meeting and the beginning of refreshments. Greta pulled out her phone and realized that she had thirty messages in the WhatsApp group for the school where her younger children went. That was definitely too many to ignore.

Greta, they're looking for you . . .
Greta, what's happened?
Greta, has something happened to Eduardo?
Greta, has something happened to Susy?
Are Michelino, Susy, and Eduardo all okay?

She interrupted that steady flow of questions with a simple "What's happening?" whereupon one of the mothers in the chat replied:

A lady, out front of the school, asked all of us about you.
She said it was urgent.

But who was she?
Did she leave any kind of message?

Yes, she said she'd be there tomorrow.
She'd wait for you.

Tomorrow, thought Greta, was a long time to wait. But she said it to herself just as a passing thought, because her mother had taught her that a trivial piece of news shows up in a hurry, pushed along by the people who pass it forward like a baton in a relay race. It's the bad, dark, horrible pieces of news that struggle to reach you, that make you wait.

She went to school to pick up Susy and Michelino, who were in third grade. Eduardo was in seventh grade, and he wouldn't be let out for another couple of hours. She started hammering them with the usual questions— How was your day? Everything all right? Everything okay? She just wanted to hear them answer, give the usual responses—Everything's fine! Everything's normal! Nothing happened at all!—to make sure that the banality of daily life could stave off the bad omen that was plaguing her.

"Greta! Greta! Gre'!"

A woman her age came running toward her, clutching her purse to her breast with both arms.

"Do you remember me? I'm Emma," she said, without even glancing at the little ones.

"Oh, right," said Greta. "Today I have to take the kids to eat." Certainly she remembered her, even if they'd never actually exchanged a word. Her youngest son was one of the kids that buzzed around Eduardo. What was his name? Oh, right, Pisciazziello . . .

"No, this is urgent," said the other woman. She continued clutching the purse, as if she was ready to take off on another sprint.

"All right," Greta said with a sigh, and pulled out her cell phone. "Give me your number. I'll call you."

"No, no, no. I need to talk to you, for real, and right away. I have to come to your house." She was talking so fast that Greta could barely understand her.

"Then tell me now, right here, *ja'*."

"No, no, there are too many people around."

"All right." And she gestured for the woman to follow her. She took off toward home at a brisk pace, with her two children struggling to catch up. Susy yanked on her mother's sleeve and asked, "Who is this lady here?"

"A friend of Mamma's," Greta replied in a tone that would clearly brook no further questions. First she needed to stare down the sense of foreboding that kept twisting her guts.

The *basso* was a window of order in the chaos of walls that surrounded it. The tags of a graffiti writer ended right up against the mahogany door that Greta polished every weekend and then started up again just past the casement of the window. She opened the door and pushed past her children, then she stood in the doorway and waited for Emma to come through it. Michelino and Susy sat down at a table already set, which marked the boundary between the kitchen and the rest of the house, while she, after triple-locking the door and closing the shutters on the only window, turned on the stove to heat the pasta with tomato sauce and meatballs. Emma found the television set, turned it on, and flipped through the channels until she found a cartoon show. After which she turned up the volume until the cartoon character Masha's voice drowned out the sound of the cars going by in the street, and then she stepped close to Greta.

"There's no good way to say this," she told her, raising the volume of her voice just enough to make herself heard.

"Spit it out, come on!" Greta replied, stirring the tomatoes in the pot with her wooden spoon the whole while.

"Eduardo has screwed up for real this time."

"What did he do?" Greta asked. The wooden spoon spun around, faster and faster, a few red splatters had already stained the ceramic tiles.

"He killed a guy," said Emma. The roar of a bear on TV prompted a burst of laughter that for a moment drowned out those words.

"No, that can't be," said Greta, keeping her eyes on the pan.

"No, it's true, it's the absolute truth."

"But what, when? What are you even talking about? Get out of here, right this second." In two quick steps, Greta stood nose to nose with the other woman. The children didn't seem to notice a thing, their eyes fastened on the TV; now there was a panda as well.

"He killed that guy. He killed Roipnol," Emma went on, "the guy they sent to take charge of Forcella. It was him."

"That makes no sense! I haven't heard anything about this, I don't know anything about these names!" Greta shoved Emma toward the door, and she was sorry she'd locked it when she came in.

"You know perfectly well that he's a member of a *paranza*, stop pretending." Even if Greta had raised her voice, Emma continued to whisper.

"You just want to shift the blame because your son didn't do what he was supposed to."

"Ah, so you see that you know all about it?" she scolded her, without losing her cool. Since the day they had tortured her eldest son, she had only one objective, to keep such a horrible thing from happening again, to somebody else. She pushed her foot against the door, against Greta, who took a step back. "You see that you know all about these things?" Another step. "You know about them, just like everybody else does: you know inside, you just don't know outside."

"Of course I know them: I hear them out on the street every day."

"It was Eduardo."

"Impossible, he's just a kid."

"Yes, I'm telling you that he's the one who did it. My son Rinuccio was on the stairs, he saw it all: Eduardo went in and Eduardo did it. Because my son went in and out of Roipnol's house all the time. They treated him like a grandson."

They grabbed each other by the hair, like a couple of girls fighting, but in silence, to keep from attracting the attention of the young twins. They held each other at bay, reciprocally, and then the stalemate was broken by three knocks on the door. The women released their grip on each other all at once, and Greta lunged to answer it, worried that outside someone might have overheard their bickering. She was ready and eager to reassure anyone who might present themselves that her children would learn the lesson, that that deafening volume was intolerable, so sorry, a thousand apologies.

Instead, what she said was "Rinuccio." Pisciazziello must have followed her all the way to the *basso*. And I'm a fool, she thought to herself. She grabbed him by the collar and yanked him through the door. Then she collapsed on the floor, bursting into tears, knees pulled up to her body: "You're just saying it . . ." she sobbed, "you're just saying it because your son didn't know how to guard the place right. You're just saying it because they pried your son's teeth out of his mouth."

"So I can see that you know these things," Emma said again, but this time there was no hint of accusation in her voice, only the understanding of one mother in the presence of another. She got down on her knees, as if she wanted to console her. She'd been through it, too.

"I know them, because people talk about them," said Greta, sniffing. "But then how do I know if they're even true? I don't understand anything anymore, I don't know anything. Who knows anything anymore?"

"I'm telling you, it's all true. And we need to say these things to each other. If we can't say them, then who is ever going to tell us? We need to save our children, rescue them. We can't let them wind up like your husband. And my husband, to keep him from winding up dead in an alley, shot full of holes, I talked him into taking work on the ships. They had him working as a lookout, too. At night, he couldn't sleep worth a damn because he knew the cops might come to take him in at any moment, or shoot him. Only with him out on the high seas do I feel safe."

"Mammà?" Susy and Michelino were staring at her with frightened eyes.

Greta slowly got to her feet and reached out to pat the little ones on the cheek. "Everything's fine, Mamma lost her temper for a minute, but now she's fine. Now the signora here is going to help me, you go outside and play, *ja'*, that way I can sit down nice and peaceful in my chair."

Only after she saw them playing happily did Greta shut the door, look down at Pisciazziello, and ask: "But did you really see him? Did you see Eduardo firing the gun with your own eyes?" But the kid just kept looking down at a point along the line of ceramic floor tiles. "Look me in the face!" she shouted.

Emma didn't like this interrogation one bit, but she knew it was the price to pay for winning Greta's trust.

Pisciazziello nodded.

"Talk!"

"Yes," he said.

"Yes, what? Yes, you saw it?"

"I saw him come out with the pistol."

"Ah, so you saw him come out with the pistol, but you didn't see him fire it!"

"No, but he went in, and then he fired."

"We need to resolve this," Emma broke in. Then she took Greta by the hand and sat her down. Greta was pale. She brought her a glass of water, then went on: "You know why they didn't kill me? Because if they had, then Micione would have looked like a fool. My oldest boy doesn't even know this. Rinuccio came to see me and told me because he's afraid. Because they're trying to find out who it was: they're trying to find out who killed Roipnol. So my eldest son gets to go on living. To say over and over again that it wasn't him, that it wasn't his *paranza*, that it wasn't the Longhairs. That's his fate. As long as it's needed, I need to make it clear that it wasn't something internal in his structure, but that it was something done by enemies. To get through this, we have to stay united."

By now, Greta wasn't even listening anymore: she'd just shut down. She didn't care that Emma knew everything, every detail, things that weren't in the police reports, things that weren't in the newspaper articles. Emma had sifted the information through the dense network, the tightly woven mesh of her own experience, and had already separated the real stories from the invented ones, the hypotheses from the legends. What she had just told her was the truth.

Biscottino had murdered Roipnol.

"Greta, there's just one thing we need to do. We both need to understand that the destiny of being a mother here is to be a soldier's mother. Have them, raise them, and then send them to die. It's just that there's no medal for this war, just shame and contempt."

War again, thought Greta, always war. Then she said: "I don't give a fuck about what people think."

"No, I'm not talking about shame and contempt that people might feel, I'm talking about my own, *lo scuorno mio*, the fact that I live off the money that my son earns from the *paranza*, that's my real shame. *'O vero scuorno.* I curse every day since I gave birth to my children, for having brought them into a world like this."

For the first time since he'd come in, Pisciazziello looked up from the floor and turned his eyes to his mother's face, as she went on: "If I could," she continued, "I'd take them and put them back inside me. But that's not something I can do. How can you even have children in this state of war? Greta, you and I, here and now, we need to settle this thing. Take the kids to your mother. Talk to your son, we need to ask for help from the police."

"But what police, what on earth are you saying?" Greta shrilled as she got to her feet. Her eyesight fogged over for a second, her legs started shaking, she tried to shove the other woman toward the door. That word— *police*—drove her once again to deny the unmistakable evidence of the facts. Which is to say, the fact that she and her son needed help.

"A social worker comes to see me," said Emma, "we talk, she helps me. She's a good person. She even works for the church."

Greta's arms lost all strength, she let them rest on Emma's, almost as if she were clinging to her. "All right, let's do as you say, I'll talk to Eduardo, I'll talk to this social worker."

"It's the right decision, Greta," said Emma. She took Greta's hands in hers and squeezed them for a second. Then, without another word, she left with her son.

Greta did as she'd been told. After lunch, she took the twins to her mother, told her that that afternoon she'd be going to pick Eduardo up at school, because they'd changed her afternoon shift at the cafeteria. Outside the school, she paced around like all the other mothers waiting for their kids, ignoring their greetings, her head filled with nothing but thoughts of that son of hers who'd betrayed her. And if he'd betrayed her once, he could do it again, couldn't he? Maybe at that moment he'd holed up in a school restroom and he was already plotting something else on his cell phone with the other members of the *paranza*. Another murder? Greta wondered.

Biscottino was one of the first to emerge and he immediately saw his mother. He walked over to her, but instead of hugging him, she smacked his backpack, accompanying the blow with a "Let's go!"

"What is it, Ma?"

"Let's go," she said again, and they traveled the distance back home in silence. Every once in a while he tried to catch his mother's eye, but Greta was looking straight ahead of her, and whenever she could tell that her son wasn't keeping pace, she gave him another hard smack on his backpack.

Biscottino hurried into the *basso* and threw his backpack to the floor at the foot of the little sofa.

"Where are Susy and Michelino?"

His mother said nothing.

"Where are they?" she echoed him, wandering around the *basso*, as if in that cramped three-hundred-square-foot apartment it was possible to find a hiding place for two eight-year-old children.

"I took them to stay with Grandma."

"What for?"

Greta switched on the television set and turned up the volume. In the *basso*, the crystalline voices of wizards and sorceresses echoed as they engaged in a chase scene on flying broomsticks. Biscottino paid those sounds no mind; he decided that his mother was furious at him for one of those usual things—disrupting class, bad grades—but still, that twist in their everyday routine smacked of something not right, excessive for anything to do with a trivial matter of school discipline. Plus, she hadn't even offered him a snack. That was strange, no doubt about it.

"What is it, Ma? Why did you take Susy and Michele to stay with Nonno and Nonna? Is something wrong? Are they okay?" And he remembered the time, in second grade, when he'd caught the mumps and had to stay alone in his bedroom for ten days, without anyone else to keep him company.

Greta just looked at him. Motionless.

"So why don't you answer me, why do you look at me as if you'd lost your tongue?"

"I'm looking at you because I'm trying to figure out if I still know you. I want to look good and hard, these eyes, this nose . . ."

Biscottino burst out laughing. "Why don't you know me anymore, Mammà! You made me yourself, I came out of your tummy! *Ja'*, turn off the television set."

"It doesn't mean a thing that you came out of my belly." She looked him up and down, from head to foot.

"Oh, *ja'*," said Biscottino, "you're just playing with me—"

"I want to understand," she interrupted him, "if there's a scratch, a wrinkle, if the color of the eyes has changed."

"What are you saying, Ma, it's me, I'm still the same!"

"No, let me look closely." She started touching him all over, scrupulously, like a mother chimp poking for fleas in the fur of her baby. Biscottino squinted his eyes, shook his head, laughed and huffed in annoyance, all at the same time, amused and irritated, the way he used to be until very recently when his mother insisted on giving him a kiss at all costs, planting her lips on those chubby cheeks of his. And he would push them away, those kisses, because by now he was too big for that gooey smooching, the kind of attention you'd lavish on a newborn baby.

"Leave me alone, *ja'*!"

"But I don't think anything changed, and maybe that's why I never noticed."

"What did you think was going to change?" asked Biscottino. He was about to ask her if she'd lost her mind, but those eyes scrutinizing him were determined, confident, the opposite of madness. "What was supposed to change?" he asked again softly, with the smile still lingering, not yet fading.

"The face changes when you kill a person."

Biscottino did the only thing he could do. Fake it.

He turned his back on her in silence, opened the fridge, shut it, then got out the jar of Nutella and went in search of a piece of bread. "What on earth are you talking about, Ma?" he asked, in the most relaxed and unruffled tone he could muster, and stuck his finger directly into the chocolate spread. "What's happening?" he asked again, his lips smeared with the brown cream. "Did someone tell you some bullshit made-up story?" But he wouldn't look at her.

At last, she started slapping herself in the face, hands open, and talking to herself all the while: "This is what you were capable of bringing into the world: a murderer son. A murdered husband and a murderer son. This is the gift you could offer this beautiful city."

"Ma, hold still! Cut it out!" Biscottino dropped the Nutella jar and grabbed his mother's arms. "Hold still!"

"This is the only gift I could give this country," she went on. Her voice was steady, but careful not to overpower the volume of the TV. "And I'm worse than this city and worse than this country."

"What's happening?"

"What's happening is that you've become a murderer, Edua'." Her face was flame red, but her eyes were still the same as before.

"What the fuck are you talking about?!" snapped Biscottino, recoiling from her gaze and slamming his fists down on the table.

"I know everything, Edua', I know everything." She kept repeating his name as if it were a rosary, as if to remind herself just who the person was that she had before her.

"Actually, you don't know a thing, Ma, you don't know anything. That's why you took Susy and Michelino to stay with Nonno and Nonna, so you could put on this show?"

"Edua', now how are we supposed to get out of this situation? How are we going to get out of it, Edua'?" And she braced both elbows on the table and took her head in her hands.

"Ma, I don't know what's happened," said Biscottino. "Who told you this nonsense, what housewife started running her mouth?"

Those words hit her like a whipcrack: she, too, had denied as long as she'd been able. Now, that's enough, she told herself, this is no longer the time for this. She reared up above him, a good handful of inches taller than him, and gave him a backhanded smack to the mouth: "Stop lying!"

"Oh, go fuck yourself," shouted Biscottino, and ran out the door, pursued by his mother, who was shouting threats: "Don't you dare, Edua'! Don't you dare!"

Biscottino leaped easily onto his mini-quad. Out of here, he thought to himself, I have to get out of here.

His mother's voice kept coming closer, but by now he'd got the key into the ignition, had one hand on the throttle, and the engine roared into life, freed of the speed limiter.

"Eduardo! Edua'! . . . Biscottino!"

Biscottino sat there, finger in midair, over the electric starter button. His mother had never before called him by his nickname, his moniker. He turned to look at her.

"Biscottino," she said again. She hurried over to him, and, where she had originally been planning to straight-arm smack him, now she reached out and caressed him. "That's what they call you in the *paranza*, isn't it? Even that name comes from me, because I always used to bring you biscotti, I always brought you cookies."

"No," he said, with a smile, "it's because when we were playing soccer, you'd shout: 'Edua', *vienet'a piglià 'o biscottino*,' but I didn't want to come get a cookie."

"Come inside."

Biscottino got off the mini-quad and went back inside with his mother. Hand in hand.

"Is it true that you killed him?" she asked him, once they were both back inside the *basso*. She got down on her knees so that her face pushed right into her son's, her eyes leveled at his. But Biscottino was staring down at the floor and wouldn't speak.

"You can tell me, can't you?"

Biscottino shook his head no, but it was a feeble gesture, incapable of undermining such a grave accusation. But to say yes, he'd have had to muster much greater strength, and, there and then, in his mamma's presence, he just couldn't find it.

She lifted his chin so he had to look at her. And her hand trembled as she did so; her hope was null, a distant gleam you can no longer put faith in.

"Let's do this: just like when you were teeny-tiny. If it's true, give me a kiss, okay?"

And her cheek received the dampish kiss, a childish kiss.

# EXCURSION TO MILAN

I n Nicolas's head, the dots were all being connected with extreme precision. Soon he'd be able to see the whole picture, which, mission after mission, was starting to become clear. After the elimination of Mojo, he'd punctually received the phone call from the lawyer Caiazzo, providing the information that he'd requested as payment: the time had come for a little excursion to Milan.

None of them had ever been there before, and the idea of that trip prompted a sort of fascination mixed with repugnance. Drone had taken care of making the reservations and buying the tickets. Six seats in car number 8 of the Naples–Milan train for the men of the *paranza* and six for their girlfriends, three cars back. Far enough away, but still reachable in no more than a handful of minutes.

Drone was taking part in the plan from a distance: what they needed was girls, and he had two or three, but utterly virtual, voices and faces, whispers and bodies that bonded with him through the screen. No, in this case what was needed was physical presence. Biscottino, too, stayed home; at his age he still thought about soccer much more than he did about women. This was the first time he wasn't elbowing his way in to take part in an operation. In fact, no, Maraja mused: at the wharf, too,

Biscottino had accepted being kept out of it without too strenuous an objection. Maybe he didn't have what it takes to be a professional killer; killing Roipnol must have troubled him much more than it had seemed in the immediate aftermath. In any case, he'd worry about that later, what mattered now was to connect the dots, and fast. "If you want to take everything for yourself, fine, take it all, but I mean all of it," his mother had told him.

Letizia couldn't wait to go: Milan, the capital of shopping, Valentino, Prada, Dolce & Gabbana, Versace, Armani! But she wanted to travel with Nicolas. "We look like we're carrying weapons," Nicolas had explained to her. "On the train I need you to keep the bags with the weapons." And he'd pulled her close, kissing her. She'd gotten a little scared, she'd repeated that she didn't want to know about it, she wanted to stay out of his business, but then he'd laid down his ace of spades: once they got to Milan, he'd take her to Via Montenapoleone, to Via della Spiga. Shopping unlimited. He'd tag along behind her without a complaint, her every wish would be his command. "I'll buy you the Madonnina off the top of the Duomo," Nicolas had told her, and she'd clapped her hands like a little girl.

At the same time that Nicolas was talking Letizia into it, the other members of the *paranza* were securing the cooperation of their respective girlfriends. The most enthusiastic of them all was Sveva, the only one who cared little about buzzing from one shop to another. It was specifically the prospect of concealing weapons and running the attendant risks that appealed to her. In much the same way that she had first found Pesce Moscio himself attractive because life with him was a dangerous adventure.

Aside from the wheeled suitcases packed with weapons, the girls would be carrying with them their boyfriends' cell phones on the train ride back, that same afternoon. Until their return to Naples, they would use the phones to send themselves a constant flow of text messages.

"The perfect alibi," Drone had summed up, when explaining that part of the plan.

They departed on time and arrived at Milan's Central Station right on schedule.

"Nico'," said Briato' from the other end of the train, as he checked his brand-new Rolex, "you see how the train gets there all punctual now. We've relieved them of the problem of delays."

They took the metro—"*Guagliu*', our metro down in Naples doesn't stink like this"—got out at Montenapoleone, and started roaming aimlessly through the streets of the center—"*Guagliu*', up here no one even looks you in the face, they're all too scared all the time." The girls fluttered along a few yards ahead of them, radiant, gorgeous, full of life. They went in and out of every single shop and boutique, each new display window even more irresistible than the last. The guys waited, leaning against the plate glass, and looked around as if they'd fetched up in a land where customs and usages were absolutely original.

"Up here, everybody's got the runs, they all seem to be on the run from something," said Pesce Moscio, trailing behind a man carrying an attaché case and imitating his frantic stride.

Lollipop was looking straight up at the lowering sky over the gleaming, grim façades.

"The sun really refuses to come out."

Nicolas, on the other hand, was looking at the people. Whatever detail, he wanted to gauge it. How much do you earn? How much are you worth? Who are you paying? Everything had a worth that could be totted up. Everything. He leveled his eyes at people, things, reading the names of the shops, the makes and models of the cars. How much does that shop clerk earn? How much is the shop where he works worth? How much did they make a month? Did they have mortgages? Were their girlfriends or wives cheating on them? What work did they do with those hands? To him, everything came down to a hierarchy of money and power.

He ran a quick appraisal of himself. Golden Goose sneakers: 350 euros; tattoos: 4,000 euros; Damiani bracelet: 2,000 euros. He smiled with satisfaction. Then he took a look at his Ulysse Nardin Caprice watch (3,000 euros); it was time to say goodbye to the girls.

They accompanied them to the taxi stand, keeping a tight grip on their wheeled suitcases and cell phones with new SIM cards, which they'd then make sure to destroy. The girls, on the other hand, were leaving with armfuls of bags and packages, a drunken binge of shoes, dresses, earrings, and bracelets, for themselves and for their girlfriends, sisters, and mothers. In their new handbags, the smartphones of their respective sweethearts. "Write to me soon," the boys said laughingly, as they watched the taxi carrying the girls heading off toward the train station.

Tucano reached his arm around Nicolas, grabbing his shoulder with the same hand that seconds before had been waving a bandanna in farewell: "So that's the only good thing about Milan: the train for Naples!" And with a laugh on his lips, he slapped Nicolas on the back.

"I never thought you were such a sentimental softy, Tuca'. You know what I say? Let's go pay a call on an old friend."

You can never really leave Naples behind you. You can emigrate to Australia, become a kangaroo rancher, and learn how to throw a lariat, but if you were born in Naples you wear your origin like a badge. Even if you left with fear in your heart and the blessing of your family, even if your name is Stavodicendo and you abandoned the Piranhas. Nicolas had talked with his mother, she was so proud of her son and the way he was building a new life for himself. "Now he's in the restaurant business in Milan," she'd finished up with pride in her voice. He'd learned the address from one of Stavodicendo's *fratocucini*, cousin-brothers, a guy to whom he occasionally sold hashish, because the mother had made it clear that she considered it a blessing that her son was hundreds of miles away from the city and especially from Nicolas and his gang. Every once in a while they were in touch, Stavodicendo and the *paranza*, but Maraja didn't want to let him know they'd be dropping by: it was going to be a surprise.

They saw him coming from a long way away. He was riding a bicycle. He was wearing a helmet and a backpack that looked like a cube. And he was almost completely dressed in pink. Helmet, sweater, backpack. All of it pink. And yet it was really him, no doubt about it. His legs were skinny as sticks, his arms were long, his chest was sunken.

Lollipop, who had stepped back into the doorway of an apartment house, had tears in his eyes, he'd been laughing so hard. Stavodicendo was riding figure eights in the middle of the empty street, like a little kid. He was close to the end of his delivery shift, and that day he'd ridden thirty miles; he couldn't wait to take a shower and sprawl on the sofa, all the more so given the fact that his roommate was sleeping elsewhere that night.

The first one he saw was Nicolas. He'd emerged from who knows where and was walking toward him in the middle of the street, arms thrown wide, as if he wanted to hug him in greeting. Then he saw all the others, to the right and left, Briato' emerging from behind the hood of a Fiat Multipla. He clamped down on the brake handles, braced both his feet against the pavement, and instinctively lifted the bike, ready to pull a quick U-turn, but in the space of a second, they were all over him.

"Madonna, what are you all doing here?" asked Stavodicendo, with more fear than surprise in his voice. He shifted his gaze from face to face of the members of the *paranza* and found only looks of amusement. Finally, he got off his bike and hugged them, one by one. He thought to himself that only a few weeks had passed since he'd left, but they were already greatly changed. They stared at him with eyes that had seen things he had missed, important things, and he felt a stab of envy. Just as he envied their clothing, their shoes, their watches, every object that offered mute testimony to the riches of easy business, free of sweat.

"*'O facchino!*" exclaimed Drago', opening the food-carrier cube and peering inside. "A delivery boy!"

"*A Pantera Rosa,*" Pesce Moscio piled on, naming the pizzeria Stavodicendo delivered for. The Pink Panther.

Stavodicendo let them mock; he felt humiliated a bit, and yet, at the same time, for the first time since he'd left Naples, he also had the sensation that he was at home; he realized that he was still a part of the group, and that a blood oath is more powerful than physical distance.

When the jeering and ribbing died down, he took the bicycle by the handlebars and set off: "Come on, you're all guests at my house."

"Fuck me, you've even got a house of your own. So you live alone?" asked Briato'.

Stavodicendo nodded, then asked a question of his own, in dialect: "*Che site venuti a fà ccà?*"

"What do you mean, what are we doing here?" Nicolas said. "We came to see you."

"Don't talk bullshit. Why did you bring those suitcases with you?"

"You've got a sharp eye, Stavodice'," said Nicolas, "the fog hasn't affected your eyesight."

"By the way," asked Pesce Moscio, "why isn't it foggy?"

"Oh," said Briato', "these people up here don't even have fog anymore. They don't have a thing, really. This Milan is a shithole."

"No, that's not true," Nicolas shot back. "I don't mind it, actually."

Stavodicendo ushered them into his cramped two-bedroom apartment, and the *paranza* took possession of the space the way it always did everything: by invading it, overrunning it. They looked everywhere, curious to see how people lived in a Milanese apartment. Then Stavodicendo let it slip that he was sharing the apartment with a young man who was at business school.

"Ah, so you see, this isn't your house all to yourself after all, is it?"

"No, that's true, but he's never here, this *guaglione*. I have the place to myself."

They tossed the roommate's clothes onto the bed—"Fuck, they even wear vests with their suits up here. *Ua'*, what a gay three-piece suit"—they rummaged around and inspected everything in the room. Nicolas sat, entranced, leafing through a textbook on political economics for a few minutes, while Pesce Moscio peeked into the underwear drawer because "Lookie here, as if the uniform wasn't enough, you've even started wearing pink underpants, Stavodice'!" Stavodicendo didn't even try to stop them, he just sat down in front of the coffee table to roll a joint, the raw makings of which Nicolas had offered him.

To complete their research into the ways and customs of northern Italy, they emptied the refrigerator—"What's all this seaweed, Stavodicendo? Is it because you don't have the sea nearby that you eat this garbage?"— and then Briato' and Pesce Moscio flopped down onto the sofa, Drago' and Lollipop on plastic chairs, and Tucano sat on the floor with his back braced against the wall.

On the other hand, Nicolas continued roaming around the apartment, interested but not anxious, as if setting his thoughts at rest. "Your mamma is so proud about how her son is living in Germany"—the others snickered unobtrusively—"but does she really know how you're living?" he asked him. "I'm not even going to ask you how much money you make delivering this crappy food to the Milanese. But if you're happy to deliver up here, you might as well come back and do deliveries for your own *paranza*, because you'd earn more and sweat a lot less."

Stavodicendo nodded, taking a long drag on his joint. In those past few weeks, he'd done nothing but brood over the money he'd lost, every blessed day, and every blessed night he went to bed with the unwavering conviction that, come sunrise, he'd get out of bed, hammer that fucking bicycle into junk metal, and head for the station to catch the first train home. But he lacked the strength to do it, and when morning came, instead of wrecking the bike, he stood up on the pedals and started churning out the miles, delivering hot meals for the miserable pittance they paid him. But now he felt safe, at least, no gunfire, no blood feuds. Now that the mountain had come to Muhammad—as his grandfather always liked to say—the *paranza* had finally given him the courage to dump it. "What are we supposed to do?" he asked, therefore, though speaking to no one in particular.

"'O Tigrotto," said Nicolas. "We need to pay a call on him."

Stavodicendo nodded. "Why do we need him?"

"For a trade. When the Striano-Grimaldi feud was going on, the deal was: L'Arcangelo in a cage and 'o Tigrotto in exile."

"Nico'," Tucano broke in. "Tell him where 'o Tigrotto is."

"He's become a German, too, 'o Tigrotto. That bastard lives in Rho."

"What the fuck kind of name for a town is Rho?"

"Rho's like, I don't know, say, Cardito, or Cicciano."

"No, but those are names, at least. What the fuck kind of name is Rho?"


They budgeted four days for their stakeouts. They'd take turns, setting out in pairs from Stavodicendo's apartment early in the morning, riding the metro out to the Rho Fiera stop, and returning in the late afternoon to report in. They'd evicted the roommate, forcing him to move back in with his parents. On the evening of the fourth day they all met up in the bachelor-sized living room, eating takeout sushi that Stavodicendo, on the verge of quitting his job anyway, hadn't bothered to deliver. They analyzed the situation. 'O Tigrotto was confined to a wheelchair, and left the apartment twice a day, in the morning and at four in the afternoon, and when he did, his wheelchair was invariably pushed by a tall blonde with the broad shoulders of a swimmer, no doubt from Eastern Europe.

He always followed the same route. Newsstand—a café called Al Posto Giusto—glass of white wine—home again. The caregiver accompanied him up to the fourth-floor apartment, then went home for lunch. "She lives with a Milanese guy thirty years older than she is," Lollipop had discovered. "She resumes her duties at 'o Tigrotto's place at two on the dot. She's like a stopwatch."

"'O Tigrotto has turned into a little old man," Briato' commented. Of the firm, impassive man, the man of steel, whom he'd once admired at the trial, all that remained was the sheer bulk, crammed into that half-rusted-out wheelchair. He pinched his numb leg and decided that, sooner than wind up like him, he'd make sure he shot himself.

"What the hell," said Nicolas, "that guy's not just on the run. That guy's terrified, he has the ghost of the Grimaldi clan riding on his back."

Catching him out in the street would be impossible. He was always surrounded by other people, and they weren't operating in *paranza* territory, they couldn't count on lookouts or allies. They had no structure up here. To keep on staking out 'o Tigrotto in the hope of finding a breach in his daily routine would be nothing but a waste of time. And for Nicolas it was always a matter of time.

"The apartment building," Nicolas asked, "what's the apartment building like?"

Tucano had sneaked in and roamed every floor. Eight stories, four staircases, two apartments on each landing, eight apartments per floor.

"And who lives there?"

Tucano shook his head. "They come and go and never speak to each other. No one talks here, Maraja. These Milanese have constipated mouths."

"*Guagliu'*, there's a narrow elevator. 'O Tigrotto's wheelchair and the slut can both barely fit in it."

There were no alternatives. They'd catch him at home, when the caregiver was with her man. All they needed was some bait on the hook, someone who could go upstairs to 'o Tigrotto's apartment, undisturbed, ring his doorbell, lure him to the peephole, and get him to open the armor-plated door.

"*Stavodice'*, be ready to make your last delivery," said Nicolas, putting on the table the pink food carrier that Stavodicendo was already dreaming of tossing into a dumpster.

Stavodicendo wasn't ready.

"But . . . I was just saying, what am I supposed to do? I was just saying . . ."

"Nothing," said Nicolas, "nothing you haven't done before."

"Yeah, but, I was just saying . . ."

"You were just saying that you really are just an 'I-was-just-saying.' A Stavodicendo. Give me five, come on," Pesce Moscio broke in.

Stavodicendo seemed to calm down and offered the rest of the *paranza* a joint.

"Just taste what the weed is like in Milan."

"But that weed is good because it comes from Naples. Obviously. Everything good comes from Naples."

Stavodicendo had already established a reputation as the one who was always running away from his responsibilities; now it was up to him, and he was going to prove that he was up to the challenges of returning to the gang. He shoved the pistols into his cube and set off, boarding the metro with his bicycle at the Lambrate station, fifteen minutes before the rest of the *paranza*. The same way they had done with the girls, the others would follow him a couple of trains back.

Stavodicendo could feel the eyes of the other passengers focusing on him. Why had that female college student who'd sat down next to him suddenly stood up and moved to another seat? What about that gentleman with the newspaper who was pretending to read but actually kept peeking over at him?

As soon as he got out at the Rho metro station, he started Google Maps and put in 'o Tigrotto's address. Stavodicendo was the only one who hadn't gone out on any of the stakeouts, to keep his face from getting a little too familiar in that neighborhood. With the cube on his back, he walked the 495 yards indicated by the map to reach his selected destination. He walked slowly, as he'd been told to do, a little bit to flesh out the image of the delivery boy who didn't know how to find his way around the outskirts of town, and a little bit to give the *paranza* time to catch up with him. They took delivery of the guns a couple of blocks before he reached his destination, leaving two handguns inside the cube for safety's sake. Stavodicendo, on the other hand, was supposed to continue to his destination unarmed, to avoid arousing suspicion; after all, they'd be right behind him and they'd have his back.

An elderly lady was just coming out the front door of 'o Tigrotto's building, and Stavodicendo lengthened his stride to hold the door and ask if she minded letting him go in, because he had a delivery for Signor Onorato. "He's such a wonderful person, you know that? It really is a shame that he's in a wheelchair, but thank God, he has Svetlana." The slut, Stavodicendo thought to himself. "She takes care of everything, and she always has a smile on her face." Stavodicendo nodded with great conviction, even though he hadn't been able to make head nor tail of that last phrase. Every so often, the old people spoke a language that belonged to them alone, and when they died, that language would go extinct. He thanked the old woman, waited for her to round the corner, then left the door half open for the *paranza* and started up the stairs.

When he reached the appropriate floor, he took a minute to catch his breath and then he rang the doorbell.

"Who is it?" came a voice. It arrived together with the sound of creaking metal and had the mocking tone that you'd expect from someone like him, not an ancient relic in a wheelchair.

"A delivery for you, sir." Stavodicendo forced himself to imitate that ex-roommate of his, to give his accent the most neutral cadence possible.

"I didn't order anything."

"I see the name Svetlana written on this order. Doesn't she live here?"

Silence. Then: "No, she doesn't live here. She's my housekeeper."

"I was just saying that on the order it's also written that it's a special delivery: Svetlana ordered you a bowl of pasta with sardines."

Nicolas had told him that he knew 'o Tigrotto's weak spot, namely, food, and food from back home, down south, must surely be something he missed sorely, living around all those polenta eaters, as the southern slur for northern Italians went.

Stavodicendo heard a sound of keys falling on the floor, then the metallic creaking of the lock—Nicolas's information had proved accurate, that big cat hadn't been able to resist the siren song of the southern seas in his food bowl. After four turns of the key in the tumblers, the door swung slowly open and 'o Tigrotto appeared, in his usual wheelchair. Didn't he ever break character with that pantomime? Stavodicendo took a step forward to fill the doorway and keep the door from being shut. And as he bent over to take the food carrier off his back, Nicolas appeared behind him. And so did the other five. That was when 'o Tigrotto, as if he'd heard the question that Stavodicendo had framed only in his mind, leaped to his feet like a spry young stripling. His face was pale, so that he himself looked like one of those ghosts that had occupied his body.

"San Gennaro has performed a miracle, he's up and walking!" cried Nicolas, raising both arms, and thus placing the pistol in a clear line of sight. He lowered the gun immediately, leveling it straight at him.

'O Tigrotto's hands darted to his shorts. Conditioned reflex had led him to reach for his pistol where he'd worn it all his life, but Nicolas immediately smashed his head into the man's face. 'O Tigrotto lurched back into his wheelchair, hands cradling his face, while his eyebrow, cut by the head butt, gushed blood.

"You've gotten rusty, Tigro'," said Drago', entering the apartment with the others and shutting the door behind him.

"Wait, what are you doing? Who sent you here?" 'o Tigrotto said again and again, groggy and bewildered. Lollipop on one side and Tucano on the other pinned him down to the armrests. Drago' and Stavodicendo got behind him and grabbed the handles. They took him to the kitchen, while 'o Tigrotto kept begging them, between spurts of blood: "Wait, wait, wait, wait, wait!"

"He's like a little kid who's afraid of getting a shot," said Briato'. "Let's get this done!" Then, turning to 'o Tigrotto as if to console him, but actually to twist the knife: "Don't worry, you won't even feel it."

As he heard those words, Nicolas put his gun away, stuck his right hand into his jeans pocket, and pulled out the knife. "Hold him still, *ja'*, I just had an idea."

# THE SOCIAL WORKER

While the members of the *paranza* were aboard the train taking them back home, and Stavodicendo was speculating about the effect that his surprise return would have on his parents, Biscottino was behind the *basso* with Pisciazziello.

In that courtyard they'd spent days at a time making two-pronged attacks, running in parallel and passing the ball, tighter and tighter and faster and faster, lofting it back and forth through the air until one of them launched a thunderous shot into the goal and the other swerved to embrace his teammate. The goalpost twins. Biscottino was a player who never hogged the ball: he was always willing to pass to a teammate. When they played on the mini-field, or when they played in the classroom, balling up sheets of copy paper and Scotch-taping them into rudimentary soccer balls, kicking penalty shots between the desks, and even when they played in the piazza in front of the sanctuary of Loreto Mare. He lived for the assist. His greatest joy came when he was able to outrun and outfox both opposing defenders and goalie and then lightly loft the ball to the striker, but only when he was in perfect position, right in the goalmouth.

But today the ball seemed to be glued to Biscottino's foot. He caressed the ball with the sole of his shoe, and then with a light touch lofted it into the air, cushioning its fall with his instep.

Pisciazziello started waving his arms, as if he were defending at the San Paolo stadium, but Biscottino didn't even deign to glance at him.

"What's the matter, Biscotti', aren't we friends anymore?" asked Pisciazziello. He felt guilty because he'd let slip the story of Roipnol to his mother and from that point on, things had started moving so fast that it wasn't clear anymore just where they'd wind up. He knew that Biscottino was trying to keep Signora Greta calm by staying home, good and obedient, and having as little as possible to do with the Piranhas: he felt hemmed in. But what Pisciazziello didn't know was that earlier that morning, awakening, his friend had been confronted with another surprise.

Since the day he'd murdered, he'd never again used it, his Desert Eagle, he hadn't once taken it out of his bedroom. He'd emptied his Pokemon card holder and hidden his gun between the album's rigid covers. Then he'd stuffed it under his bed, just far enough out of sight to escape notice, but still well within reach, close enough to feel it there, as he sat on his sheets; he only needed to swing his heel and he could tell that his weapon was there, available. But that morning, the swinging heel had encountered no resistance. Biscottino had dropped down, belly flat on the floor. There was nothing under the bed but dust. At that point, he'd walked over to where his mother was sleeping with his two younger siblings on the sofa bed, and he'd listened to the deep breathing of the three, only then beginning his silent search. He'd looked everywhere, even rummaging through his mother's underwear drawer. He'd pushed away the wave of shame as he'd lifted and peered at bras and panties, and when he'd stumbled upon his father's old shirts in the same drawer, shirts that Greta still held on to, he'd felt a lump in his throat. Then he'd searched in the bathroom. Nothing. The pistol was nowhere to be found. Biscottino had gone back to his bedroom and found his mother there, waiting for him. She hadn't even let him open his mouth. "Now is the time to swear an oath," Greta had told him. "What oath?" Biscottino had asked her. He was standing there in underpants and undershirt, his arms held before him, like a soccer player facing a penalty kick. Greta had stood up and pushed his arms aside to hug him tight, and then she'd forced him to swear: he would never fire a gun again in his life, not even straight up into the air. Biscottino had nodded, what else could he do?

Pisciazziello asked again: "Aren't we friends anymore?"

"You could have kept your mouth shut, Pisciazzie'." That was the response, and Biscottino's voice was so faint and hard-edged it practically drew blood.

"What could I do? They did crazy things to my brother, you know that . . ."

"And now you can see all the comings and goings at home." He lofted the ball back into the air and started dribbling the ball all on his own. Foot, thigh, head, juggling it and never letting it hit the ground. And never passing it.

"The social worker again?" he asked. For the past week, or nearly, that woman had been showing up every day at Biscottino's *basso*, and a couple of times Pisciazziello, too, had crossed paths with her. She showed up every now and then at Pisciazziello's house, too. A big tanned woman who accompanied every single phrase she said with a smile that smacked of mockery, and on the occasions when she had spoken to the two of them, explaining that she needed to speak to "*Mammà*" about "important matters" and "all alone," she had uttered the words clearly and loudly. "We're not babies," Pisciazziello had told her, and in response she had given him a smile.

"Yeah, her again, I'm afraid," Biscottino replied. "I'm starting to get scared, Pisciazzie'. What if now my mother tries to send me to boarding school? In that case, I'd rather wind up behind bars, *adda murì mammà*. And what the hell does this woman have to say? Every time she comes they talk for two or three hours. It's a good thing she brings us food."

"*Ua'*," said Pisciazziello, "it's not like she brings us free food."

"Eh, maybe that's why your mother's here, too, talking with her, maybe she wants to get some free food."

Foot, thigh, head. The ball still hadn't hit the ground.

"I'm starting to get scared, too," said Pisciazziello. He'd stepped closer to Biscottino to steal the ball, but the other boy slid it around to his side and defended it with his body. "For the next six months, my brother's going to be living on nothing but smoothies, you realize? He's always on edge, and not just because of the beating he took. He's in and out of the house every hour of the day and night, and Mammà is out and about a lot more, and she's always talking with your mamma, too."

He stuck out his left leg to put Biscottino off-balance and then surprise him on the right, and so the other boy used his elbow to ward him off. Stalling for time.

"You didn't say a thing to your brother, right?" asked Biscottino. He'd already asked Pisciazziello that question a thousand times, and every time Pisciazziello had answered in the exact same words: "*Adda murì mammà*, not a single word, and not even that!"

They battled for control of the ball for a while, until Pisciazziello suddenly retreated, but Biscottino remained planted on the spot, well balanced, and started juggling the ball again. "But are you sure," he asked him again, for the second time since that whole thing with their mothers had started, "that Carlito's Way doesn't know anything? Look, it's not in your interest for your brother to know, because he'll put the blame on you, too, if he finds out I killed Roipnol. Your mamma knows that, right?"

"Don't worry. Mammà understands that this is a huge problem for everyone. We're not crazy, you know." Pisciazziello swung his foot at a bowl full of cat food. "Biscotti', in this whole mess, if there's one person who can feel good about things, it's you, because at least you had the balls to kill a boss. Even though I actually loved Roipnol and 'a Culona. They'd let me play on the computer, they'd take me out to go shopping." He slid into thick dialect: "But now I'm friends with a guy who's got a huge pair of balls."

Biscottino smiled; maybe he'd be able to forgive him for his loose lips.

"I'm pals with someone who murdered a person," Pisciazziello piled on.

"If a person gets himself murdered, it means he deserved it, right?"

Biscottino lofted the ball in the air just enough to get himself in position and get ready for a scissor kick against Pisciazziello. The impact was sharp and hard, a perfect *pock* sound, and his friend put both fists together to ward off that cannon shot. The ball lofted high and ended its arc right at the entrance to the courtyard. The two of them sprinted to take possession of the ball. Pisciazziello got there first and immediately passed the ball to Biscottino, who raced off, brushing against the walls, and then kicked a gentle cross that the other boy headed sharply into the goal. They'd made peace.

They stopped to catch their breath, sitting on the sidewalk. "*Adda murì mammà*," said Pisciazziello, "inside, they're talking about us."

Biscottino pointed up to a long narrow window about a yard off the ground. He dragged a trash can over, laid it on its side, and climbed onto it.

"What are you doing!" exclaimed Pisciazziello, looking around.

"You said it yourself, Pisciazzie'. They're talking about us inside," said Biscottino. He grabbed the side casements of the narrow window and, levering up with one leg, hoisted himself up onto the foot or so of windowsill. He remained there for a few seconds, studying what part of the body he should try to insert first into that opening. He looked like a little bird perched on a branch.

Biscottino slid his legs through the narrow window, got a foothold on the toilet bowl, and leaped down onto the rubber mat without making a sound. He looked out into the courtyard in the middle of which Pisciazziello was still standing, motionless.

"Pisciazzie'," he whispered, "you're up to your neck in the same shit. It's worth your while to come listen."

In a flash, Pisciazziello was in the bathroom, his ears pressed against the door.

"He really screwed up, and it's no laughing matter!"

The voice belonged to Pisciazziello's mother, and he tried to flatten himself against the door, as if by adhering as closely as possible to the panel, the sound would reach him more clearly. He didn't understand why he was at the center of the discussion; after all, he wasn't the one who had pulled the trigger.

"Yes, he really screwed up, my boy Eduardo," said Biscottino's mother. Pisciazziello couldn't help but heave a sigh of relief, and he shifted slightly away from the door. Next to him, he felt his friend's body stiffening and felt a surge of shame at his reaction. He put a hand on Biscottino's shoulder, who looked over at him with terror in his eyes.

"The only thing to do is to cooperate with the police," said Emma. The sound of shoes scraping on the floor. Mamma's not happy, Biscottino thought to himself; he was all too familiar with that habit of hers, the way she'd scrape her feet on the floor, like an animal seeking shelter.

"You really think so?" said Greta. "Give me time, let me think it over." More scraping, followed by the creak of the springs in the sofa. She'd gotten to her feet and now she was walking across the room. Pisciazziello and Biscottino stood up and turned toward the window, the only way out. Then they heard the sound of the kitchen faucet and a glass emptied all in one splash. They pressed back against the door.

"If we think too hard and long, we'll just screw up," said Emma.

"I know that's what we need to do, but I have three children. Where would I go?"

The little half bathroom beat with the two hearts of Biscottino and Pisciazziello, pounding hard, and every heartbeat, which they could feel in their chests but also in their mouths, in their throats, in their wrists, just punctuated that back-and-forth between their mothers. It seemed like the background music of one of those thrillers they so loved to watch together on TV.

Biscottino felt a hole opening in the pit of his stomach. In the past few days, he'd thought of every possible outcome, except the possibility of having to leave the city. He would never again see Pisciazziello and the others, he'd never again play soccer in the courtyard. He felt a wave of fear much more powerful than the one that had swept over him when he'd set off to kill Roipnol. He retreated to the narrow window to get a breath of fresh air, but the hole in his stomach just kept getting bigger. And here came the cramps. He sat down on the toilet seat cover and pulled his legs up to his chest. The pain subsided a little.

"You can't do these things halfway: either you do them or you don't." The social worker had taken the floor, interrupting the conversation between the two mothers. The woman's high-pitched voice reached Biscottino clearly, as he rested his head on his knees. "And you should be happy to do them, because you're saving your children's lives."

Pisciazziello wrapped his hand around an imaginary erect penis and pretended to jack off with it, smiling in Biscottino's direction, who instead grimaced back: another cramp.

"I'll get in touch with the police and I'll start a conversation with them,

I'll start briefing them on the way matters stand, the situation . . . but you needn't worry, because I won't mention any names. But I'll also tell them that you need to be convinced and that you naturally demand certain conditions," the social worker continued. She articulated her words very clearly, the same as when she spoke directly to Pisciazziello and Biscottino. That wasn't a good sign, thought Biscottino. "Where would you like to live, Signora Greta? I'll take care of everything myself."

If it hadn't been so perfectly silent in the bathroom, they wouldn't have been able to hear the whispered reply: "Venice."

Biscottino felt his intestines sag downward, and instinctively he tightened his sphincter, clamped his butt cheeks together. A rivulet of cold sweat ran down his back, ending in his underpants. How could it be his mother was falling for the arguments of that bitch of a social worker? What did she even know about them?

"Eduardo needs to be kept out of this whole story," said Greta. Biscottino felt he'd been reborn.

"And he'll be kept out of this story, I told you: no names." The social worker pressed the point home. "And the same for your son, Signora Emma. You need to be careful, too."

Pisciazziello sat down on the edge of the bidet and looked at Biscottino. "You, too," his friend whispered, pointing his forefinger right at him. "You're ending up just like me, no better, no worse."

"But it's tougher for me," Pisciazziello's mother told the social worker. "Probably better, Signora Lucia, if we leave my boys out of it . . ."

"Remember that I'm on your side and the side of your children," said the social worker in the tone of voice of someone who'd repeated the concept over and over again. "I want us all to come out of this situation together, like a team."

Then Greta's voice: "We'll turn him into an informer, *pentito* . . ."

Biscottino's and Pisciazziello's hearts plunged into cold water, as they held their collective breath: "Never," they said to each other, breath within breath.

That deadly word, *pentito*, rushed past outside the door like an avalanche sweeping away everything in its path: in the void that remained, Biscottino's fart rang out.

The cramps had resumed. "I can't take it anymore," Biscottino said under his breath. The stench immediately filled the bathroom, and Pisci-azziello lifted his elbow to cover his nose.

"Is there someone in the bathroom, Signora Greta?" asked the social worker.

"Those are just noises from the courtyard in the back, they do every-thing you can think of out there," Biscottino's mother promptly replied. Looking out the window, she'd noticed that the bathroom window was ajar.

"Greta," the woman resumed, "it's my job to protect people, especially minors like Eduardo and Rinuccio. But you have to understand that it's up to them to let us help them. If you let them speak to the police, no one would hurt a hair on their head."

A second fart was covered up by the roar of a passing scooter. Biscot-tino waved his hand in Pisciazziello's direction: it was time to get out of that bathroom, they'd heard all they needed to hear.

On the other side of the door, the three women were all talking at once, interrupting and drowning one another out.

Pisciazziello climbed up onto the narrow windowsill while Biscottino gave him a boost, pushing from behind.

"Never!" Biscottino told himself again. He went out the window and started running through the alleys and *vicoli*, followed by Pisciazziello.

# THE GIFT

Like all the residents of the city, Nicolas felt a chill the minute he stepped away from its streets, but he hadn't suffered in Milan, and he wasn't suffering now that he and his *paranza* had returned from the north. This morning they'd all awakened to intermittent rain showers, as if a gang of ill-intentioned clouds were having fun swooping back and forth over the city, and every time they emptied their rainwater the temperature dropped precipitously, making the hairs stand up on your forearm. Then the sun insolently managed to wedge itself back in, just making it clear once and for all that this was his personal territory, and the temperature bobbed back up, bringing with it the smell of tar, of the condensation that still hadn't had time to issue forth, releasing that aroma of hot asphalt, a whiff that blocks your nostrils.

The souvenir needed to be delivered promptly to L'Arcangelo. Actually, the gift consisted of two separate items. A box of mozzarella—a foam container that they'd jammed with ice cubes—and a panettone that they'd bought in Milan at a pastry shop in the city center while the girls were shopping in the boutiques.

When they returned, the city had welcomed them with rain, and that morning, too, the rain continued intermittently to shove the sunshine aside.

Nicolas had tugged loose the handle made with adhesive packing tape on the box of mozzarella, and he'd done the same with the cord on the panettone package. Then he'd hauled them up into the crook of his elbow so he could have both hands free to drive the scooter, and he'd bought a rain poncho to keep the gifts for L'Arcangelo dry. He climbed aboard the TMAX, taking care not to dent the boxes too much, and once he was securely seated, Briato' put the poncho on him from above, lowering it over his head.

Maraja went straight to the industrial parking lot on the A3 highway. He looked like a scarecrow that some fluke of the wind had shrouded in a chance trash bag. Aucelluzzo was waiting for him at the camper cemetery. He'd rather just take the downpour like a man, Aucelluzzo had said, and then had proceeded to complain about how sick he was of being a postman. Nicolas didn't even comment. Five minutes later, he was climbing the stairs to the apartment of Professoressa Cicatello. With one arm stiff, holding the box of mozzarella from below, and the other arm behind him, holding the panettone. He set both boxes down carefully on the marble floor of the landing and rang the doorbell. No answer. He tried again. Nothing. And yet he knew there had to be someone at home, because if he placed his ear against the door, he could hear the sound of slippers sliding across the floor. He rang a third time, leaning on the button for a long time, so that he knew L'Arcangelo could hear him from upstairs. Then he realized that he just needed to resign himself to the fact that he'd have to wait there for a while, who knows how long, serving out the penance that L'Arcangelo had ordained for him.

In the meantime, the sun had come back out, and the sudden spike in the temperature was threatening his souvenir. Nicolas started pounding on the door: "Signo', my gift for Don Vitto' is going to go bad, this is the finest mozzarella, please, I'm begging you, let me in—" The sound of more slippers on the floor, this time a more persistent sound, and at last the door swung open, with four brusque turns of the dead-bolt key. Professoressa Cicatello was wearing yellow kitchen gloves and she raised them toward

Nicolas as if to push him away, but he didn't give her a chance, because he pulled out a hundred-euro bill and placed it on her cheek. "Signo', my hands are full," he said, as he was already running into the kitchen. At an angle, precariously, his eyes fixed on the narrow rungs, he climbed the ladder like an acrobat, careful to keep from tipping the mozzarella box too sharply. The ice in the box must have melted by now. When he reached the trapdoor, there was nothing he could do but start shouting: "Cicogno', it's me, Nicolas! Cicogno'!" Another penance, he thought, and then he tried: "Cicogno', please open up, my surprise for Don Vitto' is going to go bad."

'O Cicognone opened the trap door, and then stood there to relish the scene of a sweaty, panting Nicolas, and in the end he informed him that he could come up, but then he'd have to wait awhile because Don Vittorio was up on the roof, choosing whores.

Nicolas managed to get up the last two steps, objecting that he'd paid his penance: enough was enough.

"He's on the roof, I told you, put your things on the table."

"No, I have to go up . . . it'll go bad!"

'O Cicognone shrugged and vanished into the kitchen.

Nicolas climbed the spiral staircase concealed in a built-in armoire at the end of the hallway. That was how Don Vittorio got to the roof, by climbing up a vertical tunnel that penetrated through twenty feet of reinforced concrete. Don Vittorio was proud of those narrow shafts that he'd had driven through the whole building, allowing him to move freely. "The circulatory system," he called it. It never occurred to Nicolas that he might set the boxes down, because he knew 'o Cicognone would stick his beak in them for sure.

Once he reached the roof, he saw a very different Don Vittorio from the last time. Gray trousers and a light blue shirt, loafers, and a Rolex on his wrist. He was freshly shaven, and not only because he was going to meet his girls, as he called them. There was still a sense of slovenly neglect, such as a dark stain at the knee of his trousers or the hair that was too long at the nape of his neck, but overall, he looked like a different man.

In front of him, five prostitutes were shielding themselves from the sun in the shade of the dish antennas that Don Vittorio had had put in for all the tenants. The black clouds were moving away in compact formation, and Nicolas retreated under a dripping rain gutter.

The five women looked like sisters. Probably South American, short, dark-skinned, with enormous breasts. Look at that, L'Arcangelo really likes women, thought Nicolas. Don Vittorio paid him no mind, simply beckoned the prostitutes forward one by one by crooking the forefinger of his right hand, then he'd spin the finger in the air, and the prostitutes would show off a pirouette, and when he bent his first two fingers at the knuckle, they'd bend over at the waist, and finally, he'd tell them to walk back and forth with a movement that could easily be mistaken for a head-shake of rejection. Five times in a row, each the same as the last, until the last prostitute blew him a kiss and he said, never once taking his eyes off her: "Nico', let me fuck this one, and then I'm all yours."

"Don Vitto', I came to make my apologies," said Nicolas. He grabbed the two boxes and lifted them off the floor.

"Ah, so it's one of the Three Magi, bearing gifts," said L'Arcangelo without bothering to turn around. "You waited awhile, didn't you? Well, wait until I have my fuck."

"No, no, it's important," Nicolas objected. All that effort to get to that point, and the gift for L'Arcangelo was going to be ruined for a stupid fuck with a whore. "Don Vitto'," he tried again, but now he was interrupted by the prostitute who'd been selected by L'Arcangelo. She slipped her hand between his shirt buttons as she rubbed her hip against his crotch. "Vitto'," she whispered in the voice of someone promising honey, "I'll wait for you, in the meantime I'll have a bite to eat."

"Mary Magdalene has come to the rescue of the Wise Man bearing gifts," said L'Arcangelo, planting a kiss on the prostitute's forehead.

"*Grazie*, signori'," said Nicolas.

They went down the spiral staircase. The old man went first, moving with slow, exasperating caution, setting one foot on one step before committing to the next one, waiting to make sure that the other foot was lined up properly. Behind him, the young man was seething with impatience, certain that L'Arcangelo was going to welcome his surprise. And how.

Don Vittorio took a seat in his armchair and lit a Toscano cigar. He stared at a point just above Nicolas's head, an inch or so, no more, making sure not to look him in the eyes. If Nicolas moved, L'Arcangelo followed him, but always gazing up just a little.

The first gift was the panettone.

"I was in Milan, Don Vitto', have you ever been there?"

"Of course I have," he said. "We owned Vi.Ga Construction. One time I even went to see a game at the San Siro. We put in three goals against Milan. What a night."

"That's the only good thing they have," said Nicolas, pointing to the panettone.

"And what does the mozzarella have to do with anything?" asked L'Arcangelo, setting the panettone aside. He had always refused to eat panettone when he went on his missions among the industrial sheds of Brianza, and he wasn't about to start now.

"This isn't mozzarella. This is a cake for the celebration."

"What do we have to celebrate?"

Nicolas opened the mozzarella box on the table. *Tock*, went an ice cube. That's a good sign, thought Nicolas, and he called 'o Cicognone.

'O Cicognone had seen dozens of boxes just like that one in his life, and he'd prepared dozens more. He knew that you had to take great care in opening the box, otherwise you ran the risk of spilling the mozzarella milk, leaving the mozzarella high and dry in nothing more than a sad puddle of liquid. He yanked the lower end of the length of adhesive tape and started pulling, steadily and without jerks. Once he'd removed the vertical tape, 'o Cicognone proceeded to the horizontal, which connected the lid to the box proper. As he removed that strip, an increasingly pungent stench rose to his nostrils. He pulled off the last length and— "What the fuck!" he shouted, stumbling backward until he ran up against a credenza.

"He won't bite anymore," said Nicolas, his eyes focused on L'Arcangelo and the smile of someone ready to savor the scene. "Do you recognize him, Don Vitto'?"

L'Arcangelo was motionless, his face white; 'o Cicognone, covering mouth and nose with the bottom of his T-shirt, stepped close to the box again. In a greenish fluid, with black veins running through it, studded with worn-out magic pine tree deodorizers, floated a man's head.

"Why, it's 'o Tigrotto, Don Vitto'," said 'o Cicognone in the piercing voice of a little boy on his birthday.

"Now your son Gabriele can rest in peace," said Nicolas.

L'Arcangelo got up from where he was sitting, took a step, getting close enough to peek into the box, and then collapsed back into the armchair. Nicolas was now looking at a decrepit old man, stunned, mouth agape, the same man who just a few weeks earlier had kicked him out of the house. He'd dropped his Toscano cigar on the floor, while 'o Cicognone continued to shout, "'O Tigrotto! 'O Tigrotto! 'O Tigrotto!" extremely excited, to the point that he actually stuck both hands into that purulent water and hauled out the head of Gabriele Grimaldi's murderer.

"Put down this death's head," L'Arcangelo ordered, then went over to hug Nicolas. He held him tight, and stood there for a while like that, chest to chest, his arms crossed over Nicolas's back, like a couple of lovers who hadn't seen each other in far too long. At last Don Vittorio straightened up, placed both hands on Nicolas's ears, and pulled him close. A kiss with lips clamped. Nicolas was overwhelmed by L'Arcangelo's cologne. He felt his stomach contract, but only for a second, because he actually felt fine. On his tongue, he felt the silence that is created between father and son when they make peace.

All was forgiven and now they could start over. They were even now— but from two different positions; the father who punishes and absolves, the son who learns and grows, surpassing the parent.

'O Cicognone had come back to the kitchen to get the Chivas Regal so they could drink a toast, caught somewhere between a repressed urge to vomit and a proliferation of sweet words in memory of Gabriele and libelous insults against 'o Tigrotto.

Nicolas wanted to tell him about the general Hasdrubal Barca who lost to Scipio, who then sliced off his head, which is the way of victors. He'd watched the documentary on the History Channel, even he couldn't have said how many times he'd sat through it, and he'd prepared very specific words to say to L'Arcangelo. But that impetus Don Vittorio had shown, and the way he was still holding him tight, had jumbled that little speech in his head, so all he could get out was the question: "Don Vitto', is this loyalty enough to make you trust the *paranza*?" And as he said it, he realized that he ached for another one of those fatherly kisses. "We're allies," he forced himself to continue, "we're a single thing, united," and in the meantime he wondered if this was what it felt like to be a son.

L'Arcangelo gazed at him contentedly, nodding his head almost imperceptibly, stroking Nicolas's cheek. The sound of clinking called them out of that embrace. 'O Cicognone had come back with three champagne flutes full to the brim. For that very special occasion the whiskey had to be consumed out of party glasses.

"Cicogno'," said Don Vittorio, jabbing his thumb at 'o Tigrotto's head, "go throw this garbage in the garbage. And look out for the video cameras."

They were alone again. "Whoever avenges a son becomes a son," said L'Arcangelo, accompanying Nicolas out onto the balcony. The air was hot, suffocatingly so, but still better than the air in the apartment: 'o Cicognone would take quite a while to get rid of that stench. Side by side, hands grasping the railing, they looked out in silence at that expanse of buildings and streets, and farther on was the heart of the city, invisible but perceptible. All the way down was the sea. Nicolas knew that it was up to Don Vittorio to break that silence. He had brought him the head of his enemy; now L'Arcangelo would return the gesture by revealing a secret to him. It's by sharing secrets that you distinguish a real relationship from a false one.

"Maraja," said Don Vittorio, and then he stopped. He'd used his title and it was right to let it hover between them for a while.

"Maraja," he continued, "a contact is like water, everyone drinks it but they don't know where it comes from. Only one person can know the contact. But not even all of that person: the ears can't hear, the stomach can't digest it, the mouth can't even know who it is. Only your heart can know it. The more people know your contact, the more your contact is burned once and for all."

Nicolas knew all these things, and L'Arcangelo knew that he knew them, but that's the way it had to go.

"I'm giving you the keys to the safe, Maraja."

Nicolas nodded. He knew that, too.

"The contact's in Albania," he said, looking into the distance again, "his name is Malen Duda, aka Mario 'o Bross. I'll call him. Starting tomorrow, you're me as far as he's concerned. 'O Bross does business from four to six in the morning, but he decides which days. Now I'll arrange a date for you to go."

Nicolas turned to look at L'Arcangelo. "Don Vitto' . . ." he began, but then he stopped immediately. Everything had gone better than expected. He'd won forgiveness, regained trust, and got access to the cocaine, hashish, and marjiuana. He had everything. What should I do, he asked himself, say thanks and go?

"Are you wearing fresh underwear?" L'Arcangelo asked, surprising him.

"Yes, Don Vitto'."

"Then that's all you need."

"Why do you ask me that?"

"Because you're leaving right now."

# THE CONTACT

On the Naples–Tirana flight, Nicolas Maraja had had the impression he was flying straight into the heart of his kingdom, and he'd fallen asleep amid fantasies of elephants, plantations as far as the eye could see, and flying carpets. I'm going to take my scepter, had been his first thought upon reawakening, as the plane descended into the Albanian capital.

His first flight had gone just fine, and when the wheels touched down on the runway, he'd shown his approval of the trip's completion with a burst of solitary applause. Now he was looking out the windows of the car that had picked him up at the airport. He'd climbed in with a hunch that this was the Range Rover that Aucelluzzo had described to him when he'd given him the airline tickets. The interior of the car was austere and bare, it was like being in a tour bus; the doors had no handles on the inside, and this detail, rather than unsettling him, reassured him: he was in the right place, that certainly had to be the car that Mario 'o Bross used to transport people. The driver, concealed behind a panel of smoked glass, still hadn't spoken a word. He was driving the Range Rover through traffic, pushing at speed and with arrogance, and before long Nicolas saw Tirana spread out before his rapt eyes. Big, square, majestic buildings, which he imagined just as teeming with people as those in his own city—though these buildings bore the marks of the passage of time differently. You could clearly see a before and an after: the rough gray of the façades shifted sharply in color, and then dulled back to gray after just a few yards. "It looks like the work of some crazy painter!" he said aloud, as if the driver really was someone you could chat with.

The car slowed to a crawl, now the traffic was intense; outside the window, Nicolas heard music he hadn't noticed before. The eighties hit song, popular with Italians living overseas, "L'italiano" by Toto Cutugno.

"Fuck, we have quite the musical connoisseur in the front seat," he commented sarcastically. The volume sank until the music was indistinguishable from the rumble of the engine, turning at low r.p.m.

"We're almost there," said a voice in perfect Italian, with a light Pugliese accent. It came out of a loudspeaker hidden somewhere in the car, and Nicolas spoke loudly in response: "Is this the road to Lazarat?"

A harsh, metallic burst of laughter filled the interior of the vehicle, followed by hacking coughs, the coughs of a smoker, and of someone who hadn't laughed that hard in quite some time. "Son"—the driver's voice this time had gained a hint of warmth—"Lazarat is just a sweet dream. Before you get there, you have to go to the office."

The Range Rover lunged forward and Nicolas grabbed the headrest to keep from being slung against the car window. Outside, the great anonymous apartment blocks had given way to modern apartment buildings, looming high in the sky. Fountains, well-tended streets, busy, well-dressed people. His disappointment over Lazarat passed quickly: it's in these buildings that the decisions are made, he told himself, the plantations are postcards for tourists.

"Here we are," the driver said at last, turning down the ramp to an underground parking structure.

*Livello* –2. The metal panel was written in Italian, as were the directions to the elevator. The driver had pushed a button to pop the door open: "Go up to the sixth floor, someone will meet you there." Then, again without setting foot outside the Range Rover, he added a "*Buona fortuna, ragazzo,*" a phrase that somehow rang spectral. Nicolas hurried toward the elevator, four walls covered with fake wooden planking.

It's all a fake, Nicolas thought to himself. He felt strangely at ease in that city, it reminded him of the time—a time that seemed all too distant—when he had put together the *paranza*. No means, no resources, just a burning ambition to reach the top, to become number one. Tirana was small, not yet powerful, but it dared to pose as a financial center, like that building with an old freight elevator that ran down to collect its visitors directly on the parking level. The point was to churn out business, and who the fuck cared if the floors weren't polished to a sheen or the wall-to-wall carpeting was coming up at the corners.

The elevator doors slid open onto a reception area.

"You would be Signor Fiorillo?" asked a woman of indeterminate age, who seemed to have been waiting her whole life for his arrival.

"Yes, I'm Signor Fiorillo," said Nicolas. No one had ever called him *signore* before.

"Please go right in." And she pointed the way down the hall on Nicolas's right.

In the conference room the executive chairs were still wrapped in plastic. The ficus plants and coffee machines, the luminous whiteboard and the black conference table with outlets for laptops—everything there was ready to be inaugurated. A corner window looked out on the neighborhood below, but before Nicolas had a chance to take anything more than a perfunctory glance, a man's voice from behind him summoned his attention: "Signor Fiorillo." Two men in suits and ties, both bald and with wired earpieces running under their shirt collars, stood looking at him, arms crossed on their chests, as they might have seen in some film about CIA agents.

Either their suits are too small, Nicolas thought immediately, or they spend too much time working out.

"Come with us," said one of the two men, while the other stepped close to Nicolas, and together they escorted him to the office across from the conference room.

Nicolas couldn't see Mario 'o Bross because he was circumfused with light. The light came pouring in through a skylight over the door, bouncing off a painting that L'Arcangelo's contact had arranged to have hung behind his back (a red cube contained inside a yellow cube). That flood of light overwhelmed the visitor, who, for an instant, found himself blinded. Slowly, Nicolas was able to focus on the aluminum desk, the 27-inch iMac, the white sinusoidal office chair. And last of all, the contact himself, the broker. Handlebar mustache, black hair parted to one side, white shirt without a tie, jacket with a blue pocket square. And for an instant, Nicolas felt as if he'd stumbled onto the set on an old porn film, except that really the man was a perfect copy of Nintendo's plumber. Mario. The spitting image, thought Nicolas.

Mario 'o Bross gestured for him to take a seat.

"Why didn't you blindfold me when you brought me here?" Nicolas asked, rudely dragging the chair closer to the desk. "That's what Pablo would have done."

"Signor Fiorillo, this isn't an episode of *Narcos*," the other man replied with a smile. "Things are decided by accountants, bureaucrats, and business consultants these days. We make the numbers work, and the numbers make things work. There's no such thing as Pablo anymore." He, too, spoke a passable Italian, but a few words now and then struggled to get out right. He double-clicked on his Bluetooth mouse, and then did it again: he'd found the file he was looking for and now he was scanning it.

Nicolas thought about the gentle slopes of Lazarat, saw himself as he'd imagined the scene during the flight: intently stroking the tops of marjiuana plants stretching out as far as the eye could see, discussing the properties of the soil, the quantity of water required for irrigation. All the same, he had to confess that those words—*signore, business, partner*—did make him feel bigger, greater somehow.

In Naples the term of address *signore* would have been considered effeminate by the *paranza*. But overseas, it was the first step toward his dream, which was to call himself Don Nicolas Maraja.

"*Vabbuo'*, Marietto," said Nicolas, but the other man didn't seem to take the nickname assigned him amiss. "So now what do we do?"

"Now what do we do?" 'o Bross parroted back to him. "Signor Fiorillo, that's something you need to tell me. In your opinion, do you think I built this import-export waste business by asking questions of the sort?" Nicolas understood that, in spite of his outward calm, the man was starting to lose patience.

"How much is the ante?" Mario 'o Bross asked. A quick swipe of the mouse, just one click, as if closing the file that he'd opened before.

"The ante . . . ?" Nicolas stammered.

"The system administrator. Who's sysadmin?"

Nicolas hesitated and 'o Bross inundated him with new questions: "Who's taking care of customs? And the cover shipments. What cover shipments have you arranged? You need to have a man at every stop along the way. Do you have enough men?"

He'd stood up and now he was planting both fists on the desktop. "Don't you know that the job of system administrator is the most highly paid position in this whole line of business?" He'd lost all his composure, and in his vehemence he was spitting out drops of saliva along with the words. "Don't you know that without a system administrator, any broker or one of those narcos that you're so crazy about would be forced to deal door-to-door without ever being able to set foot outside his neighborhood? Don't you know that a system administrator might not even see the stuff once in his whole fucking life?"

"Of course, I know all that," Nicolas bluffed. He, too, had got to his feet, and now he was staring straight into Mario 'o Bross's eyes.

"So where do we situate him, huh? Where do we place him?" 'o Bross attacked him. Not even schoolteachers bore down so hard during oral exams. But then he lowered his voice: "But why do they send me little kids? Grow up, Fiorillo, and then we'll talk." Mario 'o Bross strode toward the door, and in the blink of an eye he'd walked through it, shutting it behind him. Nicolas chased after him, shouting, "Hey, what the hell!" and threw the door open and grabbed Mario 'o Bross from behind, but the two body-guards lifted him physically and carried him back into the office. They set him down on the chair and then stood on either side of him, like a pair of gendarmes. After a few minutes, Mario 'o Bross returned to his seat at the desk, calmer now: "The only reason I don't just eliminate you is respect for L'Arcangelo."

"It's not L'Arcangelo who saved me," said Nicolas, "it's the fact that you need the money that the Piranhas can bring you."

"We'll use the money from your *paranza* for coasters under our beer glasses. Show some respect. Let's start over from the beginning, Fiorillo. Who is your system administrator?"

Mario 'o Bross simply wanted to make his own earnings as high as possible and depress the *paranza*'s to the lowest. Nicolas crossed his legs and knitted the fingers of both hands together on his knee.

"We don't have a system administrator," he replied.

"You see, you know the answers already, Fiorillo! So let's do this. I'll pay the system administrator up front and we'll deduct that from your end."

In the two hours that followed they settled all their issues. Varying quantities and qualities for weed, hash, and cocaine, cover shipments, numbers of containers, methods of recovery, emergency fallback plans, percentages, systems of communication. Everything.

At the end of this intensive course on how to become the compleat narco, Nicolas felt exhausted and ravenous. He felt happy, and he felt the impulse to tell Mario 'o Bross so, but he restrained himself.

"*Grazie*" was all he said.

"*Grazie a lei*, Signor Fiorillo," retorted Mario 'o Bross, couching his "thank *you*" in the formal *lei* that they'd started out with, now that the meeting was about to end. "One last thing," he added as he buttoned his jacket. "You understand that you're now in possession of extremely sensitive information and I can't just let you wander around Tirana. Your plane takes off in thirty-six hours, and I need you to spend the time here, in my office. But don't worry: my men will bring you provisions, enough to keep the wolf from the door. So long, Fiorillo, it's been a pleasure."

"Fuck, thirty-six hours. But where do I sleep?"

"The wall-to-wall carpeting is very comfortable."

Nicolas was tempted to say, "This just isn't happening," but he swallowed his words and watched Mario 'o Bross leave the office, followed by his bodyguards, who locked the door behind them.

# THE BIRTHDAY CANDLE

**W**hen he got back to Forcella, the neighborhood was fast asleep, even if it never quite seemed to sleep completely, as if the sleep was always provisional, with a watchful alert just in case. Everyone ready to leap to their feet, people and stones, and even the stones never fully slept.

As soon as he opened the door he was practically knocked down by Skunk. The dog loved him, and Nicolas had grown fond of her; on Lollipop's recommendation, he'd bought her a treadmill so that she could gallop and stay in shape while he, stretched out on the sofa, read and watched videos on YouTube about decadent emperors and victorious armies. He patted his dog, palpating her firm flesh, the powerful muscles ready to lunge and strike out—he already knew where he was going to take her for her first fight. "You're almost ready for your baptism by fire, *ja'*!" he told her, scratching her coat right behind her shoulder blades; then he set her paws, still anchored to his jeans, on the floor. It was only as he was straightening his back that he noticed a dim light coming from inside the apartment, beyond the front hall. "Mammà," he ventured, hesitantly. Mena had turned silent. When he returned home and she came to welcome him, it seemed as if she held her breath until she saw him, almost as if she were expecting from one day to the next to find herself face-to-face with a ghost.

But out of the darkness a lovely silhouette emerged: "I was waiting up for you, my love," came Letizia's voice. "Come with me." She took him by the hand, then stopped to embrace him, gave him a kiss, and sat him down on the sofa. She wrapped both her arms around his neck and straddled his legs. Now that he could look right into her face, so close up, Nicolas noticed the radiant mouth and the cheeks bursting with joy, and in fact her whole person was so eloquently overflowing with that emotion that it was already starting to infect him.

He almost felt like laughing: "Sweetheart, what is it, what's got into you?"

"Shut your eyes."

"What is this, a surprise party?" he asked, darting his eyes around in search of other shapes hidden behind the furniture, outside the doorways. "It's not my birthday . . ."

"A party, sure, but just for me and you. I even sent your mamma away this evening." And then, in a voice that pretended to be stern, she said again: "Now close those eyes of yours!"

He felt confused, the way you do when you just can't wrap your rational mind around something, but your body has already intuited the answer and knows it, even if it won't explain it to you.

He heard her get up and make a few motions around the room, a giggle, and then in his ears the first few notes of the lullaby "Go to Sleep, Little Baby," and then: "Now you can open your eyes."

In front of him was a small chocolate cake and, at the center of it, like a birthday candle, some sort of thermometer. He turned to look at Letizia.

She nodded her head yes, and threw her arms around him. The hug lasted the blink of an eye, then she pulled back to get a better glimpse, her smile already fading: "Nico', but are you happy, or aren't you?"

Unable to answer, practically incapable of drawing a single breath, Nicolas picked up the pregnancy test, and sat there, enchanted, gazing at the two little red lines, phosphorescent in the dim light. For an instant he wondered, given that color, what sex the child could be . . . Then he looked at Letizia, and she seemed even more beautiful to him than before, such a woman, such a grown-up in comparison with him, and so perfect for the miracle she was working even now. She looked like the Mother of Dragons.

His gaze must have seemed dopier than it was dreamy, though, because Letizia shifted uneasily on the sofa cushion: "Nico', what's wrong? I waited a little while before telling you, but now the situation is real. Did I do something wrong? Tell me something, at least . . . should I be worried? Aren't you happy?"

Nicolas felt ashamed because in his mind he heard the words that others had uttered a million times before, "Having a baby changes your life," and he'd sworn he'd never say them himself, along with all the other bullshit that grown-ups never tire of spewing out. And yet . . .

He turned serious, putting the thought out of his mind.

"If it's a boy, we'll name him Christian. And if it's a girl, Cristiana," he told her, and started caressing her all over, softly, delicately, with a care he'd never shown before. And on Letizia's face the smile reappeared, as did the tenderness in her eyes for that man of hers, whom she'd never before seen so fragile. And while he planted a kiss on her belly, his lips barely brushing her skin, and told her what their life together would be like, the three of them, all the things he'd buy to make them happy, the way everyone would treat them like little Prince George and Princess Kate, or even better, like the Beckham family—that's how they'd treat them; and while she laughed and wept and he laughed and melted and turned into a child and then, seconds later, felt like a father, seeking her caresses and caressing her himself, Skunk was celebrating after her fashion, with her face plunged in the cake.

# CLAIM OF RESPONSIBILITY

CAMORRA: OLD CLANS DECLINE AND FALL

THE CHILDREN'S PARANZA KICKS THE OLD FAMILIES
OFF THE THRONE

TWO MURDERS BRING THE FAELLA CLAN
TO ITS KNEES

Once it had become blindingly clear that the murder in Rho, in spite of the barbaric beheading, had nothing to do with ISIS, the local papers, and even a few national publications, had added two and two and gotten four: they'd lined up Roipnol's murder and 'o Tigrotto's murder and had reckoned that the power of Diego Faella, 'o Micione, was weakening. On account of the Piranhas.

Micione, sitting at his kitchen table, looked embalmed as he ignored the espresso getting cold in his demitasse and the headlines that, even in the regional press, were proclaiming his decline and fall. 'O Pagliaccio was trying in vain to crowbar him out of his catatonic silence when the ring of his cell phone managed to do the trick: on the phone's screen could be read the name of the lawyer Caiazzo.

"Counselor," Micione began, "should we sue *Il Mattino*?" And then he burst into a very tense peal of laughter. Caiazzo's voice croaked out the name of a restaurant and a lunch date, an urgent one. Micione agreed to the time, ended the call, and finally seemed to have emerged from his funk. 'O Pagliaccio allowed himself to ask a question he'd been meaning to put to his boss for some time now: "But why don't we just rub out all these little snotnoses once and for all and be done with it? Why just kill one? Let's kill them all! We have the first and last names of everyone in the *paranza*. We can go fetch them one by one. And then rub them out one by one."

"Paglia', then I have to think you haven't understood a single fucking thing so far! Can't you get it through your head, that if I start waging war against a gang of kids, then I might as well just hang it all up, put on my best suit, and get comfortable in my grave and wait for the end? It's not possible!" Micione grabbed a chair and hurled it through the open door, down the hall, until it scratched the glass of the aquarium. "It's not possible!" he said again, as he sat back down. "Killing children means you're already dead in the eyes of the other families. Neapolitan, Calabrian, and Sicilian. It means we're nothing, less than nothing, that we're not good enough to scare a bunch of children, or even to get them on our payroll. We shoot kids, and everyone else will start shooting us."

"*Ua*'," said 'o Pagliaccio. "It's great to be kids in this city. Anyone who touches you becomes a little weaker. Whoever hurts you gets hurt. It's the greatest. I want to become a kid again myself."

In the meantime, Micione's temper had subsided. "Tomorrow take 'a Ranfona to Forcella," he ordered. "Give her the shop that we owe her. Let everyone know that we killed Roipnol."

"How do you mean?" asked 'o Pagliaccio.

"That we decided to eliminate him."

"Like with 'o Mellone?"

"Exactly. We'll rip off their dead. And if someone steals your dead, they're stealing your living, too."

"Which means that . . ."

"Right."

Deep down, 'o Pagliaccio heaved a sigh of relief: he was no good at comforting people with words, but with his pistol he'd restored justice plenty of times. While Micione crumpled up the pages of the newspapers and threw them on the floor, methodically, and sheet by sheet, adding detail to the mission he was entrusting him with, 'o Pagliaccio felt himself regaining his territory: at last, they were going to take action.

Anyone who saw them coming from a distance couldn't help but think of a joke. He was short and had a crazy headful of hair shooting out in all directions, while she was practically a foot and a half taller and had a head of hair worthy of Morticia Addams. For each of her long-legged strides, he had to take two. 'A Ranfona gesticulated everywhere. She pointed to apartment buildings, streets, and even cars, saying: "All this used to be our territory!"

'O Pagliaccio stopped in front of the metal roller gate of his auto deal-ership. It had recently been repainted, and the smell of fresh paint wafted in the air. Everything was ready for the inauguration scheduled for the next day. With a gentlemanly gesture, 'o Pagliaccio waited for 'a Ranfona to step inside and then, his smile never flagging for an instant, he turned and lowered the roller gate behind them again. She looked around the in-terior, satisfied; she liked the space, the depth of the storefront. "This is a good location, there's plenty of foot traffic. Down there"—and as she said it she spun her finger in the air—"I want to hang my brother's painting."

'O Pagliaccio let her finish and then pulled the trigger three times. Two gunshots in rapid succession, and the third after a few seconds. The sound echoed, amplified by the sounding board of the empty garage, res-onating clearly through the surrounding *vicoli*.

The metal roller gate rose rapidly and 'o Pagliaccio appeared, a broad smile still on his face. He looked quickly to right and left, then strode off in the opposite direction from the way he'd come with 'a Ranfona. The message had been sent to the neighborhood at large. The evening newspapers and the ones that would come out the following morning would put the lie to all the banner headlines of earlier that day: Micione was claiming responsibility for the murder of Roipnol. Micione still ruled.

In the meantime, Micione set down his fork after gulping down his last mouthful of crème brûleé, rolling it around in his mouth to savor it to the utmost. He felt like celebrating now.

"What did you want to tell me, Counselor?" he asked, rinsing his palate with spumante.

Caiazzo courteously declined a topping-off of his glass. "I have an important piece of news. The police have issued an arrest warrant for the murderer of your colleague."

"Colleague?" Micione stiffened.

"'O Tigrotto," Caiazzo hastened to clarify.

Micione's mouth split in a beaming smile. He narrowed his eyes and leaned toward the lawyer, bracing himself with both palms on the table-top: "And just what's the name of this traitor?"

"Vincenzo Esposito."

"And who is he? Where is he now?"

"Everyone calls him Stavodicendo . . . he's a member of Maraja's *paranza*."

Micione sat back down in his chair. Oh right, he thought, smiling smugly to himself, you're trying to screw Diego Faella, now? You'll have to kill quite a few more people before you can pull off that trick. "Where is he now?" he asked again.

"I don't know," the lawyer replied, throwing both arms wide as if he were reciting the Our Father.

"Well, we'll find out right quick," said Micione, and grabbed his cell phone to summon 'o Pagliaccio.

Now Caiazzo felt reassured he'd managed to avoid betraying the Faellas. He drained the rest of his espresso and made his courteous farewells, making way for 'o Pagliaccio, who had just come hurrying in.

It was a matter of tracking down Stavodicendo as quickly as possible, so as to shut the mouths of those who said that these days Micione wasn't in charge anymore.

"But isn't he a *Bambino*, isn't he untouchable?" asked 'o Pagliaccio, after Micione told him about the tip.

"Sure, but now he's killed one of my men, and so this Stavofacendo . . . or whatever his name is . . . must die. But without making it clear that I'm the one pulling the strings. And anyone who is supposed to understand will understand, just wait and see."

"First thing, we've got to find him," 'o Pagliaccio concluded.

That morning the lawyer had awakened Nicolas with his phone call: his sources informed him that Stavodicendo's cell phone had pinged the cell tower of the district that included 'o Tigrotto's house. An arrest warrant was about to be issued in his name, they had a couple of hours before the police could get out to pick him up.

Stavodicendo was the only one who hadn't gotten a replacement cell phone, that was one detail of the plan that Drone hadn't taken into account. Nicolas had sworn an oath: "*Mannaggi' 'a maronna*, how can it be that even when we organize every last detail, someone always screws us?"

The lawyer had recommended hiding Stavodicendo for a while in the De Gasperi district: "That's the safest solution . . . and after all, he's in Ponticelli."

As he ended the call, Caiazzo felt that things had been handled, that debts always had to be paid and he'd settled his with Nicolas for the help he'd given him with the copper thefts. He'd run down the names in his directory and made the call.

Everyone knew the De Gasperi neighborhood and everyone had made a visit to it at least once, a fun outing, to see the doors and windows walled up by the government in an attempt to keep away immigrants and junkies who were squatting in the buildings. And so a deteriorating neighborhood that was falling apart had been transformed into a haven for outlaws and wanted men, who'd rather wall themselves in alive than leave the city. They'd live there, behind rudimentary brick walls with just a single opening to the outside world: a brick that, when removed, let in a little light, air, and daily meals. The life of a vampire. But for many it had become too challenging and disagreeable, and renovations would have attracted unwanted attention, so it had become the last haven of professional killers. They'd shoot their victims and then vanish here.

Nicolas had zipped down to see Stavodicendo on his scooter and had explained everything to him in person—his cell phone was unquestionably tapped. Stavodicendo needed to pack his bags in a hurry and then, in even less time, bid his parents farewell. He would wait for him downstairs for five minutes, and not a minute more.

"Mammà, I need to get back to Milan right away," Stavodicendo told his mother.

She practically burst with joy: "The problem is when your kids come back, not when they go away."

His father, on the other hand, understood immediately that the new departure concealed something else.

"Is everything all right, Vincie'? Why all this hurry?"

"No, it's just that I was saying, I'm not comfortable here . . ."

"Is it the *guaglioni* you're hanging out with?" asked his mother.

"Nicolas's *paranza* is operating fine," said his father, dropping the mask. "Still, though, you're better off heading up north."

"I was just saying . . ."

"And that's why they call him that, because he's always just saying."

His mother hugged her son tight. "Don't worry, Vince', as far as I'm concerned, you can say it as often as you want, this 'I was just saying,' if it makes you feel okay."

When he went downstairs, Nicolas reassured him.

"You'll stay in there for a while, good and obedient, you won't go out, you stay out of sight, then we'll solve the situation and you can go free."

"So when are we going to solve the situation?" Stavodicendo asked, his face white as a sheet. For the first time, it occurred to him that maybe his mother had been right to weep when he'd returned.

"Soon, soon," Nicolas replied, and he'd hugged Stavodicendo, holding on to him just a little too long, as if betraying with his body the reassurances he'd offered him with his voice. Stavodicendo had never received so many hugs in his life as he did that day.

They arrived at the De Gasperi neighborhood with a pick and mortar. They tore down a wall and entered the apartment where Stavodicendo was going to stay.

The reek of mold in the air forced them to cover their noses with both hands. They quickly inspected the area, two hundred square feet, ignoring Stavodicendo as he rattled on about a YouTube video that showed the most dangerous prisons on earth, and how there was one where the inmates were kept in solitary confinement 24/7/365, and many of them wound up killing themselves by hurling themselves, dead weight, against their toilet bowls.

"I was just saying that I don't want to wind up like that," Stavodicendo told Nicolas, who hugged him once again.

"But you're not alone, you have plenty of bros." Then, kissing him on both cheeks, he added: "See you soon, Stavodice'." He went back out and with the mortar and bricks, rebuilt the wall.

*Soon* had always and only had a single meaning for Nicolas: "right away." But this time, he really wouldn't have been able to assign a meaning to the word.

On the bus that took her to the cafeteria early in the morning, Greta usually catnapped to get those extra snatches of sleep or else simply shut her eyes and let herself dream a little. But ever since Biscottino had pulled off that nasty screw-up, she constantly was on the alert and the only times she allowed herself to close her eyes were when she was lying safely in her bed at home. She looked out on the city streaming past the windows, and found herself saying goodbye to it, cursing the city for having ruined her life, but also thanking it for having given her something good. Then her eyes turned to the man sitting next to her, and from him down to the pages of the newspaper he was raptly reading. That's when she saw it. An article as long as a bedsheet with that headline bellowing her Eduardo's innocence. A hallucination, she thought at first. She blinked rapidly and hard, then turned her eyes back to the paper. Again and yet again. The words were still there, identical, neatly displayed. And the more she read them, the more things they told her: Eduardo is no longer obliged to turn state's witness, the protection program is no longer necessary, no more danger, no more risks. She read and reread, and in her head a blessed voice kept saying: "All guilt has been washed clean, you can start over. But you, Greta, now you must keep him out of trouble, you need to keep your son safe, you've been warned, from now on, Eduardo needs to behave himself." She read on, nodding her head, promising everything, whatever the cost. Certainly, she nodded, I'll take care, she promised, I'll watch over him. I swear, I won't miss a thing. She didn't even care that she knew every word of it was a lie, that she was sure her son was still a murderer, nor did she even care to know why someone had taken responsibility for the murder.

She knew the real reason: it was grace from on high. She clasped her hands together and mentally prayed to the Madonna, she prayed to God who had come down from on high to give her and her son a second chance, while the passenger beside her was already turning the page, covering up the headline that attributed to Micione the murder of Crescenzio Roipnol:

LOCAL FAELLA BOSS WHO HAD BETRAYED THEM
KILLED BY THE CLAN FOR HAVING SUPPORTED
THE PIRANHAS

# THE MORTGAGE REVOLUTION

**Y**our *papà* called."

Nicolas was sitting in an armchair, his face buried in his cell phone.

"Ah, so he's still alive? And what's he looking for?" The answer came out instinctively, driven by his anger at the words he was reading. He ran his thumb over the news, and every article had the same version of events. It had happened again. Micione had claimed credit for Roipnol's murder, too, just as he had done with 'o Mellone, the piazza boss whom Nicolas had murdered in order to send a message to the people of the neighborhood. Back then, he'd been able to shout, "That's my work, I pulled off that job!" And he could shout it again now—"That's our work, we did that job!"—but he'd need to find a better way to say it, a way that would do the most damage.

Mena let a few moments of silence go by, so that her son could get it through his head that, in spite of everything, he still needed to show a little respect for his father. At last, she told Nicolas that his father had kept her on the phone for a full fifteen minutes.

"He's late on his mortgage but the bank manager told him that these matters can be resolved." She sat down on the armrest of his easy chair. "The manager wants to meet with you. Maybe that's a good thing for us."

"Meet me?"

"Yes, you."

"But what could he want to talk about?"

"How would I know? Maybe money," said Mena, rubbing forefinger and thumb together suggestively.

"All right, Mammà, tell Papa I'll go, but I'm not going alone. All my brothers have to come with me."


They arrived at the bank looking like eight grooms ready for the altar. Some of them had navy-blue suits, others wore black, and they all wore ties. Biscottino had stuffed himself into his suit from his first communion, while Briato' had gone so far as to put in a pair of blue contact lenses to make his gaze even more riveting. Only Drago' wore his usual clothes, a pair of tight jeans and an artfully faded T-shirt. On the *paranza*'s chat, Nicolas had explained that they had been summoned by an important person, good things might come of this. Not even for an instant had the idea passed through his mind of going alone. It was all of them or none of them. It was about money, and the *paranza*'s money was a subject of discussion for all of them together, even if some of them—and here Nicolas gave Drago' an extended glance, from head to toe—hardly seemed to share that opinion.

A security guard, clearly on the verge of taking his pension, peered out through the glass, and when the first of them set off the metal detector, thought he might be about to have to use the pistol that had never been fired since it was manufactured.

"Don't be afraid," said Nicolas with a wink, "I've got this under control. It's pinging because my dick is made of steel." The kids burst into a loud round of laughter that undercut the tension of finding themselves in a setting where they didn't know the rules: none of them could ever have imagined that their first experience of being in a bank would be to walk in through the main door, stripped of their "girlfriends." Nicolas took a step forward and pulled out the keys to the TMAX. One after the other, the members of the *paranza* rid themselves of their metallic objects—

chains, bracelets, lighters, electronic cigarettes, coins. At last, they were permitted inside. People were waiting in line, while the tellers counted out banknotes and typed rapidly on keyboards. Tidiness and order, that's what the bank reeked of.

"What now," said Drago', annoyed and in a loud voice, "do we have to stand in line?"

"It's all taken care of. Come on, come right this way."

The manager, thought Nicolas. Drago' was the first to head off after him. He was curious to know just what Nicolas planned to do with his money. He body-checked the security guard with his shoulder and turned down a hallway, followed by the others, who filed past, waving into the video cameras.

"You're all over eighteen, aren't you?" asked the manager as he sat down in an office chair that actually looked more like an armchair. He didn't seem bothered by the fact that Nicolas Fiorillo had shown up with his entire gang.

"Sure," said Briato', and all the others followed suit, affirming their age in chorus.

"No," muttered Biscottino, alone in replying in the negative.

"All right, all right, that's enough," said the manager, without paying any mind to that guy with his hair in a mohawk, and then he ran his fingers over the mustache he didn't have. He was so tanned that his flesh practically glittered, and Nicolas immediately felt an intense surge of dislike for that fat little banker, that *chiattillo*.

"Forgive me if I lured you here under false pretenses, so to speak. You know, you're quite famous in the city and I always keep my eye out for the up-and-coming players in the territory."

"Players?" Pesce Moscio asked.

The manager ignored him. "Let me get to the point, Nicolas Fiorillo, or should I call you Maraja, which is how everybody knows you. Your considerable liquidity runs the risk of being counterproductive. I have a solution that can satisfy everyone. *Win-win*." He emphasized the unfamiliar phrase in English.

"*Ua'*, listen to the fucking way this guy talks!" said Pesce Moscio.

"Let him talk," said Nicolas, encouraging the man to continue.

"Very good. As you know, liquidity is the real problem these days.

Those who have too much, and those who have too little. Our lending institution has plenty, heaven knows, we're perfectly solvent, but on the weekends our ATMs are having trouble; how can I put this, they're running out of oxygen."

Maybe this guy wasn't so bad, thought Nicolas; after all, he didn't talk all that differently from them.

"Here's our offer: we hold on to your cash, which we'll use to supply our ATMs, and in exchange we'll underwrite mortgages for your families. You give me a hundred and twenty, and I'll return a hundred to you, brand-new bills, fresh from the mint. That leftover twenty is our commission, the cost of the dry cleaning."

"But I want my own account!" Lollipop said instinctively. The others nodded in a buzz of voices.

"I want American Express," said Tucano.

"I want Visa," said Briato'.

"But why would you want to give a gift to the tax office?" said the manager, trying to make them listen to reason.

"But with the money that we bring you, you don't just fill up your ATMs on Saturday. You fill at least another four. So?"

"So your parents come in here, and we'll set up a mortgage for them. The money comes in on one side, and then we hand it back out to your families."

"Maraja, I don't trust him," said Biscottino, and the other members of the *paranza* grumbled in agreement.

"*Guagliu*'," said Nicolas, "he's offering us money laundering."

The manager threw both hands in the air, as if defending himself. "What a thing to say, Maraja!" Then he turned to Biscottino: "Close that door, if you please. More than anything else, it's about helping your parents. The money remains yours."

"I'm in," said Nicolas. It was a win-win opportunity, the manager was right.

"Me, too," said Drone.

"So am I," said Briato'.

They all seemed to agree. "So, basically, we're in agreement," Nicolas summed up.

"Very good," said the manager, "the procedure is quite simple, first of all—"

"But why would we want to give our money to our parents?" Drago's voice interrupted him, after remaining silent until that point. "No disrespect, boss, but my family won't do a fucking thing with a mortgage."

He was the only one of them who lived in a house that was paid for, and his mother had no trouble making ends meet. They lived pretty comfortably, all things considered, even though certainly not the way they'd lived in the days before his father, 'o Viceré, had had his reputation ruined by a miserable informer uncle of his; why should he give up any of the money he earned?

"Gentlemen," the manager explained, "this is only a proposal. If you're not interested, no problem. Friends like before."

"That's fine, friends like before," said Drago', and he turned and left the office.

Nicolas went right after him, and the two of them started arguing, impassively, in front of the other customers.

"Nico', but they're making fools of us here. Do you really think they're doing us a favor? These guys will just take our money and we're even supposed to hand over a percentage to them. And then they come up with this bullshit twist of giving the money to our parents."

Nicolas leaned in, nose against nose. "No, didn't you understand? We're walking into a bank. Of course they're going to fuck us, aren't they? That's just the way things work, Drago'. You're either fucked or you're the fucker. And right here and now, they're fucking us, but that's okay. They take the dirty money from the piazzas off our hands and then they give it back to us, nice and clean, to put in our wallets."

"Why do we give a fuck about whether the money's clean or dirty, legal or illegal? It's not like somebody takes a look at a fifty-euro bill and asks, 'Is that a legal fifty-euro bill?' It's just a fifty-euro bill. They're stealing our money with the excuse of making it legal."

"Eh, no, Drago', if you think like that, we're just stuck being a two-bit little *paranza*, and small fry they can fish with a rod and reel. We'll never get anywhere. We need to be able to walk into banks. That's the path to follow. Make our money work for us."

Drago' didn't seem entirely convinced, but he decided to give it a try, and went back in with Nicolas.

They agreed to bring in the cash the following day, then it was time to say goodbye.

"*Arrivederci*," said Nicolas, extending a hand.

"Who are you?" the other man replied. "I'm afraid I haven't had the pleasure . . ."

"What do you mean, who am I?" Then he saw the smile on the bronzed face. "Oh, right, of course, we've never met." Then he looked up at the video camera. "What about that?"

"No worries, it isn't working today," said the manager. "It's been giving us trouble for a while now . . ."


A few days later, Tucano showed up at the bank, accompanied by his parents. The manager came to welcome them and ushered them into the usual office. He'd already prepared all the documents, marked with Xs where Tucano's parents were supposed to sign, their faces bewildered and ashen with disbelief, like someone who's won the lottery but just can't wrap their mind around it. As soon as they got home, the two of them emptied the master bedroom and gave it to Tucano so that he'd be more comfortable, with the hours he was keeping. They moved into his little bedroom, thus sanctioning on the basis of profit a switch in roles and status in the family hierarchy.

After them, it was the turn of Briato's and Drone's parents and Drago's mother. Pesce Moscio brought the bank documents home, waving them in the air, with the words: "Mammà, they gave us a mortgage!" The reactions were all the same. Tears and hugs, heartfelt thanks and still more tears. At Stavodicendo's home, a letter arrived by certified mail: his father was out of his mind with jubilation and he threw his arms around his incredulous wife, stunned by the gift that made the fact that their little boy was wanted by the law a little less of a bitter pill to swallow. "My son," Lollipop's mother went on repeating, now that they could buy the building that housed the gym and expand their business, "my son, my son, my son . . ."

Biscottino had returned home with his backpack overflowing with brochures from the bank, brochures that offered an array of investment possibilities. He had left the documents for the mortgage, on the other hand, in a folder on the table, open to the page with the amount being financed. Eighty thousand euros.

Greta had noticed the file immediately and she'd understood everything even before Eduardo started blathering confusedly about money, mortgages, and banks. She'd closed the folder and told Biscottino that she couldn't stand being made a fool of.

"Ma, it's all true, trust me. Now we can buy a real apartment!"

She'd slapped him in the face. "This *is* a real apartment!"

Since the day she felt she'd been pardoned, she'd become that much stricter with him. She'd given up on the program of protection, but the social worker never tired of telling her it was dangerous to go back, and said she'd already discussed the case with the police (though she didn't admit it to her, she'd also mentioned their names), shouting that she couldn't change her mind now.

Instead, she most certainly could, she told herself: first of all, that was the only path, and now it was no longer necessary. Emma, too, kept calling her, asking her to rethink it, or else she'd swing by the house to see her, but she was certain. She was so confident of her decision that one night, on her way to the hospital to start her shift, she'd detoured down to the port. She'd worked her way as close as possible to the sea, made sure that nobody but the seagulls were there to witness what she was doing, and she'd reached into her purse and pulled out a bundle of rags and tossed it into the water. She'd wrapped up that rough bundle of rags to make sure she could forget that contained inside it was the pistol her son had used to commit murder. The ball had floated on the surface for a few seconds, then it had unraveled, letting the pistol drop to the seabed. Now Eduardo was no longer in danger, as long as he behaved properly. Instead, rather than behaving like a little lamb and staying out of trouble, he had brought her that patent fraud of a mortgage, which clearly involved the Piranhas, and this alone was an outrage in the face of Providence itself.

Nicolas, in contrast, rather than going directly to Mena, had dropped by the clothing shop across the street from her cleaning-and-pressing shop, with its umpteenth owners in the course of just a few months. He walked in with a bag full of cash.

The new owners were a couple of newlyweds with a chihuahua that spent all day in the doorway. He found them behind a glass counter, folding the items to be put on display.

"Here you are," said Nicolas, putting the bag on the counter. "This is for you."

"What do you mean, what's happening here?" asked the proprietor, shifting his gaze from Nicolas to his wife.

"What do you mean, what's happening? Open the bag, why don't you?"

An untidy mass of cash poked out of the open zipper. Every last banknote was a hundred-euro bill.

"Well?" said Nicolas. "After all, this shop is going out of business, isn't it?"

"No," said the proprietor, and before he could add another word, his wife had grabbed him by the wrist.

Nicolas noticed and said: "Listen to your wife. This shop is going under. Take the money and shut up."

"But the store is worth more."

"Eh, I know it's worth more. But then what if it burns down? Then it stops being worth not very much and becomes worthless." Nicolas liked doing things alone, without any need to have his brothers around him.

The owner took the money and turned and went into the back of the shop.

Nicolas was leaving, and the lady went so far as to hint at a thank-you: "As long as you make sure we have no trouble, Nico'."

"You have my word."

Nicolas crossed the street at a run, scampering like a little kid, back when he heard that his father had come home and that his parents were getting ready to leave for the camping site in Minturno. Just like when he couldn't wait to climb into the car, him, Christian, and his parents.

He walked into the pressing shop practically laughing: "Mammà, here you are, washing and ironing clothes, and over there"—and he pointed to the clothing shop—"you'll be selling them."

Mena was radiant. That son of hers never made a mistake, he really was special.

Mena knew where her husband was holed up. He'd bought a one-bedroom apartment in Vasto. It was on Via da Forcella and close enough to the station for him to be able to kid himself into believing that one of these days he'd hop on a train toward a new life, or at least that's what Mena thought. She found him waiting for her in the doorway. Mena restrained a smile; they looked like a couple trying to put things back together after an episode of cheating. Instead, what hovered between them was a death in the family, followed by his act of cowardice, and now the embarrassment of those unpaid mortgage payments.

After a somewhat awkward exchange of greetings, she sat down and showed him the papers from the bank: "You see?" she said. "It's all taken care of. Paid in full. Even the part of the mortgage that hadn't been paid, all that's needed here are a couple of signatures."

He flopped down on the sofa and undid a button on his shirt. Mena, on the other hand, was fiercely proud of her son, the way you'd carry a saint in a procession.

"No," he said, after building up a sufficient supply of oxygen in his lungs. "I'll never accept."

Mena's lips twisted. She headed for the door, without a word of farewell, then she turned and said: "Look, they accepted them all, every last one. You're the only one missing, you and that other idiot woman who lives in the *basso*. Think it over carefully." And she slammed the door behind her, violently.

The security guard had a very simple directive—"never set foot outside the bank"—but there was something about the guy who'd been walking back and forth for nearly an hour that just didn't seem right to him. At first he'd thought the guy might be a nutjob, his hand constantly in his hair as if trying to suppress a thought, and that mouth that never closed in silence. He was talking to himself, and seemed to be caught up in a complicated line of reasoning. Every so often he peered into the bank, going so far as to shade his eyes from the light with the palms of both hands. But he was too inept to be the lookout for a gang of bank robbers, the security guard told himself, and he regained his equanimity once he saw that the man was finally leaving.

Just half an hour after Mena had left, Nicolas's father pulled out his cell phone and stood there staring at it for a good long while, undecided as to whether he should call his son, whom he hadn't talked to in months now, or even Mena herself, to tell her that he'd changed his mind. But had he, really, changed his mind? He'd come all the way over to the bank, and he was standing outside, finally discovering that no, nothing was going to turn him aside from that refusal, that rejection of terms. He looked up, recovering the fierce pride that had held him together—since the day that he'd lost everything, Christian and everything else in his life—and he found himself looking at a well-dressed, elegantly groomed woman who was heading for the bank with the same hesitant stride that had just carried him there, too. It was as if she was expecting someone and, at the same time, was afraid of an unpleasant surprise.

Nicolas's father ran a quick hand over his hair, happy about that apparition: he'd seen Greta only once before, he couldn't even remember where, and she'd struck him as different from the others.

There was only one way to find out: "Are you here to pick up the winnings from the lotto that our children bought tickets for?" he asked.

Greta smiled and then turned serious again. "You're the father of . . ."

"That's right, I'm the father of Nicolas Fiorillo . . . the father of Maraja."

"I'm Eduardo's mother," said Greta, and she added nothing else, because it cost her too much grief and pain to utter that other name, it was bound up too tightly with the pistol she'd found under the bed. "You know, I didn't even believe in this story of the mortgages. I just came to check it out. And so you, too, have found that it's true." She twisted her hands, and then gazed at him as if he were a doctor who was about to give her a diagnosis: "What should we do, Professo'?" There they were, not thirty feet away from a signature that would have taken care of them for the rest of their lives. And Greta was asking his advice as a father and a family man, in the stead of that dead husband with whom she could no longer discuss matters, but also as a more highly educated person than her.

"We're reaping what we've sown," he replied.

"So you think we ought to take this money?"

"No, I don't think so, we can't become a *paranza* ourselves," he said, the words coming out in a rush. He realized that he needed to be clear with this woman, and he returned to the decisive tone of voice he'd used with Mena. "If we've come to this point, it's because we've sown the seeds of evil."

"Sure, but this money . . . I have three children, Professo'. And you can't raise children on nothing but good manners, education, and empty words. You also need this damned money." Greta adjusted the strap of her purse over her shoulder and then took a step toward the entrance to the bank.

"I used to have two sons, two children, of my own, and it's precisely because I couldn't convince them to stay away from this money that now I have only one, or maybe I don't even have him anymore." He took a step, too, but only to reduce the distance between him and Greta.

"That's true," she said, and gave up her attempt to get farther away from him. "But now, with this money, I'll take them away from here. I'll move house, away from this city. We'll leave, but we won't be running, we'll leave by the light of day."

"Signora, do you know how they made this money—"

"*'O ssaccio buono,*" she interrupted him: I know very well. Raising her voice a little, she went on: "But there's something else I know. If I dress them warm and decent, if I make sure they get enough to eat at every meal, if I let them travel, if I keep them safe, if I make sure they study, then this money from the devil? I'm spending it the way God Almighty would spend it."

Nicolas's father stopped short—another few feet and he would have been walking with her through the front door of the bank. "What can I tell you, signo'?" Greta was already rummaging through her handbag for metal objects to put in the tray before entering and, without the courage to even look him in the eyes, asked: "So you're sure you won't go in?" An attempt to split the guilt, and feel its burden a little less. Or perhaps even one last attempt to let herself be convinced not to go in.

He said nothing, just turned his back on her and the bank, and walked away.

# CHICCHIRICHÌ

caught him."

Not a "Can I talk to you?" and not even an "I come in peace, Maraja." Chicchirichì hadn't even looked him in the eyes, he'd simply uttered those words, "I caught him," and Nicolas had lengthened his stride, leaving him behind him, standing there, outside his house. He had no time to waste on that jackoff, he told himself. Chicchirichì had been in the Longhairs forever, he might even be older than 'o White, and he still was basically serving as a *guaglione*, a foot soldier. In the past, he would have taken the unannounced appearance of the Longhairs' bagman as a clumsy attempt at an ambush, but the truce that had ended hostilities in Forcella was crucially necessary to the *paranzas*: a dead man in the street in the center of the city would have unleashed complete chaos.

The next day, he found him there again, and he repeated the same words, but with an addition that convinced him to give him a hearing.

"I caught Agostino," he said.

Agostino 'o Cerino. How long had it been since he'd been kicked out of the *paranza*? Since the day of his ejection, he'd simply erased him.

He leaned in close to Chicchirichì: "Caught him doing what?"

"Taking messages to Micione . . . The messages that Copacabana smuggles out of Poggioreale Prison? That bastard takes them to Micione."

Chicchirichì was holding his head low, and Nicolas grabbed his mohawk. "Look me in the face when you speak to me," he said, jerking his head up with violence. Chicchirichì's eyes spoke eloquently of sleepless nights, of tormented thoughts. "Have you read what they're writing to each other?"

"No, I barely got it." Then, rummaging in all directions with his glance to make sure there was no one within earshot, he added: "'O White doesn't know anything, he doesn't even know I'm here right now."

Nicolas weighed that confession without releasing Chicchirichì's mohawk, then decided he could afford to give him ten minutes.

He took him up to his apartment and made him comfortable in an armchair. Then he rolled a joint and offered it to his guest. He looked like a zombie. After three hits, though, his tongue loosened.

"So they're right across from each other, right?" Chicchirichì began, and Nicolas nodded in confirmation, though he actually had no idea.

"So they haven't given Copacabana the forty-one bis," the so-called hard-prison regime, a sort of extreme solitary confinement. "That bastard. There are friends of Copacabana who get their girlfriends to put their hands on their dicks, right? And basically the minute the guard sees it, he's 'Hands on the table, hands on the table,' and at that exact moment, under the table, they exchange shoes. Agostino gives his shoes to Copacabana and Copacabana gives his to Agostino. And that bastard Copacabana puts the letter in his shoes."

Just a few seconds of distraction, but quite enough time for Copacabana to get his *pizzino*, his Mafia letter, out of the prison. Once the visit was over, Agostino would shuffle away in Copacabana's size 10 shoes toward the exit, while the prisoner returned to his cell in Agostino's size 7½s.

"Ah, so Agostino' o Cerino is basically a mailbag," said Nicolas, who rolled the tip of the joint in cocaine and then offered it to Chicchirichì. "But are you sure?"

"I'm telling you. He's taking the messages to Micione."

"Which messages?" Nicolas asked. He was trying to figure out whether the *paranza* of the Longhairs had sent Chicchirichì to pretend to sell him out.

"I told you, I haven't read them. But I followed him, and I do know that they're getting ready to screw us . . . they're planning to sell Forcella to outsiders again."

"So you really think Copacabana is that much of an asshole?"

"If you ask me, yes, he is!"

"So why did you start following Cerino in the first place?"

Chicchirichì lifted his knuckles to his eyes and started digging. Furiously. When he turned to look at Nicolas again, under the burst capillaries, you could glimpse a glistening veil of moisture, and his voice now sounded like that of a young man who'd understood that there was no future for him. He'd expected money, Chicchirichì: a crumb of power, but instead, he'd got nothing. He'd remained 'o White's personal slave, while all the others pursued careers. And so he'd gone to his boss with the story of Agostino and he'd suggested calling Maraja, to ask him for help. 'O White had spat on his shoes and then told him to go take a walk. And to come back when he had less bullshit to spew.

"Maraja, I took that walk, and it led me to you," said Chicchirichì. "Forcella is our property."

"Is Forcella your property or our property?"

"Maraja, Forcella belongs to whoever can take it. But now it's our turn. I'm sick and tired of getting my balls busted. The piazzas need to belong to us. Now I want to graduate to the major leagues. I've had it with being left behind."

"So you and me together, a sort of recycling."

"I've been stuck in the minor leagues for too damned long. Now Copacabana needs to understand that it's our turn."

"You mean we need to get a turn to play?"

"You and us both. No way they're going to farm it out. The center of Naples belongs to the people who were born there. Now you guys have the piazzas. But for how much longer? If Micione and Copacabana decide to install another one of their men, after Roipnol?"

"Let me get this straight," said Nicolas. He'd stood up to rekindle

Chicchirichì's joint, which was drawing no smoke by now. "I'm supposed to solve the problem of Agostino for 'o White because he doesn't have the balls to solve it for himself? And then what? It's a gift package, a courtesy service we provide? Or really, a gift outright, to you."

"Maraja, do you want to be under Micione's command?"

"Micione can blow me," Nicolas replied. "But what's your objective here? You're not some kind of Luca Brasi, are you, sent by the Corleone family to sell out to the Turk?"

"Luca who? Who the fuck knows him?" said Chicchirichì, who wasn't a big *Godfather* fan.

Chicchirichì reached up and touched his mohawk, straightening the tip, which was hanging limply to one side, and then laid out his demand: "I want the piazza at the train station. I sold there for years. You can even ask Stavodicendo, who used to work there with me, when he was just a kid. So anyone who sells there, I manage them. The shit that's sold there, I get to buy it. That becomes my piazza."

"Good job, Chicchirichì, now you got what was eating at you out into the open," Nicolas said, with a fleeting smile that faded as fast as it had appeared. "And what the fuck do I care if you want the station? You're not in my *paranza*. You don't belong to me. You belong with the Longhairs."

"I report to 'o White. But if 'o White loses this battle, you lose it every bit as much."

"I don't lose, Chicchirichì. We have the shit, we have the piazzas, we own Forcella. We have the heart of Naples in our grip. Whoever's on top now will be under later. Game over."

"But if you ask me, we lose the game if we play against Brazil."

Nicolas no longer followed what he was saying.

Chicchirichì had stuck a hand into the back pocket of his jeans and pulled out a crumpled scrap of paper, which he then handed to Nicolas. Maraja sat there staring at the scrap of white dangling from his hand, and for an instant he felt as if they were playing Capture the Flag. Then Nicolas grabbed the piece of paper and set it down on one knee to smooth it out. It was the conclusion of a lengthy line of reasoning that had begun who knows how long ago. It sanctioned a new king for Forcella, in fact, a queen. Copacabana's wife, Fernanda.

Chicchirichì had lied, he'd read the note, he just hadn't admitted it right away.

"It's true, Maraja, what I told you was bullshit, I read the message!" Nicolas continued puffing at his joint, made of a cigarette emptied of its tobacco then refilled with hash and a portion of the original tobacco filling.

"You see how they're sticking it up our ass?" Chicchirichì went on.

Nicolas balled up the note again and flicked it at Chicchirichì, hitting him square in the forehead. "So what? So they want to put Copacabana's wife in command, the Brazilian slut? Who gives a fuck? We'll cut her head off, too." But he said it without conviction. "So where did you get this note? Have you become a magician? How do I know that you didn't write it yourself, asshole?! Get out of here."

"Maraja, just listen to me."

"How did you get this note?"

"The guy was over at Micione's house," he explained, "he spends lots of time there fucking with his girlfriend. While they were yanking out Carlito's Way's teeth, and everyone was there, 'o Micione, 'o Pagliaccio, 'a Ranfona, I managed to get my hand into the pocket of the jacket that was lying there, on the table, and I stole the letter. That's what I did, while Carlito's Way was spitting blood and shrieking like nothing I've ever heard before, Maraja. In the meantime, 'o Cerino was just standing there laughing and saying: 'How nicely Carlito's sings.'"

Chicchirichì looked up; his eyes were welling over, the memory had shaken him deeply.

"Thanks for the visit and the message, Chicchirichì," said Nicolas as he stood up. "Now we'll decide . . . what we need to do next."

# VIDEO

The video that Nicolas received from Scignacane lasted just two minutes and fifty-eight seconds. One of his men had filmed it at Nisida Reform School with an old Samsung that Scignacane had given him in person.

At first, Nicolas thought the video was a prank, some sort of flash mob in a prison setting. You could see a hallway, lined with flaking paint, and a double file of boys walking toward the video camera. Then another boy entered the frame, his back to the camera, wearing a sleeveless T-shirt that left uncovered his skeletal shoulder blades and a pair of basketball shorts that extended to the middle of his calves. When he went past, all the others turned their faces to the wall; only once he'd gone past did they resume their march.

Fade to black for a couple of seconds, and cut to the next scene, which begins in a cell. The guy on the bed, lying on his back and staring at the springs of the bunk above him, no doubt about it, was Dentino. He'd lost weight, his beard had grown out, there were dark circles under his eyes, but it was him, there was no mistaking those rabbit incisors. He was dressed like the boy who at the beginning of the video was walking against the stream of inmates in the prison hallway.

Nicolas turned the volume up all the way, but the video had been recorded without audio. In the footage, Dentino got up from the bed and left the cell, heading over to two other inmates who were talking together, and trying to join the conversation. The two inmates went on talking without even looking at him. So Dentino walked past them, but he started to be bodychecked by anybody in his path, and yet the others went on as if nothing at all had happened. Dentino walked up to another convict and tried to talk to him, too, but all he got in return was a glance that penetrated his body. He was a phantom surrounded by human beings in flesh and blood who couldn't see him. He didn't exist for anyone there.

Another gap, two more seconds, and then a public shower. Dentino was soaping himself with slow, dreamy movements, always in the same area of his chest, dazed, and then a corpulent convict grabbed the bar of soap out of his hand, just as naturally as if he'd taken it from a soap dish. He scrubbed his dick with it, long and thoroughly, and then put the bar of soap right back where he'd found it, in Dentino's hand.

The red dot that marked the progression of the video had almost reached the far right. Another cut and then the final scene, five seconds long. Dentino, naked in his cell, banging his head against the wall. Body rigid, hands at his sides, no movement but the rocking of his neck, back and forth, back and forth, back and forth.

The End.

Nicolas watched the video again, then wrote back to Scignacane:

**Maraja**
You were right. This is worse than death.

"Those who hurt us once can't be allowed to hurt us again," his mother had said. Her wish had been granted. Christian wouldn't come back to life, they'd never see him again or wrap their arms around him, but at least now he could rest in peace. And now Mena, too, would finally be able to put her heart at rest.

He'd shown her the video and she'd watched in silence. That vendetta without a dead body required a little longer to take in.

"Mammà, he's become a living ghost. He suffers every blessed day.

But enough about him. I have some good news to give you. I didn't want to tell you right away, because before the third month, it's bad luck to talk about it, but now we're almost there, and so . . ."

Mena understood instantly.

"I'm going to make you a grandmother," Nicolas concluded proudly.

Mena hugged him tight: "My son, my boy. You're my one and only, my true love."

An innocent creature was preparing to enter their lives. And tomorrow, at last, Nicolas was going to see it for the first time. He fell asleep as light and airy as someone who'd completed a grievous task and could now devote himself entirely to the future, but instead his night was troubled by a ghoulish nightmare of which he could remember nothing upon reawakening.

But he didn't let it ruin his day, anyway. He went downstairs to pick up Letizia, in front of her building, and when he saw her emerge from the front door, it was like witnessing an apparition. She looked like Botticelli's *Spring*, exactly as he had seen it at the Uffizi: she walked forth as if riding a wave, and everything in her and around her was blooming and flowering. That's how Nicolas saw her, eating her up with his eyes, hungrily, and then he walked next to her, letting the world see how pretty she was and how lucky he was. Looking at her, and touching her ever so slightly rounded belly, he felt the fullness of happiness. They were strolling through Forcella hand in hand, invincible, heading for their first meeting with that tiny bean that was the product of the union of the two of them, alone. This was the first sonogram.

Downstairs from the gynecologist's office, though, Letizia lost her confidence, and her skin blushed pink. "What if there's something wrong? What if this little baby is missing a piece?" And she started weeping, just like that, out of the blue sky.

Nicolas wasn't expecting it, it really hadn't occurred to him that there was even a passing chance that the two of them could produce anything less than a tiny creature of the utmost perfection. "What are you talking about, Leti', how can you even think such a thing? It's bad luck to even say it!" And he extended forefinger and pinky finger to ward off the evil eye. "Don't worry, you'll see, everything will be fine. This is Maraja's son."

"What the fuck does Maraja's son have to do with anything?" she said, as if she couldn't stand those words, the arrogant blather of a member of the *paranza*. Nicolas took her face in his hands.

"Letizia, look at me now: don't worry, or the creature that's growing inside you will sense that you have some doubt. There can't be any doubts. Things are fine."

Even he didn't know how he'd done it, but he'd found the right words. She pushed the button on the elevator and they rode up, leaving all hesitation behind them.

Nicolas shot a video of the examination on his cell phone, and when the doctor asked him: "Could we possibly avoid that?" he replied to her with: "No, we can't avoid it. That's my baby, my baby's in there."

The video was a mess: you couldn't make out a thing, and where the gynecologist was taking measurements and Letizia was melting with enchantment, all he saw were a few indistinct patches. And to think that he'd expected to glimpse the tiny creature's face. Or at least determine its sex. Not a chance, you couldn't even tell which way it was facing.

But he could hear the heartbeat. It was pounding loudly, filling the whole office with its rapid beats. How could that tiny creature have such a powerful heart? It really was his child!

But most of all, how could Letizia have that life enclosed inside her? This was the first time that he'd seen live anything similar to the wonderful documentaries he'd watch for hours on end, enchanted, captivated, on YouTube. But it was so immensely more thrilling than any of that. Even if he wasn't doing a damned thing; even if he wasn't even slightly at the center of attention in that scene. He couldn't catch his breath for a few seconds when Letizia, who seemed perfectly at her ease lying there on the doctor's bed, with the handle of the sonogram traveling over her belly, took his hand and laid it right *there*, where that second heart of his was beating. She was radiant. Within her, she had the greatest power on earth. A power, he understood, that had nothing at all to do with the fact of whether or not someone was in command. He left his hand resting on her belly for as long as he could.

# THE CONFEDERATION

White and his men were in their clubhouse, absorbed in a game of pool. Outside, one of those typical winter days, enveloped in a cotton ball of cloud cover; inside, nothing but the click of pool balls and the occasional curse.

In the midst of that silence, a gush of water, as if a torrential rain were inundating the gutters on the roof, echoed in his ears like some deceptive enchantment. Through the windows, a white carpet of clouds, but not even a drop of rain.

"What's going on?" 'o White asked, and mingled among the customers of the café who were stepping out into the open to find out for themselves. The splashing of drops had by now dwindled to a rivulet.

Lined up out front of the bar/tobacco shop like a line of schoolchildren, the Piranhas. Maraja, Tucano, Lollipop, Drone, and Biscottino were resheathing their penises after carefully shaking them dry, and only Drago' was still emitting the last few drops. Briato' and Pesce Moscio had stayed in the lair, because they didn't want to talk with the Longhairs after they'd broken their legs just a few months ago, on account of the fuel truck they'd hijacked from Roipnol's gas station.

On the asphalt, a puddle of urine was spreading, licking at the toes of 'o White's shoes where he stood in disbelief. He looked around for the men of his *paranza* and saw them mingling among the few rubberneckers who had had the nerve to stick around, unlike the others, who had taken to their heels at the sight of that declaration of war.

"Let's go slice these shitheads' dicks off," he incited them.

"Hey, what the fuck do you think you're doing!" he shouted at the Piranhas.

'O Selvaggio, Carlito's Way, Orso Ted, and two other Longhairs strode forward, shoulder to shoulder, each with a hand behind their back or stuck down their trousers. Only Chicchirichì hung back, because he really hadn't expected that move from Nicolas.

By now there was no one left in the *vicolo*; the shutters, which had been left open until a few seconds ago to catch whatever whiff of cool air might stir, were now shut tight. The field of battle belonged entirely to the *paranzas*.

"I haven't killed you so far," said 'o White, speaking to Nicolas. "And you come and piss in front of my house, in front of my clubhouse. But now I'm going to put your blood down on the asphalt. That way your mothers can bring a wreath of flowers for all of you here, on top of the piss you've spilled." 'O White gripped his Beretta hard, hoping to conquer the shaking of his hand. "I'll put a bullet in your mouth!" he shouted. "I'll shoot you all, every last one of you!" But the arm holding the weapon remained glued to his side, he could feel it weighed down, as if there were a forty-pound dumbbell attached to that hand. The Longhairs had unholstered their guns, but without hearing his go-ahead, they all hesitated.

Nicolas calmly grasped the wrist of the hand with which 'o White was holding his Beretta: "They've fucked us again, you know that, don't you?"

Maraja could feel 'o White's tendons relaxing. The plural first person that Nicolas had employed had made matters crystal clear: the Piranhas' affront fitted into a larger line of reasoning that now even 'o White had understood. "Let's go upstairs," he said.

Maraja opened his hand, the Longhairs put away their weapons, the Piranhas regained control.

They followed 'o White into the game room and then through the galley kitchen behind the counter of the bar, until they reached a metal staircase that in two flights took them up to the roof, a rectangle of tar that the Longhairs used as their conference room. From there, it was like looking down at a forest, and the crowns of the trees were the roofs. Tufa stone and cement, illegal structures, gorgeous ceramic tiles, storerooms and solariums. They seemed to move in the breeze, just like treetops. Naples from the sea, Naples from the land, Naples underground, and then the roofs of Naples, where you'll find everyone in the city.

Nicolas was forced to raise his voice to make himself heard by 'o White, who had taken up a position with his men just a few yards from the brink.

"Look here," said Maraja, and he tossed a scrap of crumpled paper, which landed on the ground. 'O Selvaggio lunged to grab it, but Nicolas put his foot on top of it. 'O Selvaggio returned to the ranks. "Do you know what we found in the shoes of that piece of shit 'o Cerino?" Silence. "Do you know what's written on that piece of paper, 'o White? What's written is that they're not going to let us have Forcella. They're not going to give it to you all, and they're not going to give it to me. Copacabana is sticking it up our asses again." He moved his foot and gestured for 'o White to come over; he picked up the note and started reading it aloud.

"'It's best for Forcella to be led by a person we can trust. I recommend my wife, Fernanda . . .'" He scanned the rest of it, reading but silent, then he crumpled up the *pizzino* and tossed it down into the alley.

"All right, then, Maraja, what does that mean to me? He's buried behind bars at Poggi Poggi. We're out here, free as birds."

Nicolas started clapping.

"Good for you, 'o White. I see that you've actually understood the whole thing. Not that I'm surprised, eh! You're all really good at sucking Micione's cock. 'O Selvaggio managed to run the piazzas of the Faella family, eh? Micione, Micione's brother, Micione's uncle, all of them cousins. You turned Carlito's Way into Freddy Kruger, Chicchirichì is the chauffeur, and the minute Don Diego says a word to you, you bend right over and . . ." Nicolas emitted a low whistle and pushed his hand back and forth like a piston.

For the first time, 'o White's face colored slightly. "What do you know about it? What do you know about us?" Nicolas limited himself to cocking an eyebrow and gesturing for him to look around. Carlito's Way had raised a hand to his mouth to cover up the jagged stumps of his teeth, and at the opposite corner, Chicchirichì was shifting his weight from one leg to the other, his eyes fixed on Nicolas. 'O Selvaggio and Orso Ted wore the expressions of those who don't really understand but can guess that something brand new is happening.

"This is your *paranza*, 'o White. We've taken everything away from you. We have the drugs. We own the piazzas. You don't see the money anymore, just a few coins here and there, and you go around carrying a beat-up old Beretta. Do you still know how to shoot it?"

From the alley came the shouts of a mother berating her son, and then a faint young voice swearing: "I won't let it happen again, Mammà."

"You're just like that little boy," said Nicolas, jutting his chin. "Micione spanks you, and you say you're sorry."

'O White said nothing.

"You've always shat in your pants," Nicolas went on, "but you've never fired a shot. And do you know why not?" He let the roar of a souped-up scooter disperse into the air. "Because there's just one thing that you all want, too. Naples. It's just that we're working hard to take it, while the old men who issue the orders, those piece-of-shit old men, they stay in their houses, behind their shutters. They want to defend their family, the rules. They're afraid of dying."

Drago' shivered; it wasn't that he disapproved of Nicolas's words, taken each for each; more than anything else it was an involuntary reflex, because he came from one of those noble families. The memory of his grandfather, 'o Sovrano, and the thought of his father, 'o Viceré, made him feel he had a stake in that conversation.

'O Selvaggio had come over and was standing beside 'o White now. "Maraja has a point," he said.

"Let's fight a single battle," Nicolas went on, "with a single enemy. Just one."

"Fuck, who's Juventus," Tucano piled on. "Juventus are all those old shitbucket families of Naples. The families of Marano, the families of Secondigliano, the families of San Giovanni a Teduccio. All those people who are thirty, forty, or fifty years old. All those ancient pieces of shit." Then he spoke to the city's roofs: "The streets belong to us, *guagliu'*."

The Longhairs, who had so far been standing off to one side, on their own, now stepped forward, converging, attracted by the proposal: for some time, they'd been sick and tired of loitering on the edges of the action, and Maraja was offering to bring them in, to join forces against a common shared enemy, the old clans. But 'o White remained silent. He was thinking about after they'd defeated Micione. He was thinking about Nicolas, who would then take the few remaining piazzas that the Long-hairs still controlled because, if he wasn't afraid to present himself in that fashion in their own meeting room, in their clubhouse, then what would stop him, once he'd gotten what he wanted, what would keep him from simply getting rid of them, too?

"With what you're telling me," was all he said in reply, "all I need to do is say the word and Micione will come to your house and shoot you and your mother, seeing that he's already taken care of getting rid of your brother. And in exchange, I could take all your piazzas, easy as pie."

Nicolas cut his line of argument short. "Don't let's waste time on this bullshit, 'o White. You kill me, and he'll kill you. I'm offering you the oxygen that you and your *paranza* need."

Chicchirichì nodded as if it were up to him to accept Maraja's proposal.

"So, just where did you get this letter?" asked 'o White. It was over. The offer had been accepted. That change of topic was worth more than any simple yes.

Nicolas pulled out a pack of Marlboros to pass around between the two *paranzas*, as if to seal their confederation, but when it was Chicchirichì's turn, Nicolas lit his cigarette personally.

"There's someone in your *paranza* who's been smarter than you, and who knew who he should take it to."

Chicchirichì stood motionless, frozen to the spot, with his cigarette dangling from his lips.

"And now?" asked 'o White.

"And now?" Nicolas replied, taking two long drags.

"And now we need to make it clear to Copacabana that he needs to keep his mouth shut. We'll send him the message through 'o Cerino, we'll make him do a round-trip, make the information flow the other way."

Nicolas extended his fist and 'o White did the same. Fist bump. Knuckles against knuckles.

"Now we're at peace," said 'o White.

"Now we're at peace," said Nicolas.

"So now you can leave 'a Koala and her baby alone."

"We're at peace," Nicolas reiterated.

"Give the kiss of matrimony," said Tucano, and they planted kisses on each other's cheeks.

Now it really was all over, and they were free to break ranks. The members of the *paranzas*, the Children and the Longhairs, pulled out their smartphones: who could say what had happened in the meantime, in the streets far from that roof? 'O White lit a cigarette and took off at a run, heading straight for the edge of the roof, as if he were about to take off into thin air, but instead he slammed his shoulder into Chicchirichì, who attempted a halfhearted pirouette, but his hands grabbed only empty air, and now Chicchirichì plummeted down into the *vicolo* below. A three-second fall, and then a tremendous symphony of alarmed shouts and car horns. Silence on the roof.

'O White took a deep drag. "That traitor killed himself, because he fucked up big."

Nicolas stuck his head out and pulled it back in immediately. The sprawled body of Chicchirichì lay in disarray, surrounded by the first-chance good Samaritans, but it was clear that there was nothing anyone could do now to help him. The act had been too spectacular, too theatrical, a demonstration of something he hadn't yet fully grasped. "So what is this supposed to mean?" he asked.

"Because we can't have any traitors in our ranks. I've eliminated my traitor, Maraja. What are you planning to do about the traitor that you've got in your *paranza*?"

# PART TWO

# THE BOY KINGS OF NAPLES

**A** *child isn't a child, in Naples. A child isn't a* bambino, *a child is a* criaturo. *"Teng'a creatura," I have a child, a creature, says a mother, and she butts into line at the bank or leaves her car double-parked in front of the nursery school, shouting those words at the traffic cop on duty. The creature dictates a law all its own, it takes advantage of the rights that belong to it, unquestioned, more than any law passed by the state. Does a window get broken because a back-alley goalie failed to block a kick? Ch'amma a fà, so' creaturo: what can we do, kids will be kids—that's the all-encompassing justification of the janitor, the hall monitor, the schoolteacher, the mother of one child who's just beaten up another.*

*These creatures are very close to all of creation. They belong to it like the shameless blue sky that hovers over the off-kilter TV antennas on the rooftops, the wind that whistles at the intersections of the alleys and* vicoli, *the hollowed-out tufa of the car parks and storehouses that, not that many years ago, were actually private homes.*

*That is why, in Naples, creatures are sacred, holier than elsewhere. Sacred is what brings the gift of life, in absolute terms, with no knowledge of the death that it carries within it. Like animals, like plants, like the fertile* soil of the vegetable gardens at the foot of the volcano that, were it to re-awaken, would devour everything and everyone.

Everything that has substance and meaning takes shape around children: families, the neighborhoods from Forcella to Vomero, from Chiaia to Secondigliano.

That's why the child is the king of Naples; the only king that no one has ever tried to hurl from his throne. But like a young dauphin from the old days, the child, the creature—'o criaturo—enjoys none of the rights of childhood.

Creation does nothing to educate, it does nothing to protect, it teaches no distinction between good and evil. Creation knows nothing but the sacred potential of existence and transformation, remaining forever immortal. The creature comes into the world in imitation of it. The creature grows. It learns to clear a space for itself, or else to submit. It learns by playing, like all puppies do, which, in order to keep them from wandering into mortal danger, must be grabbed by the scruff of their neck and held back. But some are always lost. Some invariably wind up in the jaws of a predator.

All the children in the world believe that they're immortal. Any newborn appears to its parents like a book of blank pages on which the world will ink a history that they dream will be better than theirs. The creatures of Naples, though, don't have that time before them.

They define at every instant in this existence what they are and what they will be, just as creation itself decides without deciding, concerning a tree felled by a lightning bolt, a seed that gives birth to a flower in the midst of an arid, hardscrabble flower bed.

Baby kittens are blind and toothless, but soon enough they will become hunters. Baby rats are born hairless and pink, but those that survive will become long, fat, and hairy, learning young to go out at night, alone, under cover of darkness. Only little human creatures must establish which among them will become prey, and which will become predators.

It's not merely out of black hunger yesterday, or for an iPhone today, that the children of Naples steal, shoot, and occasionally murder. Rather, it's because the life of each and every criaturo defies death, just as it ought to: until death comes and finds them, and takes them in its talons.

# THE VISIT

orcella at dinnertime is made of cork just like any manger scene, and like a manger scene, the lights all go on at once. Inside the apartments, one after another, as if they were torches taking flame from sparks borne on the wind.

Drago' was in his bedroom, lying on the bed, captivated by the stories of those American characters who bid on storage units that have been abandoned and put up for auction. The last season of *Storage Hunters* promised big surprises but still never seemed to answer the question that Drago' always asked himself: How could anybody forget all those valuables in and among the worthless knickknacks?

His mother, in the kitchen, was making dinner, and as she did, she kept her eyes on Renato in the soap opera *Un Posto al sole*, while in the armchair his sister, Antonietta, twelve years old, a faint swelling of breasts flaunted with pride, was playing with her smartphone.

The roar of an engine distracted him from the screen. It was too full-throated and powerful to be a car from the neighborhood. He sat up and craned his neck to see if he could guess the model. "Audi S8," he said. He leaned out the window and smiled; he'd guessed it right.

"What the fuck is a car like that doing in Forcella?" And he dived back onto the bed, alarmed. He grabbed his phone.

**Drago'**
*Guagliù*, there's a strange car.

**Maraja**
Cops?

**Drago'**
Impossible. It's serious-looking.

**Lollipop**
So who is it?

He didn't have time to formulate a hypothesis before the doorbell rang, announcing a visitor: the Audi was there for him. "I knew it."

He stuck his cell phone in his pocket, his gat down his pants, and rushed toward the front door. His mother had just pulled away from the peephole, wiped her already clean hands on her apron, and opened the door.

Viola stepped through the door, ceremonious and impeccable, from the permanent in her hair to her well-tended fingernails. She leaned down to kiss Drago's mother, brim of her hat in her face. Then she did the same with Antonietta.

"Look what happy, shiny faces you have!" she said, pretending her feelings had been hurt. "And to think that I've always entered this house by kicking the door with my feet."

"What does it mean that she always came in with her feet?" Antonietta asked her mother.

"Your cousin will explain it to you." Viola brushed her cousin's hair back behind her ears. "There, now you look like a real princess. Don't you remember the gifts I brought you?"

Antonietta nodded decisively.

"And how do you think I could get into your apartment with all those packages in my arms?" She planted a kiss on her forehead.

"Has something happened, Viola?" Drago's mother was uneasy; Viola certainly hadn't dropped by just to say hello.

Viola went on, speaking to her aunt. "Is this what we've come to, that when you see me, it must be because of some piece of bad news? I can't just come to my aunt's home, I can't come visit my cousins?"

"I'm just saying"—Drago' began, leaning against the hallway door-jamb. Viola seemed to notice he was there at that very second, but Antonietta was the only one who could believe the look of surprise that she displayed on her face—"but the last time we saw you, the last time you set foot in this apartment, it was when your father turned state's witness and you rushed around swearing up and down on a stack of Bibles that you hadn't been part of it, but no one in the neighborhood believed it for a second."

"Eh, times have changed," said Viola, waving her hand in the air with a gesture of nonchalance. As if she'd been invited to make herself comfortable, she stepped forward, gazing around with a blend of curiosity and indifference. "Ah, but here I can see that everything's remained exactly the way it always has been."

You're wrong there, Viola, thought Drago'. Absolutely nothing's the way it was. Now we're the bosses here in Forcella, he thought, and your husband gives us blow jobs. Times have changed.

Viola slipped a handbag out of the shopping bag that hung off one of her shoulders. "Come here, little one," she said. "*Mamma mia*, you're a woman already. And a woman needs a nice purse."

Antonietta turned beet red in surprise: "*Ua'*, Viola, are you serious right now?"

"Nothing less, and when you come to Rome, and you stop by my store, I'll give you more . . . all the purses you want!"

Antonietta clapped her hands, grabbed the handbag, and clutched it to her breast. It was a Saint Laurent Kate! It was the actual Kate Moss bag! If it hadn't been for her mother's stern glare, she would already have taken a selfie and shared it with her girlfriends.

Viola ran a hand over her hair: "Antonietta, these pretty eyes of yours can only match up with a purse like this one. Never settle for less, you always need to want more than you have."

"*Grazie, grazie, grazie!*" Antonietta thanked her in a high-pitched singsong, hugging Viola, who ruffled her hair like she was a baby doll.

Drago' watched this scene, annoyed by that faux-cunning move of openly buying the sympathies of the littlest one in the household, but also by Viola's sheer physical appearance. All that overstated personal care smacked of arrogance, as far as he was concerned. In the meantime, his mother had gone back into the kitchen, followed by Viola and Antonietta, who were walking hand in hand.

"Aunt, can I help you?" asked Viola.

"No, take a seat in there," said Drago's mother. "It's all ready to eat."

Viola was going to be staying for dinner, and without even asking. Drago' started feeling uneasy.

"Thanks, Auntie. How pretty you are," said Viola. "I don't think you've aged a single hour since the last time I saw you. Even though I know how hard your life is. Two children, a husband who's retired like an old lion . . ."

At the stove, Drago's mother said nothing and Viola went over to sit at the head of the table, in front of a plate turned upside down, to keep off the dust.

"That's Papa's seat, get out of it," Drago' snarled. He took his plate and turned it over, and he did the same with the other two. He would have preferred to just keep everybody from eating.

"Eh, *mamma mia*, 'o Viceré wouldn't have been offended," Viola replied in a dismissive tone of voice.

"What do you know about it?" Drago' snapped. "Why are you trying to put words in my father's mouth?"

"Because I've come to pay you back for all the pain and sorrow that 'o Viceré has been carrying deep inside, and that you've all been carrying, too."

"We don't talk about these things at the table," Drago's mother put in. "The table belongs to the Lord and money belongs to the Devil. Come on, everyone, sit down and eat." And she turned the bowls over on the table, including 'o Viceré's bowl. Then she served the spaghetti.

"Your hair looks nice the way you have it fixed, Drago'," said Viola, but he went on eating without waiting for anyone else, and without answering her. The tomato sauce immediately burned his stomach, and he tried to put out the fire with a glass of red wine.

In the meantime, Viola went on with her show. At every mouthful of spaghetti, it was a shimmying and shaking of ringlets in a sign of approval: "They're heavenly, Zietta," Viola said, "just heavenly," and Viola kept talking to her increasingly captivated niece. "Look here," she said to her cousin, and showed her a selfie with Chiara Ferragni that she'd taken at the Los Angeles airport.

"*Ua'*, Chiara Ferragni! Viola, your hairdo looks exactly like hers. Your hair looks good, not Luigi's, he looks like a baby chick."

"I got it done in Rome, *picciri'*."

"*Ua'*, I wish I could spend a few weeks in Rome," said Antonietta, dreamily.

"When you grow up, I'll take you on to work in my shop. It's in Rome, on Via Bargoni," said Viola.

"Swear you will!"

Drago' put his fork down in his bowl: "Don't you worry, when Antonietta grows up, she won't need to come work as a cleaning lady for you."

His sister glared daggers at him, her eyes glittering with rage and despair: in that improvised family meeting, only Antonietta enjoyed the presence of the guest, and everyone else was just waiting for dinner to be over so they could get to the real reason for Viola's visit.

Viola had already lost interest in her; she ran her napkin over her lips, tinging it with her lipstick, then set it delicately down on the tablecloth. Then, looking hard into his eyes, she said: "So, Drago', can I speak to you, as a *soracucina* to a *fratocucino*?"

"Antonie', *ja'*," said Drago's mother, quickly stacking the dishes. "Help me do the dishes, and then we'll go to sleep. Say good night to Viola."

Before vanishing reluctantly into the kitchen, the girl went over to plant a kiss on Viola's cheek: "But, seriously, I want to come to Rome," she whispered in her ear.

When she heard the kitchen door shut, Viola was able to explain the reason for this visit: "I'm here to bring you a message from Micione," she said.

"I don't have anything in common with your husband," Drago' retorted, and found himself unsurprised at what Viola had to say.

"This is important, Luigi'. You need to come out to San Giovanni a Teduccio to see us."

"What have you got to tell me?"

"Good things, Luigino!"

"Micione has always turned his nose up at us. Why on earth has he changed his opinion now?"

Viola touched her bangs with one hand, as if to make sure her eyes were free of interference so she could look at him more intensely: "You have the same blood as I do, as his wife, and he's never turned his nose up at you."

"My blood is mine alone. It's not shared, it's not a post on Facebook."

"Luigi, we share the same blood. Diego, 'o Micione, he's borrowed blood," Viola promptly retorted, "but the family is ours. It's always the Strianos who command."

"Nice—so is he blood lent to you or are you blood lent to him? Seeing that he sold out Forcella . . ."

Viola got to her feet, her first sign of impatience since she'd walked in the door.

"You listen to me," she said, "tomorrow morning 'o Pagliaccio is coming to pick you up. Make sure you're ready for him!"

"What if I'm not, then what happens?"

"You can tell me another day and we'll come get you ourselves," she concluded, with a flexibility that deprived Drago' of his urge to bite. Viola recovered her smile for the farewells: "Auntie," she said, stepping through the kitchen door, "give my best to Uncle. Tell him that he's the pride of our family, that he saved our honor."

Drago' had remained sitting at the table. Inside him, there was room for curiosity. Curiosity about what Micione wanted to offer him.

# AT THE ROYAL PALACE

I n the Hummer, sitting next to 'o Pagliaccio, Drago' felt calm, even relaxed. Viola's little speech about affiliation and loyalty hadn't had that much of an effect on him. Luigi Striano felt that he wore in his flesh both faces of the city, and he lived that, it strengthened him: he bore the marks of birth and rebirth as if they were two badges, his noble blood and the flaming wings tattooed on his back. He was a Striano, but he was also a member of the Piranhas. And most of all, he was a brother to Nicolas.

"They're old, we're new." In this simple phrase that he kept repeating in his mind, the *paranza*'s whole philosophy was summed up in a few words. Micione had screwed them with the sly trick of Roipnol's murder, but they'd find a way to reclaim that corpse, the same as they'd figure out how to reclaim all the piazzas. In the meantime, gaining access to Micione's private residence was a privilege, so he was savoring the excursion. He got out of the Hummer and admired his reflection in the smoked-glass windows, straightening his hair, which had wilted a bit during the drive. While 'o Pagliaccio searched him carefully from head to foot, Viola was already waiting for him, smiling in the doorway. She was impeccable, as always. She looked as if she'd just stepped out of the beauty parlor.

"You look handsome, just like Grandpa, Luigi'," she told him, and her smile widened. Drago' wondered when Viola had become so syrupy and cloying: was her father's turncoat betrayal to blame, or was it a result of mixing her blood with the diabetic blood of the Faellas? He followed her inside, eyes on her ass, which if anything had improved with age. Captivated by that swaying sashay, he didn't notice at first the hollow sound that Viola's heels made on the floor. But when he lowered his eyes, he found himself gazing down on an enormous stingray swimming under his feet, followed by a school of electric-blue fish. Drago' leaped away, hurling himself with his back to the wall, legs shaking in fear.

"What the fuck is that?" he managed to stammer out when he finally realized that he wasn't plummeting into the void.

Viola emitted a high-pitched, careless laugh: "Come on, *ja'*, Diego is waiting for us."

Micione was wrapped in a cardinal-red dressing gown, but a closer look revealed it was one that a boxer might have worn, not a man of the church. The furnishings were sober, understated, probably the result of Viola's hand. And then there was glass everywhere, and mirrors. They liked each other and themselves, and they liked looking at themselves.

"Luigino *bello*," Micione began, shaking hands with him. "Or what is it you call yourself now? Drago'. You look exactly like the cartoon character." Drago' didn't react. "Do you know that once, when you were little, you came here before? You were tiny, knee-high to a puppy, you were a *scignatella* . . ."

"I don't remember . . ." Drago' replied in a flat voice.

Micione had finally let go of his hand, and now he was pushing him toward Viola. "Of course, it's understandable, you were too small," she put in.

"My father, God rest his soul, Antonio Faella," Micione went on, "when he had my brother's first communion, you know, 'o Gialluto, he invited all the Strianos. That was when I fell in love with my Viola." He pointed Drago' to an egg-shaped chair and chose for himself a leather armchair that had nothing to do with the rest of the furnishings—his favorite. "We've always been family," Micione went on.

"I don't remember a thing," Drago' said again, still standing and doing nothing to conceal his mistrust. "How long is this yammering going to go on?"

Micione took the rude words without blinking an eye. "But why," he asked, "is someone expecting you?"

"Come on," Viola broke in, pulling her chair closer, "sit down, Luigi'."

"Viola, do me a favor, get the photographs, would you?"

She sprang to her feet and grabbed a couple of silver picture frames on display on a shelf behind her. She set them down on a coffee table in front of Drago'. They were two group photographs, in black and white: men and women, elegantly dressed, celebrating who knows what, arms around one another; familiar faces, forgotten faces, some of them entirely anonymous.

Until that moment, Drago' had been there but not really there at all; he'd left a substantial chunk of himself outside, standing sentinel, maintaining a safe distance from this invitation that smelled of a trap. But then, in one of the faces in those photographs, he recognized his grandfather, and decided that yes, he was handsome, he was fierce and proud; he saw his mother, very slender, and a man who laughed and put his arms around her, and who was trying, in the other photo, to kiss her on the neck while she feigned offense: that was his father.

"*Ua'*, look at how young Papa is there," said Drago', feeling for a moment as if he were truly in a family.

"Ah, how much fun we had . . ." said Micione, troweling it on. "Then Feliciano pulled the fucked-up move that he pulled." And he tightened the sash on his dressing gown, shaking his head as he did. "But even if the party's over, all the good that your grandpa 'o Sovrano did, the balls that 'o Viceré, your father has, all of this can't be wiped out by a traitor, it can't be erased by a turncoat who ruined everything, Luigi'," Micione said. He'd stuck a hand into the pocket of his robe and pulled out a rectangular plastic object. He rubbed it a couple of times over the red satin and then he said: "Lui', do you remember your grandpa?"

"Not much . . ." Drago' replied.

Micione snapped the rectangle of plastic he was holding and extended it right in front of his eyes. "Look here. Who do you see?"

Drago' fell silent. In that little hand mirror he saw a reflection of his father, his grandfather, he saw the faces that he'd admired in the photographs.

"You see?" asked Micione, nodding at that silence as if it were an admission. "You only need to glance in the mirror to see it." He snapped the hand mirror shut and put it away in the pocket of his dressing gown. "Now let me show you another creature who had plenty of heart, and fears nothing, just like your grandpa, another king of the earth."

He walked over to a double glass door and waved for Drago' to follow him into the elevator.

They stepped out into what once must have been the garage. Micione had gutted the place. Gone were the individual stalls, gone the partition walls, gone the roof that separated them from a small garden. Replacing them now were cages for animals, and a plexiglass ceiling to let the sun filter through. The air reeked with the stench of excrement. It felt as if they were in a subterranean zoo. Micione placed his arm around Drago's shoulders and led him past several empty cages, while Drago' wondered whether the man kept racehorses down there, or what.

"Look here," said Micione, taking his arm back. Drago' grabbed the bars and stuck his head through, but he could see only bales of hay piled up and a giant food bowl, still dirty. He was about to ask how long he was going to have to wait to get to know this other king of the earth, when a lion emerged from behind the wall of hay bales, heading for the bathtub that he used as a drinking trough. Drago' leaped backward, fetching up against Micione's belly.

"*Ua'*, that's so cool," he said, excited and scared at the same time.

"Let me introduce you to Genghis Khan, the white lion. This is my son."

Drago' leaned toward the bars.

"You know the name? You know who Genghis Khan is?" Micione asked him.

"I do know," Drago' replied. "I know. A king, the best king of all of them. The king of Mongolia." He'd been infected with Nicolas's passion for the History Channel, because, Nicolas always said, if you're going to learn something, you might as well learn it from the greatest. And who had ever been greater than Genghis Khan? Not even the ancient Romans had built an empire as vast as his. He, no doubt about it, had been the king of the world.

"And do you have the balls to go in there?" asked Micione.

"If you give me a club, sure," he said, starting to laugh.

But he realized right away that it hadn't been meant as a joke.

"Why, does the lion have a club?" Micione asked him, in fact. "What he was born with is what he uses to defend himself. So what you were born with, use *that* to defend yourself. You need to fight on equal terms."

Drago' went back to staring at the lion, which by now had started to pace in circles. The cage was broad and deep, but it was clear that Genghis Khan felt cramped in there. He would pace to one end of the cage, then he'd pace back, and so on. He'd certainly appreciate a little unprogrammed entertainment.

"Well, so, do you or don't you have the balls to get to know the emperor up close?"

"Are you trying to get me eaten by Genghis Khan?" Drago' was striving to keep a little lighthearted banter in his voice, but deep down he was shitting his pants.

"Don't be ridiculous! Genghis can tell the difference between people he should eat and people he should lick. Go on, get in, don't wet your undies."

He stuck the key into the lock and pulled open the door to the cage. Genghis took a step back, trying to determine whether Drago' constituted a threat. Drago', too, took a step back, frozen with fear. In the meantime, Micione had stepped into the cage and was petting Genghis's back. He ran his hand with the coat and then against it, roughing up the lion's white mantle. He grabbed his head and pulled it close to his own, as if begging him to start purring. Micione the kitty cat and his *micione*—his kitty cat, thought Drago', and he felt a little safer.

"*Ja*', just pet him," the other man cajoled him.

At that point, Drago' sidled over to the lion the way you'd sidle up to a dog if you were terrified of it. He brushed the lion's hindquarters and then moved his hand up to the middle of its back, following the curve of the spinal cord. He could sense the repressed tension, the power ready to lunge. And kill. He increased the pressure; now he was stroking the lion the way you might a tame, well-behaved Labrador. "Genghis," he whispered breathlessly.

"So you like the conqueror?" Micione asked him.

Drago' nodded: "He's beautiful. Can I take a selfie?"

He pulled out his iPhone and raised it to frame as much as he could get into the shot. He inhaled the odors he remembered smelling when as a child his father took him to the circus, and he wrapped his arms around the lion's head. That head was so large that in order to embrace it fully, he was forced to press his face against Genghis's whiskers, cheek to cheek. He smelled the rank breath, and his arm around the lion's neck went up and down with the animal's heartbeat. He stretched out his free arm to snap the selfie, but he was trembling too much, it was bound to come out blurry, so instead he started recording a video. "The lions of San Giovanni," he said, and then he stopped recording because Genghis was starting to show some signs of irritability.

"He's a lion because he was born a lion," said Micione. "You were born a lion, and now you're just being a sheepdog. If you were born a lion, you can't turn into a sheepdog."

Drago's face twisted, and his eyes filled with suspicion. "I've got to go now," he said, and he darted quickly out of the cage, as if escaping a trap. "Ciao, Genghis, I'm sorry they have to lock you up in this aquarium."

They rode back up in silence, and 'o Pagliaccio and Viola were gone now. Micione took off the dressing gown that he wore over his clothing and carefully folded it and put it away. This was the signal that the visit was about to end, and in fact his expression, too, was no longer cheerful.

"You need to take the Piranhas in hand," Micione said to him, without any beating about the bush, as he took his seat behind the desk. "Naples is under the control of the *guaglioni*, and the *guaglioni* don't want to be under my control. The Longhairs' *paranza* doesn't have the balls for this. And Copacabana, all he's ever worried about is leading *la bonne bonne vie*, going bowling . . . how can a self-respecting boss spend time in a bowling alley? Throwing a ball at a bunch of pins. It means you're gay or a child, right?"

Drago' said nothing; the conversation wasn't over.

"Now he's locked up at Poggi Poggi," he said, referencing Poggioreale Prison, "so he's no good to anybody anymore. Children want to be commanded by children. And you have the blood to command."

"In the Piranhas we're all in command, we're all brothers," said Drago'.

"Drago', Forcella is yours by right of blood!" He slammed a fist down on the desktop.

"Micio'," Drago' replied, "Forcella belongs to the *paranza*: you need to just pull out of the center of Naples. Those streets belong to us, we took them over one by one."

"That's where you're mistaken: those streets belong to Nicolas Maraja. You just bring him pastries, he takes them and eats them."

"That's not true," Drago' retorted, raising his voice. "We aren't like the old Camorra. Each of us has a piazza all our own, and everything we earn we share equally. We're not like you. We're true brothers."

"And you believe that?" asked Micione, regaining the same comfortable tone of voice with which he'd first greeted him on his arrival.

"No, it's not that I believe it, it really is like that. That's the way it is," Drago' said again. His family lived on Vicolo dei Carbonari, not in San Giovanni a Teduccio.

"There are only two positions in a *paranza*," Micione said. "There's the people who give the orders, and the people who take them. Do you see that chair over there?" And he pointed to a golden throne in the far corner of the room. "That's the throne of Francis the Second of Bourbon, the last king of Naples, and it seats only one. God summoned him to that throne. Now the family has summoned you. Think it over."

Then Micione picked up his phone: "'O Pagliaccio, he's coming downstairs."

The excursion was over.

## A PERFECT SHAVE

There were two things in life that Copacabana loved unreservedly: the ass of a Brazilian girl, and getting a barbershop shave. He'd married a fine Brazilian ass and, after ten years of marriage, he'd never found another one like it, and that was considering that in all his time in Rio, while running his hotels, he'd enjoyed his fair share.

He would never give up his shave with hot lather and a straight blade, not even in prison, and especially before any meeting with his lawyer. It was a sort of family tradition for him: his father had been a barber, and so had his grandfather before him. Both of them, when he was a youngster and had decided to grow his first goatee, took him aside and remonstrated with him: "Pasqua', what do you think, is your face like your dick, that you'd let hair grow on it?"

Copacabana laughed at the recollection, as he sat in his cell in Poggioreale Prison, while his trusted barber, Peppe, another convict in his early fifties, was finishing off a sideburn. Peppe was famed throughout the house of detention. He'd stolen a Luca Giordano painting from a museum and shot two security guards. He'd only meant to kneecap them, but the bullets had severed both men's femoral arteries.

"What do you say, you like it, signo'?"

Copacabana looked at himself in the mirror. Peppe knew what he was doing, he had to admit it.

"But I haven't seen your cousin lately," Peppe went on, "the kid with the red hair."

"Eh, no, he can't come anymore. Health problems."

"What kind?"

"Problems with his feet . . ." said Copacabana. "Now do the other sideburn." And he handed back the mirror and returned to the shave and his own personal thoughts. They'd caught Agostino 'o Cerino, and he hadn't been replaced yet. It had happened before, couriers had been picked up or rubbed out, but usually in no more than twenty-four hours they were promptly replaced, as a sign of unaltered trust. Not this time, though. Micione's message was unmistakable: Copacabana's wife, Fernanda, was not going to become the queen of Forcella, and he, Don Pasquale Sarnataro aka Copacabana, was going to rot in his cell in Poggioreale. End of relationship. That's why he'd requested an urgent meeting with his lawyer. He hadn't had time to prepare for the meeting, and that meant he was going to have to improvise. Copacabana didn't really know how to improvise, though.

"Counselor, things aren't going well," Copacabana said. "I need to get out. Once again half the city is shooting at the other half, and if we don't get rid of the *paranzas*, we're going to wind up like a firecracker with a wet fuse. They're all rabid animals, we just need to put them out of their misery, one after the other." This was the first time he'd told his lawyer the way things stood, without camouflaging his meaning or couching his terms in disguises and half measures.

The lawyer didn't appreciate the straight talk: "Signor Sarnataro, I'm afraid I must warn you that if you continue to speak to me in these terms, I'll be forced to withdraw my services as your legal counsel. I fully realize just how tough life can be behind bars, but I don't subscribe to a single word of what you've just told me. If you wanted a Camorrista lawyer, you could have found a hundred thousand of them. I am working strictly on the legal aspects of your trial. And let me point out, while we're on the subject, that the fact that you haven't been subjected to the forty-one bis regime isn't merely a victory: it's an absolute triumph of the lawyer's profession. If you can only impose a measure of self-discipline, then we'll also be able to take care of this trial, and you won't be forced to sit in this cell until you're a bent and feeble old man."

Copacabana leaped from his seat, the few hairs that still dotted his balding cranium pointing in all directions. He started shouting at the lawyer, explaining that half the judges in the country checked into and out of his hotels, along with all the political kingpins of the right, the left, the up, the down, who knelt down before him to ask him for votes. They were all friends of his, all listed, with their phone numbers, in his address book, and if he owed a speck of gratitude to anyone or anything for having been spared the sheer torture of the forty-one bis regime, what he owed it to was his own fucking address book. He was ready to eat that lawyer alive, swallow him whole, but a guard had stepped in to take him back to his cell. "Courts are just so much theater," said Copacabana as he was being led through the steel-reinforced door to his wing of the prison, "but the script is written elsewhere. You have to believe that, if you want to be a good actor!"

He returned to his cell even more desperate and terrified than before. He started smacking the walls with open-handed blows, as if he were beating the whole prison of Poggioreale. No one looked out from any of the neighboring cells, not even when Copacabana started yelling that he was a big-time businessman who had transformed a village in Brazil into the Naples of South America. "I was born to appreciate beauty," he ranted. "There are butchers to take care of the business of killing."

Peppe. He needed Peppe. It had only been a few hours since his shave, but when he ran his hand over his cheek, he could already feel a faint fuzz starting to sprout. Plus, Peppe had always appreciated his thoughts about beauty.

"Your skin is looking irritated, Don Pasqua'," Peppe said to him, before tossing the cape over his chest and fastening it around his neck.

"Will you put a hot towel on my face?" asked Copacabana, and the young man replied that he'd be glad to. "You're just too good-hearted, signo', you've never killed anyone, and these people take advantage. Don Pasquale, you simply fly too high, too close to the sun."

"Truer words were never spoken," said Copacabana, and he shut his eyes and settled back to enjoy the warmth on his cheeks. "How many years do you still have in here?" he asked.

"Another twenty, signo', the road is long," Peppe replied.

"At least you're behind bars because you were searching for beauty."

"What beauty? They would have paid me four million for a Luca Giordano . . ."

And with his straight razor, he slit Copacabana's carotid artery. The man who had guided Peppe's hand on the day of the theft in the museum had today guided his hand directly onto Copacabana's throat. And that man was Micione.

# DRIVING SCHOOL

The *paranza*'s new cars were having their maiden run, a baptism by rubber along Via Posillipo to Marechiaro, and back. They never went any farther, because it would have meant disturbing the shoals of Nisida. "That bitch Nisida never gave in to Posillipo, instead she jumped into the sea," as Nicolas had told the story rooted in ancient mythology.

Briato' showed up at the New Maharaja in a fire-engine-red Porsche Cayenne brand new from the dealership.

"*Ua'*, let's try this car out!" Lollipop suggested immediately.

Back and forth, the members of the *paranza* took turns taming the Cayenne; even Susamiello claimed his run, but that privilege was still denied to the little ones. "Did you wash your hands?" Briato' asked them.

Nicolas alone stayed off to one side, punching words into his smartphone, indifferent to everything that was going on in the parking lot of the New Maharaja.

"Nico'," Briato' shouted, "it's your turn. Nico'!"

Nicolas shook his head and pointed to his Rolex. There was no time, he still had to hand out the monthly paychecks and then go by to pick up

Letizia. "Maternity class," he explained, pointing an imaginary pistol at his temple and pulling the imaginary trigger.

In about half an hour, Nicolas divvied up the cash and said goodbye to his men, but before he could hop on his TMAX, Drago' came over to him: "Hold up, Nico', let's drive part of the way together."

They rolled along, scooters side by side, in silence, until Drago' asked: "So, have you ever driven a car?" Nicolas sped up, putting a good fifty yards between them, but then he let Drago' catch up with him. It would do no good to lie.

"Then let's set up this driving school, *ja'*," said Drago' in such an inviting tone that Nicolas found himself obliged to accept.

The first stop was at a hardware store; they needed a drill bit and a roll of duct tape. It was simple physics: if they used the butt of a pistol to break a car's side window, it would make a tremendous racket. If they taped the drill bit to the pistol butt, and then hit the window with it, the glass simply imploded. A nice clean piece of work.

"Maraja, choose the car!"

They buzzed along Via Nuova Marina and pulled over by the cars to consider them. They felt like they were in *Grand Theft Auto*. Drago' knocked on the driver's window of a big sedan and signaled for the guy to roll it down. The guy was so fat that the transmission was completely hidden.

"Is that an automatic?" he asked him.

The guy tried to accelerate, but the two of them were on him in a flash, and Drago' repeated his demand, whereupon the guy nodded his head. "Queer," Drago' commented.

At last they laid eyes on a perfect car. A Mercedes SLC the driver was parking, using the stick shift. They shut off the street, Nicolas hopped off the scooter, shattered the driver's window with a quick blow from the butt of his pistol, yanked open the door, and hauled the unfortunate man out onto the pavement.

As soon as Nicolas started up, he acquitted himself admirably. The car shook a bit and touched the curbs from time to time, but he drove along reasonably well. Drago' rode along next to him and gave him instructions through the broken window—"Shift, brake, downshift"—but he couldn't keep Nicolas from taking a turn too tightly and scraping the side of the

Mercedes and, more important, wedging it irremediably in the narrow alleys, or *vicoli*. They just dumped the car there: Nicolas climbed out and got behind Drago' on his scooter; he stopped a short while later.

They chose another car stuck in traffic, a Fiat Panda, easier to handle. They shattered the driver's window, hauled the owner out, thoroughly terrorizing her, and off they went again, back to driving school. Nicolas ground the gears as he shifted from second to third, and lurched forward a bit, but for a brand-new driver he wasn't doing badly at all. Drago' hit the horn a couple of times to celebrate his pupil's progress, and Nicolas responded by banging his fist on the roof of the car. The *vicolo* widened slightly, allowing Drago' to rev the TMAX and ride along on the driver's side. From there he'd enjoy a better view of Nicolas at work.

Something wasn't quite right. The engine was revving too high, it should have been in third gear by now, but Nicolas had his eyes glued to his rearview mirror. Drago' turned to look behind him and he saw what Nicolas had seen: motorcycles belonging to the Falchi squad of the police. We need to do something, thought Drago', and Nicolas must have been thinking the same thing, because he'd drawn his pistol. Drago' kicked the door of the Fiat Panda: "Nico', let me take care of this. You get out of these *vicoli* and out into traffic." The Panda accelerated and Drago' fired four shots into the air so the Falchi came after him. There was a fork in the narrow lane, and Nicolas veered to the left, while Drago' turned right, leading the police.

If I can only get to Piazza Mercato, then from there I can cut over to the station, and I'm safe, thought Drago'. He'd aim at pedestrians and veer away only at the last second, forcing them to leap out into the street and hoping that would slow down his pursuers. In the meantime, Nicolas was driving through the *vicoli*, trying to find his way to Via Nuova Marina, and as he drove he typed into the *paranza*'s chat:

**Maraja**
Cop emergency. Come on your bikes.
Kids come too, come on, *guagliunciell*!

And he sent the Google Map coordinates.

Here's the marina, and there's my scooter, Nicolas thought to himself.

He jumped out of the Fiat Panda without even bothering to switch off the engine, leaped onto the TMAX, and took off in the direction of Corso Garibaldi. Knowing Drago', he would have veered into the messy labyrinth of the neighborhood around the station to elude his pursuers. He just had to stay out of their reach long enough for the *paranza*'s network of protection to leap into action. It was a strategy they'd been employing as long as they'd been alive: bewilder, confuse, and make as much ruckus and turmoil as possible.

Drago' had practically reached the station. As he roared through Piazza del Mercato, he realized that the motorcycles chasing him had gone from two to, now, three. He was racing as fast as he could, leaning into the curves at angles approaching forty-five degrees, and in the end he'd emerged onto the last stretch of Corso Garibaldi. The Falchi were still right on his ass. In his pocket, his cell phone was sizzling on his thigh, buzzing with the growing stack of text messages and notifications.

Drago' stood up on the scooter's deck to get a glimpse of the road ahead, beyond the cars: at the far end of the piazza there were two squad cars full of state police, and from the right, over near the station, a car full of city traffic cops was arriving. He was surrounded. Drago' considered whether to just dump the scooter and continue his flight on foot. There was a small knot of Africans who were bivouacking next to the monument; with a bit of luck maybe he'd be able to use them as human shields. He released the throttle, determined to make that last desperate attempt, but he saw a 50 cc scooter coming in the opposite direction, pulling a wheelie as it arrived. Driving it was Susamiello. Yes, none other than Susamiello, and right behind him was another scooter, driven by one of the youngsters, one of the other two *guagliuncielli*, he couldn't even remember his name. They darted suddenly to one side, in an incursion into the lane that Drago' was occupying, roaring straight at the car full of city traffic cops as if challenging them to a reckless duel.

The anti-police had arrived. And the more Drago' looked around, the more scooters he saw appearing; in fact, there was even a young kid riding a BMX who veered over close to one of the squad cars and with a well-aimed kick shattered one of its brake lights. Drago' felt as if he'd fallen into one of those old Westerns that his father could never get enough of: the police were the regular army, organized, methodical, predictable; the *guaglioni* of Naples were the Indians, courageous, skillful in exploiting the territory, deeply anarchistic. Here was mayhem, here was salvation. Drago' sped up and shot past the two squad cars that were now busy trying to thread their way through the buzzing swarm of scooters, and left the piazza, free at last.

That evening, at the New Maharaja, they celebrated their exploit. Drago' had sidled over next to Nicolas, whispering: "Congratulations on your new driver's license," and they'd clinked their flutes of Moët & Chandon together, sloshing at least half of the bubbly onto the floor of the private room. Just a short time before that, Drago' had awarded Susamiello and his comrades their prize. He'd stepped out of the club and found them waiting there, as usual in single file, facing off with the unruffled and unrufflable bouncer. Drago' had wrapped his arm around the human refrigerator's shoulder and then pointed at those three, who burst out in exultation when they saw the gesture, only to turn and relay the same signal to a small group of young girls waiting behind them. The bouncer waved in the three youngsters with their chosen damsels, and they vanished into the long night of the New Maharaja.

Nicolas, too, had a gift for Drago': he handed him a set of keys.

"The car comes from our dealership," said Nicolas. "They weren't fast enough to deliver it, these jackoffs." Drago' looked down at the set of keys in his hand: a Maserati SUV.

"Since when did you buy a dealership?" Drago' asked. Nicolas had locked arms with him and led him to the parking lot. Day was dawning.

"Ever since we started offering him protection, the owner keeps giving us cars. He says that if we drive them, then everyone is going to want to buy one, that same model. Can you believe it, we set the fashion." Nicolas was talking with his eyes narrowed to slits. Too much Moët, too much cocaine, too much New Maharaja.

"Everyone wants to be like you," said Drago'. "Nico'," he went on, "I have something I need to tell you," and he started relating his tale, beginning with Viola's incursion. "If it had been up to me, I'd have laid her out dead outside my front door, but she's still blood of my father."

"Drago', these guys are getting scared, don't you get that? They want an armistice. We're succeeding! We've busted the toilets!"

They slapped each other five, then Drago' told him about that morning with Micione, starting with Genghis Khan and showing Nicolas his selfies in the cage.

"He has a real lion?" asked Maraja.

"Real as can be."

"Fuck me, after the Dogo Argentino, what I need now is a tiger, *adda murì mammà*," and the idea made them all laugh.

Drago' described the repeated attempts by Viola and her husband to bring him into their family: "'You've been here before,' 'We're all one family,' 'All the good your grandfather did in his life can't be wiped out by just one turncoat,' all that kind of bullshit, Nico'."

He spoke and gesticulated, a whirling of hands as if to sum up the idea that the encounter had been an overwhelming meat grinder, but that he'd been capable of emerging from it intact.

"And then he told me that I needed to take over the *paranza*." He said it with the sense of immediacy with which Micione had said it to him. At the home of the Faellas, he had reacted by contesting each point: But how would Nicolas react?

"And what did you tell him?" asked Nicolas, never taking his eyes off his face.

"I told him that the *paranza* belongs to all of us, that we're brothers, that we own the *paranza*, and that we're all bros."

"And what did he tell you?" The confession had turned into an interrogation, but Drago' sensed in Nicolas's question curiosity more than concern, as if Nicolas wished he could have been in his shoes, gaining access to the headquarters of the Faella clan.

"He told me that now everyone in the city wants to work under us, and that I have the blood to command, not like Copacabana, not like 'o White." Drago' paused: "Not like you," he said, and he stopped before adding that the way Micione saw it, he was nothing more than Maraja's houseboy.

"Not like me," said Nicolas, with a hint of a smile, and he thought to himself that that was exactly his strength: he never laid claim to his realm on account of any rights of birth, he conquered it through his own merits.

"These guys really are old. They're still worrying about blood. Fucking nobility, my ass."

"Maraja," said Drago', his gaze level, "my blood is the blood of my brothers."

"I know that, Drago', I know it," Nicolas replied. He'd learned that whatever happened, more than an interpretation, what was needed was a reaction. You always had to respond. He said: "One of these days, let's take a ride up to Rome and visit your cousin."

Drago' returned home the morning of the following day. Nicolas had decided that they'd leave the New Maharaja only once they'd emptied all the fridges. Once he arrived on Via Nuova Marina, he veered sharply toward the Inner Port, roared past a couple of shipyards, and stopped at a wharf.

"Filthy water," he said loudly, and shoved the scooter into the waves.

## TOURISTS IN ROME

Tucano was practically in tears when he told Nicolas that he couldn't go to Rome with him and the others because he had to take care of his six-year-old sister and feed her.

"She comes home from the parish church summer day camp and she eats like Pesce Moscio." Tucano excused himself in the face of the round of mockery from the members of the *paranza*, who only doubled down on their ridicule when they heard that statement. At last, Tucano told them exactly what had happened. His father had lost his temper with his mother for her latest acquisition: a six-hundred-euro smart TV. "You're eating me out of house and home," Tucano's father had said, "it's just my bad luck! What did I ever do to deserve this family?" Whereupon his wife had stood up to him defiantly: "And to think that if we have a paid-off mortgage and a roof over our heads it's certainly no thanks to you." And the veins in his neck had bulged and swollen: "I won't allow you to say these things in the presence of our children," and so on and so forth. In the end, his father had taken a swing at his mother, and she had retaliated with a good hard punch, and Tucano had stepped into the middle of it, he'd gotten shoved back and forth, but it hadn't moved him a quarter-inch from where he stood, because his father still thought of him as a child, but with his legs solidly planted, he was unmovable. Tucano had gone to his bedroom and come back out with the Colt Trooper revolver from his bedside dresser and had aimed it directly at his parents' faces: "Now pack your bags and get out of here, the two of you. From now on, I'm in charge around here, I'm the head of household, I'm the one who brings in the money." And he'd looked at his father. "Now get out and never set foot in here again! You no longer live here, you've busted my chops once and for all!"

Obviously, they hadn't believed him and they'd waited for him downstairs, but he'd put his hand on the Colt Trooper's bulge on his hip, and they'd moved along, meekly and obediently.

"So now you have to be a babysitter?" Lollipop asked.

"What else am I supposed to do?" Tucano replied.

None of them had ever been to Rome, and Nicolas's idea had been welcomed with enthusiastic cheers: "Take us to Rome / Maraja, take us to Rome," along with further mockery directed at Tucano: "*Ua'*, don't forget about the evening feeding, Tuca'!"

Drago' and Briato' would take care of the means of transport. Nicolas would occupy the front passenger seat of Drago's SUV, with the duties of navigator, while all the others rode in Briato's Cayenne. There would be no problem with parking in the center of Rome; after all, the cars were registered in the names of strangers. Drone, happy to finally be part of an away mission, had laid out a tourist itinerary custom tailored for the *paranza*. Even Biscottino had willingly agreed to come along; his mother was looking for a job out of town and had less time to worry about where he might be, and was less of a helicopter parent these days.

In the neighborhood around the Termini station, they halted for the day's first purchase. And it was Nicolas who insisted on paying. Seven pairs of light-up devil horns and seven pairs of eyeglasses with blinking LEDs at a Chinese gift and novelty shop. Then he also purchased a centurion's short sword, but he kept it for himself, promising that he'd award it to his most loyal soldier. They trooped along in a herd, like tourists eager to consume whatever Rome had to offer, little did it matter whether that might be the Trevi Fountain—into which Lollipop went ahead and tossed a fifty-euro bill—or all those shops they'd never dream of setting foot in back in their native city: but here everything was picturesque, everything was "*romano.*"

Drone made them wander down Via del Corso and Via Condotti, where, with an oversized shopping bag each, they looted Valentino and Armani. And also Louis Vuitton, Tiffany, and Chanel, but also the market stands selling tripe, white pizza, and pangiall'oro cakes. Gobble everything and then discard the leavings: the *paranza* had always lived according to that simple rule of capitalism.

The tour ended with the Colosseum. They convinced one of the gladiators standing around outside the monument to let all seven of them hold him up in the air, and they managed to mix in with a guided tour. After they abandoned the group of Japanese tourists, Nicolas pulled out the short sword and waved it in front of his men, who broke into a rhythmic cheer, their hands cupped over their faces—"Spaniard! Spaniard! Spaniard!"—reenacting their favorite scene from *Gladiator.*

"What's Viola's shop called, Drago'?" asked Drone, tapping on his iPad.

"Celeste. You know, sky blue. Like her eyes and her father's eyes."

"But why is the shop named after another color if she's called Viola?" asked Pesce Moscio.

"Because Viola has blue eyes, no?"

"What are you talking about? Viola has pale blue eyes, not sky-blue eyes," said Lollipop.

"Yeah, but there's no difference. Sky blue . . . pale blue . . . it's all the same."

"What do you mean? Pale blue is the Napoli jersey, while the Lazio jersey is sky blue, can't you see that it's a more faded color?"

Viola's shop, Celeste, was 4,000 feet from their current position, according to Google Maps, a good fifteen minutes on foot, hordes of tourists allowing. The *paranza* had all the time they needed to duck in somewhere, get a bite to eat, and review their plan. They chose a tiny local trattoria ("Dal Principe, Prince's, it only seems right," Nicolas had commented), as small on the outside as it was narrow and cramped on the inside, and in fact the *paranza* filled the entire restaurant after forcing a German couple to get out: Briato' planted himself, legs akimbo, and stared at them, impassive in the face of their "*gibt es ein Problem?*" until the two of them got up and went to the cash register to pay for their meal and leave.

They would use Drago's car to shatter the plate-glass display window of Viola's shop. "But why my car in particular, it's brand new!" he'd complained the whole way, but that's what Maraja had decreed: "That's only fair, Drago', this is the only way we can do this incursion," he'd said, and Drago' had gone into a funk, sulking miserably. Drone had already taken care of the shop's alarm and the video cameras in the neighborhood, operating remotely. That night, neither alarm nor cameras would be in operation. There was just one detail still to be taken care of, which Lollipop identified after pulling aside the checkered curtains in Dal Principe. An Indian vendor was patiently and methodically arranging the flowers that were on display in the rear of his Fiat Scudo van. At first, Pesce Moscio tried to buy the vehicle off him, but no deal: it wasn't for sale. Then it was Lollipop's turn to try, and then Drone's, but the Indian continued shaking his head. At that point, Briato' glanced at Nicolas, reaching for the waistband of his trousers, but Nicolas shook his head; shooting the man just wasn't in the cards that evening. Before Lollipop and Drone finally gave up, Drago' rushed outside and started bidding against them, as if they were in the middle of an auction of a storage unit in Las Vegas and the Indian was the auctioneer.

"Two thousand," offered Drago'.

"Three thousand, you miserable wretch," retorted Lollipop, who had immediately picked up on the idea: there wasn't a member of the *paranza* who didn't watch *Storage Hunters*.

"Four thousand," shouted Drone, curling his forefinger into a comma.

The Indian listened to each successive bid with his hand in his hair. Those guys kept touching his things, his flowers, as if they were for sale, so he did everything he could to reiterate his ownership of each item. But in the end he gave up, the numbers they were offering him amounted to more than he could make in a year. He took the keys out of the ignition and handed them over to Lollipop, joining his hands in a gesture of respect.

The *paranza* had just paid ten thousand euros for a delivery van that might be worth half that, optimistically, but an extra five thousand euros was a tip they could easily afford. Briato' took the wheel, while the others handed out roses and tulips to the girls they met on the street: "You're a flower among flowers," "A rose for a rose."

Viola's shop had three plate-glass windows on a corner: Drago's SUV would shatter the display window with a swerving side impact and then it would be able to continue on its way. The job would be simpler that way, and they wouldn't have to clean out the car to loot the shop. Drago' shook his head: "Destroying my brand-new Maserati is one fucked-up idea."

"Just the tip of the car's hood, Drago'."

"Fuck off, Nico'. Let's just use the delivery truck, no?" Drago' tried again.

"So how are we going to take the stuff away from here?"

"There's always Briato's Cayenne."

"No, it rides too low. We need your car. *Adda murì mammà*, you've busted my balls once and for all, Drago', I'll buy it off you," Nicolas snapped, and Drago' realized he had no choice but to give in.

The "Celeste" sign was purple. A clash of colors that was annoying, but apparently the owner of the shop had decided to claim it openly and with determination, considering that in one corner she'd placed her initials with flourishes and curlicues: *VSF*, Viola Striano Faella.

Lollipop went to get the SUV; he was going to drive it as a battering ram. Drago' would drive the Fiat Scudo. Now they just had to wait for Rome to empty out a little bit, so there was less traffic, fewer people.

Around midnight the noise in the streets subsided and, like in a fairy tale, the city seemed to put on its slippers.

"Out in sixty seconds, are we ready, *guagliu'*?" Nicolas asked, but it wasn't a question.

None of them tried to conceal their presence: they just stood there, some smoking cigarettes, others with their arms crossed as if waiting for a bus, as untroubled as professional safecrackers. The SUV with Lollipop at the wheel appeared, moving slowly—if it rammed the shop window of Celeste at 60 m.p.h., there was a good chance the driver would spin out of control and smash into the building across the way. Instead, the plan was to limit the sharp, fast acceleration to a final sprint of the last few yards. Lollipop rolled to a distance of about a hundred and fifty feet from the expanse of glass and shifted into first gear. The grinding manual transmission echoed in the Roman night.

First came the noise, like a waterfall crashing down onto boulders. It was almost a peaceful sound, reassuring, and in the end the shattering glass built up incrementally into a terrifying roar. Drone filmed the whole scene with his high-definition smartphone: the powerful silhouette of the SUV shunting through the havoc of breaking glass and screeching metal, and all around, a hail of crystal shards. He ended the video with a wheeling panoramic shot, to record for posterity the lights switching on in the apartments and the shutters timidly swinging open.

Ten seconds or so after ramming through the front window, Lollipop stepped out of the Maserati unhurt and triumphant, twerking the way he'd seen Jamaican girls do on YouTube. In the meantime, the others had darted into the store, while from the same street the SUV had come down, Drago' was approaching at the wheel of the Fiat Scudo, with the side doors already open.

"Fifty seconds," said Nicolas.

The *paranza* grabbed everything they could lay their hands on. Shoes, boots, handbags, but the paintings on the walls too, the carpets, the armchairs.

"Thirty seconds."

Viola was going to have to answer "Everything" when the carabinieri asked: "What did they take, signora?"

"Ten seconds: get out of here!"

The *paranza* piled into the Cayenne, while Nicolas leaped first onto the hood and then the roof of the Fiat Scudo. He pulled out the knife that L'Arcangelo had given him and, next to the logo, complete with fluttering curlicues that Viola had placed under the name of the shop—VSF—he carved the letter and numbers F12. He jumped down and got behind the wheel of the Scudo, which placidly puttered out of Italy's capital. In the seat next to him, Drago' gazed out the window, sunken in the springs and upholstery, his eyes on the abandoned Maserati.

The *paranza* was celebrating its knockover at the Casilina Ovest roadside diner when Viola woke up Micione, shaking him by the arm.

"They robbed me, Diego! Those traitors! Those snot-nosed kids!

Doesn't family count for anything anymore, Diego? Answer me! Do something!"

Micione sat up and tried to focus on his wife, who was already fully dressed and made up. What time is it? he wondered, but what he said was: "What's happened, my love?"

"It's the Piranhas. They destroyed Celeste. They took everything. We've got to do something, Diego!"

"Are you sure it was them, my love?"

"Those pieces of shit basically signed their work."

Micione sat back down, propping the cushion comfortably behind his back. Those kids were overdoing it now. First the piazzas and now his legal businesses. What were they driving at? Then he, too, stood up and went over to hug her. Viola is right, Micione thought, I have to do something.

While Nicolas and his men were playing at being tourists, Stavodicendo was lying on his bed, repeating the mantra that he had used as a child to make the time go by: "Garella, Bruscolotti, Ferrara, Bagni, Ferrario, Renica, Caffarelli, De Napoli, Giordano, Maradona, Carnevale, Romano, Marino, Volpecina, Sola, Muro, Bigliardi, Di Fusco. Coach: Ottavio Bianchi."

That handler of wanted men on the run, whom Nicolas had hired to pass meals for him through a hole in the wall, along with scraps of information, had also brought him a tray of cookies as an extra treat. He knew that that night the *paranza* was going to ram its way into Viola's shop, and that then they'd give the authentic handbags to the vendors along with the counterfeits. To insult her. To mortify her. The plan amused him and he was happy that the *paranza* had sent those crunchy pastries as a way of drawing him into the celebration, but having a valid excuse not to take part in the operation also relaxed him. No one was going to look to Stavodicendo to display the courage that he often lacked: all things considered, being on the lam had its advantages.

He was so sick of being on the run that that squalid little apartment had struck him, after just a few days, as a cozy and welcoming nest. When he'd been in Milan, it had taken him a while to stop jerking in fear at every small sound, at every insistent glance, but here, where not even daylight could penetrate, he felt protected. The fears that he'd expressed to Nicolas had evaporated, because now he understood that it was just a matter of being patient.

To kill some time, he thought about soccer: he'd been thinking about it, truth be told, but in here it was a passion he could easily cultivate. He'd asked the hands that provided him with food to bring him a championship calendar and from then on he'd obsessively studied it for days at a time. He was anxiously awaiting the Naples-Juventus game. It wouldn't be long now. From the walled-in neighborhood, the echo of the city reached him, muffled, and it seemed to him that it wouldn't be too very dangerous to sneak out for the ninety minutes of the match. He'd studied the door that sealed him in for quite some time now and he'd noticed that the bricks weren't solidly connected, they looked like stacks of Lego piled up by an apathetic child. If he gave it a hard shove, he could knock it down. Or at least he'd give it a try; it would be worth it. In the meantime, he waited for the day and ate his pastries.

The next day, Micione summoned 'o Pagliaccio and 'o Gialluto and started questioning them.

"All right, how many shops and cafés pay monthly protection to the *paranza*?"

"How do I know?" 'o Gialluto replied.

"Pagliaccio, which ones?"

"How do I know?" 'o Pagliaccio replied, following suit.

Micione blew up: "You never know a fucking thing, how can it be? How much do you make a year, you? Two million euros. And you? Four million. And that's not counting the shops, the business, everything you do. You exist because I exist. And you don't know a fucking thing."

"Give me my orders, and I'll execute them."

The historic center filled up with new faces, as if a foreign army had marched out of San Giovanni a Teduccio to sow terror. A man walked into Zi' Pe's delicatessen and fired a shot into the counter—the bullet came to rest in a mortadella. "Next time, that bullet will wind up in the middle of your forehead, if you keep paying off the Piranhas." Another man from the Faellas' gang fired a burst of bullets from an AK-47 into the clothing store, and before turning to go, shouted that they must never again pay so much as a penny to Maraja. They stuck knives into the tires of a delivery van that was unloading merchandise and warned the driver that from that day forward, this territory was off limits to him, if he dared to go on paying the Piranhas.

The terrified shopkeepers complied, some of them felt relieved, as if they'd been liberated from a tax. "So now who do we pay?" they asked, but received no answer, because Micione had issued no instructions on that point. 'O Pagliaccio and 'o Gialluto coordinated their soldiers, scolding them good-naturedly when they overdid it a little, and in the end they, too, went into a pastry shop, ordering pastries in abundance, but when the time came to pay, drawing their handguns: "If you continue to pay the Piranhas, this is the money you'll be paid in, pure lead."

When they told Micione about it, he paid them no mind. He'd been exposed; now he'd publicly acknowledged the power of the Piranhas, who had been able to buy the shops that he had just ripped out of their grips. What could I do? he justified himself. When they lay hands on your wife, there's no such thing as strategy, you just have to lash out blindly.

It was Drone who informed Nicolas, who already knew everything.

"No one's paying us anymore, they're taking our shops away. Even the restaurants we're protecting have gone back to the shitty old online reviews."

"Well, that must mean that the restaurants we're protecting serve bad food," Nicolas replied sarcastically. He'd already worked out his anger by destroying a few of the tables in their private room.

"What are you talking about, Nico'?" asked Drago'. "When on earth? It seems as if you're living on another planet—here they're taking everything away from us. If you don't know how to protect, you're not protected. And you know that very well."

"And where the fuck were you all? When you want to piss and moan, you all come here," said Nicolas. He could sense the violence from before starting to surge up inside him again, and he kicked them all out, all except Tucano.

"We need to impose our will," he said, "we need to send a signal, we need to show our strength. Go challenge 'o Gialluto's dog."

"But Skunk isn't ready," said Nicolas.

"But 'o Gialluto's dog is a piece of shit, he's an all-black German shepherd, they just make sure he wins because he's 'o Gialluto's."

Nicolas nodded his head, unconvinced and worried about Skunk. But she was a member of the *paranza*, too. A female soldier of the *paranza*.

'O Pagliaccio's men were working full-time. They entered and left Forcella, making it clear that the Piranhas were no longer in command, and then they started hunting down Stavodicendo. Micione had made it very clear. He wanted the head of Vincenzo Esposito, aka Stavodicendo, he wanted to get his hands on that kid who had made him look like a fool in the newspapers, by adding 'o Tigrotto's death to Roipnol's murder.

'O Pagliaccio was heading out to an ARCI organization restaurant and club in Forcella. But first he was going to see the Naples-Juventus game, and then he'd play his usual game with the proprietor. Maraja was done. The Piranhas were done.

And that's where he saw him.

Alone, sitting at a table, with a Red Bull in his hand. On the television set hanging in a corner, the game was under way. He couldn't believe that he'd just stumbled upon him, that he had him at his mercy, here and now. 'O Pagliaccio walked in, indifferent to the few witnesses; this was an opportunity he couldn't overlook. He stepped a little closer and fired.

The bullet entered Stavodicendo's cranium and exited on the other side, lodging in the wall. A perfect hole, cauterized instantly. Only then did the heads of the other customers swivel in that direction, but 'o Pagliaccio had already taken to his heels.

# PYRE

I t was a warm winter. School was soporiferous, for those who still attended, and the afternoons drowned in lassitude. The supply that was supposed to arrive from Mario 'o Bross was nowhere to be seen and the *paranza* had nothing to do: they got bored, just like in the old days. Maraja, on the other hand, was increasingly edgy, continually making phone calls to talk to the system administrators, the Albanians in charge of transporting the cocaine. He frequently seemed distracted, absentminded.

"That's normal," Briato' had said. "Now he's about to become a father, he has a lot of responsibilities."

"And he wants a mortgage for the place in Vomero," Pesce Moscio added, since Nicolas had asked him for some advice about the neighborhood. "And then there's 'o White, who expects his end, you can imagine how he pounds his balls . . ." Lollipop had piled on. They'd all started laughing and decided that the next day they'd do something different to distract him. Tucano suggested: "Shall we have a grill at the lair?"

The lair had undergone progressive improvements, technological upgrades that Drone had installed personally. The thing Drone was proudest of was the Bluetooth audio system that he'd connected to the *paranza*'s phones so that when they were still on the stairs all they had to do was touch their screens and in the apartment the woofers of the four Marshall Stanmore speakers were already pumping out bass notes. They'd agreed by unanimous vote on the password to connect to the system: "Stavodicendo."

After a long back-and-forth with Drago', they'd gutted the old television set and used its carcass as a narcotics safe for their own personal consumption. To replace it, Drone had opted for an 84-inch 3D Ultra-HD television set.

Nicolas had chosen to shuffle his playlist of Enzo Dong, and he'd sprawled on the sofa, taking up every inch of its length, while the others busied themselves around the grill, claiming superior knowledge when it came to barbecuing meat. Lately he'd thought back frequently to 'o White's accusation, that there was a traitor in his *paranza*. At first he'd taken it for one of the usual pieces of bullshit, but then he'd noticed a series of details, muttered words, and he'd started doing a few stakeouts.

The smoke from the grill filled the lair, and Briato', limping quickly along with his cane, ran into the bedroom to open the window to create a draft. A two-door red Smeg refrigerator that occupied almost half of the bedroom wall had for some time now been set aside as their cooling unit, and so the beers started circulating. The party could begin.

Eight young men spending their time eating steaks and drinking beer, mocking one another savagely and tenderly cultivating their dreams, sitting cross-legged on the floor as if they were out in the woods camping. That's what they were that afternoon. Money, drugs, L'Arcangelo, the confederation with the Longhairs—it all seemed to be put in parentheses and postponed until tomorrow. The redemption of youth.

Briato' grabbed the ketchup bottle and drowned his steak in red sauce. "*Adda murì mammà*," he said after taking a bite. "Fucking disgusting!"

Lollipop talked about his new girlfriend, the umpteenth. She was at the university and liked threesomes with another girl.

"Oh, fuck off, Lollipo'," said Drago', "the girl you're talking about is Rosie, your five-fingered girlfriend." And he tossed him a chunk of sausage that stained his white shirt. They all burst out laughing, even Lollipop.

In the background, Enzo Dong was saying that on the Italia 1 TV network they did more dealing than he ever had, while Nicolas regulated the volume with his cell phone. Every so often a chorus would start up: "'O Sicario! 'O Sicario! 'O Sicario!" and Biscottino was forced to take a drink from his can of Heineken.

It was a time for fucking around, when you discover that even more than members of the *paranza*, you're just friends.

Pesce Moscio sang along with Enzo Dong's lyrics, adding a few of his own, while the others bobbed their heads up and down. All except for Nicolas. The others were keeping their eyes on him and they noticed it immediately.

"Maraja," shouted Drone, "go on, slice this provolone!" And he tossed him the cheese. Nicolas, still sprawled on the sofa, caught it in midair, though he had to jam the steak he'd been gnawing on into his mouth in order to free up his hands. Then he undid the string on the provolone and wrapped it around his wrist: "The provolone *paranza*," he said, and the others all burst out laughing.

"Tuca'," said Nicolas, "pass me the cleaver." The "cleaver" was a knife with an eight-inch blade that he'd found while rummaging through the kitchen drawers.

Nicolas started slicing the cheese. He would cut a slice and then lay it on the blade of the cleaver, and extend it to the others.

"Let's take communion, Maraja," said Tucano, cautiously receiving his slice.

"*Ua*'," said Briato', "now Maraja is handing out the bread to the Apostles."

One at a time, they all gathered around Nicolas, who continued to slice the provolone. Lollipop fell to his kness, hands clasped in prayer, and let Nicolas slip the piece of cheese directly into his mouth.

"Everyone take some," said Nicolas.

"Amen," they replied, amid gales of laughter.

"Bless me, Father! Bless me!!!" shouted Pesce Moscio, pretending to talk in tongues, and he took his piece of cheese over to the grill to toast it.

Drone got down on his knees and raised his arms, as if he were venerating a holy man.

"Come on, Drone," said Nicolas, "I'm going to let you take communion, even if you're a Muslim infidel."

A general round of laughter, and the sound of pull tabs on beer cans.

When it was Biscottino's turn, Nicolas called for silence, laying on the hands, and everyone stopped talking, with no sound in the air except for the noise of mouths chomping on provolone. And the music pounding away.

"'O Sicario! 'O Sicario! 'O Sicario!" Lollipop started shouting, jumping up and down on the cushions, and the others followed him in that savage dance.

"'O Sicario! 'O Sicario! 'O Sicario!" Biscottino shouted along with him, raising high his can of beer. After all those difficult weeks, he finally felt relatively carefree.

Nicolas stuck the cleaver in the back pocket of his jeans, and once again displayed the palms of his hands.

"Maraja! Maraja! Maraja!"

Then he stood up and, starting to sing along with Enzo Dong, invited them all to form a circle, the arms of each on his neighbors' shoulders. They started singing and spinning faster and faster, in the smoke from the grill that the wind was once again pushing indoors:

"Maraja! 'O Sicario! Maraja! 'O Sicario!"

We've never been so united, thought Nicolas, as he observed the sweaty faces of his *paranza* as they circled around him. Drago'. Drone. Lollipop. Tucano. Briato'. Pesce Moscio. Biscottino. Just how beautiful are we, right? he told himself. A step in one direction, a step in the other, and off they went in a dizzyingly fast complete rotation, with Drone falling and then being jerked upright with a massive tug from Drago', and then they were off again, spinning in the opposite direction, and this time it was Briato' who lost his balance, hopping along on his good leg, he too hauled back aboard like a man who had fallen into the sea. In the end, they'd all come to a halt, packed close, panting into one another's faces.

*Oooh, I have fun only if the one*
*Who dies is a Higuain, a traitor.*
And everyone:
*Oooh, I have fun only if the one*

*Who dies is a Higuain, a traitor.*

When the next verse came around, Nicolas turned and faced them all, drowning out their voices: "The best team is one with me and only me."

He looked at each and every one of them, pulled the cleaver out of his pocket, and speared what remained of the provolone. "'O Sicario wants to play on a team that consists of him and him alone," he said.

Drago' laughed, and the others laughed with him. Nicolas's voice was deadly serious, but after all, it was a Carnival afternoon, every joke was allowed.

Only Biscottino wasn't laughing: "I don't play alone," he said. "I always pass the ball."

"*Ua*', Maraja, 'o Sicario has a point here," said Lollipop, and he slapped Biscottino generously on the back.

"How true," said Nicolas, "but still, he does play alone."

"Maraja," Biscottino defended himself, "I performed the ritual with the rest. We're all part of the same blood, we're all bros."

Nicolas lowered the volume on the music to zero: "Are you really sure, Biscotti', that we're brothers? Because if you ask me that blood oath wasn't worth a thing, it didn't do a bit of good."

"What do you mean?" Tucano exclaimed. "Afterward my dick grew to twice the size!"

More laughter and voices that overlapped, hastening to contradict Maraja, like in some new game of that afternoon's fiesta: "So did my wallet!" said Drone.

"And I go wherever I go, but I always feel that I'm with my brothers," said Drago'.

Biscottino, on the other hand, stood there, silent, his big eyes focused on Nicolas.

When Nicolas shouted the refrain into Biscottino's face, though, the others finally realized that this wasn't a joke.

"You're not a *sicario*, not a paid killer," said Nicolas. "Biscotti', you're a Higuain."

The euphoria had evaporated. The smiles were slightly twisted, the eyes narrowed to slits.

"We put our balls in his hands, and now he's going to get us all arrested," Maraja went on.

"Nico'," Lollipop tried to say, "I don't . . ."

"There's the social worker who comes to talk to your mother every blessed day. Tell the truth, you took money and sold us out to the police," Nicolas accused him, at last.

"Maraja, Biscottino is a bro, he's the one who put a cap in Roipnol's ass . . ." said Drone. And Biscottino did the only thing that Maraja wished he hadn't. He confessed it all.

"I didn't tell anyone but my mother. She's the only one who knows," Biscottino blurted out. "She knows that I'm the one who shot Roipnol and 'a Culona, she found the pistol . . ." He decided it would be best to leave Pisciazziello out of it entirely, in part to limit the damage of who all knew the truth, and in part because Pisciazziello was his friend. "But I only confessed to my mother." He exhaled. He felt better now, with a weight off his back. There, he thought, the worst is over.

"Hey, he talked to his mamma!" said Nicolas, but it was clear that that answer didn't satisfy him.

"Wait, hold on, let me get this straight, what did you tell her? And who did your mamma talk to?" asked Drago'. He was pale, the ends of his hair glued to his sweaty brow.

"No one," Biscottino stammered.

"Did you mother talk to the police?" Drago' persisted.

"*Adda murì mammà, no!!!*" Biscottino practically shouted, but his voice came out thin and faint.

"What about the social worker, did she talk to the social worker?"

"Sure, but she's all right . . ." said Biscottino.

Drago' tried one last loophole: "Can you retract your statement?"

"Eh," Nicolas broke in, "and now here's the lawyer who'll fix the situation for us."

"Maraja, it's just a social worker." Drago' tried to minimize.

"And who do you think the social worker would talk to? You know that they've already searched the *basso*, and maybe they've already found the pistol he used to kill Roipnol."

"No, that's not true. My mother threw the pistol into the sea."

"Right, into the sea of cops. There's a cop car in front of your school and another one that follows your mamma everywhere. You're already under police protection."

Biscottino took a step back, terrified, and whimpered, "It's not true, it's not like that." He didn't even have the strength to cry, the tears just wouldn't come, he could only stare at the blade of the cleaver buried in the cheese.

But it remained right where it was.

That blade seemed like the pivot around which the entire room was spinning; everyone was staring at the steel knife but no one was moving: by remaining motionless, perhaps they thought they could make time stand still, or even make it run backward, walk out that door and never walk back through it, instead go home and have sex with their girlfriends, walk into the New Maharaja and get drunk, delete this whole experience.

For the first time, Biscottino felt small, extremely young and small around them. Nicolas walked around behind him, rapidly untethered the string from the provolone that he'd wrapped around his wrist, grabbed both ends of it, pulled it taut, and then wrapped it around Biscottino's neck. He'd moved so quickly that Biscottino noticed that Nicolas was behind him only when he realized that he could no longer breathe. The others, too, had been caught off guard, a couple had started to make some movement or other, but nothing more than that. Nicolas was executing Biscottino.

The body compensates, it's programmed to do that. It takes energy from one part and channels it where it's needed most. Biscottino scraped his throat raw as he struggled to fit at least a finger between cord and flesh. As less and less oxygen reached his brain, the most obvious defense snapped into operation. It's in that fraction of a second that the body tricks you. Even though he weighed a good forty or fifty pounds less, if it had occurred to Biscottino to struggle, to kick Nicolas in the balls with his heel, maybe he could have wriggled free, or at least staved off the inevitable for a little longer. But instead he focused on the cord.

"What the fuck are you doing!" Drone broke in after a few seconds.

He grabbed Nicolas by his belt buckle and gave it a yank. Biscottino managed to get a gulp of air into his lungs, but Nicolas shoved Drone away with a kick to his shins, yelling: "Get back!

He stretched and pulled, and yanked again, and Biscottino's eyesight blurred, his legs gave way beneath him. He fell to his knees, his hands still on the cord, which by now was cutting into his windpipe, the fatty odor of the provolone wafting into his nostrils. Then he sprawled headlong onto the floor, his legs shuddering in convulsions. He looked as if he were climbing a tower. Drone and Briato' had left; the other boys gathered around Biscottino, watching motionless, staring at their feet: to meet the eyes of any of the others would have meant to share in the scandalized indignation at the murder of one of them. He might well have been a traitor, a Higuain, but he was still Biscottino.

"That's enough," said Drago', but he didn't take a step toward that diminutive body, now motionless.

Nicolas relaxed the straining tension in the cord. His fingers were starting to hurt. He ran a hand over his sweat-drenched forehead, then he reached that same hand out to close the eyelids of the one who had always been the puppy of the *paranza*. For a moment it seemed as if the boy were still breathing. He knelt down and stroked the dead boy's hair.

It's over, he thought, it's over. When he stood up from Biscottino's body, there was no one else in the room but Tucano.

"Now what, Maraja?" he asked.

"Now let's light a bonfire."

They went down into the street, where Biscottino's mini-quad was parked between their scooters. Nicolas grabbed it by the handles and Tucano by the rear faring. More than a hundred pounds, carried by two guys up three flights of stairs.

They overturned the mini-quad in the middle of the room and unfastened the cap on the gas tank. A dense wave of nearly transparent gasoline spread across the floor, licking at the sofa, the cabinet holding the 3D TV, the coffee table. Licking at Biscottino.

Then Nicolas jumped over the puddle of fuel and went into the bedroom. It had to be in there somewhere, maybe over the bed, no, next to the armoire, there it was, right next to the big mirror. A framed photograph. The *paranza*, all of them together, at someone's birthday party. Every last one of them. Even Dentino. And Biscottino. They all had their arms over one another's shoulders, just as they had been a short while ago, there, in the lair. Nicolas shattered the glass against the corner of the bed, pulled out the picture, and rolled it up. He went back to Tucano, who was waiting for him, his Zippo open and lit. He held the picture, as if it were a wick, over the lighter's flame and waited for it to catch.

"Now it really is over," he said, and tossed the photo into the gas.

# FRIENDS

What he needed to do first and foremost was reassure the piazza bosses, make it clear to them that there would be no more highs and lows in the supply chain. From now on, the shit would come in steady, with outstanding quality and punctual deliveries. He decided to summon them all to the New Maharaja, and he asked Oscar to prepare the club as if he were holding a convention. The pushers arrived one by one or in small groups. The woman who worked in Vicaria Vecchia showed up, dressed to the nines, as if she were going to a ball after all these years; another pusher, who ran Piazza Cavour, came with his children; the guy who ran Piazza San Giorgio walked in, arms crossed over his chest, perplexed, and preferred to remain standing the whole time. Outside, Drone videotaped it all from above with a Yuneec Tornado, making sure there would be no unwelcome surprises. That little jewel of a drone had given him nothing but satisfaction, and he also used it to keep an eye on the comings and goings in the various piazzas.

Once they were all there, the lights dimmed and the UEFA Champions League theme song started up, which in its turn triggered the smoke machine. The man from Piazza San Giorgio raised both arms over his head and shouted: "What did I tell you?! 'O Maraja is poisoning us, this is a gas chamber!"

A surging wave of people moved toward the door, but as soon as they saw the lasers, they understood that it was all part of the theatrics and they relaxed.

"Friends," Nicolas began, emerging from behind a curtain in his elegantly cut suit. Friends? he thought to himself in a fleeting split second. He'd only even laid eyes on most of them a couple of times, at best, and from the *paranza*, there were only Tucano, Drone, and Pesce Moscio, and then there was 'o White and Carlito's Way. Fuck, Nicolas said to himself, where's everyone else?

None of the piazza bosses had ventured to take a seat, as if gluing your ass to one of those plastic chairs might somehow mean giving your implicit consent. Certainly, that boy had shown that he knew what he was doing, and they'd all made money, but he still wasn't fully reliable. Just as his people weren't fully reliable.

It had happened a week ago. Pesce Moscio had passed through Piazza Bellini and he hadn't been happy, not one little bit, with what he'd seen: three kids, maybe twelve years old, peddling drugs in broad daylight. The piazza that had once belonged to Stavodicendo and now belonged to Pesce Moscio simply wasn't getting adequate supplies, there had been a general shortage of drugs for a while now, and the piazza boss expected Micione to take back control soon. In the meantime, Piazza Bellini had become prime territory for self-made drug dealers to infiltrate. So Pesce Moscio came back carrying a Kalashnikov and with a chattering sweep of automatic fire, he'd laid them all low, piazza boss included. But that was strictly a temporary solution. Pesce Moscio knew that, and so did Nicolas, who was now going to explain why it would no longer be necessary to fall back on such extreme measures.

"Friends," Nicolas said again.

A man stood up, about sixty years old. Since he was twenty, he'd been working at Piazza Bellini.

"Before we start, Maraja," he said, "I wanted to talk to you, in the name of us all."

Nicolas was annoyed by the informal *tu* the man had used.

"We're coming here," the man continued, "and we're coming at our own risk. You've supplied us with product and it's always been first-rate shit. We started selling it, and with the money we made, we were able to pay a tax to Micione. Then we stopped paying that tax. But after that, your product stopped arriving, and now we're going back to selling Micione's product. We don't want to get shot, either by you or by Micione."

There was an approving round of applause. Nicolas let it die down and then went on: "Friends, the rules are the same as always. They're the same rules that applied before I was born, before my father was born. You're the piazza bosses, you know how this works. Either you sell the product of the clan that commands your piazza or else you pay tribute to the clan and you sell product that you buy from whoever the fuck you please. But now the *paranza* is establishing another rule: in our piazzas, you can sell any drugs that you want. After all, we have the best product at the lowest price."

One of the bosses stood up: "So are you saying that I can sell someone else's shit and you won't shoot me?"

"No, I won't shoot you. Because if you're selling someone else's shit, it just means you're a fool." Nicolas stared at the heads of each and every one of them to see if they nodded, and focused on the heads of the ones who hadn't nodded promptly, gazing hard at them. It was a liberation for those who worked on the piazzas.

"If you sell good product, you're not afraid of the competition. Now that's enough, we've talked too much."

Then came champagne, lots and lots of champagne.

"Freedom! Freedom! Freedom for everyone!"

"Long live the *paranza*!"

They'd just made the best deal of their lives. As long as the *paranza* survived, they'd be free to sell whatever and as much as they pleased, and whenever they liked. For each and every piazza boss, the dream of becoming a small businessman had suddenly come within reach.

One by one, the piazza bosses shook his hand. 'O Maraja clasped back with vigor. This seemed like the end of everything, the moment when you exchange compliments for the outstanding results achieved—but actually, it was the beginning. Now they had to organize the transport of the product, carefully and efficiently, from the first shipment, which would soon come into the port of Salerno, distribute the narcotics to the piazzas, arm and supply 'o White and his *paranza*, who had been peppering him with texts and phone calls since the day of their confederation: he could smell the money waiting to be made, and he wanted to make up for lost time.

"Thank you, friends," Nicolas was saying, but where were Drago', Lollipop, and Briato'? Where were his friends, his brothers? Were they at home, now that the lair no longer existed? Nicolas finished the last handshake and decided to go home himself, where a female friend was waiting for him, a friend he knew would never betray him.

# DOGFIGHT

Nicolas dropped to his knees to pet Skunk. The bitch kept eating up the miles on her treadmill, and she arched her back slightly, as if to return the caress. Under his fingertips he could feel the bands of muscle moving in time to the galloping pace. Skunk could have taken his hand off in a single bite without warning, but she never would, no, Nicolas was sure of that, because the day he'd presented her to the *paranza* with that name, the name of the female marijuana plant, the fertile plant that gave birth to others, the bitch had clenched her jaw. He'd seen it. She was his.

"You're a beauty," Nicolas told her, increasing the pressure of his fingertips on her back. The harder he pushed, the stiffer her back became, in a sensual exchange of pressure and the release of tension.

Skunk's first dogfight was scheduled for the following night. Right up to the very last minute, Nicolas had been uncertain whether to confirm her presence; after all, Skunk had never faced off with another dog, she could get badly hurt, she could even be killed. But she was ready: his dog couldn't be one of the world's losers, she was certainly a world-beater. She'd kick their asses, all of them, he decided as he filled her bowl, she was going to be a champion.

The fight was scheduled to take place in Marcianise. The dogfight ring had been set up in a pit, six feet square, that years ago had been readied as a resting place for tons of garbage, but had never been used. It was one of those places that seem to exist only if you believe in them, like Hogwarts, and only when you become the owner of a fighting dog.

Nicolas arrived as the sun was setting, and the headlights of the cars and motorcycles parked facing the pit all started flicking on. He parked off to one side and, with Skunk on the leash, he headed over to that hole in the earth. Smooth walls, sheer, impossible to scale, so much so that the trainers of the fighting dogs had to climb down and up on a ladder, like painters. And every time they went down there, the mockery started to rain down from the audience up above—"Go on, give him a bite!"—after which the trainers could climb up out of the pit and the real battle would begin.

Anyone could be hiding among the ordinary spectators and the dog owners, from retirees who spent their days at home or at church but who had a private lust to see limb ripped from limb, all the way up to a rival gang member, an enemy of Nicolas. Atop the rampart that years ago had been a wheat field, the people were all equal, all the same, and all of them had their heads turned down toward that hole in the dirt. Any other place in the city, 'o Gialluto and Nicolas would have drawn guns and started shooting the minute they saw each other, even if it was a chance encounter in the aisle of a supermarket. But here, 'o Gialluto was no longer a Faella, no longer Micione's brother, he was just the owner of a fighting dog. With one hand on Skunk's powerful neck, Nicolas waited for 'o Gialluto to arrive, and while he waited he watched the first dogfight.

Facing off were a rottweiler and a Dogo Argentino, but a bigger one than Skunk, certainly a male. The two animals wasted no time studying each other, they just lunged into the fray. All around Nicolas, people started shouting and cheering them on: the rottweiler was more aggressive, he'd make hamburger out of the Dogo, no, the Dogo was just parrying his opponent, don't you see how it's staying on its back paws? Kill him. *Accìrelo.* Rip him limb from limb. *Staccace 'a faccia.* Take his face off. Rip his throat open. Tear his ear off. Nicolas felt as if he were sitting in the front row of an ancient Roman amphitheater, singing the praises of the gladiators in exchange for sweat, blood, and dirt.

Then the rottweiler and the Dogo slammed together, jaws wide open, the first vertical, the other horizontal, forming a violent cross. Nicolas prepared to hear an explosion of shattered fangs and torn fleshy tissues; instead what he heard was a loud *clack*, as if gearings had meshed and then ground to a halt.

The trainers descended into the pit, warily circling the two animals locked together, searching for the best point of access, and then lunged at the beasts, lifting their rear legs into the air. The dogs instinctively broke apart, and then resumed the fight. The furious combat didn't last long, only until the two challengers stopped sinking their teeth into each other, exhausted like a pair of gladiators who had decided to spare each other, to spare themselves. No winner. Jeers and whistles from the disappointed audience.

The next bout was announced by the chattering of the spectators.

Scar tissue from the most recent wounds glittered in the headlights: these were a pair of veterans, the two dogs in the ring, even Nicolas understood that. They stood at the corners of the pit for a good solid five minutes, indifferent to the shouts of the onlookers. But when they lunged together at the center of the ring, the fight didn't last long: the cane corso went for the bull terrier's throat, and the dog hesitated an instant too long, unsure whether to dodge the attack or attack in response, and in a second he was on his back. The cane corso went for him, getting in a couple of solid bites, but by doing so he exposed his throat, and the bull terrier took that as an opportunity to rip out the other dog's jugular.

The night went on like that, an assortment of bouts, bets, and lacerated flesh.

Nicolas watched the remaining dogs, and was starting to feel anxious, and that anxiety quickly infected the dog. He didn't see 'o Gialluto. It was the audience that announced his arrival. Everyone started shouting: "'Totò! Totò! Totò!" 'O Gialluto's dog, the Belgian shepherd that was going to face off with Skunk, had finally arrived. Their turn had come.

Nicolas caught a distant glimpse of 'o Gialluto's jaundiced skin, which seemed to glow a phosphorescent yellow. Neither of the two spoke a word, they had eyes only for the dogs they were taking down into the pit. As soon as her paws hit the dirt floor, Skunk started to snarl, tensing every muscle in her body, the nape of her neck, the neck itself, thighs, hocks, her whole white coat swollen with fibrous protuberances.

Skunk lunged at Totò, who elegantly sidestepped her, dodging each attack, ensuring that the Dogo slammed against the walls of the pit. Nicolas followed each move, teeth on edge, and every time Skunk slammed into the wall his hands went to his head, fingers yanking his hair till it hurt, but each time she immediately charged back into the fray, nothing daunted. On her fifth charge, however, while the Belgian shepherd dodged left, Skunk skidded to a halt and whipped around in a new direction. The two dogs locked in a whirling melee of limbs and fangs, kicking up a cloud of dust into which, for a few seconds, they both vanished from Nicolas's sight. When the cloud subsided, Skunk was panting and looking up at her master, tongue lolling. Nicolas took a step closer to get a better look; that chunk of flesh dangling from Skunk's lips couldn't be hers, it was too rubbery. Then his gaze shifted to Totò, writhing on the ground and spitting out gobbets of blood. Skunk had ripped his tongue out.

"Skunk!" Nicolas waved his arms up and down, as if trying to incite the mob. "Skunk! Skunk!" But the dog stood impassive. Whereupon Nicolas simply flung himself into the pit without bothering to use the ladder, and rolled on the ground, arms wrapped around his championess.

# WAKE

'm sick and tired of everything."

"That's the way things go."

"Even Nicolas. I'm sick and tired of him, too," Drone went on.

"Good things and the things we do badly, well, we just have to do them and not ask why. Once you've decided to live this life, that's the way it is. Today we're here, tomorrow we're gone. That's the way it is, it's not up to us."

"And who decides it?"

"Who decides it . . . who decides it . . ." Drago' stuck both hands in his pockets. "Uh, no one. Things decide for themselves."

He lengthened his stride; he was running late for Biscottino's wake.

Greta's voice could already be heard, loud and powerful, dozens of yards from the *basso*. She didn't sound like a woman annihilated by her loss, as Drone and Drago' had imagined her; instead it sounded as if she were delivering a courtroom summation. If anything, she looked and sounded like one of those preachers you see in American movies.

Drago' took a deep breath, screwed up his courage, and entered the *basso*, dragging Drone behind him—Drone who had changed his mind now and couldn't bring himself to go in. This had been a friend of theirs.

Nicolas had killed him, and by doing so, he'd killed the *paranza*. You can't look a woman in the face who's just lost her son, especially not if she's lost him the way Greta had lost Biscottino.

"So don't look her in the face," Drago' had replied, but there was nothing brash about the way he said it. Just the determination to fortify his courage and choke back the tears that had been stinging his cheeks before Drone could get a look at him. He didn't know whether or not Biscottino really had become a traitor, a Higuain, but one thing was certain, he'd been a friend of theirs, a member of the group.

Inside the apartment, the coffin looked white in the dim light: it had already been welded shut. Inside it were Biscottino's charred remains; they couldn't even have an open casket for one last farewell caress. Greta kept a hand on it, almost as if it were a lifesaver that prevented her from slipping under the water, and in the meantime she spoke to the women of the neighborhood, mothers like her.

"Being men, being boys, is a terrible thing. This is the fate that awaits males. First my husband, and now Eduardo. This country is cursed, and so is this government, and if they want to know the truth, they have to get it from an eleven-year-old child. They couldn't find the truth on their own!"

More women kept arriving, hugging her, then coddling the twins, dressed in mourning but not yet aware that their brother would never be coming home; they stood there, hand in hand, in a corner of the room. Then the women set down the dishes they had cooked for the wake and, with rosaries in their hands, nodded at her words. Drago' screwed up the nerve to get in line behind the women.

"My condolences, signo'," he began, when he finally reached her. "We came to let you know that you can keep the mortgage."

Greta looked at him, expressionless; she'd frozen to the spot and that chill made the hairs stand up on Drago's forearms. He'd never seen a face like hers, or actually, yes, she looked like Uma Thurman, all she was missing was that yellow jumpsuit. She pointed her forefinger right at him as if it were a gat, and then, in that preacher's voice, she bellowed: "You! You killed him! You're all beasts, all wild animals!" She advanced on him threateningly and for an instant Drago' feared that that forefinger might actually be capable of firing lead. "And like wild animals you ought to die, murdered, alone, in pain, betrayed by your friends the way you betrayed your friend. Because Eduardo, because Eduardo, because *Biscottino*, as you always called him, loved you all." And she reached out that hand to claw at him.

But at those words, Drago' had already taken two steps back, and now he turned on his heels and ran, legs trembling, with Drone ahead of him, running even faster.

The next day, Drago' passed by the *basso* once again. He didn't know why his feet had taken him there; he had fooled himself perhaps into thinking that he might be able to say something else to Biscottino's mother about the mortgage, but what he was looking for, if not forgiveness, was a little benevolence. All he found was a green sign stuck to the door and the phone number of a real estate agency. Greta had left the city.

# HERE WE ARE, HERE WE STAY

The only thing they knew about the journalist who was going to be interviewing them was that she was a woman and that she worked for a local news program.

"What do you think she'll be like? Hot, do you think?" asked Briato'.

"Hell, these women on TV, you never know if you're looking at the front of them or the back, they're so damn skinny," said Pesce Moscio in disgust, and as usual the response was a wave of mockery about the fat girls that he always seemed to pick. After the fire, they'd seen one another again at the New Maharaja or in the alleys, but never all together. Nicolas knew that this was finally the right occasion to bring the *paranza* back together: for the first time, they'd tell the world that they existed, they'd make their voices heard. And one way or another, they'd honor Biscottino's memory. But they needed to remain focused, measure their words. "We need to speak without saying." The clubhouse would serve as the set for the interview, and, for the occasion, they'd had the foosball tables and the slot machines moved. Even the poster of Stoya had been carefully folded up and stowed safely. Nothing but white, anonymous walls to make the place unrecognizable. And to make themselves un-recognizable, too, Drone had procured a set of Mephisto ski masks.

"*Ua*', that's too cool," said Tucano, snapping a selfie, and then he turned to Lollipop: "You're still a dickhead, it's not like if you cover up a dick you can't tell it's still a dick."

"*Guagliu*', I want to go on TV, too," said 'o White, but Nicolas shook his head no. "Maraja," he insisted, "now we're just one *paranza*, I have the right." Whereupon Nicolas practically spat in his face that this was an old story, and they, the Children, were the ones to put it to rest. "It's our fuck-ing problem, 'o White," he said, and 'o White swallowed his pride and gave up his claim, rather than blow up the confederation over an appearance on TV.

When Risvoltino saw the journalist arrive with a cameraman follow-ing behind, he launched a signal to Nicolas: the *paranza*, in its entirety, lined up against the wall, faces covered with black ski masks that left only eyes and mouth visible, Maraja at the center, and Drago' and Lollipop, the two tallest, on either end. In front of the wall's flaking plaster, the row of masked youngsters might just as easily have been seen on the outskirts of any of the world's big cities. That was the first thought that occurred to the woman as she entered the room and found them waiting, and if she was surprised or frightened, she certainly gave no sign. She ex-tended her hand toward the masked figure who was staring at her with a magnetic gaze, a pair of dark eyes that would pierce the television screen exactly as desired. Excellent, she decided. While her cameraman set up the tripod, she explained how she planned to conduct the interview. "Feel free to talk, and to use curse words now and then, if you like. The more at ease you seem, the better. I understand your situation, for real, I've been working on this topic for a long time, and this is finally an opportunity to shed a little light on the blighted outskirts of our country's cities . . ."

"Signuri'," Drago' interrupted her, "actually, we're here in the center of the city."

"Yes, of course, but it's your social setting that marginalizes you, casts you aside . . ."

"Like fuck, signuri'," said Nicolas, his eyes turning flinty. "Forcella is our home, and we're the ones who give the orders here."

The journalist instinctively took a step backward. Her body had sensed the danger even before she realized what was happening, a few seconds later, that these weren't the usual "disadvantaged youth" that she was accustomed to interviewing. She recomposed her face into a steady, professional smile, but maintained the distance she had established, then turned to her cameraman and told him that the interview could begin.

"Are you the boss here?" she asked Nicolas.

"Yes," Nicolas promptly replied. He was about to add something, but then his gaze buried itself deep in the black rectangle of the video camera, and it dawned on him that that answer hadn't been right. "No," he tried to correct himself, "*siamo brò*, we're brothers. No one's superior to anyone else here . . ." And here he took a pause to search for the right word. "This is a democracy."

The journalist nodded and extended the microphone under the nose of another ski mask.

"What do you want to be when you grow up?"

"I'm already grown up," Tucano replied.

"How old are you?"

"Eighteen."

"And what do you do for a living?"

"We're businessmen," Briato' replied.

"Ah, and what kind of business are you involved in, specifically?"

"Things . . ."

"Could I ask you to be just a bit more detailed?"

"Logistics and large-scale distribution," came Drone's voice, promptly.

"What do you all want to do when you grow up?"

"What we're doing now," Drone replied again.

"And when you're older?"

"I don't want to get old," said Lollipop. "That's gross!"

The journalist sat there nonplussed for a few seconds, then used that answer to plunge to the heart of the interview: "So you're not afraid of the violence on these streets?"

"We're not afraid of anything," Lollipop confirmed, and all those ski-masked heads nodded in unison. "*Adda murì mammà.*" Pesce Moscio put the seal of approval on it.

"I understand . . ." she said, and turned to look at the cameraman. Only a quarter turn. That was the signal for him to tighten the frame; she was about to ask the key question.

"Do you deal narcotics?"

Smiles and eyes turning in all directions. One of them said something incomprehensible and the smiles turned into a collective burst of laughter.

"We aren't dirt farmers," Nicolas said after a short pause, pulling the reins back into his own hands. "Signori', we don't have jobs. If there had been any jobs for us . . ."

"True," said Drago', "they've abandoned us . . ."

"Everyone's moving out of the center . . ."

"Weapons. Do you have any weapons on you?" the journalist asked, ignoring their round of complaints.

"Signori', these are things we don't talk about . . ."

"Do you consider yourselves vicious?"

"Not vicious, we just take what we want."

"And do you take these things that you want illegally, at times?"

"Dottore'," said Nicolas, "legal, illegal . . . I mean, come on, it's as old as the Cippus of Forcella. Legal is if you can afford it, and illegal is if you can't. You're illegal until you can pay to make it legal."

The whole crew burst out laughing and cried, "Wow, that's huge, brother!"

"The drive-bys, the firefights, the murders," the journalist went on. "We read all about it in the newspapers, and they say that this neighborhood has turned into a war zone. What do you think?"

"Eh, those are things that happen . . ."

"So does that mean that you're responsible for all the murders that take place in Naples?"

The ski masks all turned toward the young man who had retracted his leadership. Nicolas knew that this answer could be a double-edged sword: on the one hand, it would attract the investigators of the district attorney's office, and on the other it would make it clear to anyone else who was watching that they decided the good and bad weather in that city.

"What can I tell you? If you set foot on our streets, you'll always find us," said Nicolas.

"Excuse me, how do you mean?" the journalist asked.

"We're here. If you set foot on our streets, you'll always find us."

The cameraman narrowed the shot until those dark eyes filled the frame. The interview was over.

The journalist had left just a few minutes earlier when Drone, still wearing his Mephisto ski mask, went over to Nicolas.

"Nico'," he said in a worried tone, "you wait and see, now everyone's going to come after us."

"*Guagliu*," Drago' weighed in. "We need to put our gats somewhere else, at home, anywhere else, so we don't get caught with them."

Nicolas hoped for an incursion and search. It would be a reaction, proof that everyone was afraid of the *paranza*. He was sick and tired of seeing the old myth live on in the minds of judges, policemen, carabinieri, and financial police, the legend that children can't command the underworld, that that kind of power is vested exclusively in the old bosses, mature men. Maturity, Nicolas decided, leads to fear, and fear leads to death. They were the Piranhas, the only ones capable of managing power in their own time, here, immediately, without a thought for tomorrow.

That very same night, all the members of the *paranza* received house calls from the police.

"Please, come right in," said Nicolas's mother. "And all this uproar is for what? For a boy?"

"*Mamma mia*, what is all this? Are you busting into the house of an ISIS terrorist?" asked Drone's father.

Pesce Moscio's father, on the other hand, rushed right over to his son and slapped him in the face. "What have you done now?"

"Me? Nothing!" his son retorted.

In response to those questions, the police offered the same weary formulation: "We're just doing our job. Sit down and we'll leave as soon as we're done."

The officers turned the place upside down. They searched under the beds, in the clothes closets, in the dresser drawers, inside the household appliances. They found nothing, not even a chunk of hash, and they left with a handful of paper, their short after-action reports.

The Italian police left those homes amid a hail of insults from the families of the members of the *paranza*, and climbed into their squad cars, passing bike racks and flowerpots just a few dozen yards from the apartment buildings. Bike racks and flowerpots where the Piranhas had hidden their everyday weapons.

## THE PARANZA COMES FROM THE SEA

O n Tuesday we're going fishing in Salerno."

They were sitting around a table in a Mexican restaurant that had recently opened to great acclaim: El Pueblo, sombreros and ponchos hanging on the walls, with pictures that might have been thought to conjure up an atmosphere of warmth, including photographs of chili peppers, bulls, and shatteringly blue seas. Tucano had insisted on going; after all, at this point there was a table ready for them in any club or restaurant in the city, and he wanted to try them all. In the end, Nicolas had given in: "All right, let's hold this summit at El Pueblo."

As the bottles of Moët started taking effect ("But do they even drink *moetta* in Mexico?" Pesce Moscio had wondered aloud), the restaurant also started emptying out.

"All of this stuff has the symbol of Arcangelo on it. That's what 'o Bross told me," Nicolas told them.

"And what did you say to him, Maraja?" Briato' asked, stuffing his face with a fajita. It was the fourth time Nicolas had been asked the question.

"I told him that I'd be changing that, and that I'd be putting an *F* on it all."

"And then?"

"And then he asked me: 'F for Fiorillo?' 'No,' I told him, 'F for Forcella.'"

And off they went with another toast: "To Forcella!" they shouted to the clinking of crystal. "The sky's the limit!"

"*Ua'*, you know how Biscottino would have liked this party?" Drone said, and Tucano shot back promptly: "If you look to the past, you're going to get passed by."

Drago' slammed down his glass, noisily. "No, that's not the past," he said, "that's not the past at all. Biscottino should have been here. I never believed he was a traitor."

Nicolas decided that it was best not to overlook that comment: "The fact that we're here, the fact that we have all this under our control, is all due to the fact that we sweep all suspicions aside. Just one suspicion, and we're flat on our asses. That guy had the squad cars after him, he wasn't right for this *paranza*. He was our brother, but he isn't anymore."

"It's tough, but that's the way it is," said Drago', as he put a hand on Drone's shoulder.

"That's the way it is, *guagliu'*," said Tucano definitively, as he raised his glass: "To Forcella."


The first shipment was due to dock at the port of Salerno in five days; that Saturday, with a hot sun that had set an hour ago but was still somehow shedding light, the *paranza* was perched around the liquefied petroleum gas pumps at a service station overlooking the port. From high in the hills, they were able to keep an eye on the container ships coming in and going out, with the aid of a pair of military binoculars Lollipop had obtained through a trusted Ukrainian he employed on his piazza.

"There she is, that's the ship!" shouted Briato'. Nicolas grabbed the binoculars from his hands, but gave them right back to him after a quick look.

"*Nzù*," he said, dismissively. "I don't know." 'O Bross hadn't given him instructions on how to identify the cargo, he'd just assured him that he'd recognize it. "Does this thing have night vision, too?" Nicolas asked.

Lollipop fiddled with it, turning it over in his hands as if it were an alien object, and then, at last, said that it was all set.

"Maraja," shouted Tucano, "it's that one! Look close!"

"*Nzù*," Nicolas said again, dubiously, but this time he held on to the binoculars. He was starting to be sick and tired of this game. If the ship 'o Bross had promised him never came into port, he'd have lost everything: credibility, cash, power, the city itself. The confederation project with the Longhairs would be dead on arrival and the old men buried in their houses, shuttered in their armor-plated quarters, would go on giving the orders and calling the shots. His own *paranza*, maybe with no place to go, might well disintegrate.

Nicolas clenched the binoculars as tightly as his hands could grip. The floodlights poured into the lenses in greenish bursts, while on either side of him he could hear the others seething with impatience prolonged by their imposed immobility. Mario 'o Bross had guaranteed that the *tripulantes* aboard the freighter would take care to send him a signal. And he'd made a point of specifying: "The *tripulantes* are the ones who convey the shit from Point A to Point B. Without them, you're not worth a fucking thing."

"So this ship, is it arriving or isn't it, Maraja?" asked Drago'.

*Nzù*, he was ready to answer him again, but then he saw them. Four shipping containers on a cargo ship that had just entered the port. On each container, an enormous *F*. That was the signal.

Nicolas tossed the binoculars to Lollipop and ordered the others to get moving. "It's here, *guagliu'*, our shit has sailed into port!"

Down at the port, a rubber dinghy was waiting for them, with the propeller turning and a Maghrebi of few words and many grunts at the helm.

"Wait, you're a *scafista*!" Tucano exclaimed enthusiastically the minute he saw him, using the slang term for people smuggler.

"Are you the *tripulantes*?" Nicolas asked him.

The only answer was the sound of the propeller. And then, almost impossible to hear over the lapping of the water, his voice: "Silence."

He was taking them under the sheer hull of the container ship at demented speed, lights out, in order to lessen the odds of being intercepted in that narrow stretch of water. The engine made the bow of the boat rear up, and then periodically bellyflop, showering the passengers with spray. Nicolas took the spray in his face and smiled, drinking it in; the salt water sweetened everything he'd had to put up with over the past few weeks.

"Forcella! Forcella! Forcella!" the *paranza* started chanting in low voices, in the bass timbre of a clandestine cheer. The Maghrebi once again issued his order to remain silent, but by now Nicolas felt as if he were fully and legitimately Maraja. We are the Piranhas, he said to himself, and we always will be.

The Maghrebi silenced the motor and let the rubber dinghy pitch and roll until it was just a few yards from the hull of the cargo ship. Lollipop leaned out to touch it, feeling for a ladder to climb up to the deck, but the Maghrebi yanked on his T-shirt, making him tumble back among the seats, and lifted a finger to his lips.

"Silence," Maraja said, too, and he lifted his finger and pointed it at his ear.

In that horizonless darkness, a dull, muffled sound. Splash. And the dinghy started rocking a little more heavily.

They all whipped around in surprise; something had fallen into the water behind them.

Splash, splash. To their right. Two more heavy thuds.

Splash, splash, splash, splash. Now they were raining down in all directions.

They started searching for the bricks, sweeping the beams of their flashlights over the water around them, and trying to fish them out with their arms. In the excitement of that treasure hunt, Lollipop was the first to lose his balance, and after him, Drone plunged in headfirst, followed by Pesce Moscio and Drago'. They started splashing one another, ripping off their T-shirts and pulling one another under the surface, improvising flips and races. Then, when Tucano took his clothes off, and even his underpants, the Maghrebi, completely disgusted, abandoned any efforts to reduce them to silence. He cursed them in his language and started shouting himself, berating them for the assholes they were, for the mere children they were, and they replied in chorus that of course that's what they were, they were the Piranhas, and everyone knew it. At that point, the man threatened to leave, abandoning them there, and went back to the helm, but he changed his mind when he saw that the ones aboard the dinghy were helping the others back aboard, even though in the process Briato' pushed Lollipop back into the water, unleashing a burst of hilarity.

Once order had more or less been restored, the *tripulantes* opened an ice chest and gave each of them a fishing net. "Fish for them," he said.

The packets that they hauled aboard looked just like the ones they'd seen plenty of times before, but these were heavier, and protected by a waterproof wrapping. They fished out fifty or so, competing to see who could catch the biggest haul, as if they were at an amusement park. The Maghrebi was resigned to it by now, and he watched them with his arms crossed.

Nicolas, Drago', Pesce Moscio, Briato', Lollipop, Drone, Tucano. They'd all regressed to middle school, when all it took was any old piece of bullshit to amuse them. They looked around in search of others laughing and swapped hilarity each with the other. It was fine to be brothers again, it was fine to be a *paranza*. Since the burning of the lair, since the death of Biscottino, this was the first time they could remember sharing that feeling.

They returned to port, they said farewell to the pilot—"*Allahu akbar*"— and they hopped into their cars, heading toward the nearby quarries of Cernicchiara, where they would store the drugs before transporting them the rest of the way into the city in the days that followed. 'O Bross had told Nicolas that the most dangerous part of the whole operation would in fact not be the storage, but the final stage. They needed to think of a safe place not far from the piazzas: close enough to ensure a rapid resupply but far enough to avoid arousing suspicions.

"A gym," Nicolas had said.

"A gym?" 'o Bross had asked, cocking a skeptical eyebrow.

"A gym in a school, at night, when no one's around."

"You learn fast, Fiorillo." And for once he'd nodded.

The members of the *paranza* concealed the narcotics in an abandoned secondary tunnel, under a tarp, but Nicolas kept a brick of cocaine for himself. "This, brothers," he said, "is just for us." He cut it crosswise and scattered the white powder on a steel counter.

# FULL METAL JACKET

xygen. Nicolas Fiorillo Maraja had become the master of oxygen. And oxygen is like Google: free of charge, and vitally necessary to one and all. 'O Bross's drugs kept coming, punctually, as promised to the managers of the piazzas. Now Nicolas Fiorillo was God. He imparted life. He imparted air for every human being to breathe. And the first act of God had been free of charge. Just like Google, in fact. First to his *paranza*, infusing them with new blood and sweeping away doubts and fragilities. Then to the *paranza* of the Longhairs, to cement the alliance with the strongest bond there is, the bond of air that allows you to live.

Nicolas had given drugs to one and all, and they had all taken it around, given it to others, as if it were His word. And Susamiello, Risvoltino, and Pachi had taken him at his word. They had printed out a photo of Nicolas, and from that they had made a thousand reproductions, a thousand saint cards with his image that they distributed as they made their deliveries. At first Nicolas had lost his temper, because along with those saint cards, word had spread that he issued mortgages to whoever asked, found work for those who needed it, and even gave PlayStations to those who prayed to his brother, Christian, the martyr. Then he realized that holiness and saintliness could come in handy. Because a saint always has a flock of worshipful followers.

Then he had even distributed with a free hand to 'o White and his men a few of the weapons from the arsenal, to protect the drugs and to bind them even more tightly to him.

They had been to the beach at Bagnoli a thousand times, on outings and field trips. Now the Naples City of Science was being rebuilt, but that stony little beach was still there.

'O White lined them up before him. Illuminated by the light of the full moon alone, they seemed even paler than they were: a down-at-the-heels platoon of survivors and junkies. Carlito's Way still bore the scars of Micione's torture session—a scar at the corners of his mouth that widened his smile like the Joker's, and a broken nose, shoved to one side, like a boxer who'd had his bell rung once too often—but he didn't seem too troubled about it. Ever since he'd substituted the teeth that had been forcibly extracted with new gold teeth, he spent half his time running his tongue over his incisors, as if he was trying to polish them. 'O Selvaggio had been exercising the muscles he used to play foosball, and Orso Ted had grown even fatter, if possible, and with his head shaven clean he was the spitting image of Gomer Pyle in *Full Metal Jacket*.

We're a squad of dead men walking, 'o White thought to himself, but that thought vanished as quickly as it had arrived. Ever since the speech that Nicolas had delivered on the roof of the clubhouse, 'o White had no longer questioned the inevitability of the confederation: "Better to be the tail of the gray mullet than the head of the anchovy." He saw himself as the head of the confederation just a few years in the future, with Nicolas filling his glass with Moët & Chandon. He just needed to be patient, send Maraja on ahead, let him do the dirty work.

In the meantime, he needed to get his *paranza* in line. They needed to start shooting again, become dangerous again. Then he'd climb over Nicolas, and he, 'o White, would show them all that he was the real boss, and the only time you're a real boss is when you're not afraid to die.

He reviewed his Longhairs. He gave Orso Ted a pat on his straining belly, and ordered 'o Selvaggio to stand up straight. Carlito's Way had snapped to attention and done a downward cutaway salute. 'O White smoothed out his samurai ponytail in a sign of approval.

Orso Ted still had the backpack full of weapons slung over his shoulder. 'O White pulled open the zipper just wide enough to stick an arm in, then he went back and stood in front of his troops, holding a grenade in one hand. He tossed it into the air and caught it as it fell, confidently. He pulled the pin and tossed the hand grenade into the distance, deafening his men for a short while. He went and got another grenade: "Think quick," he said, and tossed the hand grenade toward 'o Selvaggio, who unexpectedly leaped forward and caught it with both hands.

"Almost wet your pants, didn't you, eh?" said 'o White. His grinning teeth splayed open in the moonlight. "On your feet! I said, up on your feet!" He wasn't muttering, his voice was flat and brisk and martial, and 'o Selvaggio decided that his boss had become a boss when someone else told him he never would be one. He got to his feet and clutched the hand grenade tight to his belly, as if it might explode from one minute to the next.

"Let's see how many minutes you hold it," said 'o White. "Pull the pin."

'O Selvaggio looked at Carlito's Way and Orso Ted, but they were gazing off at the horizon like good soldiers. He stuck his finger into the ring holding the pin and yanked it, without pulling it entirely out. Orso Ted and Carlito's Way dropped to the ground cursing, while 'o Selvaggio got rid of the hand grenade by hurling it into the sea the way you'd get rid of a jellyfish that was wrapped around your calf. The hand grenade went plop and sank into the black waves.

"That time you really did shit your pants, Selva'." 'O White laughed. He walked over to Orso Ted and once again stuck his arm into the backpack. Another hand grenade.

"Look here, *guagliu'*," and he walked into the water. He'd read on the Internet that the detonator on that hand grenade—an MK2—went off after six seconds. He pulled the pin, let the handle fly, and started counting in a loud voice.

"One." And he held the grenade high over his head.

"Two." And he reached his arm back behind his shoulders.

"Three." And he raised his other arm, in the pose of a shot-putter.

"Four."

'O Selvaggio felt a dense, warm liquid splash over his face. He spat it out and wiped his eyes with the back of his hand, just in time to see 'o White in the position that he remembered, but now missing at least half of his body. Orso Ted and Carlito's Way were shouting, but to him they looked like a couple of mimes—the shock wave had left 'o Selvaggio temporarily deaf.

'O White stood there for another second or two, then what was left of him flopped down into the water.

And that was how 'o White, boss of the Longhairs, left this world, betrayed by a countdown and an inaccurate piece of information.

# ASSASSINATION ATTEMPT

**M**assimiliano liked his upside-down life. Working at night, when there was no noise, and going to sleep in the morning. The graveyard shift at the repair shop had always been his, and the fact that he worked on scooters and that they had promised him an employment contract as an apprentice didn't really bother him all that much, even if he did have some considerable experience under his belt as a mechanic working on racing cars. He was striding briskly down Via dei Tribunali, and he slowed down only when he found himself face-to-face with a young man his same age hauling on a leash that was fastened to the collar of a somewhat recalcitrant dog.

"Come on, Skunk," the other young man was saying, jerking on the marine rope he was using as a leash. Massimiliano walked past man and dog without recognizing him; Nicolas, on the other hand, delved into his mental archive where he had a filing system for all the faces in the neighborhood. The mechanic, he told himself, and then went back to scolding Skunk, whose ears had pricked up: "Skunk, what's wrong?"

Massimiliano continued on his way and turned left, onto Via Duomo. Nicolas saw him vanish around the corner and at that same instant heard three distinct shots, like the sound of a scooter's carburetor as it accelerated.

Instinctively, he drew his handgun and dropped to the ground, head flat against the asphalt, pulling Skunk close. Then he heard seven gunshots, in rapid succession, or maybe there were more. When he raised his head again, he saw a man in a full-face helmet riding a scooter, roaring away. An assassination attempt, in the heart of Forcella.

Nicolas emerged onto the street, with Skunk barking at the end of her leash, and looked around, but he already knew that he wasn't going to encounter any other would-be shooters. Whoever it was that had tried to kill him had been afraid; otherwise there was no explanation for those shots in tight sequence, fired practically at random. He stuck his head around the corner of Via Duomo, and there he was. Massimiliano's corpse, hit by two bullets, one in the shoulder, the other one, the fatal shot, to the jugular. Nicolas stepped close, with respect. That poor sucker had taken the bullets meant for him. Massimiliano had saved Nicolas's life: the assassin must have taken the mechanic for him.

"Skunk, be good," said Nicolas, and at last the dog calmed down. Then he holstered his pistol, crossed himself, and turned to go.

Forcella was a teeming locus of ambulances and police squad cars, even if there had been only one victim. Nicolas had been able to make it back home before the arrival of law enforcement, before the various checkpoints and roadblocks had been set up and the neighborhood was militarized. News of the attempt had spread at lightning speed, by word of mouth, but the crucial detail of who had been killed remained unclear. Was Nicolas Maraja really dead?

At that point, the Piranhas packed into Briato's Cayenne and went over to Nicolas's apartment house, and Nicolas himself looked out the window.

"I love you all, I love you so much, too much," he said, fist raised, like a head of state who'd miraculously survived a coup attempt and whose first thoughts were for his people and their future, a future that a few rotten apples couldn't keep from being brilliant. And his people replied, in chorus: "You're a miracle, Nico', you're a miracle. Long live Maraja!"

With Mena and Letizia, the whole thing wasn't likely to go off that smoothly. His mother had come to meet him, as always, at the front door.

"You're here," she'd said, and then she'd thrown her arms around him as if to make sure that he was flesh and blood, and not blue smoke. She'd gazed at him, pride in her eyes, the pride of a mother who always sees her son taking first place. She'd turned over the palms of his hands, skinned and scraped from the rough asphalt: "These are like stigmata, you're safe because Our Lord wishes it so," she said, and stroked his hands. "You're special, Nico', don't you ever forget it."

Before he could think of forgetting it, Letizia arrived: "My love," she said, throwing her arms wide, more to be embraced than to embrace him. "Are you hurt?" she asked him a second later.

"I'm fine, my love," said Nicolas, planting a kiss on her belly. "No one can do me any harm."

"Who was it?" She'd been crying and she did nothing to hide the mascara that had run down her face to the corners of her mouth.

"A traitor, my love. Don't think about it now, don't get yourself upset." He helped her to sit down, then he got a chair for himself and sat down across from her. She made him tell the story down to the smallest detail, telling Skunk all the sweet words that she could think of for her. "Do you realize that Skunk saved your life? If she hadn't been there, Nico', what might have happened? How would that have left me and the little girl?"

That's how he found out that it was going to be a baby girl. "For real?" he asked, and he was filled with an unrestrained joy. He lifted Letizia into the air and danced her in a circle, then hugged her tight.

"Really, are you happy about it, Nico'? I didn't have the courage to tell you it would be a girl, that I wasn't going to give you a son." Her eyes welled with tears. "But then I thought you could have died today, that you could have been that young man crumpled on the ground, and you would never have known that a baby girl was about to arrive." She took his hands and placed them on her belly, as round as the globe. "Nico', you have to swear to me that you'll be more careful: you're a father now, you can't afford to risk leaving us alone. A father has to protect the future, a father has to protect his family. That means he has to protect himself." It seemed as if she had rehearsed that speech in her head many times already. "Think about it, Nico'. I'm not trying to meddle in your business, you know that, but it's different now."

"I think about it, Leti', I think about you all the time, you're my life and soul. Don't worry, I already told you. I'll take care of everything, but now you need to go away for a little while, until we can find the traitor. The place in Vomero is still under construction, but you can stay there. It's better if people think no one's living there yet. They're delivering the furniture next week. Right now, all you need is mattresses, and Mammà will take care of that."

Letizia pressed her hand over his mouth, silencing him: "That's enough now. It's bad luck to talk about these things . . ." And she gave him a gentle kiss on the lips.

Nicolas recoiled: "So what's that kiss?"

"What do you mean, what's that kiss? A kiss of affection, because I care for you."

"I don't want a kiss of caring," said Nicolas, and pulled her close.

"Careful with my belly, Nico'," said Letizia.

"I don't want the kiss on the cheek that goes with caring. I don't want the kiss on the lips that goes with love. I want the savage kiss that takes whatever it wants. That takes it all."

# THE BASKET OF APPLES

ast time you behaved badly with that hundred euros, really a bit of an oaf."

"I had that special gift for you, and I had to give it to you in a hurry, it was starting to stink."

"Still, you were rude."

"This time she seemed contented."

"What did you bring her?"

"Flowers from Capodimonte."

*"Bravo, guaglio'."*

They'd embraced and then they'd exchanged a few standard words, tokens of politeness.

Nicolas didn't tell L'Arcangelo that traveling the streets of Ponticelli was like driving a car in the Paris–Dakar rally. Potholes, lurches, sudden gaps in the pavement, lanes that sloped off to each side until they basically merged with the sidewalks. A pothole, or even a speed bump that had been sabotaged, leaving only discontinuous chunks of murderous asphalt, had caused him to swerve too sharply, chipping one of the roses in the floral arrangement. Nicolas hadn't noticed it until he was actually standing in front of Professoressa Cicatello, whereupon he'd asked her to wait just a moment; he'd found the porcelain petal mixed in with the banknotes, then he'd rung at a random door and had asked to borrow a tube of Attack adhesive. The result was questionable, the scar was quite visible, but Nicolas had never been an especially good handyman. He'd hurried back up to Professoressa Cicatello's door, apologized, handed her the centerpiece, and had finally been able to go upstairs.

They'd sat down in the kitchen because the living room was off-limits, crammed with 'o Cicognone's working implements. Don Vittorio had told him to install a more powerful air-conditioning system, and to spare no expense. 'O Cicognone had dismantled all the old equipment, which now lay scattered on plastic tarps, and he was unpacking the latest-generation machinery that would replace it.

L'Arcangelo had finally cut his hair. His locks no longer spilled over his ears and down the back of his neck in dirty curls; now his hair was neatly brushed, with a part on the right. He even smelled different, with a hint of cedar wafting off him.

Nicolas had unzipped his backpack and was stacking wads of cash on the table: four stacks of hundred-euro notes, which he was stacking one by one. L'Arcangelo let him work. He alternated his gaze between the cash and Nicolas. He lit a Toscano cigar, toyed idly with the ashtray, but never said a word. Why would he want to spoil that show?

"This month, we're selling like crazy," said Nicolas. He ran a finger over the last wad of notes like a croupier, producing the sound of rustling bills. "This is your end, forty thousand euros. Don Vitto', admit it, you're not sorry that you've taken us on as partners."

*Partner* was the word that had hovered in the air since they'd greeted each other. L'Arcangelo had thought about it and Nicolas had thought about it. *Partner* meant democracy, equal rights and equal responsibilities. There was an investor and there was someone who worked out in the field, but still, each played a role, each had a share.

"Maraja, of course I'm not sorry. And I'm even happier to know that I still have a partner."

"So you heard that they're trying to rub me out?" Nicolas replied promptly. He wasn't surprised that L'Arcangelo knew about the assassination attempt. The night before, the local TV news report had led with the story. Another innocent victim. Another dead man, collateral damage in the gang war. How much longer would this slaughter continue? Forever, Nicolas had mentally answered as he walked past a newsstand where the banner headlines of the morning papers were crowding the sidewalk. When will they understand that this city is at war? he'd asked himself. If they'd only admit that, these journalists would already have done half their job.

"The *paranza* is going to find out who did it, and fast," said Nicolas. As he entered the kitchen he'd immediately identified the place where 'o Cicognone kept the spare whiskey for when the level in the bottle on the sideboard in the living room dropped to just two fingers. He got up on tiptoes and reached for the high shelf, above their heads, and chose a bottle of Masterson's. "We're going to unleash a slaughter," he went on, "the streets are going to run red, or really I should say, they'll run brown, because that traitor's blood is brown like shit."

With the bottle in his hand, he went over to the dish rack and grabbed two glasses at random. He filled them and raised his own, in a brisk gesture at a toast, then drained it to the last drop.

"But you know, Maraja, that if everyone else is looking up, you have to look down. If everyone else is looking out, you have to look in. You always have to look where everyone else isn't," L'Arcangelo said as he sipped his whiskey. "And when these things happen, you need to look in your friends' pockets more than in your enemies' pockets. More dangerous than the basket of vipers is the basket of apples. The problem is never with the vipers."

"If you're referring to my basket, we're all brothers in my *paranza*."

"If you say so, then it must be true."

"Don Vitto'," said Nicolas. He was starting to feel a glow of heat, and it wasn't just on account of the Masterson's, though that certainly didn't keep him from pouring himself another glass. "You're saying and you're not saying—why don't you just spit out what you mean?"

"You know your business, it's your life and it's your *paranza*."

"I know how to spot traitors, and I don't have any around me, at least not for now."

"When they tried to shoot you, where were you going?"

"I was taking the dog for a walk."

"And who knows when you do that, and where you go when you do?"

Don Vittorio was pouring himself a second glass of whiskey and hefting the stacks of bills. "A hundred-euro note still weighs one gram," he said.

Nicolas on the other hand was mulling over the question that L'Arcangelo had asked him. Who knew? Everyone knew. He hadn't been so blind as not to ask himself the same question, as he sat watching TV, where the carabinieri were pacing around that red patch on the pavement, keeping rubberneckers away. He decided that he didn't deserve that fool's death, he needed to die like a boss, shot in the face or in the back of the head. He'd imagined it plenty of times before, but to die like that, while you're taking a dog out to pee, around a corner, in your own neighborhood . . .

"They'd been waiting for you," L'Arcangelo resumed. "You shit your pants, huh? Did you get a yellow stain?" And he gave Nicolas a kiss on the forehead.

"But who did it, Don Vitto'? Micione? The guys from Secondigliano?"

"Why would they want to shoot you?" L'Arcangelo asked, trying to make him think it through.

"Because I'm busting their balls."

L'Arcangelo started to pour another glass of whiskey but then decided against it. "*Nzù*," he said, little more than the sound of a clucking tongue. "*Nzù*. That's not reason enough, just because someone's busting your balls."

"Micione wants me dead."

"Then why haven't they shot you before? Because you have immunity."

"Immunity?"

"The immunity of your age, *guaglio'*. If someone shoots a kid, he's telling the world that that kid has the power to fuck him. Think how stupid that would make him look. The problem is that you're growing up, so now your immunity . . . Well, who do you think it was?"

"Whoever wants to take my place . . ."

L'Arcangelo nodded: "Huh, and who thinks they have the right to take your place?"

Those words made a suspicion echo in his mind, a suspicion that dated far back in time, a doubt that had lain well concealed until that very instant, so hidden that he'd never thought he even had the doubt. And now that he saw it, the harder he peered to minimize it and ridicule it, the more it grew and the harder it laughed at him, mocking him.

"Don Vittorio," said Nicolas, "I understand what you're trying to tell me."

"Actually, I'm not trying to tell you anything."

"But you meant Luigi Striano."

"You're the one who said that name."

"Don Vitto', Drago' is a brother to me. When he's behind me, I never think of turning around."

"Well, that's your mistake. A Striano he is and a Striano he'll always be."

"You don't understand, Don Vitto"—and now he was talking to convince both the other man and the part of him that had suddenly stirred awake—"Drago' even came to tell me that Micione wanted to turn him against me. If he was a traitor, a Higuain, he'd never have told me."

L'Arcangelo burst out laughing. "The best way to kill your enemy is to marry him." He was blowing hard on Nicolas's doubts, kindling them into flame, and that smoldering fire was kicking up a plume of smoke that clouded his memories and certainties.

"No, Don Vitto', stop . . ."

But L'Arcangelo was no longer listening to him. He'd gone over to the refrigerator; there must have been some leftover pastries from last Sunday. "First he married you, and now he's going to get them to give him Forcella, Maraja."

Nicolas felt his mouth pucker, his teeth on edge. He continued to click tongue against palate, the same way that that obsessive thought kept pounding in his head.

"Anyway," said L'Arcangelo, setting the tray of pastries down on the table. "Try these rum babas, sweeten your mouth a little, since it's turned too bitter just now."

"No, Don Vittorio, I'm fine, but thanks." He pictured himself in a puddle of blood. The sonogram sprawled on the asphalt, the flashes of photographers snapping pictures. The death of a fool.

"Come on, try this rum baba, *ja'*." He waited for Nicolas to bite into it. "Isn't it good? The best babas have always been made on the outskirts of town. In the center of town, all you can find is babas for tourists. Maraja, when you're in command, everyone's your brother and no one's your brother. The way you command is by making everyone believe that you trust them, but actually by not trusting anyone."

L'Arcangelo filled the glasses once again.

"Are you sure it wasn't Striano who shot at you?"

"I'm sure it wasn't."

"Only God can know for certain, but maybe we can find proof."

"Really?"

"Let me explain."

# PROOF

*hillo.*" Him. The one.

In the days that followed the assassination attempt, it seemed as though everyone had learned to pronounce just that one word: "*Chillo.*"

Briato' drowned him in a hail of texts. He wrote, "Keep an eye out for him," defining the whole matter in terms of the protection of the *paranza*.

"Maraja," said Tucano, "this guy must exist because he has a surname."

"*Chillo,*" Drone kept saying, and so did Lollipop, and even a few of the youngsters.

No one, except for L'Arcangelo, ever uttered first and last name, that would have been pointless, and after all, "*Chillo*" no longer deserved even the modicum of respect afforded by having been baptized.

Nicolas even reached the point of thinking that they were all in cahoots in shoving aside the most dangerous pretender to the throne, all of them rutting, competing, each availing himself of his own special skills. Hadn't he himself, when all was said and done, proven exactly how feasible such a thing really was? *Nothing is impossible* and *Just do it*, the mottoes that he'd had tattooed on his forearms, in English.

For a few days Nicolas had lain low in Lollipop's gym, after he'd persuaded his folks to keep it shut to the public by slamming a stack of bills on the table, twenty thousand euros: "Let's put in a bigger sauna, it'll take at least a week for the construction." Then when he was sick of sleeping on aerobics mats and eating takeout pizza, he decided to take L'Arcangelo's advice. He picked up his phone: fifty texts from his *paranzini*, but not a thing on the *paranza*'s chat. So then he wrote a message to everyone.

**Maraja**
Tomorrow. Warehouse.

They no longer felt the need to dress like their grandparents on a Sunday just to walk into a bank. Nicolas showed up in the sweatpants from his tracksuit and a sweatshirt with a hood, and the others also arrived dressed the way they usually did, or even more down-at-the-heels and ragtag. By now they were familiar with the procedure, just as the security guard by now knew them: they walked through the metal detector one by one, at their ease, firmly holding the garbage bags full of cash to be deposited. That was the main reason for this trip to the bank: they were all going to have to strip themselves of their weapons in order to get through the metal detector. Tucano carried a suitcase full of money. "Next time, a little less ostentatious might be preferable," said the manager. "I've already had to tell everyone that you're the soccer team my son plays on." "Sure enough, boss, we're your son's soccer team, we brought you a bag that he left on the field after the game," said Nicolas. He set the bag down on the manager's desk and asked, according to the traditional method, for a new line of credit to furnish the apartment in Vomero. He wanted to make sure that Letizia and Cristiana wanted for nothing; he was eager to spoil them and provide for their future. He'd said it to Mena, too: "When I'm not around anymore, Mammà, I've left you the shop," and tears had come to her eyes.

Everything went smoothly for the line of credit and the new deposits; the manager made a point of giving them special treatment. "*Grazie, Diretto*," Tucano had thanked him at the end. "Thanks to you, we can even skip the line in your bank," and he'd indulged in a complicit laugh.

When they left, before returning to his cloister in the gym, Nicolas said that he wanted to swing by his house to change his clothes, and everyone offered to accompany him.

"I don't need an escort, all I need is Drago'," said Nicolas.

Briato' took him aside: "That's not safe, Maraja, just him alone isn't enough."

"We'll be your bodyguards," said Tucano.

"We've just left the bank, we don't have our gats!" Nicolas retorted. "If those guys shoot, what are you going to do?" That was the end of the discussion.

They swarmed off, each taking a different direction. To Nicolas they looked like a school of minnows scattering at the approach of a predator.

"Let's go, Lui'," said Nicolas. "You and I haven't had a chance to talk in far too long."

Drago' nodded seriously. Nobody in the *paranza* had ever called him Luigi, and that name hit him now as if it had been uttered by Viola, drawing on a family connection that Nicolas had always scorned. It was true, they hadn't talked in a long while, since he'd first told Nicolas about his meeting with Micione. Then everything had been swept away in the rush of events, money, deaths. The attempt. A year ago, they couldn't wait to grow up, and now time wouldn't stop to wait for them.

In the past few days, it had seemed to him that the others were making a point of establishing a distance from him; he could especially sense the mistrust of Briato' and Tucano. The attempt had disturbed every equilibrium. Even Nicolas, who had never displayed any doubt toward him, was wavering. What was it? he wondered. Who could have pointed an accusing finger at him with such vehemence that it had made Maraja change his mind? Why had he asked him alone to go with him, and why was he letting him come upstairs and into his home?

Once at home, Nicolas quickly packed a bag with a few changes of clothes; Drago' waited for him in the kitchen, sitting at the head of the table.

"I'm going to use the bathroom, then we can head back to the gym." Nicolas set the bag down in the hallway and his jacket on the backrest of

Drago's chair, making sure the Desert Eagle knocked against the chair. The pistol stuck out of the pocket, clearly visible.

He washed up, carefully. He lathered his hands, intertwining his fingers repeatedly, and then ran them over his face, his ears, and his neck. He cupped his hands and splashed water on his face repeatedly. He pulled out a towel and wiped the drops of water off the mirror, one less task for his mother. Before heading back to the kitchen, he stepped into his bedroom to get a sheet of paper and a pen, then went back to join Drago'. He was standing, leaning against the stove. The pistol was still where he'd left it. He sat down, turning his back on Drago'. Just a few days ago, he'd been able to say, "When Drago' is behind me, I never think of turning around," and instead now he felt all the fear that L'Arcangelo had praised as necessary during their first meeting: "In order to command, to be a boss, you need to be afraid, every day of your life, at every moment. To conquer the fear, to figure out whether you're still capable . . ." He'd be capable, that much he knew, but he had the same fear: he didn't want to lose another brother.

"Let me write a note for my mother," he said. He bent over, concentrating, and started to scrawl the text of the message. He heard Drago' stepping away from the stove, heard him holding his breath, to make as little noise as possible. He moved quickly. He took the pistol out of the jacket pocket. Nicolas felt the barrel press against the nape of his neck as Drago' pulled the trigger three times. Three pointless clicks, the Desert Eagle was unloaded, Nicolas had removed the bullets from the magazine before slipping the pistol into the jacket pocket: "If he doesn't touch the pistol, he's your brother; if he's the one who already tried once to put you down, then he'll try again," L'Arcangelo had said. And here was the proof.

Nicolas shut his eyes and let Drago' get away.

Drago' sought safety toward the border of the neighborhood; he ran without ever turning around, out of fear he'd see Nicolas appear just yards behind him, with the pistol aimed at him, that pistol he'd just dry-fired three times, hearing three empty clicks. He ran until his legs felt hard as wood and there were flames blistering his lungs, but he found that that pain helped him to think more clearly because it seemed to sweep away all useless thought, and like a sieve left behind only the thoughts that could actually prove useful.

When Nicolas had taken him up to his apartment after the visit to the bank, just the two of them alone, Drago' felt certain Nicolas wanted to kill him. But instead, he now understood, it had been a test. A test he'd failed. He felt like crying, but he couldn't give in to that impulse, he had to run, run as hard as he could. In the meantime, he couldn't stop thinking that now he had Nicolas and the rest of the *paranza* against him. My friends, my brothers are all against me now, Drago' kept thinking. And what about me? What side am I on?

Outside Forcella, in the territories where he usually felt most exposed and vulnerable, he felt free for the first time.

And the thing is, I've always been faithful, always a loyal bro, even when Micione summoned me, Drago' kept telling himself, repeating it obsessively. I pointed the gun at your head because I thought you were the one who wanted to kill me, that's what he wanted to write to Nicolas. But what good would that do him? Now I'm just the umpteenth traitor the *paranza* is ready to rub out—with the image before his eyes of Biscottino dying.

The shocks that started from his calves rose to his thighs and then radiated out to his brain. Another burst of adrenaline, and, mile after mile, he wasn't even surprised to have reached San Giovanni a Teduccio. He stopped to catch his breath and turned to look behind him. No one. Drago' started to feel a wisp of hope. He'd crossed the boundary. He'd chosen what side he was on. The family had called him once, and he'd spat on his own flesh and blood, but now he understood that flesh and blood was the only thing left to him.

Below Micione's building he started shouting: "Viola! Diego!" The confidence and familiarity that allowed him to summon the big bosses by their first names brought the guards down. "What?"

"I need to talk to Micione. I'm . . . I'm his *fratocucino*," said Drago', describing himself with that term for the first time.

"Flesh and blood is all I have left," he told Micione. Diego Faella had put on the expression of a boss surprised at such brazen recklessness, but then he'd welcomed him in. Already on the freight elevator, Drago' felt right at home, just like the first time he'd entered the lair on Via dei Carbonari.

"Is Genghis all right?" he asked Micione, to groom him a little and win him over.

Micione smoothed his goatee: "He lives like a king: he eats and drinks, he's better off than the rest of us, trust me!" And he burst out laughing. He'd gone back to the cheery tone of their first meeting there. "Luigi'," he said as he laid a hand on his shoulder, "I don't want to know what happened to you. Maybe you had an illumination, I don't care. You're here, and that's what matters. You're family. And together, we're going to get Maraja."

Micione figured all he had to do was sit down by the riverbank and wait for his enemy's corpse to come bobbing along: after that good-for-nothing fool had promised to bring him Maraja's hide and then vanished after killing the wrong man, now here was Drago', having come around spontaneously. The first one had gone wrong, but Drago' had what it takes, as well as the right blood: he'd rub out all the other *Bambini*, the other members of the Piranhas, and he'd give him back the city's historic center.

"Now we need to get Maraja and that's all we need to do," Micione went on, "you don't need to think about anything else. Now get out of here." And together they rode the freight elevator down to the ground floor, but instead of ushering him out the gate, he walked him down a long hallway and then through a door that gave onto the rear courtyard. "You'd better not let anyone see that you've been here. We need to come up with a strategy," Micione explained to him with a wink.

From behind, emerging from the dark, Viola appeared, surprising them both.

"Ciao, Viola," said Drago'.

"You see?" said Micione. "He's come home. To his family."

Viola kept her eyes on Drago', studying him, scrutinizing him.

"Better late than never," she said at last. Drago' stepped close to give her a hug but she gestured for him to follow her, and walked over to a gate with a security camera. She typed a code into a luminous panel and the lock clicked open.

"I wonder how happy 'o Viceré is that you've finally found your way home. Have you already told him?"

"No," he replied, and that was when Viola quickly drew a compact revolver from her handbag and pulled the trigger. She shot him right in the forehead, right at the hairline of that head of hair that had won him his nickname.

Micione jerked, startled, blurting out a "What the fuck!" and immediately bending over the corpse of the boy, as it collapsed lifeless to the floor. Viola, on the other hand, simply put the revolver away without a word and, just as she had come, turned on her heels and left.

"Viola, *ua'*," Micione thundered, yelling after her, "what the fuck have you done? This *guaglione* could have come in handy . . ."

Viola turned partway around, as regal as a lioness: that's why Micione had fallen in love with her immediately.

"We can't do anything with someone who has nothing but lies in their eyes," she said. "Have the *guaglioni* take his corpse out and leave it in the street. Let's toss him to Forcella. If it hasn't already emptied out." She looked at the pool of blood spreading across the floor. "This has to be business."

# FORGIVENESS

He was two people at the same time. That was an idea that he'd had before, but one he'd have been unable to put into words, because he'd never known the right ones.

There was once the 'o Selvaggio who had run a piazza, attracting important customers, men from law enforcement, celebrities capable of paying with more valuable favors than mere cash. The 'o Selvaggio who, when 'o White died, had dreamed that the Longhairs could become his *paranza*; after all, he'd earned his valor on the field, and so he went to Micione directly and asked for the investiture. Micione had turned him down, but the reason he was called 'o Selvaggio in the first place is that he was a bit of a savage, capable of extreme acts. And so, in order to win an audience, he had presented himself at the boundary of San Giovanni a Teduccio with a sign and a bucket of paint. Then, indifferent to the chilly temperature, he'd stripped buck naked and painted himself blue. The sign read: "I want my piazza back."

"He looks like the guy from *Avatar*," passersby had commented. Micione's guards had intercepted him immediately, and, frightened by what he might do if they rejected him another time, they'd taken him to Via Sorrento, and in the end, Micione had come downstairs to talk to him, because he was scaring everyone away. Once upon a time, there'd been the 'o Selvaggio who'd spilled everything to Micione. The *paranzas* uniting, the war against his empire, Nicolas's upcoming moves. The 'o Selvaggio who'd been able to force Micione to make a deal. "You give me back my piazza and I'll rub out Maraja." Micione had accepted; after all, he had nothing to lose.

Then there was 'o Selvaggio who had failed, who hadn't been able to kill Nicolas, and who'd taken off at top speed down Corso Umberto, slaloming between the cars stuck in the traffic jam, until he reached the statue of Victor Emmanuel II. He'd taken off the full-face helmet and made a decision that he never dreamed he would make. He'd called his mother, he'd interrupted the chatter she poured into the phone, she didn't understand the reason for that unexpected phone call just as the whole neighborhood was seething with activity because there'd been a shoot-out, and in the end he'd told her that he was going to take a vacation. "You're coming to see me, aren't you?"

'O Selvaggio had left the scooter on the roundabout; after all, from there to police headquarters it was just five minutes on foot.

So it had been Drago'.

I always trusted him, always. To me, he was a friend, a brother, something closer than blood, Nicolas thought to himself as he rode around on his TMAX, indifferent to which street he turned down, which direction he took. He hadn't told anyone yet that Drago' had turned out to be a traitor, that the *paranza* had harbored another Higuain close to its breast. He thought back to when Drago' had told him about the way things had gone with Micione: Fool that I was, I even believed him! Who knows how long Drago' had been scheming to kill him and take his place on the throne. Envy, the desire to shed honor on his name, the frenzy to become boss, must all have eaten at him for a long time. But Nicolas hadn't suspected a thing, just went on trusting him, defending him against anyone around him who whispered suspicions about him. He searched his memory for the moment when something must have changed . . . that time that he'd taught him to drive, was he already hearing the clarion call of blood?

And during their expedition in Rome, when he'd sulked the whole time, claiming it was about the car, but maybe it was really because he didn't want to insult his cousin like that . . .

It's pointless, brooding over it won't do a bit of good, he thought, speeding up.

He'd always been good at looking ahead; turning around and looking back was just painful, because you can't change the past, there's no strategy, no action you can take, however ingenious, that can change even a jot of what's gone before. The only thing I can do, he thought, is flush Drago' out of hiding, the same way I took care of Dentino.

As he was formulating that thought, he found himself in front of Poggioreale Cemetery, where Christian now lay. Maybe it's no accident that I wound up here, he thought. He left the scooter out front, bought a spray of five small white roses from a flower vendor, and went in.

He was walking past the vaults and he saw all those pictures of old people, the women with hair cut short and light blue in color, the men with watery eyes that reminded him of nothing so much as the eyes of elephants. And then, in among them, there were *muccusielli*, youngsters, and even the occasional *nennillo*, or little child, with an angel by their name. He thought about Cristiana, as yet unborn, and already his heart was aching at the idea of all the dangers that awaited her, out in the world and in that city. But he would protect Cristiana, he wouldn't make any of the same mistakes he'd made with Dentino, and even with that traitor Drago'. He'd keep a thousand eyes glued to his surroundings, and he had plenty of money in the bank; even if he was gone, Letizia and Cristiana could live their lives without worries. He lengthened his stride; he'd almost arrived.

From a distance he recognized his father, in front of Christian's plaque. He'd taken the handkerchief out of his pocket and was now carefully dusting the photograph in which his brother smiled with cunning in his eyes. His step turned hesitant; he was tempted to turn back, but it was too late: just as he was putting the handkerchief back into his pocket, his father had glimpsed him.

Nicolas greeted him by jutting his chin in the air, and his father said only: "I come here every week, it makes me feel closer to him."

They stood together for a couple of minutes, side by side, in silence, gazing at Christian.

"Congratulations"—and once again it was his father who spoke— "Mena told me about the baby girl."

"We'll name her Cristiana." And even Nicolas couldn't say why he'd had the impulse to tell him.

"Really? That's a nice name." His father seemed contented, but in a sad, melancholy way. "Nico' . . ." he went on, turning to look at him. "Nico', enjoy your baby, take the time to be with her, because time goes by fast, and children grow up—"

"That's not right," Nicolas interrupted, with a steadily growing sense of annoyance. His father wasn't someone who could give life lessons to anyone else, least of all him, Maraja. "There's always time to raise your kid, it's the time to become boss that's running out."

"When you were both little, everything that I did, I did for the two of you. When I walked, I didn't think about my own legs, I watched to see if you were steady on your legs or falling to the ground . . . Do you understand what I'm trying to tell you? Everything changes when you become a father, Nico'. You're no longer all for yourself, you're no longer alone."

Nicolas was already thinking about Cristiana, he was already protecting her, even if she was still in her mother's belly, what did that old man think, that Nicolas wasn't worrying about her?

"No one's going to lay a finger on my daughter, it won't even be possible, it would be like . . . as if . . ." He couldn't bring himself to express what he meant to say, and that almost never happened. He saw before his eyes again the photographs of children that had looked back at him from the headstones and then Christian; who could say if Christian would ever be able to forgive him from on high. "It would be as if someone laid their hands on the Son of God, there would be flames and thunderbolts."

His father looked at him in surprise: "Nico', then you haven't understood a single thing. When they put their hands on His son, the Lord forgave them."

Those words caught him off guard.

"Forgiveness is for weaklings like you, who can't even buy themselves a house," he said at last, almost shouting, but the answer had sprung belatedly to his lips. The other man was no longer even there to hear it.

The two pieces of news reached him simultaneously. He devoted barely a second to the first one, because 'o Selvaggio behind bars in Poggioreale Prison was the last of his problems. But the second report, on the other hand, was one that he had to read and reread repeatedly. Trying to fathom why Drago's death should cause him such profound pain.

## GENGHIS KHAN

**S**ignora, forgive intrusion. In there, new boys arrived. Come and see?"

Viola wasn't even paying attention to her. For the past hour, she'd been surfing Chiara Ferragni's website, because it was the day when she expected to see the new shots of her creations.

"Signora?"

At last, Viola turned to look at her, but she really didn't seem to see her at all. "I sent her the handbags a week ago. She needs to post the damn things!!!"

The Filipina took a second to understand that that hadn't been an answer to her question. As always. That woman never listened, but she knew how to catch her attention. The one thing that Viola Faella, née Striano, was obsessed with now was five-star chefs, and the house had become a crossroads of bags and packages, deliveries that Viola insisted on always supervising personally. I'll take care of the groceries myself, she always said.

"Signora, groceries here. I take care?"

Now Viola had finally focused on her. She slammed the lid of her laptop shut with a thump and shot to her feet: "Rosa, how many times do I have to tell you that in this house, I take care of the groceries, I and I alone!"

Waiting for her in the kitchen were Susamiello, Pachi, and Risvoltino. Micione's men had already searched them, but under the spotless aprons, they'd turned out to be clean. They'd set down the bags on the marble countertop of the kitchen's island and they greeted the mistress of the house in chorus: "*Buongiorno*, signo'." Viola looked them up and down, from head to foot. She didn't think she'd ever seen these three before, but then these kids nowadays all did their hair in the Genny Savastano style, from *Gomorrah*. They all look alike, they're worse than the Chinese, she thought.

"Are you new?" she asked, but then didn't even give them a chance to answer: sticking up out of one of the bags of groceries was a white truffle pâté. She'd been waiting for it for the past week, and was dying to use it in a recipe that she'd seen Cannavacciuolo make on *MasterChef Italia*. Antonino Cannavacciuolo was really too sexy for his toque, she thought to herself with a smile.

The three of them exchanged a glance. What was this lady laughing at? Was there any chance she suspected them? Susamiello gathered his nerve and took a step forward, a heavy package in his hand. "Signo', this is the lion's lunch . . . we just wanted to ask"—and here he shot a glance at the two others—"could we feed Genghis? Please, signo'?"

They really are all just the same, thought Viola, they're just big kids. She rummaged through the bags in search of the cold cuts. "Hold on a sec," she said, sowing uneasiness among the three once again. But she did nothing that was especially worrisome: she pulled back the aluminum foil of the package of prosciutto and checked to make sure it was as fat-free as she always insisted. "To perfection! Good job, *guaglioni*!" And then, turning to the housekeeper, she mumbled: "Rosa, show them downstairs."

Rosa turned around and only then, once she was safely out of Viola's line of sight, did she allow herself to roll her eyes, now she had to be a tour guide for the zoo. Right behind her tagged Susamiello and Risvoltino with the expression of someone who already has the lion on a leash. Pachi, bringing up the rear and, as always, the most suspicious of the three, was focusing on a careful study of every last detail of Micione's house. Getting that far had been no small challenge—studying the comings and goings of the official delivery boys for three long days, beating them up, locking them in the back of the supermarket, and taking their aprons, persuading Micione's men with the right set of answers that they were legitimate substitute delivery boys, and finally setting foot inside the fortress—but now they had to make sure not to lower their guard. If he could have, he would gladly have searched under Rosa's lace headpiece.

They rode the freight elevator down to the garage, and before Rosa had a chance to open the scissor-grate doors, Susamiello grabbed her from behind while Risvoltino put a hand firmly over her mouth. Pachi pulled out a cloth handkerchief and rolled it up, then stuffed it in her mouth and sealed it with duct tape. With the same sturdy tape, they secured her to the freight elevator, after removing the bunch of keys from the pocket of her apron. Rosa behaved with perfect obedience in her new role as victim, maintaining the aplomb that was the first requirement of employment in the Faella household; truth be told, she just hoped they would kill him, that mangy overgrown housecat.

"*Ua'*," said Susamiello, "what a handsome boy you are, aren't you, Genghis? Oh, look at your fine mane!"

The two others stepped closer to the cage, wrapping their hands around the bars, wonder winning out over fear. Genghis sniffed at the smell of lunch in the air, and, with the creaky movements of his old paws, he got up off the straw pallet he slept on. A fine lazy yawn, and just as he was opening his eyes, he lunged against the bars. The three of them leaped backwards in fright, then exchanged a glance and burst out laughing. Once again, Rosa rolled her eyes.

With the magnetic card that was clipped to the key ring, Susamiello opened the metal roller gate that led from the garage out onto the street, then hastily opened Genghis's cage, while Pachi waved the big slab of steak in front of his nose. They'd drawn lots for that job, and he'd drawn the short straw—his usual rotten luck. He was practically wetting his pants now. He stepped hastily backward while Genghis went straight at him, jaws wide, displaying his few remaining teeth. Few they might be, but they were still lion teeth.

Susamiello took a selfie with the now-empty cage behind him to send immediately to Maraja: it was proof that the plan had been put into operation. He hit SEND and ran to catch up with Risvoltino, while Pachi kept the lion busy: "*Ja*', look at the gazelle . . . so delicious, yum!" And then, in a calm voice, to avoid upsetting the big cat, but still plenty angry, he called out to Susamiello and Risvoltino to wait for him, threatening them: "Hey, this isn't what we agreed on! Wait up for me or I'll throw the meat right on top of you and we can give Genghis a three-course meal!"

As soon as they were out on the little driveway that ran from the underground garage up to the street, Pachi got rid of the steak, throwing it like a Frisbee: "Come on, *ja*', run and get your nice slice of gazelle!" And Genghis really did take off as if, out on the savanna, a herd of gnu had just galloped past him in all their thunderous noise. But the gnu of San Giovanni a Teduccio made only one sound: honking horns. Genghis froze in place, bewildered by the chaos that he was generating involuntarily around him—a fender bender, the terrified shouts of pedestrians, and the surprised exclamations of people looking out windows and down off balconies, leveling their smartphones to share instantly on YouTube. In the big cat's yellow eyes flashed bemusement at a world never seen before, and an even greater fear than that of those who were now fleeing before him. He took off at a dead run, heading in the opposite direction from the steak, smashing into the door of a parked car not far away. He picked himself up off the asphalt even more perplexed than before, as the mayhem multiplied around him; he darted to one side and then kept running, disappearing in his mad gallop behind the mini–soccer field. Mission accomplished. Even before Genghis, the three young members of the *paranza* had vanished from sight.

Those videos reached Micione on WhatsApp, and even if he already knew the answer, he asked the question all the same. "Don't we have anything to put him to sleep?" 'O Pagliaccio had looked at him aghast, he'd never seen his boss cry before. It wasn't an easy job to have to tell him that they couldn't really go to the offices of animal control to steal a few air rifles firing anesthetic darts. In spite of himself, he was forced to deliver even more bad news to an already overwrought Micione. But there was no time even for that. Genghis had already been spotted on the hood of a Fiat Bravo, by now reduced to a tangle of sheet metal as the lion roared up at the surrounding balconies. The citizens of San Giovanni had called the police but Micione's men had managed to get ahead of law enforcement and stall them with a promise: half an hour, and they'd take care of everything.

Micione was roaming the streets of the neighborhood in the SUV driven by 'o Pagliaccio.

His head was sticking up through the sunroof like a poacher looking to flush his prey. But the only thing about him that resembled a hunter was his pose; his legs were weak at the knees and his face, damp with tears, was twisted in sorrow and grief.

They were rolling along through the deserted streets, following the signs of devastation. At one intersection where the traffic light listed askew they turned first right then left, where the frontage was scarred by the shattered plate-glass window of a toy store.

Micione, his voice cracking, was shouting instructions to 'o Pagliaccio, who, with the steering wheel clutched tight, was carrying out those orders, swerving, braking, doing 360s, until, in a narrow space among an array of dumpsters, he spotted the lion. He'd fallen asleep and was snoring peacefully.

Micione ordered 'o Pagliaccio to stop the SUV and got out before the vehicle had fully come to a halt. He pulled out a small-caliber Ruger revolver.

A shot straight to the heart would be enough to kill Genghis without devastating his body. That way, his mortal remains could be given dignified burial. He tiptoed over to him, then gave up all caution. He knelt down before him, stroking his mane, uttered a short prayer, and pulled the trigger.

# STADIUM

The stadium was one of Micione's piazzas. It always had been. He managed to get his hands on everything. Contracts, subcontracts. Officially or unofficially, Micione was everywhere. And the more the team won, the more money he made. But he made money even when the team lost; the important thing was to make sure that the soccer match went off with good security and no surprises. To undercut Micione's legal revenue stream would amount to inflicting a deep and lasting wound, because commercial licenses are far more reliable than the unsteady proceeds of the narcotics business. The stadium and its cash flow were the economic foundation upon which the Faella clan could rely for further investment.

Nicolas had been thinking about it for a while now, ever since they'd stolen credit for the murder of Roipnol. And now that everything was going great guns—narcotics, the piazzas, their confederation with the Longhairs, who now no longer had a leader of their own, the old clans clearly struggling—the time had come. They were taking control, which was why Micione had come after them: he was trying to win back his old power by undermining their shakedowns, by killing the *paranza*'s men. No, it wasn't enough that they had killed Genghis. We've torn Micione's heart from his chest, but now, thought Nicolas, we need to rip his money out of his wallet, and the money he'll miss most is his legal money. It's time to go after his safe.

S.S.C. Napoli was hosting A.S. Roma. This certainly wasn't anything on the order of the Champions League finals, but any match against Roma smacked a bit of the game of the century.

The *paranza*, every last man, including the Longhairs, gathered outside the hotel that was hosting the Roma players. They'd filled their pockets with billiard balls from the clubhouse, and, when the team bus arrived with the players aboard, they started hurling the heavy balls. The vehicle lurched under that hail of blows, and, inside the bus, the team members were seeking shelter by crouching between the seats. The police who were escorting the tour bus weighed in immediately with tear gas, but before the clouds of red smoke could fill the air, the *paranza* had already made its escape.

The second part of the plan would unfold at Fuorigrotta.

The police had implemented a "channeling" tactic to separate the fans of the opposing sides to as great an extent as possible. They'd even ordered an assortment of tour buses to take the Roma fans to San Paolo Stadium. There wasn't going to be a huge crowd of fans decked out in the iconic Roma colors of yellow and red, but all Nicolas needed was a group, even a small one, to start a brawl.

"We're going to fuck Micione in the ass," Lollipop kept saying. He'd arranged to procure the ski masks and bomber jackets they were wearing. In that getup they looked exactly like a gang of Black Bloc anarchists ready to attack. Anonymity and terror, that's what Nicolas had prescribed.

"That's right," Nicolas said, "we're going to fuck Micione right in the ass, good and hard," and he went running straight toward a crowd of fifty or so Roma fans. They must just have arrived, their banners still rolled up on their staffs and their faces beaming with the expression of soccer ultras at an away game. Severely outnumbered, but with the element of surprise in their favor, the members of the *paranza* started lashing out at the fans of the opposing team, delivering slashing blows in all directions. Once their charge had lost its initial brute force, the Roma fans, the *romanisti*, regrouped and started fighting back, and now the battle shattered into small splinter clashes, as fans faced off. Nicolas tried to bring the *paranza* back into a tight formation, but most of his men had been cut off in the surging fray. Pesce Moscio and Briato' were surrounded by ten Roma fans, a solid wall of flesh that was slowly tightening around them, until Carlito's Way broke the tension by tossing a trash can he'd ripped off its pole into the middle of the group. Thinking it might be a cluster bomb, the fans surged back. Tucano grabbed a Roma banner that someone had abandoned in the confusion and started swinging it through the air like a pennant at the Palio of Siena. Then he launched it, like a javelin, but it didn't go far, hitting the ground without causing injury. The *paranza* managed to form ranks and push a few yards forward. Pesce Moscio, Briato', and Nicolas savagely attacked three other *romanisti* who'd been left behind by their retreating compadres.

There it was, the brawl Nicolas had been waiting for. Fists, feet, elbows, head butts. Nasal septa shattered, cheekbones exploding in fountains of blood. In the distance, the riot police in full gear were deploying to put down the unrest. The group of *romanisti* split into two phalanxes, with the forward half doing its best to pin down the members of the *paranza*, while the rearguard retreated, seeking shelter behind the tour bus. Nicolas had knocked two of them to the ground and he'd taken a punch to his right brow. Nothing much, just a constant throbbing and a stream of blood that was sopping into his ski mask. The others had taken some injuries, too. Briato', in spite of his leg, was fighting like a bull and had put five of their opponents out of commission, indifferent to the cut on his shoulder.

The blows of the riot sticks that the police were smashing against their shields were coming closer and closer and picking up their pace. Nicolas gave the signal: "Penalty kick! Get yourself a penalty kick!"

Drone slumped down as if struck by a lightning bolt and the *paranza* surrounded him, in a tortoise formation, turning their backs to their enemies. Nicolas yanked off his ski mask, and Lollipop and Orso Ted followed suit. Drone, too, on the ground, yanked off his and waited for the three above him to paint him with the blood from their injuries.

"You don't have AIDS, do you?" Drone muttered through clenched teeth.

"Shut up!" said Nicolas, snapping a photo of him. "Right now, you need to be dead!" And then, turning again toward the Roma fans: "He's dead! He's dead!"

The fans reversed course, retreating, while others started running in the opposite direction, finding their way blocked by the police. The word *dead* had lit the fuse to a panic, as if the mere fact of being anywhere around a dead body somehow brought with it an element of guilt.

In the meantime, Lollipop had grabbed Drone by the arms and was dragging him away, still surrounded by the members of the *paranza*, who were shouting, "Murderers! He's dead! They killed him!"

"Deader, look deader," Lollipop was telling Drone, "relax your thighs! Your head, let your head loll to one side!"

As the police sensed the shift in the wind, they started halting Roma fans to search them.

Drone rose from the dead behind another tour bus, but by then the mayhem was so all-encompassing that even a group of snickering kids with bruised and swollen faces could pass unnoticed.


"I saw him! He's dead! He's dead!" Nicolas was pushing his way through the Naples fans clustered on the curve, brandishing his smartphone as he moved forward. He held the phone high, like mothers at the funerals of their kamikaze children, suicide bombers who'd immolated themselves for the glory of Allah, and at first his audience would take a quick glance, and then lock ranks until they finally recognized Maraja and let him through. The match had started only a few minutes earlier. Nicolas followed the route that the fans, as they stepped aside, involuntarily blazed for him toward the leader of the ultras, the Naples hooligans: 'o Mammuth. Six foot seven, two hundred sixty-five pounds, covered with a dense coat of fur that only opened out into clearings where there was a tattoo—such as the acronym that he'd had inked onto his youthful back: ACAB. All Cops Are Bastards. Whenever he was on the curve, rain or shine, 'o Mammuth never wore a T-shirt, and anyone who wanted to talk to him had to do so in the unblinking presence of those unfettered double-D cups. He'd become the chief due to valor on the field of battle, and he commanded the curve by virtue of a pair of arms the size of tree trunks. Tattooed on his right arm was the word *good* and on the left arm was *bad*, and he used them on the basis of what instinct and experience had taught him.

"He's dead, he's dead! The *romanisti* killed him," Nicolas went on repeating.

'O Mammuth waited for him at the mouth of the tunnel to ask him one simple question: "Who killed him, the cops or the *romanisti*?"

"The ultras! The ultras! I saw it with my own eyes. Look! They killed him!"

'O Mammuth held the smartphone up close to his face. He carefully studied the photo of Drone covered with blood, and then he gave Nicolas back his phone. He crossed his arms over his head. He'd made up his mind: the match had to be canceled.

On the pitch, the teams had stopped play because from outside word was arriving, in muddled form, of clashes between militant groups of fans, and there was even talk of a death. 'O Mammuth went over to the edge of the bleachers to repeat that signal, arms crossed over his head. In the meantime, a delegation from the home team had broken away from the knot of people at the center of the field and was heading toward the bleachers where the ultras were concentrated. Escorted by the police, the captain of Napoli went over to 'o Mammuth.

"If there's been a death, we'd be the first to stop play," he said, his voice cracking slightly, betraying his underlying concern.

"There's been one," said 'o Mammuth. "We can't continue."

The captain clasped his hands together: "Trust me, there hasn't been a death. The situation is well under control."

'O Mammuth looked at Maraja, and Maraja leveled a pointed finger at the soccer player: "We'll let you play out the match, but if things aren't the way you claim, I'll come and get you."

The captain pretended to be pleased, thanked Maraja and 'o Mammuth, and headed back to the pitch at a run. The match could resume.

Napoli won a narrow victory, thanks in part to the ultras in the curve who loudly rooted for their team, singing fight songs without a break for the whole ninety minutes plus injury time. A victory like any other, nothing special, and yet that didn't keep the fans from swarming onto the field to celebrate and perhaps also to work off the adrenaline they'd accumulated in that tense and frenzied pregame buildup. And while the players surrendered their sweaty jerseys to the feverish fans, the police took advantage of the opportunity to burst into the bleachers. Weapons, narcotics, dozens of illegal skyrockets: it had been some time since there'd been such a radical law enforcement operation in the curve of the stadium, where the hardcore fans congregated.

"*Ua*', we fucked him good," shouted the members of the *paranza*, leaping up and down on the soccer field where Micione would soon lose his contracts and subcontracts. "We scalped him."

It was a night straight out of the Champions League, with fireworks and processions of cars in the street, a carnival feeding on its own bonfire of euphoria, and when everyone went to bed, wrecked, overjoyed, pumped up with a lust for life, there was only one man weeping, and it wasn't for joy. One of the team officials had barricaded himself in his office, and seemed unable to do anything but repeat, over and over, "What fucking idiots we look like now." He'd tried to turn on the radio but the voices of the fans just made him want to throw up.

It had been a disaster. The police, the fighting, the confiscations, the conversation between the team captain and that oversized gorilla 'o Mammuth broadcast on a national network. Heads were going to roll, that much was certain, and most likely his would be one of them. But first he was going to make sure that one in particular fell, if he had to saw it off himself.

For the sports team executive, the itinerary that led to the penthouse apartment in San Giovanni a Teduccio was no mystery, and in fact he was one of the privileged few who could ring that doorbell unannounced. After all, he was one of Diego Faella's most important business partners. The neighborhood that morning was virtually wallpapered with death announcements. It was with regret and grief that the untimely death of their trusted, courageous, caring friend Genghis Khan was announced: the whole family was shaken by this loss. The man entered the elevator in a raging fury; he felt betrayed, defrauded of the trust that he'd placed in that fat tub of lard, and now he was screwed because the man hadn't been able to hold at bay a handful of snot-nosed kids.

He found Micione in the kitchen. Perched precariously on a stool, he was picking at cold french fries out of McDonald's cardboard packaging. It was clear that he'd just stopped crying, and he was doing nothing to conceal the fact.

"All hell has broken loose!" the executive began. He heard Viola and the Filipina housekeeper go by in the hallway. The mistress of the house was giving the woman instructions, but in an undertone. The situation must be pretty serious, thought the executive.

"Yeah, I saw," Micione replied. "What are you thinking of taking away from me?" And he grabbed a handful of french fries.

"I'm probably about to get fired. Now you need to pay me. I've got a mortgage on my apartment in Posillipo, an ex-wife, alimony to take care of. This year we can get the Champions League."

Micione crushed the ketchup packets that he'd set aside because the sickly sweet chemical concoction turned his stomach. Under his powerful fist, a bloodred lake began to spread. "Enough with this orchestra of yacking. I'm not in the mood for it: just tell me what you're planning to take away from me!"

"All right," said the executive, "grounds maintenance, parking facilities, bars and cafés, jerseys and T-shirts."

"Fuck me, everything," said Micione. He tried to wipe off his hand with one of the McDonald's paper napkins, but with that flimsy piece of paper it would take him a lifetime, so he just forgot about it.

"You can just thank me if we're taking away those contracts to punish you, because you failed to ensure security and safety in the curves. I'm just taking away the things that aren't under my control. The parallel market, you can keep handling that on your own," the executive said, in a gesture of generosity.

Micione got off the stool and went over to the sink. He let the water run for a while, and then he washed his face.

"So now you've taken these things away from me," he said, turning around. He looked horrible, having spent a sleepless night and cried himself sick, and now his grief and misery were visibly veering toward rage. "So now what if I decide to take something away from you?"

"There's a good chance I'm about to be ruined," said the executive, but the arrogance he'd displayed a few minutes earlier had disappeared, and now he was modulating his voice in an attempt to stir pity in the other man. "The carabinieri are going to come to my house. I'm responsible for team logistics, I vouched for you with the ownership. I'd guaranteed that you were a reliable person . . ."

"If anything, it strikes me that you need to thank me"—and now Micione was looming dangerously close—"because what you've done up till now, you did because I was letting you. I let you skim off the top on every contract. So now if I get a wild urge, I'll just take something away from you," he said again.

The other man worked up the courage to ask: "Like what?"

"What do you mean, like what? Like your life. Do I still need to explain to you that if you're still breathing today, it's thanks to me? Every contract that you've won, if I hadn't been there as the subcontractor, you never would have been able to handle it."

The executive walked backward until he bumped against the kitchen door; he was shaking his head, as if to say no, there was no reason to go that far, and anyway, things were okay now. At last, before stepping out into the hallway and turning to go, he added: "And anyway, it's just a temporary thing . . ."

While the executive and Micione had been discussing the fate of San Paolo Stadium, Nicolas and 'o Mammuth were sitting at plastic tables next to one of the bosses of San Giovanni's food trucks right outside the stadium. They were staring in silence at the detritus of bottles, glasses, cans, and garbage of all kinds, as well as clothing, shoes, backpacks, the occasional condom, banners, hats, and even a doll.

Since the sun had risen, an hour before, they'd downed three beers, all without speaking a word. At last, 'o Mammuth spoke: "How are we going to handle things with Micione? Do you think that all this is going to bounce him out of there?"

If there was one thing Maraja had been waiting for, it was to be able to make his proposal.

"I don't know, but I'll give you the shit. Ten percent."

"But they'll shoot me."

"Twenty percent."

"But they'll shoot me."

"Thirty percent."

"But they'll shoot me."

"Forty percent."

Silence.

"If those guys decide to shoot me, will you protect me?"

Nicolas nodded. "The *paranza* will defend every one of your piazzas to the death. I'll bring you the narcotics, no matter where, even to away games. We need to sell to all the friendly curves there are."

Still more silence. Then 'o Mammuth went over to the food truck fridge. They needed more beer to toast their agreement.

# BIG PARTY

On Nicolas and Letizia's wedding day, there was only one snag, though the young groom knew nothing about it. Letizia had woken up at five in the morning to allow the hairdresser and the beautician to do their job, but her mother understood that the bride was worried about something.

"What's wrong, my love, this is the happiest day of your life, aren't you satisfied?"

Letizia had shooed all the other women out of the room and had told her mother, through her tears: "Ma, I'm wearing a white dress . . ." And she pointed to the rounded belly that the Empire-style gown was softly sheathing. Her mother had shaken her fire-red dome of blazing hair and held her daughter to her breast. "Letizia, beautiful, your mamma's heart and soul, but is that why you're crying?" she'd asked, her heart melting at her daughter's concern. "The only purity that matters is what's in your heart," she'd explained, as she petted her darling. Letizia had smiled, dried her tears, and that was the end of it.

They got married at the church in Forcella. Nicolas had wanted "a red carpet like at the Oscars," and hand in hand with Letizia, he walked the red carpet through a crowd of people who wanted to make that day unforgettable, with Maraja and his bride.

"Long live the newlyweds!" the *paranza* shouted. "Long live Maraja! Long live Letizia!"

Letizia was thrilled, and every so often Nicolas turned around to look at her, to bolster her confidence. Then the priest uttered the familiar formula of the ritual: "Nicolas, do you take Letizia to be your lawfully wedded wife, and do you promise to be true to her in good times and in bad, in sickness and in health, and to love and honor her all the days of your life?" Nicolas almost didn't let him finish, and said: "I do, by all that I hold unholy!" unleashing the hilarity of the members of the *paranza* in the front rows: "Epic Nico'!"

After the ceremony, family and friends went on to the New Maharaja. The newlyweds arrived an hour later, in a silver Rolls-Royce Ghost. Oscar had arranged to cover the entire parking plaza in front of the club with red carpet, and there, gathered in a semicircle, the guests burst into thunderous applause when Nicolas—who had chosen formal attire, complete with a cutaway swallowtail frock coat and white tie—stepped out of the Rolls and went around to open the door for Letizia.

Everyone was there. The families, down to every last member, the mothers in filmy gowns, the proud fathers, the grandfathers, the friends of the *paranza*—some in pinstripes, others in black suits with Air Jordans on their feet. In the front row, 'o Cicognone and Aucelluzzo could be seen. Also, here and there, prominent soccer players with wives squeezed into minidresses, and rappers in tracksuits. And Professoressa Cicatello was there, too, off to one side, keeping a low profile, but overjoyed, as if Nicolas had been one of her students on graduation day. She was holding a box with handsome sky-blue giftwrapping, and Nicolas was afraid that she had decided to give him a piece of Capodimonte porcelain.

Still, there was nothing that could ruin the joy of that day, neither the grueling and mind-numbing church ceremony nor the even longer picture-taking session, least of all a damned porcelain ballerina. It was a day of celebration, meant of course to consecrate the creation of a new family, but also to commemorate his victory over Micione. The *paranza* reigned and prospered over the center of the city. They'd struggled and labored and now they'd succeeded. He'd succeeded. He looked at his men: Briato', Tucano, Lollipop, Pesce Moscio, Drone. And yet, as he looked at them, he also saw the ones who were missing—Dentino, Stavodicendo, Drago', Biscottino. He'd lost almost half of his brothers, and those losses hadn't been pretty. Not to mention Christian.

"Aren't we going in, sweetheart?" asked Letizia, finally at peace.

No, nothing could ruin their party. He locked arms with his wife and together they entered the New Maharaja in a shower of rose petals, without even noticing that among the waiters bowing their heads as they went by were Susamiello, Pachi, and Risvoltino. They had shown up at the club a couple of hours earlier with a group of friends, in accordance with Briato's orders, and they hadn't objected in the slightest as they were being issued their uniforms, in fact, quite the opposite: "*Ua'*, so are we dressing up as waiters so we can infiltrate the wedding and stand guard as secret sentinels?" Susamiello had asked. Briato' had burst out laughing, slapping him on the back in a way that accentuated the S-shape of that unripe, twisted body: "You're dressing up as waiters so you can lay out the silverware and bring food to the table!"

The newlyweds started dancing, while the guests all took seats at the tables and the *paranza* sang the hook of the song that was blasting out insanely loud, at full volume.

*Abbasc'addu me m'par' GTA!*
*NAP'L'!*

Mena was fluttering in her flowered dress from one table to another, and she even let Lollipop steer her out onto the dance floor. Every so often she'd shoot a quick glance at the corner table where the man who was still technically her husband was sitting. She thought she was going to have to argue with Nicolas to get him to invite his father, but instead he had replied unassumingly: "Already taken care of, Ma."

It was a big party. There was laughter and tears of joy, hugs and kisses, passionate dancing and romantic dancing, hymns to a prosperous future and to goals achieved. And then, in the end, came the time for the presents.

Nicolas and Letizia took a seat on the little sofa of the private room, ready to offer their thanks for the silver sets that would be merely a pre-lude to the envelopes stuffed with cash.

Nicolas had seen the *paranza* disappear midway through that ritual, and he'd envied them their freedom. He, too, would gladly have ducked out of that boring situation, but he couldn't. But when he saw them re-appear, with Tucano and Lollipop carrying a large cardboard box, he understood that the time had come for their wedding present.

They set the box down in front of the newlyweds and he saw that it was moving as if it were alive.

"There's no way we're getting another dog, my love, let me tell you," Letizia said, but Tucano reassured her: "Oh, come on, who do you take us for? We don't give replica gifts, you know. There's Skunk already, and she's more than enough!"

Still, the box kept moving, and when Letizia heard those words, rather than relax she got more worried. While she held her belly with one hand, Lollipop and Tucano lifted the flaps of the carton.

Nicolas leaned over, at last a gift that aroused his curiosity at least somewhat; the expression on his face was one of heartfelt surprise: "*Ua'*," he shouted.

The tiger was a frightened cub with a sweet face, and was now lying at the bottom of the box with its large paws side by side, as if waiting for a cuddle. Nicolas reached out his hand and unhesitatingly stroked its head, pressing his thumb onto the stripes that grew denser toward the top of its head. The animal put up no resistance.

Letizia had stood up and, still holding her belly, taken two steps back. "What are we going to do with this wild animal, Nico'? Where are we going to keep it?"

"On the roof, my love," Nicolas replied. "We'll have a cage built."

Lollipop launched a full-throated chant of "Long live the newlyweds, long live the tiger," and the New Maharaja echoed with the cheers and applause. Nicolas lifted the tiger so that Letizia could pet it, too, but she recoiled, because the last thing she wanted was that wild animal next to her belly.

Sveva, though, hand in hand with Pesce Moscio, envied Letizia that gift and started scratching the tiger cub behind the ears, whispering sweet words to it.

"The guy at the circus who sold it to me told me you need to feed it milk," said Tucano, who had gone to get the tiger to bring it to the party. Drone walked over to a young matron who was pushing a stroller back and forth, and returned with a baby bottle. While Tucano was feeding the tiger, thereby attracting flocks of young women who were dying to take a selfie with the cub, the DJ had already started the music and the party continued.

"Wait, is this tiger a boy or a girl?" Drone asked at a certain point, his head tipped to one side to peek between the animal's legs and answer his own question.

Tucano glared daggers at him, as if he'd doubted his own son. But then the doubt began to make its way into his mind, too, and together they started trying to determine the tiger's gender.

"Huh . . . now that you mention it, this tiger doesn't have a dick," they all agreed.

"You're right, it doesn't have one," Lollipop confirmed.

"But it has a pair of balls," Tucano pointed out.

"Call whoever sold you the tiger!" Carlito's Way suggested, and Tucano took his suggestion immediately.

"Hey, did you sell me a tigress?" he shouted into the iPhone, and then, after a couple of "Ah, ah, I understand's," in a steadily descending tone, he ended the call and loudly announced: "He says that he has a retractile penis."

"It has what?"

"Yeah, just like Pesce Moscio!" And everyone burst out laughing, even Pesce Moscio.

"So what are we calling him?"

"*Napule*," Nicolas promptly replied. "Naples, because Naples is a tiger."

"*Ua'*," said Tucano, and climbed up on a table to declaim: "What God has joined together, let no man put asunder," and then jumped down to join the *paranza*'s group hug: "Together! Together! Together!"

———

The party lasted until dawn, until there was no one at the New Maharaja but the Piranhas and Susamiello with the other kids, who were all in the kitchen cleaning up. Nicolas, exhausted, had just taken Letizia to bed. One last toast with his friends, and he'd join her. Sitting on the usual low couch, he had Briato' pass him the tiger cub. The animal snuggled up tamely to its master, but then with a swipe of the paw, it clawed him under the ear. An inch-long red stripe sank into Nicolas's neck, and he instinctively released his grip. Finally free, the young tiger started running through the club, pursued by the members of the *paranza*, who, half drunk and half exhausted, clumsily tried to catch it. They managed to flush him out from under an amplifier after a good ten minutes. Nicolas had remained seated on the couch, and when Tucano brought the tiger cub back to him, he was afraid the Maraja was going to slaughter the poor animal. Instead Nicolas pulled his bloodstained hand away from his neck and showed the wound to the rest of the *paranza*.

"*Ua'*, that's too cool! The tiger cut!"

"I want it, too!" said Lollipop, and knelt down before the tiger.

"Scratch me, scratch me, little tiger cub!" cried Tucano, shoving Lollipop aside, because, all things considered, he was the one who'd had the idea of the tiger in the first place. The young tiger tried to back into Nicolas's arms, but then it sensed that its new owner was pushing it forward and it lunged with a razor-claw that sliced open Tucano's eyebrow.

"*Ua'*, that bastard practically took out my eye," Tucano shouted to a general burst of laughter.

And in the early light of dawn, the *paranza* set out in the Rolls-Royce. Heading for the emergency room.

PART THREE

# YOU WHO EDUCATE

Y ou who have educated your children to be respectful and obedient. You who have educated them to censor their curse words, not to cheat on tests and homework, not to steal their playfellows' toys. You who have educated them to listen to the points of view of others and always to try to reconcile disagreements: to get their way without bullying, to think that violence is unjust.

You who have tried to teach them that good outcomes are the result of great effort and determination.

You who have educated your children by assuring them plenty of love, enough money, trying to discipline them and not spoil them. Urging them to be physically fit and active, preparing them for the larger world by teaching them languages, arming them with tolerance, massaging them with music, giving them examples of an upright, rigorous approach to life.

You, who have educated your children in this fashion, you've gotten it all wrong. You've given your children the promise of a just world they will never see.

*And you others, who have educated your children to be mistrustful. You, who have educated them to be capable of beating their fellow man before he can beat them. You, who have had no desire to lend a gentle hand, to be understanding. You, who have educated by showing them the differences between people, explaining that no one is the same as anyone else, and that black, yellow, white, and mulatto are all at war with one another. That living in harmony is the hypocritical art of the profiteers. You, who have educated them to do business, always and in every case. Well, you haven't prepared young soldiers, you haven't taken it to its logical conclusion. That's only viciousness—which is a form of weakness. On Mount Taygets, where according to legend the Spartan people chose between the fit and the unfit children, your offspring would have been found wanting and left to die. You educated them to be like you, knowing that they'd have you behind them. Feeling at fault for every penny you refused them, feeling yourself somehow inadequate for every achievement they failed to attain. For every trophy that proved to be out of reach, you felt that somehow you had missed the target.*

*You, too, have failed. You have promised your children, brought up to lust and covet, a world where they could win their place, but they never will, power will elude them as long as you are around.*

*You who have educated them for peace and for war, for the good and the bad, friendship and cunning, hugs and cruelty. You who have educated them according to the rules of this world, rules that are neither good nor bad: the rules of the winners. Your children will be exactly like those rules, neither good nor bad, they'll be identical to the world in which you've brought them up, in which you've educated them. The world of the winners. If you want the best for your children, you're reiterating the worst.*

*But now your children are taking back what the preceding generations long denied them: the truth.*

# MASS

The heroin deliveries had always come in punctually: once a week, Nicolas received a picture of a death announcement poster, usually an off-kilter, out-of-focus photograph, probably taken from a moving motor scooter, but clear enough to make out the scheduled time of the funeral services. The church was always the same, in Cercola, just outside the city: a safe place in Scignacane's view, an anonymous little town, though if you looked down on a map you had the impression that the township stood directly atop Micione's base of power, which had once belonged to L'Arcangelo, though it no longer did. The dearly departed, however, changed with every delivery: Scignacane in person enjoyed going online and consulting the death announcements of *L'Eco di Bergamo*, from a town in the north, and he'd download those unsuspecting, no-longer-living faces, rechristening them with distinctly southern names. Then it became the duty of a cooperative priest to await the hearse and keep the two or three little old ladies who frequented the church at a safe distance, explaining to them that the family wished to show the respect due to their late and lamented relative, and that therefore funeral services would be held behind closed doors. The little old ladies would withdraw, reciting under their breath, "Oh Lord, you who have made us participants in the mystery of Christ crucified . . ." while behind those doors, Scignacane and his men were clearing the coffin of the flowers and the funeral drapery and waiting for the Piranhas to enter through a side doorway. What came next was the exchange: to Nicolas and his *paranza* the hollow plastic Kinder eggs full of heroin transported to that church inside the coffin, and to Scignacane a backpack full of cash.

In the building of the Acanfora clan, La Zarina walked into her son's bedroom without knocking. He was catching a nap, but she threw open the curtains, swung wide the windows, and switched on the light.

Scignacane put his pillow over his face, hoping to win himself a few more minutes of peace.

"Alfredo, 'o Pagliaccio is furious," she said through clenched teeth. She was wilted, a shadow of her former self, but she stubbornly continued to pose as a cougar with push-up bras that tried to burst out of unbuttoned blouses to show off the disaster beneath.

"'O Pagliaccio is pissed off," La Zarina repeated.

"So what?" Scignacane replied. He grabbed the pillow again, this time to put it behind his back as he struggled into a seated position. "He's always pissed off."

"Ah, is that so? Well, this time, he's got good company because I'm pissed off too!" she shouted. "'O Pagliaccio was here, you get that? He asked me if I could 'kindly' ask you why the load this time was so much bigger."

Scignacane ran his hand over the stump of his missing ear, a habit that he'd developed at times when his nerves were on edge. The Tsarina, instead of feeling even a hint of tenderness, interpreted that touch as tantamount to a confession.

"What the fuck are you up to?" She attacked him, shaking him by the shoulders. "Tell me, you fucking wretch, who have you started selling to on the side?" But now her boy had jammed his head between his knees and was just trying to mumble: "Keep cool, Ma, it's nothing . . ."

"Nothing, is it? 'O Pagliaccio didn't shoot anybody this time. This time, he just wants to know who you're giving it to, that extra weight."

Never show up where 'o Pagliaccio can see you with the full load; he thought he'd made that clear to the new hands, but maybe he hadn't.

And maybe he shouldn't have delegated the task to others. His father, 'o Negus, had been right, it was always better to do business in person, even in the most no-account dealings, but Scignacane was a broker, his job was to negotiate with his contacts in Afghanistan, it's not like he could spend his life driving a delivery truck.

"It's all under control, Ma, I'll settle it myself," he said, getting out of bed and patting her on the cheek.

"That would be better," said La Zarina. "You're working with Maraja, right? I don't like that. I don't like it one little bit. Your father wouldn't have liked it either: we've always worked on an exclusive basis with Micione. Everyone knows it, it's practically written in the school textbooks. 'O Negus, God rest his soul, you know what he'd assured us of? No trouble, peace of mind. Why do we keep these buildings? Because we sell to Micione, and nobody else. We're alive because we're protected."

"I got you, Ma," said Scignacane, but La Zarina wasn't done. She struck her last blow: "Who avenged your father's death, when that piece of shit L'Arcangelo killed him?"

"Micione," Scignacane replied in a low voice.

"Exactly, Micione," said La Zarina. "We need to show him respect, and in order to respect your father, we need to respect this agreement." The Tsarina stepped close to her son: "And that guy, Maraja, thinks he's the king of Naples. Look what he's done to you, look what your old buddy's done to you." And with one hand she brushed the flap of flesh that had once held an ear.

He pushed her hand away in annoyance. "I told you I'll take care of everything, Ma." And, grabbing his smartphone, he left the room.

**Scignacane**
The shop is closed for business

**Maraja**
For how long?

**Scignacane**
For good

**Maraja**
But we're the ones who made it what it is!!!

### Scignacane
It's what Mamma wants

Nicolas tried to get in touch with Scignacane every way he could, but he'd blocked him from everything. Expelled on WhatsApp, banished on Facebook, bounced back on voice mail. He hurried to Piazza Bellini. He found Pesce Moscio talking to some guys, and Drone was there, too. Pesce Moscio couldn't figure out why everybody wanted to smoke their heroin, instead of injecting it into their veins, and when he saw Nicolas he said to him, "Maraja, everyone here is trying to be a Taliban," and he smiled.

"*Guagliu*'," said Nicolas, stepping off to one side with his men. "That piece of shit Scignacane has shut off the supplies."

Pesce Moscio and Drone assumed this must be a joke of some kind. If up till then they'd had one trustworthy partner who would never leave them high and dry, that had been Scignacane.

"Nico'," said Drone, as if he were continuing what Pesce Moscio had said, and refusing to believe it, "around here it's like we're in Afghanistan, with the poppy plants . . ."

Nicolas spat between his feet. "I'm not kidding around. He's stopped selling to us."

Pesce Moscio lost his smile. "What are you saying? All I have left is a single package . . ."

"We need to talk to him," said Drone.

"That bastard has blocked me on Facebook, and on WhatsApp. He's out of reach, in his castle." He spat on the ground again, but this time, far away, against a flowerpot, in disgust for the piazza that Scignacane was sending to the bottom of the sea.

"But we have his money," said Drone.

"What money?" Nicolas asked.

"A hundred thousand euros that we still haven't paid him. You watch, he'll come for it."

Money is always a good reason to talk, thought Nicolas, and he told Drone to send a message to Scignacane, because he couldn't have blocked the accounts of all the members of the *paranza*. To let him know at this point that if the shop had really gone out of business, then all its debts were null and void, too.

"*Guagliu',*" Nicolas concluded, "we have to . . ." But Pesce Moscio didn't seem convinced.

"We don't talk to him. We put him out of his misery. That bastard. How can he do this? Doesn't he show any respect? We give him plenty of money, outside his market because Micione forces him to sell to him alone, and instead of thanking us—"

"What's that got to do with anything?" Nicolas tried to get a word in.

This time it was Pesce Moscio who spat on the ground: "Hold on, Nico', what do you love better, your mamma or money?"

Nicolas looked at him, uncomprehending, while Drone answered for him. "If we don't make money, then even our mothers will turn their backs on us. Children aren't worth a fucking thing. People love you only if it's in their self-interest."

"Scignacane must die," said Pesce Moscio.

"But we can't go up against La Zarina," said Nicolas.

"Why not? Just us, alone against everyone." Drone had grabbed one of Nicolas's arms and one of Pesce Moscio's, and started pulling them toward him.

Nicolas nodded. "All right. But we don't need to do it."

"Then who?"


Drone immediately found the right contact. Instagram. Scignacane had posted a picture of his new motorcycle, a Honda CBR Fireblade, up on its kickstand. He was seated on the bike, leaning over the handlebars as if he were roaring down a straightaway at 125 m.p.h., and behind him, arms wrapped around him, was his new girlfriend, who for the occasion was wearing a short-short skirt, with her stay-ups in plain view. The caption read "Great bike!" and Drone immediately replied: "So to celebrate that skyrocket of a bike, are all our old debts forgiven? If so, we drink to your health."

"The fuck they are," Scignacane wrote back just a few seconds later.

"Usual church. Tomorrow. We'll settle up."

Pesce Moscio greeted Don Carmelo with all the respect due to a man of the cloth, and he replied instinctively, the way you respond to someone who comes up behind you while you're locking up your church, after a long day of hearing confession, organizing meetings at the parish rec center, masses, gatherings, and visits to the elderly in town. "I'm closing up, see the schedule for visiting times."

"Fuck! Are you the secretary to Jesus? The Madonna's cousin?"

Don Carmelo turned around and realized that he'd be well advised to hold his tongue. Pesce Moscio continued along the same line: "Don Carmelo, beautiful car you have. Same for the house, the only thing missing is a swimming pool. Cercola Beach."

Then he whispered in his ear: "You take money from me and from Scignacane. And now I'm here to ask you a favor. A small one. Just a phone call."

"What kind of phone call?" Don Carmelo looked around, making sure none of his parishioners were within earshot, so that he wouldn't be seen speaking to a member of the *paranza*.

"You have two options. Either you make a phone call or else I make your wish come true and you go straight up to chat in person with the Madonna, with Jesus Christ, and with the angels, and maybe you can even do a good turn to your mother and tip her off to a couple of numbers on the Naples lottery." Pesce Moscio pulled out a pair of twin Viking pistols and crossed them on his chest.

"This is the house of God, put those things down," said Don Carmelo, but more than an anathema hurled from the pulpit, he seemed to be imploring him.

"Eh, God has seen plenty of things in His time." Pesce Moscio laughed. "It's not like He's going to be scared of a couple of gats. Call this number. Call 'o Pagliaccio."

"And who's he?"

"You shouldn't tell lies, Don Carmelo. You know perfectly well who he is. The Faellas were in charge around here until just yesterday. Call him, and tell him that the Good Lord Almighty can't accept heroin in the church. Ask him if they can do something, tell him that law enforcement has gone missing around here, that you're battling all alone, with the force of the Lord."

Don Carmelo was shaking his head, but Pesce Moscio was sick and tired of this puppet theater. He aimed the pistols, one at the priest's heart and the other at his testicles. "You need to tell him that Scignacane is going to be here tomorrow afternoon. But don't name any names. You just need to tell him what I told you, and maybe you'll still wind up going to heaven."

The next day, the church of Cercola was decked out for a festival. Everything had been done in record time, that same morning, by the parishioners assembled by Don Carmelo with a post on his Facebook profile. He apologized for the short notice, but he had decided that the best way to honor the patron saint that the town shared with Naples was to celebrate him a second time with a festive Mass. The faithful forgathered in great numbers and Don Carmelo heaved a sigh of relief. With that crowd, no one would have the nerve to unleash a hail of lead.

Scignacane showed up riding his Honda, accompanied by another high-performance motorcycle carrying two bodyguards. When he saw the flood of people, he dismissed his men, and told them they could come back and get him when the Mass was over.

Don Carmelo appeared and delivered the shortest sermon of his life, reminding them one and all that a man's rectitude could not be judged by the material possessions he had amassed. Scignacane had taken a seat in the center of the nave, so that he could try to spot Nicolas or anyone else from the *paranza*, and to ensure he had the broadest field of view, he took part in the Eucharist. No one to be seen. Only the devout and the faithful.

Don Carmelo dismissed the congregation, and Scignacane mingled in the buzz of chattering voices, surrounded by men, women, and children.

Just as he was texting his bodyguard, he recognized one voice over the rest: 'o Pagliaccio.

"It's a good thing you took communion."

Two shots to the back of the head, in quick succession.

Silence.

# BACKLIT

At Sveva's house, dinner was served at 7 p.m. sharp. Pesce Moscio had asked his girlfriend why her folks were so obsessed with that Nordic mealtime, and she had told him that it helped to keep your digestion regular. Pesce Moscio didn't want to argue the point; at Sveva's house, everything went according to specific rules. Rich people's rules.

That evening, Pesce Moscio had been invited to dinner, the way he was every Sunday. By now, it had become a habit, a marker of the beginning of a new week. And these things, too—routines, dinner at the same time every day, cloth napkins folded on the plate before the meal could begin—were beyond Pesce Moscio's understanding. Still, he did his best, just as he tried to provide prompt answers to the rapid-fire questions Sveva's father shot at him. He was an engineer who had even built the apartment building his family lived in.

"Why won't you finish high school?"

"Why, how old were you when you finished your degree?" Pesce Moscio shot back, using the informal *tu*. They'd begun addressing each other informally at their very first meeting, as if it were the most natural thing in the world. Sveva's father believed in a flat hierarchy; Pesce Moscio was happy to leave the respectful address of *voi* to others.

"Twenty-five."

"And how much do you make now?"

"What kind of questions are you asking?" Sveva broke in. She looked to her mother for some implicit support, but instead what she read in her eyes was good-natured indulgence, as her mother smiled the way you might at a smart-aleck kid who could be forgiven anything. Sveva's father smiled, too.

"Sveva, Ciro has a point when he asks questions like that. In America, when you meet people, that's where the conversation starts, with money."

"I like America," said Pesce Moscio. "That's a way of figuring out what people are worth right away."

"What about everything else?" Sveva's father asked, calmly. "Commitment, education, love of your work?"

Pesce Moscio saw Sveva's eyes silently begging him to take a step back, but he decided to ignore her.

"You can be courteous and admired, but if you don't have any money, you stop being courteous and admired, then you're just an asshole without any money. And I've never seen a man of quality without money."

"Sweetheart!" Sveva chided him.

He changed the subject and the dinner went on without further clashes.

As soon as they left the apartment, he pulled her to him and kissed her the way he had when they first met. How pretty she was when she became a woman warrior. She still seemed somewhat put out, and so to win her back he showed her the baggie of cocaine he planned to offer her group of friends. Sveva looked at the baggie and then at him, and instead of forgiving him, asked him why he always had to play the fool with her group of friends.

"Your friends, the minute they see the sugar, they want to hang out with me."

"Just because they're from Vomero, do you think they think they're better than you?"

"Of course they do. Without sugar, without a pistol, without money,

I'm nothing to them. I mean, without a pistol, would you still have fallen for me?"

"I certainly think I would have."

"So you don't like it that I have a baggie full of sugar and a handgun?"

"No, I like everything about it, including that . . . I'm just saying that without them . . . I'd like you all the same."

"Okey-doke," he said, cutting the conversation short, "we'll see you later at Piazza Bellini."

That, too, had become a routine. Sveva went to round up her friends, and then they all joined Pesce Moscio in the piazza because he wanted to check to make sure everything was going smoothly. When he got there, Susamiello, Pachi, and Risvoltino were already there. He had asked them to work as bodyguards for Maraja. After Scignacane's death, he no longer felt safe, not even in his own piazza.

"Do you know how to shoot?" he'd asked as he handed over their weapons.

"Of course we do," "Sure," "Who do you take us for?" they replied, feigning indignation. In fact, they'd never fired a shot in their lives.

The three young *paranzielli* were waiting for him, standing to attention, proud of the job that meant they could finally pack a sidearm.

There were lots of people. As always. Tourists, students, mid-career professionals in their early forties, and good-for-nothings. Pesce Moscio went to say hello to the piazza boss, who confirmed that everything was going smoothly, but that they were just about out of heroin. Pesce Moscio reassured him, saying that they would resupply soon. Actually, though, he had no idea whatsoever how they were going to get their hands on more heroin now. It was a problem that needed to be solved, and quickly, before they could lose more customers, now that heroin for snorting was going like hotcakes. Pesce Moscio walked along, closely followed by the three young *paranzielli*, who rested their hands on the butts of their pistols, jammed down into their jeans. When the crowd that was swelling around Pesce Moscio—to touch him or just even to greet him and show off the fact that they knew a celebrity—started becoming overwhelming, Susamiello weighed in to clear a path down the street.

A young man approached on a Vespa. He wanted to take a picture of Pesce Moscio because he'd seen him on TV sometime previous. Pesce Moscio's curiosity was aroused.

"Where did you say you saw me?"

"On the news," the other guy responded promptly. "I recognized you by your eyes. You're a legend."

Pesce Moscio smiled; the heroin and Sveva and her father with his professorial advice seemed light-years away.

"So can I take your picture?"

"Sure."

The young man pulled out his smartphone and held it high in the air for a minute, as if trying to find the best angle, but he still didn't seem quite convinced.

"What's the matter," asked Pesce Moscio, "am I backlit?"

"No, no, you're perfect," he said, and with the other hand he extracted a compact pistol from behind his back. Four shots, right in the face, and Pesce Moscio fell right over, spraying a jet of blood as he did.

"Best wishes from the Acanforas," said the *sicario* before speeding away on his Vespa. Before Pachi, in the throes of sheer terror, did the same. Before Risvoltino made up his mind whether or not to pull the trigger. Before Susamiello managed to take aim but still wasted his bullets peppering the plate-glass windows of the café behind them.

# THE COPS ALL OVER HIM

**N**icolas was standing next to the DJ, in the cone of shadow cast by the floodlights. From there he could keep an eye on the club and see everyone all at once.

It was a new discotheque in Pozzuoli, just opened for business, and the *paranza* had been invited. Open bar, only for the *paranza*, the owners had guaranteed, and when they heard those two words, the *paranza* had been persuaded. Opening night was a success. The bodies weren't dancing, there wasn't enough physical space to sway and hipswivel, so people just rubbed against one another, crammed together as if in an orgy that however still maintained the boundaries of common decency. In the churn of the crowd, the guys found themselves glued against girls who were perfect strangers; they held both arms high as if trying to grab the music as it sprayed out of the speakers, and they ventured to lower their arms only if they picked up on the slightest hint of an invitation, a warm gaze, a smile, and then down they went, both hands, into the sea of bodies, where everything was hidden and their hands were free to wander—and discover.

From his privileged vantage point, every so often Nicolas would identify one of his men, arms wrapped around his own girlfriend or else eagerly focused on cutting in on somebody else's girlfriend. They were laughing, and they appeared to be utterly carefree. Nicolas, too, was laughing. But his laughter was edgy and bitter. Another brother had been killed. Pesce Moscio had fallen victim to his great undertaking. Nicolas had desired and planned out the death of Scignacane at Micione's hands, and La Zarina had found out. These old people just wouldn't stop rearing their heads; they couldn't seem to get it through their skulls that he was the one riding the crest of the wave now. He knew that these were just the last lashes of the scorpion's stinger, that sooner or later they'd be forced to knuckle under, just as you ultimately have to bow to God's will. If God Almighty actually exists, thought Nicolas, who knows if He gets these stomach pains, who knows if He, too, lies awake at night mulling over strategy, money, and accounts.

He threw back a Moscow Mule in a single gulp, and he heard the roar of the crowd. At first he thought they were objecting to the DJ and his terrible music, but the minute he leaned out to look down he understood what was going on.

At the center of the club a small gap had opened in the crowd and all eyes were turned to Lollipop and a young man in torn jeans and a white skin-tight T-shirt. They were quarreling. Lollipop held both arms crossed behind his back, chest puffed out in a provocative stance. Behind him, handbag clutched to her oversized breasts and eyes downcast like a violated virgin martyr, stood Gloria, or whatever the hell her name was, Lollipop's latest girlfriend.

"What do you think, that this good-looking *guagliona* is waiting for you?"

"Who the fuck do you think you are?" the other young man replied. "You're too little for this *guagliona*."

"Too little! Now I'll take a shit right in your mouth."

"Before I talk to you, you need to put your thoughts at rest, I'm not understanding a thing."

Nicolas had seen it all, he'd heard it all. The guy had come on to Gloria. Gloria was Lollipop's girlfriend. She was part of the *paranza*.

He rushed down to the center of the dance floor, where Lollipop greeted him by slapping a hand on his chest to make it clear to the other young man that things were about to turn very dark for him. The young man with the torn jeans recognized him and took a step back. The mass of spectators eager to relish the clash formed a sort of compact barrier, the perimeter of which the young man navigated while Nicolas stepped up to him, sniffing at him, first his head, then his neck and shoulders, and while the other young man did indeed start retreating, he never once took his eyes off Nicolas.

"So you get the point now?" asked Nicolas, and gave him a couple of slaps in the face.

The young man planted both feet wide, solid as a boulder. He's not afraid of me, thought Nicolas, he's not lowering his gaze, he wants to penetrate my eyes. He pulled out his pistol and killed him with a single shot to the forehead. Behind him, the smiling faces of the young crowd were splattered with blood.

A brief moment of silence, and then utter chaos. The security doors were taken by assault, but even then, they didn't open instantly, creating swirling whirlpools of screaming bodies. Then, at last, they were flung open, and in the blink of an eye the club emptied out, even Nicolas's *paranza* was outside now—perhaps swept away in the rush of the crowd, perhaps tugged away by their girlfriends. He left the corpse behind him on the floor, tucked the pistol into his pants pocket, and watched the discotheque empty.

The first to get back in was none other than Lollipop.

"Maraja," he said, yanking on his arm, "what did you do that for?"

"He looked at me," Nicolas retorted, and tried to shake loose from Lollipop's grip, but now Lollipop grabbed his other arm as well.

"Hurry up! The sirens! Don't you hear them?" And he dragged him toward the exit. "The cops are coming! Get moving!"

"What the fuck are you talking about!" But even as he was replying he recognized the shrill sound.

Yes, he could hear them now, and they sounded very close.

The *paranza* was waiting for him outside and they'd even already started his TMAX. They all took off, bent over the handlebars, heads lowered to cut through the air, like a flock of sparrowhawks. Behind them, the timid rays of the rising sun mixed with the flashing lights of the rushing squad cars. Then, nothing but the increasingly dense orange of broad sunlight as the new day got under way. The sirens were dying away now, the squad cars must have stopped at the new club. They slowed down a little. They'd made their escape.

They were heading away from home and toward the water, which was already blazing bright. Nothing could be more beautiful. They rode past Castel dell'Ovo, opening out in a fan shape like boats cutting across the water.

Briato' slammed on the brakes, and Drone, riding right behind him, braked hard in his turn to keep from hitting him.

"What the fuck are you doing?" he said, but then he noticed the police car stopped at an intersection. Inside, two officers were staring out at them, but they showed no signs of being about to pursue them. Drone immediately veered away, and so did all the others: two other cars were now cordoning off the intersection they'd just passed through.

"Maraja . . ." yelled Tucano, but Nicolas didn't let him continue, and instead pressed his thumb down on the TMAX's horn. In the sleepy morning, that blaring sound was like a blasting cap. Out of the windows of the surrounding apartment buildings alarmed faces appeared here and there, and even the street began to fill with a few rubberneckers, who'd popped out of who knows where.

"Shoot," Nicolas yelled, "put somebody down!"

Lollipop was the first to get his Beretta out and leveled, and he fired off a shot at an elderly man who hadn't been quick enough to retreat behind the front door. He was still dressed in his boxer shorts, and a white sleeveless T-shirt covered with wrinkles clung to his skinny body. The bullet caught him in the belly and his creased old body, without resistance, folded up and dropped slowly to the sidewalk.

When Lollipop turned again to look for Nicolas, he'd already turned down a side alley. The cop cars took off, tires screeching, while people poured out of the buildings and into the streets, moving in the opposite direction from what instinct would have advised, as if salvation were out there, in the open. Tucano, Drone, and Briato' revved wildly into the small knots of people forming on the sidewalks and found gaps that let them escape into the alleys.

Lollipop saw them vanish as he shoved the pistol down his pants and took off a few seconds later. But too late.

The cops were all over him.

# ON THE RUN

**N**icolas meant to live his life on the run with his head held high. Ten days, a month, a year, ten years. He'd never been to Nisida Reform School, just as he'd never been behind bars at Poggioreale, but now he found himself where a crime boss sooner or later is bound to wind up. That's why, even while he was still fleeing the police, he'd put in a call to 'o Cicognone with excitement throbbing in his voice, an excitement that had then been transformed into feverish expectation when he'd seen 'o Cicognone waiting with pick and mortar in Ponticelli, outside the walled-up apartment building where, some time earlier, Stavodicendo, too, had lived out his brief time on the run. But he wasn't going to make the same mistake, he wasn't going to let them catch him the minute he set foot back out on the street, he'd sworn to himself while Briato' and Tucano used the pick to demolish the wall that 'o Cicognone rebuilt, depriving him—brick upon brick— of both light and air. He'd transform that building into a tower from which he could issue commands to the outside world. With discipline. 'O Cicognone himself had assured his personal comfort with a brand-new generator: "This is a gift from L'Arcangelo," he had told him, and Briato' had done his part, with a PlayStation.

That very same day, toward evening, he'd received the first message updating him on the outside world. It announced the umpteenth name to cross off: "They arrested Lollipop for the old man's murder. Nisida Reform School." The videos of the murder taken in that discotheque that was fairly bristling with online video cameras had already gone viral, according to the handwriting on that scrap of paper. Then they sent him the front pages of the newspapers. For the first time he appeared, with pictures and his full name. All things that gave luster and purpose to his time on the run.

Without Lollipop, now, the ones who remained were Tucano, Briato', and Drone. There were also still a few Longhairs, and then there were the *paranzielli*, he knew, the youngsters of the *paranza* like Susamiello, Risvoltino, and Pachi, hard workers who would do anything to become full-fledged members. Even if they weren't quite ready yet, as had been clear with Pesce Moscio. They needed to be educated, they had to be brought up to their new responsibilities. It was only natural, Nicolas kept telling himself, living things renew themselves, rejuvenate, and the Piranhas had to belong to kids. The old are put in the world to die, the young to take command, that had always been his imperative. Still, shut up in that cage, he'd been reminded of L'Arcangelo, confined not that far away from the walled-up neighborhood. The truth was that lately Don Vittorio struck him as younger, cockier, but that was only thanks to the "Google strategy," he knew that . . . no, in any case, he'd never become his own jailer. He'd never be overwhelmed by the fugitive's anxiety: you have all the time you need to relive things, and not enough to live.

To keep faith with the promise he'd made, in those four months, Nicolas had stuck to a strict program. Out of bed, breakfasting on the food left over from the day before, then physical exercise. Up and down the stairs of the apartment building, knees high, like a U.S. marine at boot camp. After which, he'd go back to his apartment, wait for the hands from outside to remove a couple of bricks and shove in food (always cold, occasionally a bowl of pasta, mostly sandwiches), and eat a meal, relaxing with the PlayStation as he ate. He'd spend the afternoon playing *Grand Theft Auto* and penalty kicks between Napoli of the nineties and some other domestic team. When he was sick of games, he'd switch on his

Motorola StarTAC and get some work done. He'd issue orders, sending out his digital *pizzini*—the short notes of a mafioso—like a real old-time boss. Before dinner—another sandwich, washed down with still mineral water—he'd call Letizia. Her belly was growing. She said that she felt ugly as sin. He retorted that she was simply gorgeous. I love you, Nico'. I love you, Leti'.

From the last farewell to his wife to the moment when the generator turned off was exactly fifty-three minutes. Nicolas would start the count-down on his iPhone and begin his exploration: that was the only activity that could keep his mind off the impending night.

The place was a museum. In the apartments he was able to gain access to, abandoned objects glittered with life, with the lives of dozens and dozens of fugitives from the law who had occupied those rooms before Nicolas. Geological stratifications of walled-in criminals on the lam. Porn DVDs, a rifle broken in half, a waterbed, ripped open, that must have offered a taste of luxury in the two hundred square feet of that cell. A whole life, frozen in place, that reminded Nicolas of the lives immortalized forever in Pompeii and Herculaneum. A coffee table with a hand of cards lying on it, left in the middle of a round of solitaire, women's panties the fugitive must have sniffed until he'd worn out their smell, a painting of the sea, the freedom of water. But the thing that had enchanted him most were the writings scribbled on the walls: the names of children, wives, surrounded by timid hearts, unconfessable feelings revealed on the walls of a man's cell. One time, Nicolas had found a pencil stub and had sharpened the point by rubbing it against the wall, and then he had written the letter C. Christian or Cristiana, a memory of the past or an announcement of the future, even he couldn't say. Then he'd hurled the stub against the far wall. He'd get out of there, eventually. When it was five minutes until dark, he'd race back to his apartment and curl up in his bed. Soon the generator would switch off and the nightmare would begin.

Rats. They emerged in the darkness and filled the hollow spaces between walls, scurried along the baseboards, squeaking out those high notes, filthy creatures that they were. At first he had believed that those vibrations and thumps from inside the walls merely indicated a structural weakness, and that had frightened him; he'd ventured out onto the staircases to check it out, and as he climbed one flight of stairs he'd slipped on something soft and slimy at the same time. A rat. That's how he had discovered them. Nicolas had always hated rats. How many of them he'd shot, how many he'd crushed, he'd even blown one or two of them up. And now they were having their revenge, now that he was defenseless, now that he couldn't even see them. In that darkness, they seemed to be immaterial, ghostly, a form of torture designed to deprive him of sleep. Even the walls in those nights lost the reality that established the perimeter of his days, and they drew in on him, so that every space became claustrophobic, suffocating.

It was hours before Nicolas managed to get to sleep, and in his dreams, the rats were gnawing right and left, even chewing into his skull. When he reawakened, he checked himself all over for bite marks. After which, he left the night behind him as if he were destined never to return to it, and his last thought was of the stupid mistake he'd made, that bullet he'd fired into the cranium of some random asshole. But the guy had looked at him, he'd stared at him, as if he'd raped him. Those eyes ought to have been lowered: if you let them look at you, then you've lost from the outset.

The nights all followed the same terrible script and the days rolled on monotonously, except for the business he needed to handle from there. It wasn't bad, giving orders from a distance, but he missed his *paranza*, the admiration of the youngsters, and that sensation of being recognized on the street. He consoled himself with the thought of what his return would be like.

One afternoon, though, Letizia intruded into his solitude.

"My water has broken," she told him over the phone. She was heading for the hospital with her mother.

Nicolas kept his cool as he did in all emergency situations, and given the distance, it was easier, in that case. He reassured her, then he called Tucano and told him to escort her and stand guard, to make sure that no one got it into their head to do what he'd tried with Dentino's son.

Then he called Letizia and stayed on the phone with her until the generator turned off.

It was only the next morning that the usual hand that brought him food also stuck an A4 sheet of paper through the hole, printed with a photograph: Letizia and Cristiana were beautiful.

He had the sensation that this new life of his was taking something away from him, that he had lost something that he really would never be able to get back, and for the first time he thought back to the words his father had spoken, at the cemetery.

# THE HIDING PLACE

Aza had wept only once in her life, when her mother had died, and then she'd promised herself she'd never do it again, because how could there ever be a greater sorrow, a harsher pain?

The signora had died in her sleep, after letting out a scream that had awakened her. Aza had raced into her bedroom, she'd seen her motionless as usual, and, seized by a presentiment, she'd lowered her ear to the signora's chest. Nothing, and not a breath from her mouth. She'd left the room afraid, and then she'd felt tears roll down her cheeks, salt on her lips. The taste of her mother.

Before calling the ambulance and the signora's children, Aza had taken the time to say a prayer. They'd loved each other, Aza and the signora, in spite of the Alzheimer's tireless efforts to delete their relationship. Aza had mothered her, right up to the end.

The signora's children showed up the next day, by which time Aza had already made all the arrangements. She didn't trust those three ungrateful wretches who had made no more effort than a weekly phone call, at least not since Aza had taken up her duties: "Everything okay, Mammà?"

The heirs entered the apartment with the gait of someone finally taking possession of a territory. The two sons were accompanied by their wives; they barely said hello to Aza and then headed for the bed where their mother had slept for almost her entire life, but they didn't sit down next to it. They brushed the dead woman, with either a sleeve or the back of a hand, but none of them bent over to give her a kiss. Worried she might be an unwelcome presence, Aza went back to the kitchen, where the youngest daughter was sitting at the table, smoking a cigarette. She was clearly working up her nerve to go into the bedroom, or maybe she just wanted to be alone when she saw her mother; she didn't get along well with her sisters-in-law. As soon as she looked up at Aza, she asked whether her mother had said any final words before dying.

"Your mother hasn't said a word in months," Aza replied politely.

"Ah" was all she said, and then she made up her mind to enter the bedroom.

After not even five minutes the sons and the daughters-in-law were already sifting attentively through cabinets and drawers, rummaging at first discreetly and then with increasing gusto, eyes narrowed like someone hoping to unearth buried treasure.

Aza stayed in the kitchen, looking out the window as she waited for the hearse to arrive from the undertakers'. Only the undertakers would be able to silence those jackals, as they pawed over the dead, she raged inwardly. She was furious, she wished she could kick them all out of the apartment; in fact, she was tempted to pull out one of the weapons that she was watching over for Nicolas and mow them all down in the living room. She froze, gripped the window casement, and berated herself for her stupidity. The weapons! How could she have failed to think of it? She'd had a whole day to make the weapons disappear, and now the apartment was full of people poking and prying in every corner.

While the signora's children were busy in the living room, keeping an eye on one another, she slipped into the hiding place, stood on tiptoe, and glimpsed a corner of the green duffel bag. That was enough to reassure her. In the living room, she found the children sitting on the sofa with unhappy looks on their faces: they hadn't even bothered to shut the drawers, to tidy up in the aftermath of their revolting treasure hunt. Which still wasn't finished.

"Mammà promised me that she would give the apartment to my daughter Giorgia," said one of the daughters-in-law.

"What are you talking about?" the signora's daughter rebelled. "Mammà promised it to me."

"Sweetheart," the other brother said acidly, both hands in his pockets, a serious expression on his face. "Mammà was sick and didn't leave a will."

"Teresa," the other brother drove in, "you don't have any children. What would you even do with Mamma's apartment?"

The doorbell interrupted them. The undertakers, at last. Aza got up to answer the door while the others went on arguing about lawyers, notaries, and inheritance taxes. She ushered the four men through the front door, and, hats in hand over their belt buckles and in silence, they approached the heirs.

"Our sincerest condolences," said one of the undertakers, a guy with a pair of legs as long as stilts, so that he looked like an oversized wading bird.

The children and the daughters-in-law murmured "*grazie*" a couple of times, but it was obvious that they'd been interrupted and just wanted to get back to their discussion. The men from the undertaker exchanged embarrassed glances, whereupon the tall skinny one said: "We're here to take care of the signora."

The tension still showed no sign of subsiding, and Aza spoke before she even realized she'd done it. "A moment of silence for the signora," she said, without anger, in the tone of a priest inviting the faithful to kneel. They all turned inward in a brief moment of prayer, then the heirs left the apartment with the excuse that they couldn't stand being there for the closing of the coffin.

Aza showed the men the way to the bedroom where the dead woman lay and remained with them as they gently lifted the signora's withered little corpse and delicately laid it in the coffin. They'd hold the wake in one of the rooms designated for that purpose at the funeral parlor.

Transporting the coffin down the stairs was hard work. Aza helped the three pallbearers carrying the casket by giving them directions: "Higher, look out for the railing, hold on, careful." Down in the street, the signora's family had resumed their earlier discussion, and it was only at the very last that they even noticed the coffin being placed in the hearse.

In the chilly little room, under the anguished eyes of a Madonna painted on a pennant, Aza went on praying, for herself, for the dead woman, and to hold at bay her unhappy thoughts about her own future: Now what would she do? Where would she find another position, another job? And to bring down a benediction on those big green duffel bags that, she hoped, would still be there upon her return. She'd been a very capable custodian of them all this time, Nicolas would have to recognize that much at least.

She came back on the bus nearly three hours later, and she hurried straight over to the hiding place. The bags were gone. She pulled out her cell phone and angrily texted Nicolas.

**Aza**
The signora's children. Those pigs took
everything and carried it off.

# FROM EARTH AND SKY

One morning, Nicolas heard a sound he'd never heard before, coming from outside. The police? Impossible. They wouldn't have made all that noise. Those were scooters, and there had to be hundreds of them, maybe thousands. The roar seemed to emanate from the earth itself, like the rumble of a tsunami about to slam into the walled-up apartment building.

Nicolas lay flat on his belly, his ear glued to a crack between the floor tiles. "Motor scooters, sure enough, I wasn't mistaken," he said aloud. Then the noise suddenly stopped. He pressed his ear back against the floor. "Maraja! Maraja! Maraja!" A chorus of voices. I've lost my mind, he thought. He got up off the floor as if to move away from that hallucination, but even so, standing in the middle of the room, he could hear his name, "Maraja! Maraja! Maraja!" chanted faster and faster. Then he saw dust and chunks of plaster falling from a wall, and finally the tip of a pick penetrating the walled-up door. His hand darted rapidly to his pistol, but the light was already pouring in from outside, and his eyes were so unaccustomed to the sun that it took him a while before they could withstand the intensely blazing light. The shouting voices continued to chant his name, and more and more light filtered through his eyelashes: there was now a big hole in the wall. And then there was a crowd of young men outside, all on scooters, singing Maraja's praises. Among them, he was able to identify Susamiello.

"You see?" the youngster said to him. "We came to get you." Nicolas squinted and tried to focus. They each had both hands raised and crossed. Their fingers were bent to make a symbol. The left forefinger was pointing at the sky, the right forefinger and middle finger were raised in a V for victory, but held horizontally, intersecting with the nail of the left forefinger. Those three fingers were forming an *F. F* for Forcella.

It was time to go back to the city. Escorted by hundreds of scooters: his army. The army of children who hadn't betrayed him. His army, an army that feared no one.

Drone's garage was like a warehouse of discarded technology. The shelves were piled high with hard drives and modems, the floor was cluttered with dusty monitors that progress had made obsolete. Nicolas walked in and for a moment he almost missed the walled-up neighborhood.

"I have to see Cristiana," he told Tucano, even before greeting him after all those months. The apartment in Vomero would be the first place they'd look for him, so Tucano convinced him to wait. "Too dangerous." At first Nicolas put up some resistance: How dare he tell him what he could or couldn't do? Whether he could or couldn't see his baby girl? He started shouting, he didn't give a fuck whether his voice echoed through the garage and down the apartment building's hallways.

"L'Arcangelo wants to see you. Tomorrow," Briato' said in a flat tone, and Nicolas quieted down.

"I have to go see the arsenal, I have to understand," he said, and he wouldn't brook objections on that point.

They arrived in Gianturco with Nicolas concealed in the trunk of Briato's Cayenne, while Orso Ted and Carlito's Way went ahead to scout things out. Aza confirmed what she'd texted two days earlier, and Nicolas couldn't get any contradictory information out of her; the young Eritrean woman was telling the truth. At a certain point she threw herself at

Nicolas's feet, and he helped her back up: "It's all right," he told her, but the glance he shot at Briato' and Tucano conveyed the very opposite.

Drone heard the sound of helicopter blades. It was exactly the same as in *Call of Duty*, there was no mistaking it. He emerged from his room and ran down the stairs; he had to find some way of warning Nicolas that they were coming to get him. But Nicolas had already figured it out: that helicopter kicking up a wind had already made him run far away.

Drone stepped out the downstairs front door and a policewoman floored him with a billy club to the stomach. Drone folded over at the waist and then fell to his knees. Another policeman yanked him back onto his feet, and a third cop handcuffed him. The police cars had come to a halt in a semicircle in front of his building, and now he could clearly see the helicopter high overhead, monitoring the neighborhood. Drone turned around when he heard his mother sobbing. Next to her, his father was staring at him, impassive, while Annalisa had a hand over her mouth, as if trying to choke back words she preferred not to say. The three policemen dragged him toward the squad car, but Drone dug his heels in and the officers loosened their grips slightly, to give him one last moment with his family. Drone leaned forward to give his sister a kiss. He wanted to kiss her on the mouth, in the traditional act of a clan boss sealing a pact of trust with the one who will manage their business while they're away. It's the kiss of death, which sentences the one receiving it to death if they then cheat or betray. He stretched, lips pursed, but Annalisa turned away. Then he tried the same thing with his father and then his mother. No good. It had been them after all. Annalisa had brought them around without much effort, once they found out that the boss of the Piranhas was hiding in their garage.

"Bastards! Rotten blood! Shitty traitors! I paid your salaries! I paid for your construction projects!" he shouted at his father. "I don't want to be near you, even in the cemetery!"

His family stood watching, forcing themselves to remain silent. Only when his body was already half inside the squad car did Annalisa take her hand away from her mouth and say: "Better to come see you at Poggioreale Prison than in Poggioreale Cemetery, behind a marble plaque. Better behind bars than underground."

It was almost time to head back to the garage when Tucano asked him: "What does L'Arcangelo want, I wonder?"

Nicolas shrugged. Actually, he was worried that he'd disappointed L'Arcangelo with that stupid murder, which had kept him far from his business for months. Again, he shrugged his shoulders, but Tucano was already looking elsewhere. He was staring at the sky. Nicolas sped up his pace, but Tucano seized his arm and dragged him into a hallway. A helicopter darted between the buildings, nose down to cut through the wind, as if it were abandoning the theater of operations. Nicolas and Tucano stepped back out into the open, made sure that the street was empty, and continued toward Drone's house. One more corner to turn, and Nicolas would be safe again.

The sirens of a couple of squad cars split the air, and Tucano and Nicolas flattened themselves against a wall, like a couple of clandestine operatives surprised by the fall of the curfew. Nicolas leaned out and just managed to glimpse Drone's head vanishing into a police car, and his family trooping back into the building.

"What now?" Tucano asked, stammering.

"Now we go to the lair. It's all burned . . . not even a dead man would hide out there."

## TOWARD THE CORONATION

**W**hy did you always make me come up through Professoressa Cicatello's apartment?"

In front of Nicolas was a metal platform that would have been able to hold at the very most four people. A panel with just two buttons—UP and DOWN—controlled the mechanical arms of that jury-rigged freight elevator, without walls or even railings, without a roof.

"This is L'Arcangelo's private elevator. Here, if you fall, there's no insurance," 'o Cicognone said with a laugh.

Nicolas nodded. Tucano and Briato' had escorted him from the lair to the porticoes, and then Cicognone had taken delivery of him and had walked him around to the back of the building. The rear façade was falling apart and the vegetation that grew over it all covered the elevator to perfection.

During his time on the run, Nicolas had felt just like that backyard. In order to cut his beard, first he'd had to use a pair of scissors, and then an electric razor. He'd left the walled-up neighborhood like a castaway brought back to civilization who discovers that under the filth, a man still exists.

"We heard you let someone steal the arsenal." 'O Cicognone drove the point home as the elevator was taking them up. "L'Arcangelo took a little offense at that." The blade of the hoist jerked violently and Nicolas's breath caught in his throat; he was forced to plant his legs wide to maintain his balance. Cicognone's words didn't bode particularly well for the interview to which he'd been summoned. For the past several hours, he'd done nothing but talk to his *paranza* about the upcoming meeting: There had to be something big behind it, but what?

The freight elevator stopped a few yards short of the roof. Painted the same hue as the wall, a small metal door swung open when pushed, giving onto the stairs that led to L'Arcangelo's apartment.

Nicolas leaped across the yard of empty air between the freight elevator and the door and waited for Cicognone.

"Now you know the way," Cicognone said, and pressed DOWN.

Nicolas felt his carotid artery pounding against the flesh of his neck. He took the steps calmly, guided by L'Arcangelo's voice, which carried all the way up there. He couldn't make out exactly what the man was saying, but he could tell that he was in a good mood because the belly laughs were unmistakable, and then he caught the timbre of a different laugh.

L'Arcangelo was sitting in his usual armchair, and in the armchair next to him was a man whose wrinkled face suggested he might be the same age as the master of the house. But if L'Arcangelo carried the marks of the passing years with great dignity, as if showing off a glorious past, the other man masked his age with an excessive tan and bangs with an orangey hue that hung diagonally over the oval of his face.

"You have guests and you don't inform me?" Nicolas began, on the attack.

"No," L'Arcangelo retorted. "I also forgot to tell you that I took two shits today, are you offended about that, too?"

Nicolas tried out a conciliatory smile, and stood there as if he were being interrogated the whole time; Don Vittorio made no introductions, nor did he invite Nicolas to take a seat. Instead it was L'Arcangelo who stood up, went over to a shelf to get the bottle that had stood there, enjoying pride of place, for years, the bottle that Gabriele had given him, the bottle that every so often Don Vittorio would look at, as if in its place he could see his son's face. This time, however, he took it down, held it up to the light to admire its dense reddish hue, which reflected on his olive complexion, then calmly got out three wineglasses and uncorked it.

"What's happened, Don Vitto', to make you pop the cork on this exceedingly fine bottle?" Nicolas asked, his voice cracking with expectation.

"Take a seat, Maraja, and sample this wine," Don Vittorio replied. He half filled a glass and took a quick sip. "Ah," he said, and he clucked his tongue. "Excellent. Bordeaux, ninety-five percent merlot. A 1990, an excellent year." He took a longer drink, slowly, and then set the glass down on the armrest of his chair. "It's important to celebrate, Nico', otherwise every hour of the day is the same."

"True words," added L'Arcangelo's guest.

"Nico'," Don Vittorio went on, "do you know Don Arturo Lauretta?"

"Of course. Don Arturo 'o Sciroppo."

"My reputation precedes me," said 'o Sciroppo. "All the same, there's only one rock star in this room," he added, and extended his glass toward Nicolas, who returned the gesture, relaxing a little in his chair. But he still couldn't figure out for the life of him what 'o Sciroppo was doing there, nor why Don Vittorio had organized this meeting. Everyone knew the Lauretta family; they'd been solidly ensconced in Marano from time out of mind and their alliance with the Sicilian Mafia had made them an all-powerful enclave to the north of the city.

"Let's take a selfie, Maraja," said 'o Sciroppo. "I'll send it to my grandchildren."

Nicolas gulped down the Bordeaux, letting that guy give him a hug and ready his pose for the selfie. In the meantime, L'Arcangelo had poured himself a little more wine. He raised the glass to the ceiling and started declaiming: "The kings of the inhabited earth will be gathered . . ."

'O Sciroppo smiled and snapped another picture.

"And I saw the beast, and the kings of the earth, and their armies, gathered together to make war against him that sat on the horse, and against his army."

"What is this prayer?" Nicolas murmured to 'o Sciroppo.

"But the fearful, and unbelieving, and the abominable, and murderers, and whoremongers, and sorcerers, and idolaters, and all liars, shall have their part in the lake which burneth with fire and brimstone," Don Vittorio went on.

"Don Vitto' . . ."

"And their flesh shall consume away while they stand upon their feet, and their eyes shall consume away in their holes, and their tongue shall consume away in their mouth." And with that he drained his glass to the very last drop. "It's the Apocalypse, Nico'," he explained at last. "Revelation. Zecharaia. The Bible, you have to read the Bible. You learn a lot of things!"

All this way, the risk of coming all the way out here while wanted by the police, to listen to this bullshit? thought Nicolas.

"The Apocalypse is what's happening," Don Vittorio went on. "Micione has surrendered. He wants to meet with me." At those words, Nicolas sat up straight, attentive now. "The historic center, Maraja, he wants to give it to me. He realizes now that there's nothing he can do to stop you, and he can't afford to unleash a full-scale gang war. So he's decided to turn to an old friend . . ."

"Don Vitto', what the fuck are you talking about?"

"Now, now, don't be rude, Nico'! Things are changing around here, for real." A hint of hope bloomed in Nicolas's mind. "Don Arturo, here, and his family have agreed to a meeting in Marano. He'll serve as guarantor. Micione and his men will be without weapons. Only . . ."

"Only what?"

"Only instead of me going, you'll go."

And at that point everything became clear to him, and Nicolas understood what was being celebrated that morning. At last, his was to be the kingdom and the glory.

"You walk in and shoot him right in the face. At that point Forcella goes to you, and I take back San Giovanni, my old home. And there's nothing finer than going back to your old home. You can travel the world 'round, but there's nothing finer."

Nicolas visualized the scene, Diego Faella's big moon face blasted wide open. Their victory would be definitive, the Google method of savage price cuts in order to corner the market triumphant now, *i Bambini*, the Piranhas, winning against the old folks, against all the jacks of hearts. A smile escaped him, but he concealed it by raising the glass to his lips.

There was just one detail that didn't quite add up, and it needed to be cleared up immediately. "Excuse me, 'o Sciroppo, but if you're the guarantor, won't Micione's family take it out on you afterward?"

"The minute you walk out of that room," said 'o Sciroppo, with the confidence of someone who had gone over the plan countless times already, "we alert our men, who are already in position to rub out 'o Pagliaccio, Viola Striano, and all their men who are willing and ready to take a shot."

The idea of Viola and Pagliaccio dying pleased him greatly, almost more than Micione: Viola had denied him the pleasure of settling matters personally with Drago', but she'd still left him with the burden of that death, the slut, he thought to himself. While 'o Pagliaccio had killed Stavodicendo, according to what the patrons of the bar who'd been watching the game had told him. "So why are you doing it?" he asked 'o Sciroppo.

"What are all these questions!?" L'Arcangelo blurted out. "How dare you question the motives of the Lauretta family?"

"No, Don Vitto'," said 'o Sciroppo. "The rock star wants to know, and that's only right. You know why I want to do this thing? Because now you'll buy our drugs. Since you started bringing in weed from Albania, ours hasn't been moving anymore." And he smiled again. Perfect teeth, straight out of an ad for oral hygiene.

"This *guaglione* is a smart boy!" L'Arcangelo told 'o Sciroppo, as if Nicolas wasn't even in the room. "You really are a smart boy, Nico'. I've taught you well," he said then, addressing him directly. L'Arcangelo rarely paid compliments, and usually Nicolas took great pleasure from them, but right now his excitement about the future that he'd played and replayed in his mind every day in the walled-up neighborhood, easily a hundred times a day, was finally there. The last time he'd felt an emotion even remotely similar was when he was watching on the screen of his cell phone the first few moments of life of his little Cristiana, the princess of the historic center.

L'Arcangelo poured him another glass. "And now let me tell you another thing: 'o Sciroppo, here? His wife is my wife's sister. And Micione's mother is his mother's cousin . . ."

"*Ua*', L'Arcangelo, but what are all these relatives? I don't understand a fucking thing!"

"Nico', I have to say, you are one rude young man, there's nothing to be done about it," L'Arcangelo scolded him. "I told you this so that you'd understand why Don Arturo is acting as guarantor between me and the Faellas. He's got blood from both families in his veins."

"I don't care about all this chain of relatives, cousins, and mixed blood," said Nicolas. "A person counts for the balls they have, not for their balls' cousins. And Don Sciroppo, if you don't mind my saying so, after I kill Micione, you'll have half your family gunning for you."

"We're all ready to do it," 'o Sciroppo replied. "Let me say it to you once again."

"You're ready to betray your flesh and blood?"

"How's it feel, Maraja, to become the king of Naples?" L'Arcangelo asked, changing the subject. "When I took San Giovanni and Ponticelli all those years ago, in 1992, I wasn't walking: I was flying."

"Of course you were," Nicolas replied, willing to lessen the tension. "You're the Archangel, after all."

L'Arcangelo smiled, then quickly put in: "Sure, but don't kid yourself. After you fly, you know how many ass-fuckings you have to sit still for? Commanding isn't easy. You become the father of everyone, and if there's one thing I know about children, it's that they bust your balls. Anything that turns out right, the credit goes to them, but anything that goes sideways is *your* fault—"

"Don Arca'," Nicolas interrupted him. All that talk about blood and power was *his* territory. "Maybe you've forgotten how to command, but I haven't. Here, the Piranhas take care of things; my brothers will get you out of this sewer."

L'Arcangelo looked at 'o Sciroppo contentedly. He was visibly displaying his paternal pride. For a son who was becoming a man while following his own path, in spite of everything.

"Come on, let's drink," he said: there was still plenty to talk about. And L'Arcangelo gathered the various threads of the plan for the ambush: "Let's go back over it. You go to Cupa dei Cani, tonight. How many guys do you take with you? Who are you taking?"

"Tucano and Briato'."

"Fine. What weapons will you be carrying?"

"I'll have my Desert Eagle. Tucano has a Smith and Wesson, Briato' has a Glock."

"A Glock? A woman's gun? If you'd told me that before—"

"What am I supposed to do about it? They stole the arsenal . . . There's no time—"

"Sure, I know, but I'll give you the weapons, 'o Cicognone'll take care of it."

"But how will we get into Cupa dei Cani? Micione's men aren't carrying, but—"

"'O Cicognone will take care of that, too. Briato' will be stationed outside the immediate area, as a reserve force, but a force that can take action on a moment's notice," L'Arcangelo said calmly. "That way, whatever happens, say the police arrive or Micione brings someone else, he can take action and shoot him." Nicolas nodded. "And you'll go alone with Tucano."

"All right, Don Vitto', then it's all taken care of. I'm ready." He was eager—that evening seemed too far away, he wanted to go to Cupa dei Cani straight from there.

"This is exactly the way I expected him to be, Don Arca'," 'o Sciroppo spat out. "You can see he sprang from your loins."

"The only loins I sprang from are my mother's, Don Sciro'," Nicolas shot back.

They all burst out laughing, and Don L'Arcangelo stood up from his armchair. "Come here," he said, and shook hands with him. Then, unexpectedly, he hugged him, but Nicolas didn't mind, it was a special day.

He found Briato' and Tucano waiting where he'd left them, with 'o Cicognone and Aucelluzzo, who greeted him by placing a fist in the open palm of the other hand and leaning slightly forward. Nicolas told his men to exchange weapons: they handed over their own and Aucelluzzo handed out two AK-47s and a pump shotgun for Briato'.

And then off to Forcella. To kill time before the coronation, to drink a toast in their charred lair.

# FLESH AND BLOOD

**M**araja seemed dressed for another wedding, but instead he was going to take the scepter that awaited him.

"Maraja, get moving," said Tucano, checking the clock on his phone for the umpteenth time. "We're running late, and Briato' is already there."

"My wedding and this: these are moments I'm going to have to remember for the rest of my life, deep down," Nicolas said, fastening the top button of his jacket. He'd had it custom tailored along with his wedding suit, intentionally, and Pachi had gone over to Letizia's to get it. She had it stored carefully, wrapped in tissue paper, beside the wedding suit.

"But when you got married, people were looking at you," said Tucano, who was wearing a black Urban Classic jumpsuit. "No one here is going to remember your good suit." Then he laughed and leveled his AK-47.

Nicolas let him talk, this was his moment, and he could take it, all the rest was nothing but words. At first glance, Micione would understand it all. He would read the symbols, he would glimpse the new king, and Nicolas couldn't wait to see the look of dawning awareness of his impending fall on that piece of shit's big moon face.

"Are you ready, Maraja?" Tucano was buzzing around Nicolas like a horsefly.

"*Ua'*, Tuca'," said Nicolas, chuckling. "Are you in a hurry? The party can't start without us, don't worry."

"I'm in no hurry, Nico', it's just that I want to make sure there aren't any surprises."

"What surprises! You've done all the on-site inspections, haven't you?"

Tucano had spent hours doing the on-site inspections. He'd tried out the fastest route, the longest one, the one that went around Capodimonte Park and the one that followed the ring road.

Cupa dei Cani. It was there, in that bit of Marano outside Naples, that Don Vittorio had arranged the meeting. Nicolas hadn't reacted when L'Arcangelo had informed him of the location where it would all be decided; he would have looked like a child whose parents have just told him that the family was going to Euro Disney Resort: Marano, Poggio Vallesana, Nuvoletta, Cosa Nostra . . . The list of connections could go on endlessly, extending over decades of Camorra wars and Sicilian infiltrations, illustrious murders and corpses dissolved in acid. A legendary place, where the fate of Campania had been decided, along with plenty more. L'Arcangelo had chosen well, Nicolas thought inwardly.

Tucano had procured a brand-new scooter for Nicolas, a nondescript Honda like so many others going by on the street, with documentation that checked out perfectly. Nicolas climbed aboard, taking care not to get anything on his suit. Tucano rode ahead, checking out the situation and reporting back to him through his earpiece, to alert him to any potential checkpoints or suspicious cars.

Nicolas was driving no faster than 35 m.p.h. and the wind burrowing into his sleeves made him feel as light as a kite.

"Everything all right, Maraja?" Tucano asked in his earpiece.

"Everything's all right," Nicolas replied, clearing his throat. Unintentionally, he went back to where it all began, his bedroom at home. "The less we have now, the more we'll have later," he used to say to Christian, and he'd said it to Briato', too, to Drago', Dentino, Stavodicendo, Biscottino, Cerino, and Tucano . . . to all his friends. He hadn't yet been carrying the burden of all the tragedies, betrayals, disappointments, and errors: back then, all he'd had was potential, endless potential.

They'd been driving for ten minutes or so when Nicolas managed to rid himself of his memories and noticed that Tucano was leading him in circles.

"Tuca'," said Nicolas, "what kind of fucked-up route are we taking? We're still in Vomero."

Silence on the other end of the line.

"Tuca', for fuck's sake—" Nicolas said, more sharply. His second-in-command had slammed on the brakes and Nicolas had narrowly missed crashing into him.

"I made a surprise for you, Maraja."

"We don't have time for this bullshit—"

"Hold on."

Nicolas hadn't noticed that they were driving by his apartment building, because he'd never been to that building in his life. On the third floor, the green curtain that was covering a French window pulled back like a curtain on a stage. Letizia was wearing a dressing gown, and over that, a white blanket. Her hair hung loose, all brushed to one side. In her arms, she held Cristiana, who was fast asleep, swaddled in a pink blanket. Letizia blew him a kiss with one hand and then pointed to her daughter, smiling at him, as if to say, look what a nice life our daughter has, she just eats and sleeps all day. Nicolas smiled, too, and after getting off his scooter, he did a pirouette, so his wife could admire him, and his wife slowly enunciated: "You look wonderful."

"So do you," said Nicolas, pointing his forefinger up at her, as if there were other women up there beside her. He cupped his hands together: "I love you," he shouted, and Letizia started, a sob of emotion choked back to keep from awakening the little one. "We love you too."


Nicolas and Tucano got there a few minutes early. The car was there, right where it was supposed to be. A white Alfa Romeo, parked half on the asphalt and half on the dirt berm that marked the edge of the fields. They left their scooters about fifty yards away, as per instructions, and continued on foot. The key was supposed to be in the wheel well, directly above the right rear tire.

And in fact, there it was. Nicolas looked around. From there, they could see the roof of the building where the meeting was supposed to be taking place. Red brick, no antennas, not even a chimney pot, the place was an open-air bunker. It was situated right at the center of a slightly raised expanse of dirt, higher than the cherry orchards that surrounded it; L'Arcangelo had told him that the only way to reach it was by a dirt lane.

"Is Briato' in position?" Nicolas asked.

Tucano fooled around with his cell phone and then held it up to his ear.

"Yes, he's there. He's still in a quiet area, off to one side. He's waiting for instructions to head into the hot zone."

They got in the car. Nicolas started the engine, and the Alfa Romeo turned over, coughing and wheezing. The two of them exchanged a glance with the same thought in mind: Let's hope they don't hear us coming. They took the first left turn, into a dead-end street that ran alongside small detached houses surrounded by metal fencing. Nicolas was driving at about five miles per hour, his eyes focused between the cherry trees to identify the lane. They reached a fence that marked the boundary of the last detached house. Nicolas made a U-turn.

"Where the fuck is this lane?" asked Tucano. "Is this still the quiet zone?" He was sweating and he kept mopping his forehead with his forearm. Nicolas veered sharply right; he'd spotted something in the distance, a gleam, perhaps a reflection of the sunlight on a mirror, or a sentinel standing guard. It was worth checking out.

"There it is," said Nicolas.

Tucano leaned out the car window. A lighter strip of earth compared with the surrounding terrain, and a few signs of truck traffic that the sentinels had apparently failed to erase sufficiently.

They rolled slowly forward, even though by now the sentinels must have spotted them. The first checkpoint consisted of two men who waved for them to slow down. L'Arcangelo's men, Nicolas had crossed paths with them a few times before. He only needed to lift his foot off the accelerator pedal and pull the hand brake. The guards checked the license plate and let them proceed. A hundred feet later, another checkpoint, and two more of L'Arcangelo's men checked the license plate again.

The cherry trees gave way to the enclosure wall, which stood at least six feet tall and was topped by sharp chunks of tile. The way into the estate was through a white gate before which a tall, slightly bowed man was strolling, as if measuring its extent.

"That's 'o Cicognone," said Tucano. Nicolas drove up to him and lowered the window.

"*Guagliu'*," 'o Cicognone said, "go straight ahead, along the wall. There's a sort of stable, just pull your car in there. Shut the gate, pull out your guns, and wait." He opened the gate just enough to get through and then vanished behind it.

They followed the wall around the estate until they came to the sharp right turn, where there was a large open area with a tumbledown stable, where two horses were chomping hay. Nicolas steered the car around and backed into the stables, next to the horses, which showed no signs of concern.

"*Ua'*, look how pretty they are," said Tucano, jumping out of the car to pet them. "I'll bet these boys are fast, what do you say? And I know the whole Lauretta clan are crazy for horses."

Nicolas grabbed the gate with both hands and started to pull until he noticed that Tucano was out in the open.

"What the fuck are you doing, Tuca'?" asked Nicolas, in a low voice. "Why are you playing with horses?"

"Nico'," said Tucano, "come and see."

So Nicolas followed him, crouching down in the brush. They could hear engines in the distance and soon enough three jeeps and an SUV rose over the hill from the opposite direction.

"That's Micione with his bodyguards," said Tucano.

In those cars, Nicolas reckoned mentally, there could easily be as many as fifteen men, armed to the teeth.

"They've laid an ambush for us," said Tucano, his voice climbing by a good octave.

"Ssssh, shut up," said Nicolas. He leaned out to get a better view, but the cars had turned the corner and all he could see was the brake lights on the last jeep in line.

They heard the gate to the estate opening with creaking noises and one of the cars accelerating to go through the opening. Then the repeated *beep* of the SUVs backing up. The bodyguards were leaving; Micione was going in alone, and of course, unarmed, just as L'Arcangelo had told them.

This was the moment. They waited for the noise of the cars to die down before moving forward.

"*Ua', guagliu'*, what the fuck are you doing out here?" Aucelluzzo had emerged from the stables, out of breath. "You were supposed to wait inside."

Nicolas crossed the road, arms thrown wide. "That's just the way it went, Aucellu'."

"Get moving, come on, come get your girlfriends," said Aucelluzzo.

"Calm down," Nicolas told him, smacking him in the nuts with the back of his hand. Tucano and Nicolas got out the AK-47s they'd hidden in the trunk.

"Let's go, Tuca'," said Nicolas, with a smile, and cocked the automatic rifle. He'd use it only if necessary, if the situation went sideways. He was planning to kill Micione with his knife, the one that L'Arcangelo had given him.

"Where is he?" he asked Aucelluzzo.

"There's an office, the minute you go in. He's in there. I'll take you."

Aucelluzzo led them to the big white gate and kicked it three times to alert 'o Cicognone.

"Leave it open," Nicolas told him, after stepping into the broad open plaza that overlooked the estate. Briato' must be somewhere in the area, but he'd never be able to get over the wall to come to their assistance if something went wrong.

Nicolas ran a hand over his collar; he was drenched with sweat, and the tattoo at the nape of his neck seemed to be covered with a greasy sheen.

"Are you afraid?" 'o Cicognone genially needled him. "We still have time to call it off."

No, Nicolas wasn't afraid. He was about to bring the scepter back to Forcella, how could he be afraid? He was about to become the boy king, how could he be afraid? He was about to kill the man who had destroyed his *paranza*, how could he be afraid?

"'O Cicogno'," said Nicolas. "It's time."

The front door opened into an enormous empty room; at the far end, next to a large planter, was a closed door.

"He's in there," said Aucelluzzo.

Nicolas made sure he'd loaded the AK-47, and then he took off, without giving it a second thought, because he'd already thought far too hard about that moment: now the time had come, and he just needed to act.

The door swung open easily, without resistance. "'O Micio', it's all over now," he said, aiming the gat at him. But Micione's face showed neither terror nor astonishment, just the usual mocking grin. Diego Faella really did have a pair of balls on him, he thought to himself.

"It's all over now," Nicolas said again, and only then did he focus on the people sitting at the table with Micione. There was La Zarina, 'o Sciroppo with his smarmy, untroubled face, and, as if he'd sprung out of some short circuit in his brain, Nicolas saw L'Arcangelo in person, his feet propped up on a green duffel bag, with the guns sticking out of it. The guns. His guns. The *paranza*'s arsenal.

He squinted, shutting his eyes, but when he opened them again, L'Arcangelo was still sitting right there.

"I don't get it," said Tucano in a loud voice, right behind him. "What's happening?" Dreamily, in a daze.

"You see," said Don Vittorio to Micione, pointing to the Rolex on his right wrist. "He showed up right on time. What did I tell you? 'O Maraja is always right on time."

"Don Vitto', what the fuck is going on here?" asked Nicolas. He was holding his AK-47 aimed right at Micione, but his finger on the trigger hung limp.

"And now that we've gotten the *paranzas* out of the way," L'Arcangelo went on, "I'm taking central Naples all for myself, with everything that's in it . . ."

"Not everything," said Micione, looking at La Zarina. "You supply the piazzas and I provide protection for the businesses . . ."

They were haggling. They were actually in the final phases of divvying it all up, the instant before the final signatures.

"Don Vitto', what the fuck are you doing? You're selling off my zone!" Nicolas was shaking, and the vibration was making the metal components rattle. At last he made up his mind to do what he'd planned to do from the very start, and he jammed his finger down on the trigger and angrily started spraying the AK-47 back and forth, the way a little kid might do with a toy weapon. Micione lifted both hands to his belly. "Oh, no, aaargh, Maraja's killed me," he said with all the seriousness that little kids put into it when they're playing.

Then Tucano in his turn pulled the trigger. *Click*. He'd set it to semi-automatic to improve his aim, and he knew that if he wanted to fire again, he needed to pull the trigger. *Click*. It was an empty sound, like a wet firecracker. He pulled the trigger again. Nothing happened.

"They gave us piece-of-shit guns, they're no good! Nicolas!" cried Tucano, furious.

L'Arcangelo stretched his legs to push the duffel bag out of the way and get to his feet. He was even more elegantly dressed than the last time Nicolas had seen him, even more elegantly dressed than Nicolas was.

"Maraja, Maraja," he said, and for an instant Nicolas secretly hoped that this, too, was part of their agreement. Don Vittorio was stepping lightly on the terra-cotta floor; he looked twenty years younger. He placed his hand on the barrel of Nicolas's AK-47, pushing down on the front sight. And then he kissed him. On the mouth. Hard, violently jamming his lips against Nicolas's, until he opened them. Then their heads separated. "What have I always told you? That if everyone else is looking up, then you have to look down. If everyone else is looking out, then you have to look in. You always have to look where everyone else isn't. This time, you just didn't look."

"You fucking bastard!" Nicolas shouted, his face twisted with rage.

I'm the one who's falling now, I was on top of the sky and now I'm going to eat dirt, he thought, and he shoved the older man away, hitting him flat on his double-breasted suit with his Kalashnikov. But L'Arcangelo continued smiling, as if he were looking at a ferocious animal rebelling against captivity. At that point, Nicolas brandished the AK-47 and tried to swing the rifle butt to hit L'Arcangelo, but in the meantime 'o Cico-gnone had appeared behind him. He shoved him against the wall, and L'Arcangelo was still talking, he still wouldn't shut up, Nicolas was still being forced to listen to his lessons: "Nothing's happening, Nico'," he said. "This is all normal, it happens to everybody sooner or later, don't worry about it."

Tucano dropped the AK-47 and lunged at Micione, but a blast of gun-powder and lead from a revolver knocked him back a yard onto his back. Micione holstered his handgun and leaned forward to contem-plate Tucano, lying there with his throat torn open, like a sheet that once you start a tear in it, you can simply rip open. Tucano was thrashing on the floor, trying to get air, but he was slowly choking to death. Red bubbles oozed out of his mouth, large and round as soap bubbles, but instead of popping they just built up, forming a whitish foam, until they were rinsed away on a gush of blood.

"Nothing's happening, Nico'," L'Arcangelo said again, "you're just about to die is all. It's perfectly normal."

Nicolas could no longer breathe. He heard Tucano die, he could hear the sound of his friend's teeth shattering in his final convulsive clench-ing, then a gurgle and nothing more. He writhed, slamming his head against the wall in an attempt to find enough wiggle room to break free, but 'o Cicognone's hands held him braced against it, crushing his throat, as if he were squeezing a lemon.

He was going to die now, in an ambush, out of sheer stupidity; be-cause he hadn't been smart enough to foresee this—he who had become Maraja because he kept strategies in his head. The small gulps of air he managed to take in through his mouth made him retch repeatedly.

"Nico'," L'Arcangelo said again, "it's nothing personal, for real. There are those who command and those who take orders; you commanded, you did what you wanted, but children remain children, even if they're all dressed up. The jack of hearts might be slow, but when he gets there, he gets there. So long to Google, not that anyone even knows what it is, something that's in the air, not in your computer. We're on top of a table."

Nicolas looked at La Zarina. Everything that was happening was real. The Tsarina was sitting at the table with the man who had killed her son.

Don L'Arcangelo was sitting at the table with the man who had killed *his* son. It really is true, he thought, nothing matters but money.

L'Arcangelo looked at Cicognone: "Strip him," he ordered, and Cicognone crossed Nicolas's arms while, with the other hand, he undid the two buttons of his jacket that were still fastened.

L'Arcangelo was using his thumb to try the edge of his little black switchblade knife. He looked Nicolas in the eyes, as if paying him a final tribute, the honor of arms, and with a sharp jerk, buried the blade in his belly.

The air that until then he'd been trying to pull into his throat now poured out of it, as if Nicolas had finally found relief; even his face was relaxed. The black needles of his eyes were fixed on L'Arcangelo's eyes, but he couldn't see him. He would have liked to imagine his daughter's face, Letizia's eyes, but instead nothing came. He could only feel the burning blade of the knife in his belly, and the *scuorno*—the humiliation—of dying that way.

L'Arcangelo slowly pulled out the blade, careful to avoid staining his suit, and 'o Cicognone released his grip on Nicolas's throat.

Nicolas staggered forward, the rapidly spreading stain on his shirt darkening the light fabric. L'Arcangelo stabbed him again, just inches from the first wound, and then again. There was no thump, just one knee, and then the other, and finally down on his side. His temple hit the floor. And he saw Tucano. He tried to say something, to tell him not to be afraid, but he lacked the strength. He felt a great chill wash through him, and his legs started to thrash. It was over. He'd imagined dying so many times before, but he'd always believed it would be much faster. A light being switched off. Instead he could feel the parts of his body as they left him. At last, he stopped feeling the pain, because he simply stopped feeling anything.

Briato' had heard a single shot, and no texts were coming in on his cell phone, so he walked straight to the farmhouse and, without a hint of caution, threw the door open, his pump shotgun leveled, his lame leg extended as a brace. And he saw.

"No, no, no, no, no," he shouted. He aimed at L'Arcangelo, pumping the trigger. He fired three times before realizing that all that was coming out of the barrel was a puff of air, a fart of gunpowder. Then he hurled the shotgun at him and turned to run.

"Take him out," Micione shouted.

"Let's do like in *Apocalypto*," Aucelluzzo proposed, as he watched Briato' drag his leg after him, slam against the furniture in the room, and then trip over his own feet, after traveling in thirty seconds roughly the same distance that 'o Pagliaccio, who'd appeared in answer to Micione's call, and 'o Cicognone had covered in little more than five. It was like chasing a baby bird with broken wings.

"*Apoca* . . . what?" asked 'o Cicognone.

"Fuck, didn't you ever see *Apocalypto*?" asked 'o Pagliaccio. "The scene where the guy is painted blue all over, he's trying to run away from the human sacrifices, and the others all throw rocks and stones at him, shoot arrows . . . if he can get over the line, they're safe, but if he's caught they die."

'O Pagliaccio hauled out his pistol and started firing. Briato' had reached the center of the plaza, and when he heard the gunshot, he instinctively ducked, lost his balance, and sprawled headlong.

'O Cicognone gave him time to get back on his feet, then fired. Briato' ducked again, but this time he managed to stay on his feet, and the white gate was just a few yards away, within reach.

"Oh, this guy is really getting away," said 'o Pagliaccio. "Let's go get him, 'o Cicogno'."

"Eh, *ja'*, let him run, after all, we can just go pick him up at home . . ."

"Quit kidding around, knucklehead, we can't let word get out that we killed them, these guys from the Piranhas."

"Oh, what a pain in the ass . . . but why?"

"That's how L'Arcangelo wants it. The Children are a threat, even when they're dead."

'O Cicognone took off running, his long legs getting in the way of themselves. In the meantime, Briato' had reached the cherry trees; he grabbed the thin trunks of the trees to swing himself forward. If I can just reach the street, he told himself, if I can manage to get hidden in one of these little houses, then I'll hunker down, keep quiet, and tomorrow morning I'll sneak out of here and be safe.

He looked behind him. There was no one. He resumed his flight, even his injured leg seemed to be working better. I swear if I ever get home, I'll start physical therapy, he told himself. Aucelluzzo was bent over his scooter, elbows out, aiming straight at him. Briato' tried to dodge to the left and then swerve back to the right to outfox the scooter's trajectory, but the snout of the TMAX scythed into him at knee height. Briato' was lofted into the air and landed on the scooter, which had slid over on its side. Aucelluzzo got to his feet, cursing roundly, and started kicking Briato' savagely in the gut.

He continued kicking him until 'o Pagliaccio arrived, and then knelt down over Briato' as if to impart some final benediction and finished him off with a bullet to the temple.

They left him lying there, along with Aucelluzzo's wrecked scooter, and headed back to the estate, discussing *Apocalypto* as they went.

In the office, L'Arcangelo was still talking.

"Now that we've gotten the Piranhas the fuck out of the way, my men need to be in charge of all the children in Naples: 'o Cicognone and Aucelluzzo, they'll be giving the orders to the local kindergarten."

L'Arcangelo bowed his head, over the bodies of Tucano and Nicolas, and went on, as if he were speaking directly to the corpses: "The Piranhas were all good *guaglioni*. They'd done what we never did. They had the courage that no one in this room has. This one, lying on the floor"—and he jutted his chin in Nicolas's direction—"had more balls than all the rest of us. We were willing to be shut in, we started to become afraid of our own shadows. When you want something, you have to up and get it, and instead we all started dancing tarantellas, making pacts."

"Arca', I'd almost say you want him to come back to life," said Micione.

L'Arcangelo shook his head, without taking his eyes off Nicolas. "No, it's more like he brought me back to life. We're like vampires, we need young blood, we need to suck ideas we can't come up with ourselves." Then, at last, he turned back to the others: "All right, come on, we're done here."

"All right, then, order has been restored. The cake has been shared out. And no one had better overeat," said La Zarina. Micione filled his glass with Barolo and passed glasses to L'Arcangelo and 'o Sciroppo. He poured the first glass onto the floor: "The first toast is for the dead who have made it possible for us to live."

The Barolo ran over the desk, the chairs, the armchairs.

L'Arcangelo poured his glass over Tucano and Nicolas.

"The shit that gets sold in the historic center of Naples has to be bought from me. And the heroin from La Zarina." Everyone nodded at L'Arcangelo's words. "And now that we've founded the United Nations of Naples, let's make sure it lasts."

Then 'o Cicognone and Aucelluzzo arrived with two black trash bags and put the lifeless bodies of the two members of the *paranza* into them. They took them away, one after the other, dragging them across the floor.

# F12

I t was all the same. The gulf of apartment buildings, the street that twists its way to the little piazza, the bar on the corner. Even the street doors, the windows, the square yards of soil that held the palm tree, all the same. Actually, though, everything was different. The graffiti on the plaster of the wall right behind the palm tree stated that this had once been a war zone. The warriors who had ruled over this territory and had fought there had left their insignia behind them, in eternal commemoration.

F12.

Letters and numbers ten feet tall. Nicolas Fiorillo. And his soldiers.

"Was it really them, did they do it themselves?" asked Giacomino 'a Lucertola. Jimmy the Lizard.

"Wait, what, don't you know?" Salvo replied.

The school backpacks on their shoulders were bigger than they were. They sagged limply behind them because they'd left their textbooks to serve as goalposts in the playground behind the school where they played soccer.

"I know a guy from the Piranhas," Giacomino said. As he talked, he was looking at the graffiti.

"I don't believe it, Lucertoli' . . ."

"No, for real. I swear it, *adda murì mammà*."

"What are you talking about?" asked Carminiello, the third member of the group, and he took a selfie in front of the graffiti with his brand-new iPhone 7. "And who the hell is he supposed to be?" The selfie was already on his Instagram profile. "It's impossible . . ."

"No, I really know him."

Spaccanapoli. On the run. Their backpacks bouncing off their backs and all three laughing, no different than the laughter of all the other little kids happy to be out of school, with the whole long afternoon lying ahead of them.

At a certain point, Giacomino 'a Lucertola threw both arms wide, and without slowing down, even at a run, he started grabbing old advertising and election posters off the walls. The two others imitated him immediately, and from under a piece of copy paper that offered Latin tutoring there emerged another logo, another F12, but by now the three were already far away, they were already in Forcella.

"Look here," 'a Lucertola gasped. "You see these three bullet holes?" And he pointed at three holes, close together, between the door of a *basso* and a clothes drying rack groaning under the weight of laundry. "The *paranza* made these three bullet holes during a *stesa!*"

"Nooo, that's too cool!" said Carminiello.

"*Ua'*, I can't believe it," said Salvo.

They stuck their fingers into the holes. They felt their edges, careful not to peel away the plaster, and then they stuck their fingertips into them, back and forth. Salvo even stuck in his tongue. "I'm licking the bullet hole . . ."

"What the fuck are you doing?" 'a Lucertola asked him with a laugh.

"I want to see if I can still taste it . . ."

Giacomino 'a Lucertola started running again. He zigzagged right and left as if he were following an itinerary he'd covered plenty of times before. In the end, he stopped in front of a building with the blinds lowered over the windows.

"Risvoltinooo . . . Risvoltinooo!"

A man came out of the beauty parlor across the street, shouting at him to cut out that racket, but Giacomino ignored him.

"Risvoltinooo!" Both hands cupped over his mouth.

A roller blind on the fifth floor rose, creaking. "What the fuck do you want?" Risvoltino's eyes were shut, he was still half asleep, but he'd recognized Giacomino from his croaking voice.

"Come downstairs for a minute, *ja'*, please."

Risvoltino shouted insults at him, but five minutes later he was down in the street, still wearing the Boston Celtics shorts he slept in.

"Is it true that you were in the Piranhas?" Carminiello asked. He'd pulled out his iPhone again, ready for another selfie.

"Of course, why not . . ." said Risvoltino. "Nicolas was a brother to me."

"For real? And did you do a job together? Did you kill?"

"Certainly, we were always doing jobs together . . ."

"But is it true," 'a Lucertola broke in, "that when you were clearing the streets, when you were out on *stese*, Maraja would jump straight up to balcony height so he could shoot right into people's houses?"

"Fuck, I saw him do it myself . . . He looked like Spider-Man."

"*Ua', 'o ras* himself . . . The boss."

Risvoltino was leaning his back against the building and he'd lit a cigarette. He was smoking greedily, making a special effort to produce smoke rings.

The three stood gazing at him, slackjawed, without being able to work up the nerve to ask him the most important thing.

"All right," said the ex-*paranza* member, as if he were able to read their minds, "let's go take a stroll."

The first station of the Via Crucis of Nicolas Fiorillo Maraja was the building where he'd been born. The kitchen window was always closed these days, though in the past it hadn't been, not even after Christian's death.

"There, *guagliu'*, that's where he lived, his mother is still there . . ." said Risvoltino.

They went up to the intercom and pressed the button. Mena replied with a sigh. Kids were constantly ringing the doorbell, asking her all about Nicolas, and it was a pleasure for her to tell them about her son, see those kids who understood the worth of what Nicolas had done and who took him as an example. It seemed to her that it was a way of letting him live on a little longer, inside those youngsters; she saw them a little bit as his heirs, since he hadn't had any male offspring and she, Mena, no longer had any children at all. But there were also times when she would like to be alone, you can't always be a stranger to your own grief. And on those days, her anger boiled up and she had it in for everyone and everything.

At the other end of the intercom, the youngsters stood in silence. What do you say to a hero's mother?

In the background, they could hear a dog barking, then Nicolas Fiorillo's mother blew up: "Leave me alone, go ring your own mothers' doorbells!"

"*Ua'*, the mamma is like the son, a real hardass!" said Carminiello. Salvo said: "Oh, did you hear the dog barking? That must have been Skunk, Maraja's Dogo. *Uànema*, I've heard Skunk killed a hundred dogs."

"Is it true that Maraja had a tiger, too?" asked Carminiello.

"It's true," Risvoltino replied. "They say that there are days when you can still see it walking around Forcella."

Then he led them to the lair, the second station of the cross.

"Everyone used to come here . . . Drago', Lollipop, Tucano, Pesce Moscio . . ."

"I saw Pesce Moscio once!" Salvo cried.

"Shut up!" the Lizard retorted.

"No, for real! I saw him! My cousin went to school with him . . ."

And off they went again, because Maraja's city was a big place to tour.

"Here's where we beat the shit out of the immigrants . . ."

"That's where they killed Christian, may he rest in peace."

"Here all the shops were ours . . ."

"The clubhouse. This is where the Longhairs used to hang out."

"Roipnol. This is where that traitor lived."

Risvoltino went on like that until evening, when they ended the tour right where it had begun, downstairs from Risvoltino's house. They took the last selfies and thanked him again, then the three of them ran home—they all lived nearby. As they had that morning, their backpacks slammed against their sweaty T-shirts, but they felt older now, they'd learned a bunch of things, they had the impression they'd fought a hundred battles. Suddenly the Lizard stopped in his tracks and the other two slammed up against him. They'd passed that way a few hours earlier, and Risvoltino had explained that this had been the *paranza*'s official hairdresser, and that after the whole episode with Roipnol and the exploits that had ensued, the kids in the neighborhood, and from outside the neighborhood as well, had basically overrun Santino's hairdresser's shop. The shop was still open and the Lizard walked in without the slightest hesitation.

"We're getting ready to close, *guaglio*'."

"I want Maraja's trademark," Giacomino replied promptly.

The hairdresser smiled and, with a flourish of the barber's cloth, invited him to take a seat. Nicolas hadn't made it long enough, his time in hiding had also deprived him of those small pleasures of life, and so Santino had never been able to show him his new technique. He got the hatchet out of the sink and a carpenter's hammer out of one of the pockets of his smock. Like a sculptor with a chisel, he gently placed the hatchet on Giacomino's right temple and started tapping with the hammer against the back of the blade.

"*Ua*', how cool," said Salvo.

"This is a work of art," said Carminiello.

Once he was done with the right side, Santino started carving the back, leaving narrow strips of hair. F12.

"*Ua*', you busted the toilets!"

"Maraja! Maraja!"

Just as they were exulting in front of the shop, Aucelluzzo appeared on his scooter. The Lizard turned just in time to glimpse the new boss of Forcella riding his TMAX directly into the shop. The three friends cowered against the wall in sheer terror.

"Go right ahead, Aucellu'," said Santino, who'd kept his cool. "The boys can finish later."

"No, no," said Aucelluzzo, turning off his scooter. "Let them finish, it's on me."

Twenty minutes later, they were back in the street, hands touching

Maraja's trademark carved into their scalps. Aucelluzzo left the shop with them, then left the seat of his TMAX and pulled out a brick of hashish.

"A little brick like this, how fast do you think you could sell it? You think you could get it done in a week?"

"Oh, sure," said the Lizard, "for sure, every one of us!"

"Hold on, what are you, everyone else's lawyer?" asked Aucelluzzo. He pretended to take offense, and then the smile came back to his face. "Let the others talk!"

The others nodded their heads, eyes sparkling. It was a deal: a hundred euros a week, just to start, Aucelluzzo had told them. Then they'd see. The sky was the limit.

The next day, they were back again. Same piazza, same backpacks slung over their shoulders, same eyes looking up to admire the graffiti.

"Look what I've got here . . ." 'a Lucertola finally said, rummaging into his backpack. A dented Desert Eagle, but still looking fierce.

"*Ua*' . . . The gat," said Salvo, and he stepped forward to touch it, and so did Carminiello, but 'a Lucertola dodged their hands and put the gun away.

"Risvoltino gave it to me," he said, and then, before his friends' incredulous eyes, he added: "He said that this was Maraja's first gat."

Again, silence. And then, at last, he said, in a serious voice: "*Guagliu*', you want to start a *paranza* all our own?"